The Story of Sassy Sweetwater
by Vera Jane Cook

...

Copyright © Vera Jane Cook, 2016. All Rights Reserved. Except as permitted under the U.S. Copyright Act of 1976, no part of this publication may be reproduced, distributed, or transmitted in any form or by any means, or stored in a database or retrieval system, without prior written permission of the publisher.

...

This book is a work of fiction. While references may be made to actual places or events, the names, characters, incidents, and locations within are from the author's imagination and are not a resemblance to actual living or dead persons, businesses, or events.
Any similarity is coincidental.

...

Chatter Creek Publishing
Distributed by Bublish, Inc.
www.bublish.com

...

ISBN-10: 0-9974875-0-X
ISBN-13: 978-0-9974875-0-3

...

Publisher's Cataloging-In-Publication Data
(Prepared by The Donohue Group, Inc.)

Names: Cook, Vera Jane.
Title: The story of Sassy Sweetwater / Vera Jane Cook.
Description: [New York] : Chatter Creek Publishing, [2016] | [Place of distribution not identified] : Bublish, Inc.
Identifiers: ISBN 978-0-9974875-0-3 | ISBN 0-9974875-0-X
Subjects: LCSH: Mothers and daughters--Fiction. | Civil rights movements--South Carolina--Fiction. | Identity (Psychology)--Fiction. | Man-woman relationships--Fiction. | Beaufort (S.C.)--History--20th century--Fiction. | LCGFT: Historical fiction.
Classification: LCC PS3603.O65 S86 2016 | DDC 813/.6--dc23

The Story of Sassy Sweetwater

by Vera Jane Cook

CHAPTER ONE

Mama said I was born by a stream named Sweetwater. She called me Sassy the moment she realized I was a girl. Mama said girls should be sassy, gives them sex appeal. So I was named Sassy, after an attitude, and Sweetwater, after a stream. The year was 1949, and the place was a dirty, back-road shack in a dusty, little town in South Carolina. Mama never could remember the name of the town, but she told me that it might have been Cottageville or maybe even Ridgeville. Didn't matter much what it was called, though. I never saw it again, and as far as I knew, Mama didn't either.

Some people think a gray, tumultuous sky is an omen of discontent, especially if one's entry into this world is shadowed by blustery clouds and thunder's emphatic roar. But my mama said that heaven welcomed my birth with great horns blowing and mighty cymbals clashing and omens sent by mighty seers bring the blessings of miracles, not the doom of devils.

"Gave you its gray," she said. "Passed it right on to you."

I always knew she meant my eyes, gray as the weather on the day I was born, and sometimes showing up hazel when the sun confronts the gloom and demands I show some color.

"Gave you its temperament, too, and its mystery, girl. Women need a little mystery. That's what turns a man's head. Beauty has nothing to do with anything more than that."

It always sounded like the great god Poseidon was my father the way my mama tells it. Where else could I have come from? No man had ever come forth and claimed me as his own. Not that I didn't wonder who my father was, but when I asked I always got the same reply.

"You came from the sky, Sassy Sweetwater; clear as the stream I bathed you in, fierce as the wind that blew away the storm, the one that welcomed you here with great aplomb, and tender as the aftermath of nature's roar."

In other words, I was born an ambiguous bastard by a stream in South Carolina, and my seventeen-year-old mama was not about to tell me whose handsome smile had won her over. He was obviously too young or too old to pay for his mistake. I would find out one day, of course. When you ask as many questions as I did, the answers come at you, eventually. My birth was a riddle and I wanted my mama to connect me to some kind of heritage I could claim as my own, but she only gave me new conundrums to chase down. It should have been enough; there's nothing wrong with chasing around after answers you don't have, it's how hard you're hit with them when they fly back and knock you down.

Mama had traveled at least twenty miles east in Elvira's old Chevy to give birth to me, screaming the whole way, or so I've been told. Elvira was Mama's nineteen-year-old sister and I guess they'd planned the great cover-up, and the great escape, together. Out of a family of five girls, Elvira was the sanest, according to Mama.

Of course, I never knew how they covered up Mama's pregnancy, but Mama said her family only had eyes for what they wanted to see and ears for nothing more than what they wanted to hear. In those days, abortions weren't anything you could go to the doctor for and I'm sure, with Mama's Catholic background, she would never have entertained that option, even if she could have.

I can't imagine what she went through when she found out there was a baby in her belly before she even finished high school. And I sure don't know what she would have done without her sister helping her through it. Elvira promised Mama she'd read every book on birthing babies she could get her hands on and she assured Mama that she had nothing to fear. Well, Elvira must have been pretty well versed in birthing 'cause there wasn't a damn thing wrong with me that my mama's milk wouldn't cure. There wasn't a damn thing wrong with Mama, either, except all the things you couldn't see on the outside, all the hurt she must have been feeling; and I don't mean just about having me bursting open her uterus, but the hurts inside her heart that she never spoke about. But if you knew my mama, you'd know the hurts were there. Mama had the saddest eyes, like a wounded dog on the side of the road that you really want so badly to help, but you can't offer your services without the risk of being bitten.

Elvira went back home a few days after I was born. Mama and me didn't go home for another thirteen years. Home for Elvira was fifteen miles outside of Charleston, while where me and Mama went was hundreds of miles southwest. I don't know how we got there. Mama said we hitched all the way to Louisiana. She said wasn't a person on the road that wouldn't stop for a woman with a baby in her arms. I never knew why she'd decided to settle in Louisiana until I found out from Elvira, years later, that Mama had gotten an offer to wait tables in Baton Rouge from some man who'd passed through Carter's Crossing and had taken a fancy to her. I always wondered if he was my father, but my Aunt Elvira said I'd be more likely kin to King Kong.

Can't ever figure out why Mama left Baton Rouge and wound up settling in a place as remote as Glenmora. We didn't stay in Baton Rouge 'cause Mama's boyfriend turned out to be a shithead and it wasn't long before some other guy caught her eye just long enough to talk her into following him to Glenmora, where he was assistant principal at the local high school. Of course, I don't remember much about those years, but I can recall an apartment in the back of a small rooming house where we lived. I can just about capture the features of the woman who took care of me while Mama was working. Connie was her name and I guess she owned the place. Her bosom was large, always showing white freckled skin where the crease was. The memory is good when I think back on Connie, like the talcum powder she put in my underwear and the funny little children's books she read me, taking on a different voice for each character and scaring me half to death when she spoke like the big bad wolf and kind of lurched forward like she was going to swallow me whole.

Connie was old in the ways that make being old a good thing, with a round, kind face and a voice as soft as silk lining. She made me hot cocoa before I went to sleep every night and tossed a little marshmallow right up on top that melted so nice in the back of my mouth. She picked me up after school every day too, 'cause Mama worked long hours at the Lobster Pot. Connie drove me over to the Lobster Pot for my dinner and Mama would try, as best she could, to help me figure out decimals and multiply fractions in between taking orders. I'd sit at the counter eating crawfish, not really giving a damn what one third times one eighth of anything could ever equal, and doubting if I ever would give a rat's ass about anything I'd ever have to add, subtract, or multiply.

Mama and the assistant principal wound up breaking up shortly after we settled in Glenmora and not long after, Mama starting dating Guy Grissom, her boss at the Lobster Pot. Mama made me call him Uncle Guy for years, but I never liked him. He smelled feminine, like the cologne Mama wore, and he was always breathing heavy, like he was about to pass out. You might think he should have been real heavyset 'cause he was so short of breath all the time, but he wasn't at all heavyset. He was tall, though, and big, like those football players with the phony shoulders. But Uncle Guy's shoulders were naturally broad and then he narrowed so much at his waist, he could have worn Mama's belts. I always thought he looked funny, sort of like a cartoon character, 'cause his face was square, but Mama thought he was so handsome he could have been up there on the big screen kissing blondes.

When Uncle Guy Grissom was around Mama didn't act the same. She giggled too much and pretty much said yes to anything I asked her. I knew she barely heard what I'd said 'cause he was there, making himself at home in Mama's bed. I was pretty much ignored, except of course, when Mama remembered that I was her precious lit-tle baby girl; then, all of a sudden, I became this fascinating child with the cutest dimples Guy Grissom had seen this side of Lafayette. "Wish I could adopt this child and make her my own," he'd say. Of course I knew, even back then, that he was bullshitting me as much as he was bullshitting Mama. Said he was going to make Mama part owner of the Lobster Pot and divorce his wife soon as his youngest child was out of diapers, but of course that never happened.

Guy Grissom paid Connie to take care of me 'cause I saw him give her a white envelope every Friday. She'd hide all the bills in her top dresser drawer, all but a dollar that she'd stick inside her brassiere, right down the middle where the crease was. She'd take me to the park in good weather and buy us ice cream with that dollar or sometimes she'd keep me down at her apartment listening to The Jack Benny Show or sometimes we'd watch Dragnet 'cause Connie liked crime a whole lot. I'd come home late evening only to find Uncle Guy in his underwear eating Mama's fried catfish, which might have smelled inviting were it not for his sweet cologne stinking up our room.

Uncle Guy got sick when I was about ten years old and he died three years later. We didn't really see much of him after he was diagnosed with something Mama couldn't pronounce. Mama had to stop working at the Lobster Pot, of course, and it was eventually sold. Mama couldn't pay her bills anymore, so I guess Uncle Guy had been paying most of them. Guess he didn't leave her anything in his will, though, 'cause if he did, I doubt we'd ever have seen the dusty back road of Carter's Crossing or been desperate enough to claim the McLaughlins as blood relatives.

Right after Uncle Guy died, his wife barged into our apartment and called Mama wanton and loose, not one half hour after they put Uncle Guy in the ground. Mama cried and ordered her out, but the next thing I knew we were packing our bags and I was sitting on a bus and then I was sitting on a train and then there I was on another damn bus and Mama and I were getting off somewhere in the middle of nowhere with two suitcases and soon-to-be-sore feet after walking the two miles from the bus stop to Carter's Crossing where Mama told me we had family.

Nothing about a bus is fun. Trains somehow have a romance to them that buses just can't claim. I always felt like I could be going anywhere on earth sitting on a train, all the way across the world, listening to the whistle and catching speedy glimpses of old towns I'd never step foot in. But buses are too close to home. The towns all have a sameness to them and the roads are all too long, the destination too far. You can't be anywhere on a bus but where you started from and I don't care how many miles away you think you've gone. I'd grow up hating buses. Maybe 'cause they'd always remind me of our trip back home to South Carolina and that pathetic-looking, barren bus stop in the middle of nowhere. I'll never forget stepping off that bus wondering how far was far when nothing stares back at you but road signs that signal you're hundreds of miles from anywhere you've ever heard of.

Mama turned heads, sad eyes or not. She was tall and her hair was nearly black, but her eyes were the prettiest shade of blue I'd ever seen. It made me giggle to see how many men thought the same. I used to watch them eyeing her. Then I'd bat my eyes like Mama did, but they didn't pay me any mind—just a smile or an acknowledgement and sometimes they'd pat my head. But it was Mama they were after and I knew it, even then. I was the convenient excuse to get to her. I saw more buttons disappear into white handkerchiefs and had my cheeks pinched by one too many hairy fingers and all the time they were showing me magic tricks and pretending to be so fond of children, they were ogling my mama. It made her smile, the way I'd copy her every move, bat my eyes and shake my crossed leg while these lovesick men vied for her attention and downright ignored my girlish flirtations. I always knew Mama wanted to laugh out loud, but she stopped herself.

"Time enough to turn men's heads," she'd say, holding me to her.

I guess she didn't realize I wasn't at all interested in turning men's heads. I just wanted to be like her and to look like her and act like her. Hell, there wasn't a little girl in the world that wouldn't have wanted the same. But I wasn't tall and blue-eyed and wispy-looking like Mama. I was skinny and Mama called me strawberry head, 'cause my hair was flaming red, like the hot part of the fire, something I never liked hearing 'cause strawberries gave me hives and fire made my eyes tear. I didn't have Mama's clear white skin either. I was a constant blush with pimples about as busy on my face as grass growing on the ground under my feet. Mama smeared me with this stuff called PhisoHex at night, but for every pimple down, three more had burst forth the next morning.

So be it. Mama said I was going to grow into my good looks; I held fast to that. Mama said when your eye lashes are light and thick like mine, shading my "overcast" color eyes, as Mama called them, then men were bound to fall at my feet. Mama said all men are fools for women, but for drop-dead gorgeous redheads, men are lame-brained idiots. Mama told me not to count all the wounded and brokenhearted men I was going to leave in my wake, but to just be prepared to have that effect on them.

Uncle Guy's death changed things for us, that was for sure. For one, Mama insisted we had to go back home and make amends. I never could figure out what we were amending. For another, returning to South Carolina after Uncle Guy died, and walking up that road with my mama's hand in mine, was the closet we were going to be for a long time. I always blamed the distances that came upon us due to circumstance or choice, didn't matter, distance was the last thing I wanted from Mama. But we were coming back to too many bad memories, wanting to be enfolded by a family whose arms were too short to reach us. Walking up the road that day and heading toward Carter's Crossing, I knew that everything was changing. I could feel Mama's thoughts and the heaviness in her heart. She was passing it all onto me, the way she had given me the sky's likeness. And I took it in like a great tide cleansing me and filling up my soul with my mama's heart. I would cause the weariness she wore and I felt its weight. I carried everything that was inside of her inside of me and I always would. Everything that had hurt her, and everything that hadn't, would always be a part of my every breath. In my mama, I would find my anchor, but as I held fast to the safety, so, too, I feared the drowning.

"Come along now, Sassy," she said.

I had stopped just in front of the huge white farmhouse, staring at the unfamiliarity. Taking in the strangers that were getting up off their seats to stare back at us. Way in the distance, they stood up on a porch that should have looked inviting, but didn't. The house sat at the top of a hill and everything around it was green and rolled out toward blue skies. I'd never seen so many beautiful trees stretching lazily and affectionately across the sky, like cats stretching out in the sun.

There was a sign on the white gate that read Carter's Crossing. I realized then that as far as my eyes could see everything all around me seemed to be Carter's Crossing and everything around me began and ended here at this house; Mama's house. I wondered why suddenly finding out my mama was rich didn't seem the least bit comforting.

"C'mon now, honey, give me your hand," Mama said.

She was reaching out for me, standing in the daylight in her blue dress and her flat shoes with a wide-brimmed straw hat on her head, looking like someone important. That was the thing about Mama, she always looked like she was more important than anyone else, until she opened her mouth, then she sounded not much older than me.

The dress seemed to hug her from all sides, showing off her figure. And her dark hair was long, like soft cashmere wings flowing down her back.

"I don't want to live in that house," I said.

"C'mon now, Sassy. They've spotted us."

I did not move, but the others did. The "others" being the strangers Mama said I was kin to. I think I had an early premonition, 'cause my stomach fell to my knees right then and there.

"We're better off here than we are anywhere else," I heard Mama say.

But I didn't entirely believe her. I wanted to run in the opposite direction. But these people were walking down to where we were standing and you might say I was hypnotized by them. They seemed real tentative, like they just might change their minds and run back and drop the shades and slam the door on us. I didn't know who looked more like stray dogs: them or me and Mama.

One person had remained on the porch and didn't follow the others to the road; she held her hands up over her eyes squinting through the sun. I knew she was old, even then. The old were problematic. "Old opinions can kill you," Mama used to say.

All too soon, there was a man wearing suspenders standing in front of me, thinner than any man should be. His hair was dark, like Mama's, and his eyes so blue they startled me. Mama called him Seth.

"Violet?" he said, fighting with his sight through the sunlight. "Why, I'll be. That really you, Vi?"

Mama nodded and the man stood still, his hands in his pockets, staring at Mama, but not holding out his arms, even to me as I walked near and looked up. "Why, who are you?" he said. "You have a child, Vi?"

"Sassy, this is your Uncle Seth."

I had not stopped staring at him. He was lanky, like some old tree limb hanging by a prayer. His hands were long like his hair. When he smiled, I liked him better.

"You meet up somewhere with Aaron?" he asked. "Look at that hair, just like Aaron's."

"Richard Sweetwater is Sassy's father. We lost him just a few months ago." Mama sounded like she was reprimanding him for insinuating that my father was someone named Aaron, someone other than this phantom Richard Sweetwater.

I gave Mama an odd look, and she gave me one right back. The only father I'd ever known was the gray sky and the Sweetwater stream, but I sensed I shouldn't go around mentioning that, so I didn't. Far as I was concerned, everything Mama said made about as much sense as everything she didn't say.

"We're Irish, Seth, must be loads of redheads in our family. Sassy looks like Richard, yes, she truly does."

"Okay, Vi, whatever you say." Seth bent down and held out his hand. "Pleased to meet you, Sassy," he said.

I stared at his cowboy boots. They were yellow and pointed and I wondered how his toes could sit right in them. His jeans hung low on his hip, and he smelled pleasing, like manure.

"Sassy, don't be impolite, say hello to Uncle Seth." Mama put her hands on her hips.

I didn't get it. She hadn't warned me about this. She hadn't said a damn thing to me about these so-called kinfolk. She obviously hadn't warned Seth either 'cause we were both looking at each other like some unknown species, but I knew when Mama put her hands on her hips it preceded something she was about to say that was either very bad or very good.

"Go on now, Sassy." Mama pushed me so far forward I nearly knocked Seth off his feet. I had no choice but to acknowledge him.

"Hello," I said to the ground.

"You look good," I heard him say to Mama.

Then all of a sudden, someone was running up to us. She was yelling out Mama's name and holding out her arms. They started hugging and it looked to me like they were dancing 'cause they didn't stop holding hands and spinning around like tops.

"Elvira, oh I've missed you, honey."

"I thought that was you. Oh my God, Vi, why didn't you tell us you were coming home?" she asked. "Why, I would have sent Pike or Dudley down with the car to get you."

Mama didn't say a word; once she stopped spinning around with Elvira, she stood there glancing back at the house. She was still holding Elvira's hand, but I knew she was looking at that old woman who wasn't doing much of anything 'cept rocking back and forth.

"You are just as beautiful as ever," Elvira said. "Oh, honey, I knew you'd be back, I prayed for it."

I didn't know Elvira then, but she knew me. When she finally broke herself away from Mama she pulled me to her breast like I'd just escaped being hit by a freight train. "Sassy," she said through her tears.

I glanced over at my mama, who gave me a look that I interpreted as "make me proud and don't act like a snitch," but I was speechless. Mama had told me so little about where we were going and who I was and just how exactly I was related to these people.

"You are such a little doll," Elvira said. "I'm your mama's sister, Elvira, your Aunt El."

She didn't look like Mama at all. She looked like a boy, all skinny and flat-chested, and her hair was cut short, but it was long enough to blow back off her forehead in the soft Carolina breeze. If she'd actually been a boy, she would have been real handsome.

"Are you going to say hello to your Aunt Elvira?" Mama insisted.

I continued to stare at Seth and Elvira without saying a word. My eyes must have been round as half-dollars. I wished Mama had clued me in and given me some background on these people.

"Hello," I managed to say quietly.

And then, another stranger came slowly toward me. He was running at first, but as he got closer he slowed down. Mama called him Kyle. He was young, maybe only fifteen. His eyes were sad, like Mama's. Freckles popped up all over his face like flowers blooming and his hair was the same color as the sun. Quite spontaneously, I smiled at him. There was something about Kyle that just elicited a smile.

"Why, Kyle," Mama said. "Last time I saw you, you were in diapers."

"Really," he said, shyly taking Mama in.

"Come on over here and give me a hug."

I was beside myself watching Mama hug this boy. He was nearly as tall as she was. He looked awkward and embarrassed and the minute he could, he stepped out of her embrace, but Mama held his face in her hands and gently moved the hair that had fallen into his eyes.

"You look like you've got the devil in you," she said.

Kyle stared at her like she was a movie queen. "No, ma'am," he said. "More angel than devil."

"Why I guess that remains to be seen." Mama laughed and dropped her hands to her sides. Off in the distance, some dogs started barking.

"Did Gladys have puppies?" Mama asked. "I hear more than one dog yapping up a storm."

Seth was the one that answered. I was looking around for the puppies, but not before noticing Kyle's glance.

"Gladys been long gone, Vi," Seth said, "but we got a whole litter full of her line."

"Want to see?" Kyle piped up and took my hand. It seemed so unselfconscious, the way he was holding it and walking me off.

"Can I, Mama?" I asked, looking back at her.

After catching her nod, I ran toward the barn with Kyle. The old woman on the porch was watching me and I glanced her way. Something about her made me feel I'd be about as welcome in her house as carpenter ants.

I was suddenly aware of my dirty jeans and some old T- shirt of Uncle Guy's that Mama had given me. I hadn't wanted it 'cause maybe he had died in it and it gave me the creeps. I was hoping it didn't stink.

"Cute, huh?" Kyle said as he led me to the puppies. But I was looking at him when I said, "Yes."

He didn't look like anybody else, but then again, neither did I. They all had real dark hair, nearly black, and light eyes that kind of took a person by surprise 'cause they were unexpected. But if Mama said these people were kin, then I guess they were. Kyle's yellow hair seemed an oddity and I wondered if he was just visiting. I guess he was thinking the same thing about me.

"Who are you?" he asked as I reached out to pet the puppies. There were five of them and I knew the breed right away 'cause of the mother, whose fur was soft as cotton. They were all Border collies, Mama's favorite dog. She always said she wanted to get me a Border collie.

"I like this one," I said. I pointed to a little black-and-white spotted dog, the obvious runt of the litter. The mother eyed me suspiciously as I reached in and scooped up one of her babies.

"You my niece or something?" Kyle asked.

I laughed. He looked too young to have a niece, especially one as old as me. "I'm Sassy Sweetwater," I said.

I watched as he lay back on some hay. He was wearing overalls and brown shoes with broken laces.

"Sassy Sweetwater," he said. "Never heard a name like that. Where you from?"

"Glenmora, Louisiana," I said. "Where you from?"

"Right here," he said and sat up.

It was then I noticed his right hand for the first time. Three fingers were missing. I looked away quickly. I didn't want to stare, but it had shocked me.

He must have noticed my reaction but he pretended not to. "I'm not a real McLaughlin," he said.

"McLaughlin? That's Mama's name," I said.

"Yeah, your mama and everyone else's here. You're a Sweetwater?"

"Huh-huh. Where are your parents?" I asked him.

"Don't know." He shrugged. "I've been told I was left on the porch, and Grandma took pity on me. Picked me right up in her arms and raised me like her own."

Now it was my turn to fall back on the hay. I laughed real hard. I didn't want to say it, but it didn't seem to me that that old lady was capable of taking pity on anyone, and I'd only seen her from a distance.

"Lucky baby," I said. "I guess."

By the time we left the barn, I had been promised the puppy with the black-and-white spots and I had named it June-bug 'cause it looked like it was covered with little black bugs and it was June. Kyle got a real kick out of that and laughed for a full minute.

"I guess that makes sense, Sassy," he finally said when he got his breath.

"Of course it makes sense," I said, even knowing that Kyle was going to name me stupid for calling a dog after a bug.

But he laughed again. Nothing seemed to bother him, at least not anything he wanted to let me know about.

"It's yours," he said. "Do what you want, but I think a girl dog wouldn't want to be named after anything buggy."

I followed him out of the barn renaming the puppy in my head. Maybe he had a point, but then I changed my mind.

"I like June-bug," I shouted.

I watched Kyle leap up onto the porch. I watched him look back at me, just to make sure I saw that leap. He was tall and slender with firm muscles in his arms. He might have been the best-looking boy I'd ever seen.

My mama was standing up where the old woman was, but the old woman hadn't moved from her chair. She was sitting straight as a line ruler and when she did move her head, she did it slowly; it made her look very sly to me.

Mama was leaning against the rail with Elvira's arm over her shoulder. They were talking real softly and I doubt if anyone could have heard what they were saying. The old woman was looking off, like she wasn't interested anyway. Seth was staring out in to space with a drooping mouth. It seemed to me like he was listening to sad country music. When I walked up onto the porch, the old woman eyed me like I was the sour in the milk pail.

"Aaron ever marry?" I heard Mama ask.

"Never did," Elvira said and smiled at Mama. "Nope, never did."

I looked at Mama. "Kyle gave me one of the puppies," I said. "Can I keep it?" I saw the old woman twitch and felt something in my heart that made it skip.

"He did, did he?" the old woman said. She reached out her arms and brought me to her so that I was standing there with nowhere to go, not unless I flung my arms up and disassociated myself from her reach forever, but I guess that might have appeared rude and Mama would have been furious.

"Don't look like your mama," she said. I gave her a hateful look and heard her laugh.

"Sassy, honey," Mama said. "Say hello to your grandmother…and be nice. We're going to be living here for a while, you hear?"

I looked all around me. Nothing made sense to me but Kyle. He was smiling. Everyone else looked like they'd tasted hot pepper after biting into a piece of chocolate candy, expecting sweetness and getting burned instead.

"Sassy, say hello to your grandmother," I heard mama repeat.

But I couldn't speak to that woman. She'd been punished by the good Lord. Mama always told me that the good Lord punishes evil by making sure it can't hide. And I saw it plain as day in her face. She was staring at me like I was a freak let loose from the carnival and I knew that in that moment, as I stared back with my most disdainful sneer, that I had challenged her to either destroy me or to let me live.

"You want that puppy, you better say hello to me," the old woman said, threatening like. I felt my blood run cold, but I knew I had no choice but to acknowledge the old bat.

"Hello," I said, looking at her straight on for the first time. She wasn't half bad-looking, but she was old. So many lines ran across her face, like mazes in a dirt field that never met up or led anywhere.

"Grandma Edna," the old lady said. "You'll be calling me Grandma Edna like a proper young girl that shows respect for her elders."

I shot Mama a glance real quick and I saw her nod at me and I noticed that her expression was as fierce as the old lady's.

"Hello, Grandma Edna," I said, trying to smile but failing miserably.

"Here tell it like it is, girl."

I realized she hadn't let go of my arm. She studied my face.

"Dogs earn more love than people. You treat that dog well, and I'll treat you the same."

I didn't know what the hell she was talking about, but I'd soon learn you didn't argue with Grandma Edna.

"You name it yet?" she asked.

"Named it June-bug," I said. I heard Seth laugh, and even Mama giggled.

"June-bug, huh?" Grandma Edna said, studying me like I was a damn road map. "That'll do."

She looked up at Seth. "Get Pike to make that little June-bug puppy a bed and put it in the girl's room with a nice blanket."

"Thought you didn't like dogs in the house, Mama," Seth said.

"I got used to having dogs in my house." Grandma Edna smiled.

Mama and Elvira laughed softly, but Seth didn't respond at all. He just shook his head and looked away.

"You got to care for that puppy like your own, girl. You stop caring for it, it'll turn on you like a natural child."

"What do you mean by that?" I asked.

I felt it when she let go of me, and it almost made me stumble 'cause I'd been resisting being held by her so much.

"'Thank you, Grandma Edna' is what you should be saying. I just gave you a puppy, child."

"Want to feed the pups?" I heard Kyle ask. "It's time," he added.

"Yeah, sure do," I said, avoiding having to thank the old woman as I jumped back off the porch, leaping just as high and as well as Kyle had. As I followed him back to the barn, I heard mama tell the old woman that I was usually very polite and I'd come around.

Come around to what, I wondered?

Chapter Two

It was Aunt El that brought me back to the house an hour or so later. I had been sitting in the barn with Kyle after we fed the pups. I was dying to ask him what had happened to his fingers, but I clamped my mouth shut so I wouldn't embarrass him. We had been talking about taking a walk over to Beaufort and catching a film. Kyle said he liked films a whole lot, especially ones with pretty girls.

"Wasn't a pretty girl in Carter's Crossing 'til you got here," he said. I blushed so deep I felt faint.

"Of course we got horses in the barn we could feed." He looked at me and probably knew by the look on my face that I didn't care much for feeding horses.

"Grandma Edna usually doesn't let us feed the horses, says we got servants for that, but I could ask her."

"Servants? Are you kidding?"

"Nope. Didn't you have them in Louisiana?"

"Hell no."

Kyle seemed a little confused by that and looked away, as if he thought everyone had servants, or should have 'em.

"We could take a bike ride over to Abner Creek and catch fish." He smiled back at me and I could tell he liked to fish. Unfortunately, I didn't.

"I like films a whole lot," I said.

It was then I caught Aunt El leaning against the barn door. She'd been listening to our conversation, but I didn't know for how long. Not that we'd said anything important, but I didn't much like being spied on.

She was staring at me and Kyle and I wondered what she was thinking; she looked to be a hiccup away from puking.

"C'mon, Sassy. We got your mama's room ready. You'll be staying with her. It's a pretty room. It's got white lace on the windows and it's all blue. The windows look out over the hills. I think you're going to like it."

I looked back at Kyle and he stood there with his hands in his pockets kind of rocking back and forth on his feet. I think I would have preferred being tossed naked into a snake pit than walking into that house, or anywhere near it, and I knew he was reading my mind. I knew by the way he was grinning at me.

Aunt El put her arm around my shoulder and led me out. She walked slowly and I was a bit relieved that she did. When I looked toward the porch I could see that the old lady still hadn't left her chair, which meant I'd have to walk right by her.

"It's good for Kyle to have someone near his own age to do things with," Elvira was saying. "It's been so lonely for him. You know how kids are. They're so cruel. Bad enough he can't read, but he's got those missing fingers, something else for the kids to tease him about."

"What do you mean he can't read?"

That sure took me by surprise; he'd seemed smart to me. I stopped dead in my tracks and stared at Elvira. I heard her sigh.

"He never learned to read. Can't learn, it seems. He's in some special class in school, but he just sits there. Teachers tell us he's retarded."

"Can he write?" I asked, knowing if he could write, then he could surely learn to read.

Elvira shook her head. "Nope, can't write, either," she said.

"He's got missing fingers, maybe that has something to do with it, why he can't write?"

"He's got a whole other hand of fingers. If the right one don't work, use the left." Aunt El stopped walking and looked up at the sky, like I was up there instead of where I was standing. She was tall and nearly as skinny as Seth. She didn't really look much older than me, though she was past Mama's age.

"He's retarded. Runs in this family. There was a baby born like that, years ago, retarded like Kyle."

I couldn't believe it. Kyle hadn't seemed at all retarded to me. "But he's smart," I said.

Elvira laughed and drew me close. "Maybe so," she said. "But he can't read and he can't write and most of the time he just looks off, as if there's nothing in his head at all."

"What happened to his fingers?" I asked.

She looked up toward the sky again. "He cut them off," she said. "We don't know if it was on purpose or not. But you know how boys are. He was out there playing with the chainsaw and next thing I knew he was on the ground trying to reattach his fingers."

I couldn't believe what I was hearing. It made me sick to think that something so perfect could be made imperfect by some stupid mistake.

"Doctors couldn't do it, of course. Poor Kyle. He'll spend the rest of his life like that. Whatever is going to become of that boy?"

I felt Elvira clutch my shoulder. I felt her grip.

"Pretend you don't notice his abnormality, Sassy. He's kind of sensitive about it."

Nothing seemed real. Kyle had made too much sense to me and now in an instant, he made no sense at all. I didn't know where my mama had led me or why she'd come back to this place. We could have stayed in Louisiana, gone to New Orleans or back to Baton Rouge. Mama could have gotten work in those big cities. We didn't need this family.

Grandma Edna stared at me like I was the grim reaper as Elvira led me up the porch steps. I could even feel her eyes on my back.

"Make sure you bathe yourself before dinner," I heard her call out.

As if I wouldn't bathe after being on a bus for two days. I was going to have to bite my tongue for the rest of my life living with that old lady.

The house was big and cold. Even though it was a Southern June day, the house seemed damp, seemed to carry dampness where the wood split in the floor and where the stairs creaked under my step. And out past the window, where the limb of an old oak tree drooped, there seemed to be a contradictory message between the blazing sun beyond the window-pane and the dankness.

I found Mama sitting in a large white chair. She was staring out the window like she'd noticed something that had captured her attention and her body was slightly erect, her eyebrows pinched. I sat on one of the beds and watched her.

After a moment she turned and looked at me, whatever she'd been thinking momentarily lost. I would have chased her thoughts if I could and I would have burned them up, 'cause I knew they'd unsettled her.

"You'll like it here after a while," she said.

I turned and looked out the window, too, where her thoughts had been. Perhaps if I searched diligently enough, I'd uncover them in the wind.

"This house is damp," I said.

"It's old," Mama said.

"How old?" I asked.

"Civil War," she said. "It's been in your Grandma Edna's family for several generations. She's the Carter. Her family owned everything around here. They still do."

"Do you like it here?" I asked, and she laughed. I hadn't expected her to laugh. "We could have gone anywhere," I said.

"Remember what you told me about the bus, Sassy, how you never go anywhere at all, how you never get any further away from anywhere on a bus?"

I nodded my head and noticed her eyes, how they picked up the blue of her dress, and I thought that if my eyes were like hers, I'd never wear anything else but the color blue.

"I remember," I said.

"It's like that, Sassy," I heard her say. "I can't get anywhere I need to be on a bus, not really. But I can't take a train everywhere I need to go.

Sometimes, you just have to be on a bus to get from one place to the other. You don't have a choice."

"What?" I wondered if she was teasing me.

She held out her hands toward the walls and made a circle with her arms. "This," she said. "This is my bus, honey."

I woke up when I smelled something like onions and carrots cooking in a stew. It made my stomach growl. At first I barely knew where I was and then I remembered the blue and white room and the hills in the distance that I could see from the windows. I noticed that Mama must have gone downstairs 'cause I was alone in the bedroom. Mama must have taken off my shoes and she had found a quilt to cover me with. The quilt was pretty; every square had a fancy letter of the alphabet sewn into it and I wondered if the letters stood for anything. But sometimes things just don't stand for nothing.

I heard unfamiliar voices coming from downstairs and when I looked outside I could see the sun setting. It was a beautiful burst of amber and red, like a paint box set of colors spilling across the sky. For a moment, it seemed like God was showing me his sense of humor as the sun seemed to flirt and to play with my fascination, taking its own sweet time nestling down into the earth.

I sat there and watched the sun until it finally disappeared. I wondered if there'd ever be a time that I wouldn't stop to watch the sun set and I knew if there was, I'd have no business living.

When dusk began to settle, I looked around the room I was sharing with Mama. It was still and foreign. I could hear the wind and a faint hint of music. This is where my mama grew up; these were her walls and the scent of powder was what clothed her skin. No one else could have ever stayed in this room 'cause my mama was everywhere I looked; she was in every scent I could capture. From the half-open closet I could see her sweaters and, neatly on the floor, I could see saddle shoes and flats I knew she'd worn. This was where she cried about me, knowing I was about to be born, sharing secrets with Aunt El that no one else knew. Here I'd lain in Mama's womb listening to her secrets, being within her secrets.

I needed Mama to tell me who these people really were and, if they were kin, why we hadn't seen them in all these years. I had heard nothing but bad things about Mama's childhood and I couldn't understand why she'd want to revisit it. And even though I loved the room she grew up in, she might have hated it. She always said that thinking about her childhood made her stomach heave and gave her bad headaches. I wondered how much worse it was going to be actually living here again and how soon it would be before Mama got sick and started heaving.

When I looked out the window, I realized that Mama and I could make our get away on the roof, if we needed to. We could just crawl out and slip on down to the ground once everyone was asleep. I didn't need to be here and Mama didn't need to be here, either. I'd take the puppy with me, of course, and we could go back to Louisiana and Mama could get a job, like at the Lobster Pot, and when I got old enough I could work as a waitress, too.

As I was planning our escape, I noticed a snazzy white car in the driveway. I'd just spent two days on a bus calling out car models. It was a game Mama and me played, and I always won 'cause I knew more models than she did, so I was able to recognize right away that the car in the drive way was a 1961 Cadillac Eldorado convertible. I hadn't seen it earlier and I sure would have noticed that car. I wondered if Mama's family was throwing her a big dinner party and the Caddie belonged to one of the guests.

Maybe that meant I should change my clothes. Mama used to tell me that she was never allowed to wear pants to the dinner table, so I wondered if I'd be offending anyone if I showed up to dinner with my blue jeans and Guy Grissom's old T-shirt.

But I came to the conclusion that this house needed exploring, instead of me wasting time trying on one of Mama's dresses just to please some grumpy old lady. It suddenly occurred to me I'd never eat past lunch since I didn't own any dresses, except the skirts I wore to school, none of which had been packed 'cause Mama said we were traveling light. So we sold most of our things out on the street before we left Glenmora, including most of our clothes. Mama said I could spend the summer in jeans and shorts and not to worry. Hell, if she knew I wouldn't be allowed to dinner without a dress, she would have packed one for me.

I put my shoes back on and went out to the landing. It looked like there were five or so bedrooms. I'd never seen a house this big. I wanted to hate it, but I found it was getting under my skin a little. We'd never lived in anything this grand. The banister had a shine to the dark wood and the hallway was wall papered in some beige color with diamonds in the middle that I could feel beneath my fingers when I followed the pattern with my hands. It felt like I was touching tiny, little beads. When I looked up I saw the third floor landing and two closed doors. It was where an attic should have been but it looked to me like there were two more bedrooms up there.

I noticed that the room at the other end of the hall had a porch off of it. I could see the porch clear on down the hall. The porch railing was white, and there was an ashtray on the ledge. Someone had left a cigarette burning 'cause I could see the smoke. I could even smell it. I walked toward the room 'cause it looked like it was sending me an invitation. The white curtains were moving under a soft breeze and I could hear music from a radio. Someone was singing a mournful ballad and I identified the singer as Johnny Ray. Mama loved Johnny Ray, so I got kind of good at knowing the words to all of his songs.

As I got closer to the end of the hall, I realized the room wasn't empty 'cause I could hear someone walking around. I jumped back. I figured it was Elvira's room, but the woman suddenly walking through the door was not Elvira. She didn't look like a boy, either.

"Why, who are you?" she asked.

She didn't scare me as much as some of the others, so I answered her. "I'm Sassy Sweetwater," I said.

She smiled nice and broad. "Oh? I think I just met your Mama, Violet?"

"Who are you?" I asked.

She held her hand out to me. "Earline, that's my name."

I stood there looking at her. She had real white teeth that stood out friendly-like. "You kin?" I asked.

She bent down and whispered in my ear and I could smell her perfume and see how nice her breasts looked swelling up out of her summer sundress. I thought she was real pretty.

"I'm your Aunt El's special friend," she said.

I guess I was looking kind of confused 'cause after a while she bent down to my ear again. "Sort of like a wife is a special friend."

My mouth dropped. I guess I was trying to figure out how one woman could be married to another, if that's what she meant.

"So yes, that makes us kin," she said and kissed my cheek.

"What do I call you?" I asked.

"Aunt Earline," she said and smiled.

"Aunt Earline," I said and held out my hand. "You ain't much older than me."

"So what about it?"

"Nothing."

"Well, sweetheart, I'm going down to get a cocktail. I'll see you in a bit."

I watched her head down the stairs in high-heel shoes that clacked real loud on the wood floor.

She was tiny as a Barbie doll; maybe that's why she hadn't frightened me.

I looked around the landing. Most of the doors were slightly ajar. I knew Grandma Edna's room right away 'cause she kept it dark and it smelled like an old woman's room when I walked by, sort of like lavender and talc, with a hint of medicine. I put my hand on the doorknob and pushed 'til it was wide-open. The smell did not offend me; it was nice, sort of like a bath I once took when mama emptied a whole box of red and green oil gels into the tub by mistake and I couldn't even see her standing there screaming 'cause there were so many bubbles floating around.

I stepped inside the room and observed it. I figured I'd tell the old woman I got lost if she caught me snooping through her things. Or maybe I'd even tell her that I was looking for a dress to wear.

Grandma Edna had white, laced napkins on the dresser that she used to put her toiletries on. Behind that, were framed photographs. That's what I wanted to see, those photographs. Mama had never shown me a photograph of anyone except myself as a baby. I never even knew I had a family 'til after Guy Grissom died and Mama said it was time to make amends.

I surveyed my surroundings. The bed was huge and very high. I didn't think I'd like sleeping that high off the ground, but I'd noticed that

Grandma Edna had legs long enough to deal with it. I had an urge to raise the heavy shades and let the stars shine in. I couldn't help but wonder if Grandma Edna didn't like looking at stars.

I switched a lamp on and it brought a strange luminescence to the photographs and made them take on an eerie quality, like I was looking at ghosts. But old photographs usually have that effect on me; they make me sad. I don't like the way life's moments are captured in time. It gives me an uneasy feeling. It's not like painting, something you can alter and change. Mama says people take pictures in order to remember. "It's sort of like a passion to live deeply, to capture time," Mama told me. "Description is a love affair with life," she used to say. "That's why writers spend so much time describing things and why painters try so hard to recreate what they're looking at. Why do you think everyone on this earth has a camera? They're holding on to time, honey."

I always think about that when I'm painting, but not painting the way things are, but more like the way I see them. I've been painting since Mama got me a paint-by-numbers set for my eighth birthday. Of course, I ignored the numbers and wound up painting the drawbridge over by Lilly Pond Lane. Mama tells me that painting is my way of living deeply, and I guess I can't argue none with that.

Be that as it may, photographs still spooked me, but I continued to look at the ones in my hand. I recognized the old woman the minute I saw her younger, rather attractive face in one of the photos. There I was seeing Grandma Edna on her wedding day. I found it so hard to believe. She didn't even look much older than me. I had to see it close up, I had to see it for myself, and I reached for the photograph so I could study it. For a moment I thought it was Mama, but the woman's face was rounder, like mine. She was slender and alluring, no trace of the old and frightening person who was about to bar me from the dining room for wearing pants. I guess the man she was with was my grandfather, though I didn't know a damn thing about him. But who else could he be?

I knew right away where Kyle got his looks. He must have been kidding me when he told me he was left on the porch. He looked just like the man in the photograph, whose eyes were so pretty you could see the shape and the color in a black-and-white print. His eyes were just like Kyle's, so I surmised that they must be green. Mama never mentioned having a father. I figured he was dead or he would have been there out on that porch staring me and Mama down like the others, like we were wolves coming down off the mountain to be shot.

I heard footsteps coming up the stairs and realized that I had to get out of there before I was caught by Grandma Edna. But then I saw a photograph of seven children. Some were sitting on a couch and the others were standing behind the couch. I was overcome with a compulsion to see that photograph close up, despite the consequences. The photograph was on a table over by the bed. I ran over and grabbed it as quickly as I could. Then I slid under the bed just as Grandma Edna got to the top of the stairs. My mama was in that photograph and I just had to see it. I'd never seen my mama as a child.

I took the photograph in my hands and studied it. It made me smile to see Mama so little, looking too pretty to belong anywhere on earth, but especially not among her other siblings. I hate to say it, but Seth was so skinny, he looked about to fade away, and he was frowning even then. I could pick out Aunt El, looking like a boy in a party dress. I didn't know the rest of the siblings, of course. There was an older, somber-looking boy, and three other little girls. One of the girls had something wrong with her lip and they'd put her in the back with the somber boy, sort of like they were trying to hide her. The other two girls looked alike, unfortunately for them. Mama was the only girl with a bow in her hair. She sat in the middle looking like she was trying to disappear. I brought the photograph closer to me, wanting to trace the outline of my mama with my finger. It was like I could maybe go back in time and make her feel better. But that's why I hate photographs, you just can't ever do that.

Then I did the worst thing ever. I sneezed. There must have been more dust under that bed than inside the bag of an Electrolux vacuum cleaner.

"What are you doing?"

There she was, Grandma Edna, lying down on the floor, peering at me.

I shimmied out from under the bed and put the photograph back clumsily. I quickly tried to straighten out the stupid, white, holey handkerchief

I had messed up in the process. That's when I heard something fall to the floor and crash. It was a small dish that had held what looked to be buttons, and now the dish was all over the floor in pieces and the buttons were scattered.

"See what you've done," she said, standing up straight.

I could see how tall she was from my position on the floor. I avoided looking at her face; I had seen enough of it and I knew that I preferred looking at her likeness more than I would ever come to welcome her as a flesh-and-blood entity.

I went to leave, but she barred the way.

"You're not to come in here again," she said. "It's my room and I extended no invitation to you to enter it."

I nodded my head, too afraid of her to speak.

"I'll clean up this mess, but you owe me a dish. I expect it to look exactly like the one you just destroyed. What will ever become of you, girl? You're clumsy."

"Where will I find the dish?" I asked.

"In China," she said, still giving me a dirty look.

My hands were shaking, and my knees were weak. Was she really going to send me to China for some damn stupid dish?

"Will you remember that when you get to China, that you owe me a dish?"

"Yes, ma'am," I said.

"You stink," she said.

I didn't know what to say to that, but felt my cheeks burn with shame.

"Dinner will be in a half hour. I expect you to be dressed like a girl." She looked me up and down. "I don't want confusion in my house. Unnaturalness is a sin."

"Yes, ma'am," I managed to get out, humbly walking past her and praying she wouldn't grab me by the hair and hurl me down the stairs to my death.

After scrubbing myself clean, I rummaged through Mama's things and found a dress that might fit me. It was a blue and white polka-dot dress that looked absolutely smashing on Mama, but did nothing to compliment my budding figure. So I went through Mama's drawer until I found some red ribbon, which I tied into a bow at my waist. I let the ribbon fall down on both sides instead of cutting it off, just in case Mama had been saving that ribbon for something. I was pleased with my image 'cause I could see my curves and they were just like Mama's curves. I had a waistline and even some hips. I thought I looked pretty damn good.

I put a comb through my hair and dabbed some of Mama's rouge on my cheeks. Suddenly I felt like a grown up woman. I held my head up, sassy-like, just like Mama told me I should be.

I realized then that I was completely destroying the image with the penny loafers I had on my feet, so I borrowed a pair of Mama's white high heels. But the shoes were flopping all over the floor as I walked, so I stuffed my old socks in them, hoping that would help. Even with the socks, having a heel on the bottom of my shoe gave me another attitude change. I paraded myself in front of the mirror feeling like a film siren had just taken over my body.

I found Mama's lipstick brush in the bathroom and the color she favored, Fire Engine Red. When I looked at myself in the mirror I decided that I was almost as beautiful as Mama and certainly would be once I developed breasts. It was then I got the idea to put another pair of socks into Mama's brassiere so I'd look more like her. I checked myself out in the mirror, feeling that I was really exceptionally gorgeous now, and I certainly wouldn't be wearing anything that Grandma Edna could possibly berate me for.

I held on to the banister tightly, for fear I'd fall on my head. I hadn't enough time to master walking around in high heels, especially not ones with socks stuffed in 'em. I heard children's voices, and I hoped there were no little kids running around that I just might trip over.

No one noticed me as I made my way down the stairs. But after a moment, that woman, Earline, looked up and did a double take and a huge smile broke out across her face. I saw Elvira turn and follow her gaze and then she stared at me with a dumbfounded expression, as if I'd grown a beard I was about to high tail it back to my room 'cause I suddenly felt silly, but then, Aunt El smiled.

"Why, Sassy," she said. "Welcome."

I nodded my head back at her and tried to look like I wasn't about to fall. Two little boys and a girl were running around the room acting up. I heard someone tell them to settle down.

Once I got to the last stair I wondered how I'd make it to the couch, or wherever I could park my behind before landing flat on my sorry rear end. I had no idea that high heels would be so hard to walk in.

It was Mama that saved me, of course. She came out of nowhere and swooped me up, kind of taking me in her arms and practically carrying me over to the first available chair.

"Why, Sassy, you look beautiful," she said and bent down close to my ear as she gently deposited me on my backside.

"Red lipstick is too mature for you, darling. Try pink next time," she said.

Mama smiled even broader when she noticed the toe of my sock peeking out of my left breast cup.

One of the little boys looked at me and giggled.

"Who are you?" I asked, but he just kept staring at me.

"That's your cousin, Andy," Mama said.

"Oh," I said as I settled myself.

They were all staring at me, even the other two kids. It was then I realized that the hair on my legs was fuzzy, sort of like a little dog Mama and I used to have. I never thought about the hair on my legs before, but now I was acutely self-conscious. I pulled the dress down below my knees and wondered if I could get Mama to teach me how to shave.

"That your daughter, Vi?" someone asked.

I looked across the room. Mama was calling her Erin and Erin was looking at me through a cloud of smoke.

"Yes," Mama said. "That's my baby."

The woman named Erin coughed and some heavyset man at her side told Mama I was a peach.

I wondered if being a peach was good or bad. Was he making fun of the fuzz on my legs? But then, I heard Mama thank him.

"You look funny," little Andy said to me.

"So, what happened to Sweetwater?" Erin asked and looked over at me. "What did you say his first name was, Richard? Where'd you meet him, Vi?"

Mama stood up and refilled her glass with what appeared to be wine. A Negro woman came in and started passing out some food on a tray. I saw that the dining room table was set for twelve.

"We met on a train," Mama said. "He passed away."

"Must have been sick with something," Erin said.

"Not necessarily," Mama said and winked at me.

I recognized Erin as an older version of one of those ugly, little girls in the photograph. She looked a little better now, with makeup and her hair all done up fancy-like, but she still looked like a cross between an ostrich and a rat. I learned that the kids were hers: Andy, Kathleen, and Ricky. Ricky joined his brother on the floor and they both sat there staring at me.

I suddenly got a side glance of Grandma Edna coming into the room with Kyle. He was dressed in his overalls, but he had on a clean white shirt and a short green scarf around his neck. He escorted the old lady to a large, wine-colored chair and she sat there like a queen surveying her subjects. When her eyes got to me she stopped dead and gave me a good, long once-over.

"Why, I didn't know it was Halloween, dear," she said and started laughing. "You look like a gift-wrapped box. I hope that isn't my best ribbon tied at your waist."

Now everybody was looking at me and I was looking back at them with the heat in my body burning me up hotter than hell's fire. I felt the tears sting my eyes. I wanted to sink into the ground. Then I heard Kyle say real loud, "She looks pretty damn good."

Everyone turned and stared at him.

"You look, you look, like a movie star." He grinned and came over to take the seat beside me.

"Everyone looks like a movie star to you, Kyle. Don't you ever see any plain people in the world, like policeman and barmaids?" Erin chuckled and raised her eyes. I heard her laugh in that throaty smoky growl, but then Austin Cooper, who I later learned was married to Erin McLaughlin, came over and took my hand.

"You certainly are a peach," he said. "I'm your Uncle Austin. You want to call me Uncle A? You can."

I saw Mama smiling and when I looked up, I noticed my uncle Seth had just come in the front door. He stopped at the hall mirror and combed back his hair with his fingers.

"For a moment, I thought you were your mama," Seth said as he walked into the room.

All of a sudden, Kyle jumped up and ran to the foyer. He looked back at me as he snatched a rose from the vase. He held it out toward me and smiled.

"A flower worthy of your beauty could only be a rose," he said.

"What's gotten into him?" Erin said with a smirk.

Even Carolyn, the old lady's maid, was smiling, but no one's smile was broader than Mama's.

"Well, your taste in girls, Kyle, leaves a lot to be desired." Erin put a cracker in her mouth and chewed it. "No offense to you, dear," she said and looked at me.

"Nothing wrong with my taste in women, Erin," Kyle said.

I heard Grandma Edna laugh. She laughed so hard that some of the cracker went flying out of her mouth.

Erin lit another cigarette and tossed the match into an ashtray. "My good God, Kyle," she said, "that last girl you brought home was the size of a cow. She was so fat that you couldn't sleep with her if you wanted to, if she'd even let you. She let you Kyle?"

"That's none of your damn business." Kyle's face looked about as fierce as a shark's scenting blood.

"Remember, Mother, that afternoon we picnicked over at Low Cross Lane. We couldn't get that poor girl on the ground and then we couldn't get her up off the ground once we got her down there. And when we all wanted to nap in the shade we couldn't even turn her over." Erin found her remark amusing and started laughing.

"Screw you, Erin," Kyle shouted out.

I looked across the room at Erin, whom I quickly decided I couldn't stand. She was laughing along with Grandma Edna, sort of hooting and choking on whatever the hell they had in their mouths. Poor Seth was sitting with his head down and Mama and Uncle Austin were stone-faced.

"So much for your taste in women, little brother," Erin said as she blew smoke into the room that almost made me gag.

I watched as Earline got up and poured herself some wine. "I guess you all know that a woman's charms are not necessarily determined by her dress size."

"I liked Missy," Aunt El announced. "She had a wonderful sense of humor."

"We won't talk about your taste in women either," Erin smirked again.

Grandma Edna snapped her fingers at Carolyn and I realized that as much as Carolyn was trying to keep herself detached from this unfortunate discussion, she was mesmerized. She seemed to shake herself free after she was snapped at like that though.

"Sorry, ma'am," she said and began refilling everyone's glass. "What can I get you?" she asked me and Kyle.

"Give the children lime sodas, Carolyn," Grandma Edna said.

I didn't like lime soda, but I kept my mouth shut. Though I did want to know what had happened to the girl Kyle had dated.

"Kyle," I said. "What happened to her, the girl you were seeing?"

I never was one for keeping my mouth shut, but I was really curious. However, they were all looking at me now like I was a rattlesnake that had slithered in the back door by mistake.

"She stopped seeing me," he said sadly. "She couldn't stand being teased by my goddamn family."

"Oh," I said, feeling horrible now that I'd asked.

"Oh please, Kyle," Grandma Edna said. "Don't be so sensitive. You overreact to everything. We all loved Missy and we all love you, don't we?" She stared at Erin, who kept smoking and remained silent. "But you are too handsome to have to settle for an unattractive girl."

Kyle jumped up so quickly that he almost knocked Carolyn off her feet as she came back into the room with our lime sodas.

"I don't like lime soda," he screamed out. Then he grabbed a glass and threw its contents into the empty fireplace.

"Go to your room, Kyle," Grandma Edna said, almost wearily. "We do not throw glasses into fireplaces when we don't like what is being said."

"I didn't throw the glass. I threw the goddamn lime soda." He glared at her.

I watched as he put the glass on top of the mantel and ran up the stairs. I wanted to join him. I didn't want to eat with these people any more than I wanted to live with them. I looked at Mama and I saw that her expression was pained so deeply, too deeply for me to understand.

"Can I be excused?" I asked.

"Absolutely not," Grandma Edna answered.

Chapter Three

Iknow I had a bad dream that night. Big, creepy-crawling monsters setting fire to my hair and wild, mythological birds chasing after me in fields that offered no way out. It was a premonition that would darken my morning and, sure enough, when I opened my eyes the next day, the first thing I saw was the lead player in my nasty dream.

"Get up and get dressed," Grandma Edna said. "We're going to Beaufort."

"Beaufort, what for?"

"Buy you some clothes," she said as she rummaged through my dresser drawer and threw a pair of shorts at me. "This all you got, shorts and jeans?"

I nodded forlornly and looked at her like she was crazy. "You own a blouse, child?"

I shook my head. "Just T-shirts," I said.

"Damn shame," she muttered. "Get dressed and get on downstairs for breakfast. Carolyn has made you toast. You like toast?"

"Sure," I said.

"Meet me outside by the car in twenty minutes. Dudley will take us to Beaufort."

"Sure," I said as I got out of bed and watched Grandma Edna leave my room huffing and puffing in disgust, as if I was the sorriest sight she'd ever seen.

Well, wasn't I the lucky one. I was getting to spend the day with Grandma Edna in Beaufort while she dressed me in pink and stuck one of those sissy hats on my head; the big, stupid-looking bonnets that a lot of prissy girls wore that I'd normally never, ever be caught dead in.

I wondered where Mama was. She must have gotten up early and wasn't there to save me from this woman's clutches. I guess I was sleeping so late 'cause I was upset having to deal with these people at all. I felt like Mama was abandoning me to the fire and fury of misfortune. Maybe she was going to be joining me on my journey to Beaufort. I didn't think she should be leaving me alone with some old woman who was sending me all the way to China to replace some stupid dish. And by the way, I wondered, who the hell was Dudley?

I really wished that having a Rolls Royce in my family would have made me feel better, but it didn't. It was Dudley up there driving it and he didn't look any older than me. I sure would have liked to have been the one driving it.

"Can I sit up front with Dudley?" I asked.

Grandma Edna looked at me as if I'd farted in a goddamn quiet as a mouse grand ballroom during a goddamn speech by the President of the United States.

"Act like a member of your class," she said.

I knew Dudley was smiling even though I couldn't see his face. I guess I wasn't supposed to ask to sit next to a Negro person.

I could see Dudley's personality from the back of his head. His ears stuck out a little, so I knew he was perky. I noticed he wasn't much taller than me and I knew that for sure, even though I'd only seen him sitting.

"Do you mind the breeze, ma'am?" Dudley asked.

Grandma Edna told him to raise the window a bit and then she stared out into space and didn't speak to me at all 'til we got to Beaufort.

"We're here," she said when we arrived. "We'll shop first, then have lunch."

"Yes, ma'am," I said.

Would it have mattered if I'd said I'd rather eat lunch, then shop? I pretty much doubted that so I kept my mouth shut, but I was more hungry than interested in the dumb clothes she was about to buy me.

By the time I found myself sitting in some fancy restaurant she had bought me two bonnets, five dresses, two white slips, two pair of flat shoes, seven pair of underwear, and two pair of peddle pusher pants she said I could wear during the day, 'cause blue jeans were not allowed at all anywhere on her property except on men. She also bought me several blouses to go with the pedal pusher pants in all the colors I didn't much like, like pink, purple, and yellow.

"Say thank you, Sassy," she said. "I've just bought you a wardrobe."

"Thank you, Grandma Edna," I said while I was biting into a sandwich with no meat and too many goddamn tomatoes that she insisted I eat 'cause tomatoes were healthy.

"Don't speak with your mouth full," she said. "And wipe your chin."

"How long we staying with you?" I asked.

"From the looks of that wardrobe I bought you, a pretty long time."

I couldn't stop the sigh that fell from my lips, but instead of scowling at me, the old lady was actually smiling.

"You might not like it here, but it's the best place for you to be."

"Maybe. I got a puppy now. My other puppy died."

"Really? Puppies should never die, like babies. Babies should never die, either, Sassy."

I stared at her. I wasn't quite sure what to say to that. I shrugged my shoulders and looked off. When I looked back, Grandma Edna looked sad as Mama.

"She named you right," she said.

"She named me for my sex appeal," I said.

Grandma Edna got a strange look on her face. She stared at me a long time, and it made me so nervous that one of those stupid tomatoes slid right between the bread and onto my lap.

"Hope you got a napkin there," she said.

"Of course," I said as I picked the tomato up and left it on the side of the plate. I decided then and there that I didn't like tomatoes much and would never have one inside any of my sandwiches again. Tomatoes belonged in a goddamn salad.

"She had to come back, you know. She had to come back as much as she had to leave."

"Mama had to leave?" I asked. I hadn't expected her to say anything like that at all.

"She had to. Made me mad as hell at first, but I understand now; she had to. Aside from that though, she couldn't stay here, not then, not even now, really, but I'm glad she came back. I understand. None of us knew what to do, least of all, Violet."

"What to do about what?" I asked even though I was quite sure she wasn't going to tell me.

The old lady was playing with her napkin and speaking into it more than she was speaking to me. Then she shocked me. She leaned across the table and held my gaze.

"Can you keep a secret?" she asked.

I was too startled to speak, so I just nodded my head.

"I'm going to tell you something I never said aloud before, and I don't want you repeating it. You hear me, child?"

"Yes, ma'am."

"You're an old soul is what I think, makes me feel I can trust you. Can I trust you, Sassy?"

I think my mouth was drooping to the floor, but I managed to nod an affirmative.

"I never wanted more than two children. That shock you?"

I knew my mouth was still drooping, but I didn't seem to be able to close it. I forced myself to nod affirmatively once again.

"Well, in my opinion, no woman should have more than two children, but there's no telling a man what to do or how to do it. That's the difference between men and women; the man has the deed on your life, and the woman has the task. Tasks aren't worth a thing. Tasks are just demands, responsibilities, laws uttered by those who are best served by them. That make sense?"

"Yes," I managed to get out weakly.

"You got to grow up and write your own laws, Sassy. Have no deed on your head. You can't be owned unless you agree to be. You understand that, child? Your Mama was the youngest, never would have been born if it was up to me. That isn't to say I don't love that child. Lord knows, I loved her most of all."

I didn't like her saying that about my mama, that just didn't sound right. I didn't expect her to speak to me normal-like and, despite what she said, it was kind of nice being spoken to like I was older than I was, but hearing her say my mama never should have been born made me feel like stomping right on out of there. But then, she contradicted herself by saying she loved her most of all, so I remained seated, at least for the time being.

We didn't go right home after lunch even though there didn't seem to be anything else to do in Beaufort. Dudley had brought all our shopping to the car and he was just sitting there waiting on us.

"Where we going?" I asked Grandma Edna.

"We're stopping off to see an old friend," she said.

I let her hold my hand and, even though I feared for my life, I followed her. We must have walked clear to the end of town. I kept wondering if she was bringing me to my demise. Instead she stopped in front of a café called Littleton & Son.

"You can get a soda here, a nice lime soda." She smiled at me and took a seat in a red leather booth.

I liked it there. It was a colorful place that sold candy and newspapers. It even had a whole shelf of kid's toys and a long counter for hamburgers and malts.

"I don't really like lime soda," I said as I slipped in opposite her.

She looked a bit startled. "You don't? I thought all children liked lime soda."

"Kyle doesn't, either."

"Then what do you like?" she asked.

"I like Coca-Cola," I said.

"And what does Kyle like?"

"Not sure, but it isn't lime soda."

I never thought this woman could smile, but there she sat, grinning like a jack-o'-lantern.

"Then have a Coca-Cola. I don't believe in depriving little girls of what they want."

"I'm not a little girl," I said. "I'm thirteen years old."

"When are you going to be fourteen?" she asked.

"July twenty-first," I said.

She sat back like she was counting numbers in her head. Suddenly she said, "Yeah, too bad being too blind to see."

"See what?" I asked.

She didn't answer 'cause some man came up to us and slid down in the booth next to Grandma Edna.

"Nice to see you, Edna," he said, but he was looking at me.

"Hello, Franklin," she said. "This is Sassy Sweetwater, my daughter's girl."

The man was looking at me in a kind way so I smiled at him. Kindness begets kindness, mama always said.

"She's Violet's girl?" he asked.

"Yes."

"Spittin' image."

The man put his hands through his hair and didn't say a word more. When he got up to leave he turned back to Grandma Edna.

"I'll let Aaron know," was all he said. "I'm sure he'll call you."

I watched him walk off. "Who was that?" I asked.

"Like I said, an old friend."

Grandma Edna sat forward and stared at me some more. "Don't outrun your age, Sassy. There will be plenty of time to be a woman. Too much time, perhaps."

She didn't say any more than that on the way home. She seemed to be lost in thought. I wished I could have felt better about the clothes she bought me, but all I could think about was how stupid I was going to look in pastel blouses and pedal pushers, not to mention a goddamn bonnet. Back in Glenmora, girls wore jeans and cowboy boots. Mama never had a problem with that and she never insisted that I wear dresses at all. I was just hoping I could protest having to wear them to dinner every night. I was willing to compromise with the old woman, that was for sure, but was she willing to compromise with me?

"If I please you all week by wearing dresses to dinner, don't you think you should please me on Saturday and Sunday and let me wear jeans?" I blurted out.

She turned and looked at me. I had broken through whatever convoluted thoughts she was having. I was sure she thought just about the same way she spoke—convoluted.

"What's that, child?"

"Well, I should have two days off from wearing dresses, at the very least."

"Little girls do not wear pants to dinner. I'll say nothing more about it."

"Aunt El had pants on last night."

"Aunt El always has pants on, that's why she doesn't have a husband. You'll never see her with anything else on 'cause she's stubborn as a goddamn mule and cares nothing 'bout pleasing men. But your Aunt El is over twenty-one, and she can wear what she wants."

"Yes, ma'am," I said and slid down in my seat. This woman was surely a pain in my side.

When we got back to the house, Grandma Edna told Dudley to bring the clothes up to my room and have Carolyn put them away.

"Be quick about it, Dudley, or they'll wrinkle up. Oh, and make sure to wash the car before tomorrow. I don't want to see a streak like I did last time, boy."

"Yes, ma'am," Dudley said.

Dudley winked at me then and I saw the biggest dimple in his cheeks. It was almost as though he were laughing at everybody else while everybody else was acting superior to him.

"Old bitty," he mouthed behind his hand. "Tight as lemon lips."

I broke into a roaring laugh, but Grandma Edna must have been too far ahead of me to hear. I decided I was living in a crazy house inside a crazy world and the only people I'd allow inside my bubble of safety would be Kyle and, of course, Mama and maybe now even Grandma Edna's servant, Dudley.

Chapter Four

I soon found out that Dudley was Carolyn's boy and they lived in a little white house behind the McLaughlin's property. Dudley had a brother everyone called Pike 'cause he had a long flat nose like some fish. I never did know Pike's given name. Pike worked for the McLaughlin's whenever things needed fixing, like roofs and shingles and such. James Leroy was Pike and Dudley's father. I saw James Leroy inside the house a lot helping Carolyn and wearing a tuxedo.

Carolyn had hung up all my clothes and those that didn't hang she put in my dresser drawer. Mama went through everything when she came upstairs and started giggling. Probably couldn't help but laugh herself silly knowing I'd rather eat a plate full of spinach and drink warm Pepto-Bismol than show myself in something pink or yellow to the general public.

"You're going to have to wear this stuff," she said and I could see the humor in her eyes. My mama wanted to burst out laughing.

Several sighs fell from my lips and I turned away. I would have preferred cow dung on the knees of my jeans at my own goddamn wedding than the clothes that woman had picked out for me.

"You can't hurt her feelings," I heard Mama say.

"She wouldn't let me pick out my own clothes," I said.

"And what would you have chosen?" Mama asked. "Coveralls? Cowboy boots? Shit kickers?"

I didn't laugh, though I wanted to.

"Well, that's one way to have gotten rid of her. The old lady would have had a heart attack if I'd tried on a boy's cap," I said. "She really your mother?"

"Yes," Mama said. "And she's your grandmother and this is her house, so humor her by putting on those pedal pushers. Kyle wants to take you for a walk. Wear the light blue blouse; it's not as offensive as the pink one."

I wondered if Mama had heard from Aunt El that Kyle was retarded, but if she let me go out alone with him, she probably hadn't.

Kyle took me up behind the house and we followed a trail that went across some open fields. The dirt trail wound around ahead of us and I had no idea where it would end. There were hills everywhere I looked that swooped up into the sky and roads that weren't yet paved ran straight and some ran curved, probably leading to some mysterious dead end. I think it was the prettiest day I'd ever seen. Mama used to say that some days are downright friendly and that nature was just like a person, either snarling at you like a fierce wind, crapping on you like a storm, or loving you up like the sun.

"This is a friendly day," I announced.

We'd taken the trail down through some woods and it ended at a cove. I could hear the water running, crystal clear, something you wanted to drink, or at least put your feet in. The little rocks were gray and black and the cove was shaped like a heart. Kyle took off his shoes and socks and rolled up his pants.

"You coming?" he asked.

Well I wasn't quite sure of where I was going, but I kicked off my shoes and socks and followed him out through the water. It was cold and it tickled, but it felt good on my skin. I followed Kyle onto a big rock about fifteen feet out. I could feel the sun on me, with a blanket's warmth.

"I like it here," he said, climbing up and making room for me. "It's my special place."

It was pretty there, that was for sure. You could look all around and see nothing but trees and water. There were birds in the sky that you couldn't see, but I knew they were there 'cause I could hear 'em. I could even feel 'em close by.

"We got a swimming hole, too. I'll take you there tomorrow, but it's prettier here, a whole lot prettier," he said. "I come here to think."

I wondered what a boy like Kyle could think about when he was alone and no one around him was making him mad, like Grandma Edna and Aunt Erin had the other night.

"What got you so mad the other night?" I asked. "Was it just about that girl?"

"Maybe."

"She's mean, saying things to you no mother should ever say to her own son, or sister to her own brother."

"Answered your own question."

"You do chores at the farm?" I asked.

"What farm?" he said.

"The McLaughlin's," I said.

"That's not a farm we live in, it's a house."

I was surprised. I just assumed everyone was farming something in South Carolina.

"Well, how'd they get so rich? Aren't they farmers?"

"Hell, no." Kyle started laughing. "They're industrialists. Granddaddy is a magnate."

I think my mouth dropped right into the water. So, it seemed my grandfather was still alive, just away on business?

"Your family owns steel mills, Sassy, several of them. Recently sold off a few to Bethlehem Steel, ever hear of them?"

I shook my head. I was soon to learn from Kyle how rich the McLaughlin's were. I found out that the somber boy in the photograph was my Uncle Liam and, according to Kyle, he ran things right along with my grandfather.

"What about Seth?" I asked. "And my aunts?"

"They keep Seth under lock and key. He can barely make a run into Beaufort much less run a company. They assume, of course, that I'm just like him, dumb and useless."

"What's Seth do then?"

"He drinks," Kyle said.

I looked up when I heard a whistle. I could see Dudley walking through weeds, coming up on us with his grin.

"He know about this place?" I asked, a bit surprised.

"He's my best friend," Kyle said.

"How'd I know you were going to bring that girl out here?" Dudley called out.

"She's okay," Kyle called back.

Dudley took off his shoes and rolled up his pants and waded out to us. I noticed how the water seemed to glisten on his legs, as though his whole body had been oiled. The water looked like diamonds on his arms shinning in the sun.

"Hi," Dudley said. "Can I join you?"

Kyle and I moved over and Dudley climbed up. He sat there staring at us for a bit. It made Kyle and I laugh.

Suddenly, Dudley held out his hand. "Dudley James Leroy," he said. "Me and Kyle are like brothers."

"Sassy Sweetwater," I said, shaking his hand. "I guess we weren't properly introduced."

"Oh, I'm just part of the landscape, not anyone your grandma is going to want to introduce you to." He winked at me. "Your family hates the Kennedys so what does that tell you?"

"I'm just part of the landscape, too. Not really pemanent, though," I said.

"You like mysteries, sweet water Sassy?" Dudley asked. He was grinning, of course. He was always grinning. I wondered what he looked like when he wasn't showing teeth or dimples.

"Yeah, I like figuring things out," I said.

"Where you been all this time?"

"Glenmora, Louisiana," I said.

Dudley laughed. "They used to talk about your mama. Never talked about you, though."

"What'd they say about my mama?" I asked.

"White people only talk in front of Negroes. Did you know that? Negroes don't hear so they don't repeat, you understand? And if they do repeat, they know they'll find themselves in a noose swinging from a tree. Their flesh is cheap. You know any living thing worth less than Negro flesh?"

Dudley kept his wide grin while I stared at him. I wasn't quite sure how I should react to that.

"Hey, Dud," Kyle said. "You come all the way out here to toss us a riddle?"

"No riddle," he said. "Fact. Don't you know what a riddle is?"

"Want to catch a film later?" Kyle asked him.

Dudley shook his head. "No, I can't stay long, but I seen you two heading toward the cove. Wanted to make your acquaintance in the proper way." He smiled at me, and I smiled back.

We sat on the rock tracing nothing in particular with the sticks in our hands and saying nothing at all. After a long while of silence, Dudley suddenly threw his stick far out into the water. Then he stood up and removed his shirt. I saw that he wasn't skinny at all. He had muscles that made him look strong as an ox.

"What about my Aunt El?" I said to Kyle. "What does she do?"

"Women don't run steel mills, Sassy. Your Aunt El has taken over the duties of the house, a task worse than death for a woman like her."

"You know she's married to Earline?"

"Not married like we could be," Kyle said.

Dudley slid down the rock and into the water. "You two couldn't be married, either," he said.

"What are you talking about?" Kyle asked.

"Look at the two of you, both got different colored hair. Sassy's is red-gold, Kyle's is like a lemon. Not a lot of people can say they got hair like that. Got different fathers, I think. But maybe got the same mother, you two. I knew it the minute I saw you Sweetwater Sassy. I remembered how he threw your mama out, even threatened to kill her 'cause of that boy in town, the one she got caught holding hands with. Had hair like flame, too, more than that, his face is stamped on yours." He looked at me.

Kyle stood up and put his hands on Dudley's shoulders. "That's enough, Dud," he said. "You've got no proof of anything like that."

"Truth don't need proof."

I saw the look that came across Kyle's face. I didn't know what they were talking about. I didn't understand what Dudley was getting at. Seems he didn't talk straight, he talked around things.

"No more of this," Kyle said. "I don't want to hear this talk. Hair color don't mean a damn thing."

Dudley looked at me. "I'm thirty-three years old," he said. "I remember things. I talk truth, but no one listens to a black man. We got nothing worth hearing."

"You know that isn't true," Kyle said. "I don't think like that."

"Gonna be a riot in town, black students marching into Littleton & Son demanding to be served. Whole country is gonna burn up over that 'cause they ain't taking no for an answer."

I looked off. I knew what was going on around me, lots of angry heat over black people, but Mama said it's going to all be ironed out one day and made right.

Kyle laughed. "Good thing Granddaddy is up North or he'd be down here burning crosses."

"Sure enough," Dudley said, "just not on my front lawn."

"Tell me about our family," I said to Kyle.

Kyle sat back on the rock. "Your Aunt Erin is married to a rich man and doesn't do a damn thing but smoke cigarettes all day and say nasty things to anyone who crosses her path. Your Aunt Beatrice is a spinster who lives up North and writes mystery books she can't publish. Oh, and your Aunt Peg is a cuckoo."

"A cuckoo?"

"Yeah, she's into fortune telling, works a night club in Savannah."

"I guess she's the only one I'd be interested in having dinner with," I said and laughed.

Dudley chuckled. "We're on the same wavelength, Sassy. Your Aunt Peg is a live wire, sees things like me. I like live wires."

"What do you have to say about my family?" I asked Dudley.

"Your mama was the prettiest woman I ever set eyes on. I still remember and I was Kyle's age when she left here."

"So they never said anything bad about her?"

"Perverted tongues have nothing but foul illusions to spread." Dudley looked proud of himself and grinned at me some more.

"Who's perverted?" I asked Kyle. "Aunt El?"

"I don't know what he's talking about," Kyle said.

"Elvira McLaughlin has no eyes to see. She don't even know she's a lesbian. That pretty one just humors her, tells her they're just being friendly, not to worry." Dudley grabbed his shirt and pursed his lips, sounding as feminine as he could get, he said, "Just scratch me here, sweetie. I got an itch between my legs is all, but don't stop scratching me 'til the big bad itch is done. Nothing queer about scratching now, is there?"

Kyle hooted real loud. "You're a nasty son of a bitch," he said.

"I got to go." Dudley put his shirt back on and buttoned it up. "She gave me a shopping list a mile long, the one that don't know she's a lesbian."

I watched him wade back to shore. He yelled out over his shoulder. "None of them have eyes to see, but you got eyes Sweetwater Sassy. I can see that."

I watched him walk off through the weeds like he'd never been there. "What's he talking about?" I asked Kyle and shook my head.

"Sometimes I know, and sometimes I don't, but he speaks the truth as he knows it, in his own strange way."

"What's it like going to school here?" I asked, wanting to change the subject. I didn't like talking about things I can't get at. "I'm probably going to still be here in September."

I'd asked Mama when we'd be returning to Glenmora, but she said we'd be staying a while at Carter's Crossing, that she had unfinished business. Of course I asked her what kind of unfinished business, but she wouldn't tell me. I sensed in my soul that I was stuck here for eternity 'cause most things unfinished stay that way.

Kyle found some little sticks that he tossed into the water. "School here is hell," he said.

I remembered what Aunt El had told me about Kyle being retarded and I wasn't quite sure how to broach the subject. It was probably none of my business anyway.

"You don't like to read?" I asked him.

Kyle laughed, a reaction I hadn't expected.

"That what they told you? Ain't true, just what they think."

"Yeah," I said. "I thought so."

"I act well my part," he said, with his face close to mine.

"I didn't ever believe it," I said.

"When June-bug is old enough, we'll bring her out here with us. I'll read to her and you can see for yourself." He winked at me and grinned. "I can read a book a day. I'll read to you."

He sure didn't seem retarded to me.

"'Listen to this, 'Family quarrels are bitter things. They don't go according to any rules. They're not like aches or wounds, they're more like splits in the skin.'"

I stared at him not knowing what to say. I knew he was referring to the McLaughlin family and what he had just said made sense, though I couldn't have told you why.

"F. Scott Fitzgerald," he said.

"Who's he?" I asked.

"A great writer," he said. "Like Joyce and James and Keats."

I couldn't help but stare at him and search his face. He had more freckles than me and his eyes were green, but not like mine, grayish like; his were cat's eyes, green as emeralds, light like the man in the photograph. But we were bound by something close and I probably knew it the moment I laid eyes on him. Maybe Dudley spoke truth. Maybe Kyle and I were born from the same parents. But how could that be? Mama was seventeen when she had me. Couldn't have been more than fifteen if she'd birthed Kyle. Anyway, if Kyle was my brother, Mama would have kept him.

"Do you know who my father is?" I asked Kyle. He shook his head and looked off.

"I'm going to ask Dudley," I said.

"Why don't you ask your mama?" he asked.

I started laughing. "You're not stupid, you're lying to everybody. Why?"

He sat and looked into space for a long time. All of a sudden he surprised me and slid back off the rock.

"Come on with me," he said and started wading back to where we'd left our shoes. I followed behind him and barely had enough time to lace my sneakers.

We walked back the way we'd come except that we cut off the trail about a half mile from the house. I had to keep yelling at him to slow down. Kyle hadn't said anything at all, but he was walking fast. I could tell he was determined about something, maybe it was just about leading me somewhere.

We climbed up a short hill. There was a sycamore tree flowing out against the sky, reaching for the corners of the earth.

"Look here," he said, breathing heavy.

I saw it there under the tree, a small cross. "A dog buried there?" I asked.

"A child, Sassy Sweetwater," he said. "A baby."

I was shocked. The family cemetery was way off in the other direction. Kyle had pointed it out to me while we were walking to the cove and I said I wanted to see it just to trace the names, see if any of those dead people were named Sassy. He had promised to show it to me.

"Why is he over here all by himself?" I asked.

"You don't put a body out somewhere in plain sight, not one you can't explain."

I shook my head in disbelief. "You're not saying that someone in the McLaughlin family killed a baby?"

"That's why I'm pretending to be dumber than a mule, Sassy. That's why," was all he said.

Chapter Five

A few nights later, I found myself sitting across the dinner table from a man with flame hair, just like mine. I could see the shine in it every time he turned toward the candlelight. I kept looking from him to Mama; hard to keep my eyes off Mama 'cause something was under her skin, like electric shots. I could feel it. Her heart was like a river, flowing soft under the mystery of the moon. Whether or not she noticed how I stared at her, I couldn't say. Mama had too many secrets. It unsettled me to know that. She looked more beautiful than I'd ever seen her. I remembered how she once told me that beauty is an inner energy ignited by a passion. Well, then, Mama's passions were on fire that night.

Grandma Edna sat at the head of the table and Uncle Seth was down at the other end. Me and Kyle were sitting together staring at the redheaded man across from us that everyone was calling Aaron.

"I was very honored to accept your invitation to dinner tonight, Mrs. McLaughlin," he said and politely smiled at Grandma Edna.

"I'm happy you were free on such short notice," she said.

The man called Aaron carefully put a piece of meat in his mouth and chewed it slowly. He stared at Kyle and then at me and smiled.

"Your mama and I went to school together," he said. He turned and looked at my mama like she was a thirsty man's stream of cool, fresh water. I saw something in his eyes I'd never seen in any man's eyes before, not Guy Grissom or any one of Mama's other admirers. He lingered on her, as if leaving her image might have been a painful act he couldn't bear enduring.

"I think you meant to say that you and Violet were glued together." Seth laughed like that was a private joke. "Not went to school together."

Aaron laughed uncomfortably and glanced at Grandma Edna. "We were close, yes," he said and smiled at me.

"I think you best apologize to your sister, Seth, for being glued to someone is hardly an attractive way of saying that Violet captured attention." Grandma Edna pursed her lips into a smug expression and took a sip of wine. "Especially Aaron's."

"Yes, she certainly captured my attention," Aaron said. "You look quite lovely tonight, Violet. Same as ever."

I watched my mama smile a smile I'd never seen before. Her gaze roamed over his face like some priceless, precious lost object.

"So how's business over at Littleton & Son?" Seth sat back and wiped his chin with a white napkin. "Hear tell there's trouble in town."

"We're ready for it," Aaron said. "Just hoping it won't happen."

"I'm staying clear of Beaufort," Mama said.

"Not if I have anything to say about it," Aaron said. And then, as if he'd been embarrassed by saying it, he added, "The restaurant is a lot bigger than when you last saw it. You need to come by. We're selling lots of things in there now, like magazines and toys."

Earline sat to Aaron's right and Aunt El sat to his left. Everyone was eating, even Kyle. I wanted to give him a look, but I seemed to be the only one recognizing, or giving a damn, that my mama and this Aaron feller sure looked like they liked each other a whole lot.

"Do you do well in school, Sassy?" Aaron asked. That took me by surprise. I hadn't really expected him to talk much to me at all.

"I like it well enough," I said.

Mama smiled at me. "Aaron was the class valedictorian," she said.

"What's that?" I asked him, but it was Grandma Edna who answered.

"He had the highest grades in his graduating class," she said. "That would be a nice goal for you, Sassy." She looked at Kyle disdainfully. "Someone in this family needs to show a little intelligence and fortitude."

Kyle ignored Grandma Edna and took a bite of the beef bourguignonne that Carolyn had made. "This is very, very good," he said. "I'm sure smart enough to recognize that."

"I think you're a whole lot smarter than you let on." Aunt Earline winked at him.

"What was your favorite subject in school?" Kyle suddenly asked and leaned forward toward Aaron. "Literature?"

Aaron smiled. "Actually, it was science."

"I like literature, too, especially Shakespeare. You like Shakespeare?" Kyle leaned in even further and stared at Aaron pensively.

"Yes, Shakespeare was a wise man." Aaron smiled at Kyle and Kyle sat there staring at him like he was an apparition.

"Listen to this."

Kyle stood up and looked at all of us around the table, like he was about to deliver bad news. He put his hand to his head and brooded a bit, then he began to speak while he walked and paced around the room.

"To be, or not to be, that is the question,
Whether 'tis nobler in the mind to suffer
The slings and arrows of outrageous fortune,
Or to take arms against a sea of troubles,
And by opposing, end them. To die, to sleep
No more, and by a sleep to say we end
The heartache, and the thousand natural shocks
That flesh is heir to; 'tis a consummation
Devoutly to be wished to die to sleep!
To sleep, perchance to dream, ay there's the rub,
For in that sleep of death what dreams may come
When we have shuffled off this mortal coil
Must give us pause."

I noticed that everyone was eating except for me and Mama and Aaron. I hadn't taken my eyes off Kyle. Aaron sat back and clapped. He looked a bit startled.

"How fine you recited that, Kyle. Hamlet, isn't it? Yes, quite fine. It was as if you understood exactly what you were saying. I'd say you have a feel for Shakespeare."

Grandma Edna laughed, as did Aunt El. "He read it off a napkin, I'm sure," Aunt El said.

"Ha!" I shouted. "You said he couldn't read."

"Don't be impertinent, Sassy," Grandma Edna said.

"How could he recite Shakespeare if he can't read to memorize," I yelled.

"Radio," Grandma Edna whispered as if Kyle wasn't even there.

"Bull," I shouted.

"Sit down, Kyle, and don't let your meal get cold." Grandma Edna shook her hands in a flurry. "Sit, sit. Shakespeare gives me a headache and this bourguignonne is just too good, needs to be eaten while it's still warm."

Kyle stopped at Aaron's chair and whispered in his ear, but I heard what he said. "I want to be an actor," is what he said.

Aaron looked at Mama again. "Acting is a fine profession," he said. "Would you agree?"

Mama nodded. "Nothing pleases me more than a good live performance."

"Yes, yes, acting is a fine profession."

Kyle searched Aaron's face. I saw the desperation in his expression and I wondered why this man seemed so important to him. It was like he wanted to enter into his blood stream and connect to his very organs. Then I thought about what Dudley had said and it came upon me like a beam of lightning striking before my eyes. *Aaron is my father, isn't he? Mine and Kyle's.*

"I have quite a high regard for actors," Aaron said. "It's the craft of chameleons."

"And you said he was dumb," I said to Aunt El, with a great deal of anger. "He knows F. Scott Fitzgerald, too."

All of a sudden everybody was staring at me as if I'd just farted again in church and competed with the incense.

After a moment Earline reached for another helping of potatoes.

"I played Goldilocks in grammar school. Everyone told me I should be an actress." Aunt Earline looked at me and grinned.

"Heaven spared you," Grandma Edna said. "You would have failed miserably. I hear a lisp impediment in your speech and you're unattractively short."

No one laughed at that but Grandma Edna. I looked back at Aaron and watched him eat. Everyone was being polite, not wanting to offend Grandma Edna, even though she had offended Earline.

"I don't think being short has anything to do with being an actor, do you?" I asked Aaron. "I think Earline is pretty enough to have been a fine actress."

"I do agree with you, Sassy. Earline might have been the next Julie Andrews." He smiled at me and I caught Grandma Edna's expression, like she'd just taken a bite of bitter.

"Well since everyone at this table is entitled to their own opinion let me add that being pretty would not have been enough. One has to be reasonable when choosing a profession."

"And what do you want to be when you grow up, Sassy?" Aaron asked.

He had my color hair and it was smooth like mine and straight. Aaron was boyish looking, almost cute and he barely looked much older than Kyle. He had a nice face and without knowing him well, I would trust it.

"I want to be a painter," I said and smiled at Mama. "To capture description is a passion and I'm a passionate person."

Mama laughed. "That you are, Sassy," she said.

I stared at Mama wishing she could read my mind. I wasn't quite sure how I was going to approach the subject, but I'd found an answer to one riddle, at least. This man was my goddamn father. He seemed nice enough. Why hadn't I ever met him before?

"A painter?" I heard Grandma Edna say. "How alike we are, Sassy. Of course, I would never claim to make a living at it, but it's a fine hobby. I do enjoy painting. I go often to Sutter's Fork and paint barns. Would you like to join me one afternoon? There are fine barns out there to paint. We could walk the back roads, lots of fine subjects there."

I took a sip of water and smiled slyly. "I want to paint naked people," I said.

Grandma Edna sat back with a start. "Oh, pardon me," she said.

"I want to paint lines and circles and force the realm of reality. I don't want my paintings to look like anything anyone else could ever paint. I want my inner vision exposed on canvas, splattered in color, for my vision is uniquely mine, but it is open to interpretation, not like a stupid static barn, which can only be what it is—a stupid static barn."

They were staring at me, even Mama.

"Apologize immediately," Mama demanded. I could see fire coming from her eyes.

"No need," Grandma Edna said. "I like her spirit. And besides, she's right. I never had the courage to reveal my inner expressionism. I'm too much a realist."

Aaron finally broke the silence that lingered after that. Only sound I could make out was that of Seth chewing his food.

"There's a gallery in Charleston that I particularly like," Aaron said. "The work is innovative and young, very daring. Would you like to go to Charleston with me one day, Sassy? We could go to the galleries and then to the Gibbs Museum, as well. Yes, we could go there, too."

I was shocked. Maybe he was claiming me?

"Can I go with you?" Kyle asked.

"Well, yes." Aaron looked at Mama. "We could make a weekend of it, take your mama with us. I'll get tickets to a show. Would you like that, Kyle?"

Kyle nodded so enthusiastically that his head might have detached from his neck. I hadn't looked at Mama to get her reaction, but everyone else was silent. They weren't even eating, they were just sitting there.

The ring of the phone was so loud and jarring that it made me jump. It was Seth who got up to answer it. He didn't say much, just nodded and said, "Yes, yes," a few times to whoever was on the other end. When he put down the phone, he looked at Grandma Edna, then at Mama.

"Liam will be here by tomorrow night," he said and, after a very long sigh, he added, "Daddy will follow in a month or two. There's some trouble with the Spartanburg mill, he needs to be close to home he says."

I might have noticed how silent they all got, but I was too happy to let anything in but Aaron's offer to start acting like a father.

That's what he was implying, wasn't he? Why else would he want to take us to Charleston?

"That was Liam on the phone?" Grandma Edna asked and Seth nodded.

"What do you think you should do?" Elvira asked Mama.

"Thought Daddy wasn't expected for another damn year," Mama said.

"He's about to lose another mill," Seth said. "It was unexpected."

Of course Mama didn't come up to bed right away. She was out there looking at Aaron, maybe even smooching with him. I snuck down the hall into Kyle's room. He shared the room with Seth, but Seth had gone out after dinner. He went out almost every night, none of us knew where and no one asked. Couldn't even tell you when he came home, but once I heard a car pull up the drive at dawn.

"He's my father, isn't he?" I said as I came rushing into the room.

"I hope so," he said. "I hope he's mine, too."

"What? You don't know whether he is or he isn't? How long you been living here?"

Kyle sat on his bed and stared at me. "They won't tell me who I am," he said. "Only thing anyone ever said to me is that I was left on the porch and Grandma Edna took me in. So, maybe that's the way it was."

"Well, I know I'm related to that man." I went to the mirror over Kyle's dresser and stared at my image, which so resembled Aaron's and any fool could see it.

"Your knowing don't mean a thing, we need proof."

"Proof, like what?"

"Like answers," he said.

"Only one around here with answers is Dudley." I looked at him and frowned. "But his answers don't come out straight. You have to speak Dudley talk and I can't."

"Dudley don't know a damn thing," he said. "Your mama knows, she's the only one."

"You ever see that man before?" I asked.

"What man?"

"Aaron," I said.

Kyle sat there mute. Finally he turned to me. "I've seen him in town, not here, never seen him here before."

That didn't make any sense to me and I sat down on the floor. "How come all of a sudden he's been invited to dinner?" I asked.

"'Cause your mama is here and they went to school together."

"Right and according to Seth they were 'glued together' and then my mama got pregnant and ran off," I said. "Maybe we should have a talk with Mama."

"Maybe I don't need the truth like you," Kyle said, like he'd suddenly gotten angry. "Maybe it's just fine that he comes around now. Maybe the truth would snatch him from me and I can't have that, Sassy. It's enough just us knowing. It just don't make sense, his pretending not to be our father when he is, but he must have a damn good reason for it and we should respect it."

I wanted to confront Mama no matter what Kyle thought, but she never made it back to her room, which led me to only one conclusion: she and this Aaron guy, who just might be my father, had spent the night together. I saw them from my window in the moonlight after I left Kyle's room. They were holding hands and I felt like the whole world shifted into slow motion as I watched them. They would stop walking, all of a sudden like, and stare at each other, my mama and this man whose blood I just might share. I was far from them, sitting in that window, but I knew what it was, what mama called the flame of life, when loving someone was a mirror into your soul. They held each other in the dark and it was like a song was being played. Oh, I knew what I was looking at. Their bodies moved to something beyond my hearing, but it had rhythm and heart and they danced to it. They danced the way only lovers can and I thought to myself that I had to have what Mama had, some day, in someone's eyes my soul would flourish, too.

I watched them walk off into darkness and disappear into the intimacy of their yearning. I approved. I so approved. I had a real family now. I had Mama and I had the answer and surely Mama would reunite me with the truth. I would cherish Aaron as my father. We'd make up time and whatever we had lost of it wouldn't matter from that point on.

Chapter Six

I took June-bug on her first trip to the cove the next morning. I didn't want human company, didn't want Kyle with me. Kyle was afraid of the truth, the very thing I sought. Kyle was hiding from all of them with his stupid act. I saw how desperate he was for Aaron's attention. I saw it with my own eyes and yet neither one would claim the other as father and son. I knew that if that man was my father, he better start calling me daughter. And he would, Mama would insist on it.

June-bug loved getting out of the barn. She was eight weeks old now, more than ready for the bed Pike had built for her. She was the softest thing I'd ever held in my arms and maybe the smartest dog in the state of South Carolina, for she knew exactly where I was headed and even led the way. It was like I could think something and she'd hear my thought.

Carolyn had put a blanket in her bed and Pike had carved "June-bug" into the wood. I was excited about finally moving her in to my room, maybe even into my bed when she got tired sleeping near the door. I'd speak to June-bug and tell her things I couldn't tell anyone else. Mama always said that a country road and a dog is just about the only religion a person needs.

After an hour or so playing at the cove, I sat down in the middle of a field and watched my puppy run around like she'd never been let loose before. When she tired herself out and lay down beside me, I started bonding with her, telling her things you can only tell a best friend. Lord knows, she was going to make more sense than Kyle or Dudley.

"I don't understand these people Mama calls kin," I told her. "Kyle is so confusing, cutting off his fingers like that, not wanting to confront Aaron as his father."

"Grandma Edna is downright mean, June-bug," I said. "And yet, sometimes I feel a kinship, strange as that sounds. I feel like her and me are bound in some way that I can't yet ascertain."

I put my hands behind my head and lay back. "You know," I said, "I wonder now if I didn't get my love of painting from Grandma Edna. I really do like to paint barns, but I wouldn't ever let her know that. I don't want to be like Grandma Edna, mean one moment and nice the next. I want to distance myself from being a contradiction. I wished I'd kept that to myself, about having a passion for painting. I'm not ready to share my secrets with Grandma Edna, she's too capable of swallowing everything I love with her abusive remarks and I'm not willing, quite yet, to let her gnaw on my bones."

June-bug licked my arm and I rolled over and patted her fur, staring into the warmest brown eyes I'd ever see on this earth.

"Seth is sad as can be. He's sweet, but he's not living life for the joy it is. There's a weight on him I wish I could take off and bury deep, deep enough to lighten his load, but that just doesn't seem possible when a man holds on to sorrow the way Seth does. He says he doesn't like the ways of the world. Wonder what he means by that?"

June-bug got up and chased a bird. I waited for her to return to my side and settle. Looked to me like she was smiling when she flopped down on her side.

"Aunt El is married to Aunt Earline," I said, "and no one talks about it. I can feel the way Grandma Edna hates Earline, but she doesn't do a damn thing about it 'cept say mean things. I heard her tell Seth that those two women should find themselves some husbands and get out of her house."

I had decided that when I got a chance I'd explain to Grandma Edna that Earline and Aunt El were married to each other and that was just the way it was, weird or not, and there wasn't ever going to be a husband for either one of them. Maybe I could make her understand that a person's choice is nobody else's responsibility or concern. But then she'd tell me I was too young to be smart and maybe I never would be.

I don't know what made me look up toward the hill. Maybe I felt Grandma Edna's presence, even though she was so far away. She was there though, under the tree where the grave was. She was sitting there stroking the cross and if I didn't know any better I'd swear she was talking to it.

I couldn't believe what my eyes beheld. I slid down on my stomach for fear she'd see me. Grandma Edna was sitting there talking to a dead baby who wasn't even in the family plot. I'd been hit with more shit since I stepped off that damn bus than I'd ever been hit with in my life. Why didn't my mama marry that redheaded man and give me a proper father? He seemed nice enough; why the hell wasn't he claiming me and Kyle?

And what the hell is that mean, old woman doing up on that hill talking to a dead baby?

Mama was there when me and June-bug got back. She was sitting at the kitchen table drinking down a cup of coffee. She was staring into nothing so hard she didn't even hear me enter, but June-bug went right to her and she hugged the dog close.

I was never one for pulling any punches and I was just about to tell Mama that I knew the truth now, but there was Kyle sitting on the other side of the table staring at Mama like she was someone he might never set eyes on again. Poor boy looked about to cry.

Mama looked over at me and tried to smile. She'd changed since the last time I saw her. I noticed it right away. My mama was thinking thoughts that were going to affect me forever. I felt my stomach fall.

"You out for an early walk?" she asked.

I nodded my head and looked over again at Kyle. He looked as downtrodden as Seth did on a daily basis. I knew my world was going to fall apart and I wondered if Mama had said anything to Kyle that was making him look like an undertaker had just done him up for his own goddamn funeral.

"I like Aaron," I said out of nowhere and I felt Mama's gaze shoot up to mine.

"Well, that's good, that's good," she said.

She glanced between Kyle and me. My stare was making her uncomfortable and I knew if I didn't open my mouth in the next three seconds, she'd be gone, fast as lightning and maybe even as far as Mars.

"When you going to tell us?" I said.

Kyle's head jerked up and his mouth just hung there, like he'd been struck dumb. I heard June- bug lapping up water from her bowl. I also heard Mama's breath and all the jumbled words she was trying to string together. There'd been only a few times I'd been real disappointed in my life and this was going to be one of them and this was going to be the most disappointing of all. Somehow I knew that.

"I was going to," she said.

"He's our father, right?" I blurted out.

Mama looked up briefly and then she sat there and stared at the cup in her hand. "I was going to tell you that I have to go away for a while."

"What do you mean you have to go away for a while?" I felt myself getting nauseous.

"I want you staying in one place 'til I'm ready to send for you, Sassy. I need to find a job and a place to stay. It won't be long, honey, I promise, not more than a few weeks."

"You going with him?" I asked.

Mama looked at me real innocent like. "Who?" She looked at Kyle like I'd been referring to him.

"Our father," I said.

Mama looked startled. "I'm going alone," she said. "At least for the time being, I'm going alone."

"That's not true," I said. "That's just not true. You know damn good and well you're going with him."

And Mama slammed her hand down on the table so hard that the cup fell over and what was left of the coffee spilled onto the table.

"Don't defy me. Don't you ever contradict me again, Sassy Sweetwater. I'm going alone."

"I hate you," I screamed out. "You're lying to me."

I ran back out the door and it slammed shut behind me. I saw Grandma Edna coming down from the hill. She stopped before me and searched my face.

"What is it, Sassy, what's wrong?"

I saw pain on her the same as I felt it all over me. I wanted to run into her arms, but I didn't. I ran in the other direction as fast as my feet would move, to find Dudley.

Dudley took care of the horses and pretty much drove everyone around in the Rolls Royce, ran errands, and on occasion, built and mended the fences with Pike. He kept the cars clean, too; aside from the Rolls, there was Seth's black Impala, and the blue Impala that Aunt El used.

I found Dudley in the barn tending the horses. He looked at me briefly when I walked in, but then quickly went back to what he was doing.

"Cloud over your head, girl," he said.

"Yeah, and soon it's going to storm," I said.

He laughed. "You talking Dudley, now."

"I met my father last night," I said. "You know him?"

He shrugged his shoulders. "Can't say I know him well."

"But you know him?"

"Sure enough."

I kicked something out from under my foot. "They're denying me the truth. Why?"

"Do I look like I got answers?"

"Someone does."

Dudley scratched his head and sat down on a small stool. "Yeah, they all got answers, but then again, they the ones that created all the questions. They the ones wrote the script, you know what I mean?"

"Give me some of those answers, Dudley."

"I'll give you what I can, what I know. Can't pull a rabbit out of a hat for you, though."

"Mama says she's leaving, but not with me. I swear, if she dares to go anywhere without me, I'll run away, never to be seen again."

"Best stay where your mama needs you to be. She's got her reasons."

"Aaron is my father, isn't he?"

"You got eyes, don't you?"

"He Kyle's father, too?" I asked.

Dudley looked off. "They all too blind to see who his father is. Plain as day to me."

"So why won't he own up to it? Why can't he come right out and tell me?"

"It'll cost him his life, Sweetwater Sassy. His body would be found in a ditch and no one would ever pay for it, not in this state. That's what I think."

"His life?" I asked. "Is that what you just said? What do you mean it'll cost him his life?"

"Been killing here on this land, killing of the flesh and, too, killing of the soul."

"Who killed that baby up under the tree?" I asked. "Is that what you're talking about?"

Dudley got up and stood before me. We were the same height and I met his eyes, soft and brown as a feisty squirrel's.

"Oh, so you know about that?" he said.

"Who killed it?"

"Two kind of men you best not cross: a rich man or a crazy man."

"What are you talking about?"

"You think Kyle cut off his own goddamn fingers?"

I looked at him so bewilderedly that he must have felt sorry for me. He led me outside behind the barn to a bench. We sat on it. I was surprised that he had the courage to put an arm around me.

"Fingers on his right hand don't provide much support anymore. He was born right-handed. So now, he can't write, can't do much of anything. He plays stupid, it keeps the devil away."

"Who is the devil, Dudley? What's his name?"

"You got a pretty mama. Some men love her too much, even the wrong men."

"You telling me someone cut off Kyle's fingers? Aunt El told me he cut off his own fingers."

"Why would he do that? The devil put his hand under a saw. I heard Kyle scream, and I was the one cleaned up the blood. A house full of people up there lying to stay sane. Lying and hoping the lies will transform the truth. No one loves that boy. What do you think it's like being on this earth with nobody loving you?"

I put my face in my hands. All of a sudden, I had a barrage of feelings pulling my body weight down and I felt myself tip over.

"You all right?" Dudley asked.

"Who did this to him, who hurt him like that?"

"He's hated. I don't even think they know how they treat him. They make 'em feel rage, rage for being born, wearing sin on his face. His father is a mighty mean bastard," Dudley said.

"Aaron isn't a monster," I shouted.

"Got it all wrong, girl," he said.

"Aaron is my father, isn't he? He isn't mean, he's a good man. He wouldn't hurt anyone."

"You going to lose 'em both, girl. Don't see no way you can't. Kyle should run far as he can get. I keep telling him that, telling him to get the hell out of here."

I looked him square in the face and clenched my teeth. "Talk truth," I said. "Why should he run?"

"You got to be careful here, Sassy. You got to look after yourself. Your mama got to send for you soon as she can; she won't leave you here. If he comes and sees you, he'll know who you are and he'll hurt you bad. He won't hurt your mama, though, not on the outside. Lust never been a good thing, Sassy."

"What are you talking about?"

"Talking about the devil, the one that killed that baby up on the hill. The one that should never lay eyes on you. He's got a scar your mama gave him right before she left. Just get away. I have a place I can hide you, least 'til he leaves. He always leaves, never does stay long. Your mama thought he'd never come back, must have thought that. Must have thought some woman was keeping him out of the state."

"You talking about Liam, he'll be here soon."

Dudley's gaze shot up to my face. "Seamus is the one you got to fear, but stay away from Liam, too. Eldest son born from the loins of a dark, dark man."

"Why would Mama ever come back here?" I almost wailed out the question. I wanted to scream and cry loud as I could and beat my fists on the ground. "Why would she leave me?"

"Must feel you're safer here than with her. He'll beat her up when he sees you. You don't cross Seamus. Your mama never listened to him. His whole goddamn family hates him. Why not? They were raised by the whip. They won't let you stay up at the farmhouse, trust me on that."

"I won't let anybody whip me, Dudley."

"I got a place I can hide you, Sassy. No one knows about it, no one cares about it. I been squatting on it for years, should be mine by now. If you need it, you just let me know. I got a whole town to hide you in."

"I bet my mama is going back to Louisiana, but not before that man fesses up to being my father. I'm going to force him into it."

"You're in real danger here, Sassy. Maybe your mama just come back for Aaron. Now she's got him again, she's got to go."

"Aaron will protect us, he'll take us away."

Dudley laughed. "Can't outrun a man like Seamus, Sassy. That's what your mama knows for sure."

CHAPTER SEVEN

I came back to see Dudley two days later. I don't know why I knew that one day I'd need this secret place of his, but the minute I woke up to find the blue Impala gone, I also knew that nothing in my life was ever going to be the same.

The place Dudley spoke of ran along the creek. The road that led into the town couldn't be seen at all. Dudley had to leave the truck and part the trees in order for us to drive up. We drove on a dirt road for about fifteen minutes, finally coming upon a clearing. I couldn't believe what I was looking at when he quit the engine.

"It looks like a town," I said.

"Sure enough was, Slave Town." He grinned.

There were old buildings all around us that went down a dirt street about a quarter mile and there was a large barn down a hill, by its self. It was set apart and we had to traverse a steep incline to get to it, but the barn was nice and clean. I could see inside that there appeared to be plants all set up in little rows.

"What's in there?" I asked. "Looks interesting."

"My hobby," he said.

"Hobby?"

"Cannabis."

"What the hell is that?"

"Plants."

"You like growing plants?"

"Uh-huh," he said.

When we walked back to the dirt street, I went inside the buildings. Some didn't have doors and it was spooky how deserted it was. Dust blew around from the road and dried my mouth. Tumbleweeds rolled in the wind. I could taste the dirt. Lots of yellow weeds were sprouting across the way in a field. The buildings ran up and down and faced each other on an old bumpy road.

"This place yours?" I asked.

"Whole thing is mine. Like I said, been squatting on it. Don't let anyone try and take it."

"What's it doing here? Anyone know about it?"

Dudley shook his head. "Been here since the Civil War and before. See yonder? That's cotton fields. This must have been all slave quarters. Makes it more my land than yours. I love nothing in life like I love this land, Sassy, maybe 'cause my people called this home. Your people can't claim it more than mine."

"You mean it's on McLaughlin property?"

"No one knows it's still here. No one gives a damn. Not worth anything to anyone but me."

I was pretty shocked. I kept walking in and out of the old slave quarters. Wasn't much of anything in them, but you could tell that once they were lived in.

"I'll fix one up for you," Dudley said.

He walked back over to the truck and climbed up to the front. "You seen enough?" he asked.

I nodded. I sure was happy to know it was there. My life was in turmoil and I wasn't so sure I just wouldn't be needing a new home.

"Where's my mama?" I asked as I stood in the doorway of Aunt Elvira's room.

It was Aunt Earline that came over to me; her hair was in pink curlers and there was white cream all over her face. She looked like one hell of a sad clown standing there frowning at me. I felt in my gut she was feeling sorry for me.

"She had to go away, honey, but she'll be back."

"When?" I asked.

"Go ask your Aunt Elvira, she may know."

"She leave in the Impala?" I asked Aunt El. I found her in the kitchen making coffee. She sighed long and hard when she saw me.

"I promised your mama I'd look after you," she said. "And I will."

"Where is she?" I asked.

Aunt El sat me down and filled up a glass with coffee and mostly warm milk. She slid it over to me.

"She's gone back to Louisiana, honey. Going to get a nice house. Once she gets settled, she'll come back for you. Won't be long, won't be long at all."

"How long you think?"

Aunt El reached out her hand and put it over mine. "Best not mention your mama while Liam is here. It's not a good idea to talk about your mama too much."

"Why not?"

"He'll tell Granddaddy and we don't want Granddaddy to know our business."

"Why not?" I asked.

"Oh, your granddaddy never thought Aaron was good enough for your mama, that's all. Best to just let him think they never got together again."

I was downright confused. She hadn't asked me not to mention Aaron, she'd asked me not to mention Mama.

I finished the coffee in one long gulp and high tailed it back to my room. I put on the jeans I'd come with and my sneakers and went and woke up Kyle.

"Mama's gone," I said.

He shot out of bed and stared at me. "She was telling the truth?"

"Guess so."

"Where'd she go?" he asked while he was slipping on his jeans.

"Louisiana. C'mon, I need an address."

We took the black Impala and Kyle drove us to Beaufort. We went over to Littleton & Son, but the crowd was too thick to get through, so we left the car parked and got out and walked. People were yelling and screaming like holy hell. Cops were pushing the crowds back.

"What's going on?" I asked someone.

"Idiot is serving niggers in there," some man with a very red face said to me. "Get on out of here, you might get hurt."

"What if Aaron is in there?" I said to Kyle and before I knew it, he was pushing himself through the crowd. I couldn't get past all the people; I was too small and kept getting pushed back. So I waited at the curb. There were people with television cameras there telling everyone to yell and scream. I stuck my tongue out so they wouldn't take my picture.

Must have been hours before the cops got the area cleared. I was finally able to see five black people coming out of Littleton's, smiling, but frightened, and some angry crowds throwing stuff at them and shouting obscenities.

I sat on the curb and waited at least another half hour. Finally, when I looked up, Kyle was walking toward me.

"They're both gone," he said.

"Aaron and Mama?"

Kyle nodded. "His father told me your mama came back and picked Aaron up and we'd never find them, would be dangerous to know where they were and they're not in Louisiana. Said I could pick up the Impala and bring it home. Seems they left in Aaron's car."

"I don't understand," I said. "Why is it dangerous?"

"Someone doesn't want them to be together, I guess, and Mr. Littleton told me never to mention a word about Aaron being at our house for dinner the other night."

"Who the hell would we mention it to?" I asked. "But Aunt El said the same thing to me."

Kyle shrugged. "Don't know what it's all about, but best do like he says. Your mama will be back. Aaron, too."

CHAPTER EIGHT

Liam McLaughlin was a very quiet man, but not the way Seth was quiet. When Seth smiled, I warmed to him; when Liam smiled, I recoiled. Nonetheless, I was determined to be polite 'til Mama got back. I wouldn't put it past these people to throw me in a soup pot if they didn't like something I said or did.

Liam didn't say anything outright when he walked inside the house and saw me standing there to greet him. But he studied me like I had just landed from Mars with large, limpid eyes and sinewy gray skin.

"Who's she?" he asked.

I didn't like him on sight, but I curtsied and told him my name. He was nearly thin as Seth, but nowhere near as tall. He wore glasses and suspenders and his mustache was thick as a thorny bush.

"Vi stayed with us awhile. This is her little girl. She'll be coming back for her in a month or two," Elvira said.

"Don't look like Vi," he said, "but she's pretty like her."

He walked over closer to me and stared some more. "Got her father in her, I guess."

Then, quick as a whip, Aunt El grabbed his arm and marched him into the kitchen. "Carolyn made your favorite stew. Can you smell it, Liam?" I heard her say.

I was glad he left the room, relieved to be rid of him, though I wasn't able to articulate just why he gave me the creeps.

Kyle and I had already had our lunch and we were dressed for the swimming hole. June-bug followed as we ran out the door.

"You like Uncle Liam?" I asked Kyle.

Kyle said he hadn't seen him much over the years.

"He gives me the creeps. You notice those weird eyes?" I said. "I hope he don't stay long."

We started splashing around and swimming, even jumping from the tire hanging from an old oak tree while June-bug ran around barking at us.

I ignored Uncle Liam for the next few days, which wasn't easy to do since he followed me around and kept asking me if I liked to horseback ride and offering to let me ride Misty, the sassy filly. "Sassy like you," he kept saying.

I still hadn't heard from my mama and most of the time my thoughts were preoccupied with that. Every time the phone rang I ran for it.

"Mama will be back before my birthday," I told Kyle. "Mama wouldn't miss that."

"School starts soon enough," Kyle said. "You'll have to go to school."

"Mama will be back for me before then," I said. "I'll probably be going to school somewhere else."

"Stay away from Thomas Tierney," he said. "I don't like him."

Kyle was acting like I'd be going to school in Carter's Crossing, but I knew I wouldn't be. Mama would come and tell me all about our new apartment and Aunt El would take us to the bus stop and maybe we'd come back holidays. I'd always want to come back and see Kyle and Dudley.

"Didn't you hear what I said, Kyle? Mama will be back for me long before school starts," I insisted.

"Well, just in case she doesn't," Kyle said, "stay away from Thomas Tierney."

"Why?" I asked.

"Never shuts up about my hand," he said. "Calls me Claw."

"I'll beat him up," I said.

"Oh, it'll take two of us to beat him up. He's the tallest boy in school. He's always teasing girls, too. I think he's just awkward around them and that's a defense."

I laughed out loud. "And people think you're stupid," I said. "I think you could be a magnate, too, like Granddaddy. That's how smart I think you are. Your teachers are dumb not knowing you're fooling, Kyle. Teachers here must be dumb as a square dance."

Every night at dinner, all they talked about was steel mills. I found it boring and didn't take my eyes from my dinner plate. Besides, I didn't want to have to look at Liam, who they'd placed right across the table from me. I'd look up and find him staring at me and it would give me a hot flash.

"What you gonna do 'bout the mill in Youngstown?" Grandma Edna asked.

"Not going to sell it," Liam answered.

"Why not?" Aunt El said. "That mill is never going to prosper again. Take the money and invest it in overseas mills, they're the ones going to prosper."

"Good thing you're not running the company, Butch." Liam took a large swallow of beer and wiped his chin. "Women never know what the hell they're talking about when it comes to business."

Aunt El smiled. "I'll make you a prediction," she said. "You're going to have to close three more mills this year. I say sell now and get yourself on the board of a big one, like US Steel, own the stock. Shit, you're best off with a thousand shares of US Steel than a thousand canceled contracts."

Liam laughed. His laugh was low, sort of like a snicker. It was obvious he'd just dismissed Aunt El's opinion.

Liam was sitting where Kyle usually sat, so I couldn't make faces at Kyle, but I did sneak a look down the end of the table and stuck my tongue out at him while the others argued over politics. It seems Uncle Liam thought John F. Kennedy was a disgrace to the Irish with all his liberal views.

"Mama is a liberal," I said to Grandma Edna. Then I realized I wasn't supposed to be talking 'bout Mama at all, but Grandma Edna didn't seem to notice.

"This family is split down the middle like the North and the South when it comes to politics.I, for one, like John Kennedy, but I don't want our schools desegregated. That would be a disgrace. And you, Sassy, are entitled to your opinion. Do you like John Kennedy?"

"Yes, ma'am, I like him," I said.

Liam laughed that low snicker again. "When Negroes start taking your husband's job away, you won't like him that much," he said.

"Best keep power with the white men," Aunt El said. "Is that it? No room in this country for anyone else?"

"You're just jealous," Uncle Liam said. "'Cause you can't ever enjoy the privileges of being a white man. Like it or not, Butch, you're just a woman."

I didn't think that calling her "just" a woman was a very flattering thing to say. His derogatory subtext was obvious to me, but no one said anything in Aunt El's defense, not right away, anyway. Grandma Edna continued to sip her wine and Seth kept eating. I don't know what Kyle was doing 'cause I couldn't see him down at the other end of the table, but I finally heard Aunt Earline speak out.

"Personally, Liam," she said, "if you mean killing each other in wars, smoking cigars, or going to cat houses, I'd say, I don't want 'em. Keep your damn 'male' privileges."

I laughed out loud so heartily that I spit my Coca-Cola out of my mouth. I heard Kyle snicker right before Liam answered.

"Still a man's world," he said. "Sorry to disappoint you, ladies."

Chapter Nine

I guess Uncle Liam knew about the swimming hole. It had probably been there for a hundred years, but I didn't like it one bit when he showed up there. It had been about two weeks since he'd arrived and I'd done my best to avoid him, but there I was, floating on my back and when I looked up, there was Uncle Liam staring down at me from the top of the hill. I quickly swam over to Kyle and said, "Shit, stupid Uncle Liam is here."

Kyle looked back at me and raised his eyes. He didn't want him there, either.

You had to shimmy down the hill to get to the water hole and that's just what Uncle Liam did. He was wearing dark blue swimming trunks that looked more like underwear to me and nothing else but a pair of sandals, but he managed to shimmy down the dirt pretty well. I noticed he had more hair on his body than a grizzly.

"He looks like a jerk," Kyle whispered.

Both me and Kyle were in the water swimming around each other by the time Uncle Liam removed his sandals and walked out toward us. Then he did a sudden drop out where the hole was deep. When he came up for air he was right near us. I guess he thought we wanted him there. He started telling us how he and Seth and their sisters would come down to the hole and swim with the turtles.

"You think you're standing on a rock, but you're really standing on a turtle's back." He laughed. Maybe he thought that would frighten me, but

I don't frighten easily, so I smiled so broad he might have noticed I'd never had my tonsils removed.

I ignored him, but the next thing I knew he was holding me up on top of the water, his arm uncomfortably around my stomach.

"You need to move your head like this," he said and started showing me how to breathe while swimming. He twisted my head into the water with his other hand and then twisted it back out.

"Now take your breath," he said with his hand on my neck.

I shoved myself so far away trying to get out of his clutches. I did a back paddle to the other side of the hole, but he didn't seem to notice. He swam over to me again. "This is the proper way," he said. "Look."

I turned around and noticed that Kyle had a strange expression on his face. He was thinking the same thing I was, that Uncle Liam was weird as false teeth in a pickle jar.

"You can swim here nude," Uncle Liam said quietly, like it was a secret. "No one will know."

I shot Kyle a look. Then I almost dropped dead when Uncle Liam held his bathing suit up in the air.

"Feels so good," he yelled out.

I skedaddled up out of the hole as fast as I could and hurried on up to the top of the hill, scratching myself with sticks. When I looked back behind me, Uncle Liam was walking out of the swimming hole stark naked.

"Hold on, Sassy, don't be afraid," he yelled up to me.

I'd never seen a naked man before and I stumbled trying to get away and at the same time, I looked back and stared at him out of curiosity. He didn't look anything at all the way I thought a naked man would look. I knew he had something different between his legs that wiggled like a worm, but I couldn't tell you what it was.

"C'mon, Kyle," I called, but Kyle didn't come after me.

Later that night I went into Kyle's room and I found him sitting up staring at nothing. "Why didn't you follow me out of the hole?" I asked him.

"I did, but you'd already gone."

"You didn't take off your trunks, did you?" I asked.

Kyle shook his head. "No way."

"Did he try and force you?" I asked.

"He was too busy to try and force me to do anything."

"What you talking about?"

"It was so nasty I couldn't move."

"But you did move finally, didn't you?" I whispered.

"You think I should say anything? He was standing up in front of me playing with himself, telling me he had the biggest prick of any man in the state, at least twelve inches long. He said women tell him it's the biggest thing they've ever seen. The son of a bitch is only 'bout five foot four, how is that possible?"

"Shit," I said and sunk down. "We better tell Grandma Edna."

"No," Kyle shouted out. "She'll think I'm a queer."

"Well, you didn't do anything queer, did you?"

"No, but I just stood there looking like the dumb fool I'm pretending to be when I should have punched him. I couldn't believe what I was looking at and it sure as hell was no twelve inches long, barely three. I think he wanted me to do the same thing he was doing, stand there and play with myself, too, but I got away."

"Shit," I said and sat down on his bed. "Uncle Liam is a fucking pervert."

Grandma Edna was sitting in her bedroom reading by a stand-up lamp. The sky was gray and muddy looking and maybe it was boredom alone that made me and Kyle decide that Uncle Liam's exposing himself to us was as perverted as naked old men at a Brownie meeting and that Grandma Edna should be informed. Maybe, we were hoping, she'd send him away.

She looked up when she saw the two of us standing in the doorway of her bedroom. Kyle entered first and I followed, not quite sure of how to get the story out.

"Why aren't you two in the study watching television?" she asked. "I got a book here to read and I don't feel like talking."

"Oh, we don't want to talk to you, Grandma Edna," I said. "We want to tell you something."

She seemed a bit curious and put the book down. She didn't ask us what it was, but she leaned forward and stared at us.

I thought Kyle was going to start telling her what happened, but he just stood there even though we'd rehearsed it three times that he was supposed to tell her what Uncle Liam did, being older and all, and then I'd jump in. I gave him a dirty look, but all he did was clear his throat.

"Well?" she said.

I was the one that started the story and Kyle finally took over and after a bit, we were both talking over each other, telling her how Uncle Liam was naked at the swimming hole, but I guess the both of us were too afraid to say he was playing with himself.

Grandma Edna laughed, it was almost like a giggle, as though Uncle Liam being naked at the swimming hole was as funny as the little Spanish hand puppet on The Ed Sullivan Show.

"He's been naked at the swimming hole all his life," she said. "All the kids went down there and took their clothes off. We knew about it, but what was the harm in it? What can you say to kids who just like swimming in the nude? Innocent fun, Sassy, that's all."

"Well, it didn't seem right to me," I said.

"Why not?"

"Well…" I looked at Kyle, who looked out the window.

"Did Uncle Liam do anything to either one of you? Did he touch either one of you?" We shook our heads 'cause he hadn't.

"Innocent shenanigans," she said. "Don't concentrate on stupid things, children. I will tell Liam myself to keep his trunks on at the swimming hole from now on. For God's sake, he's a grown man, but he didn't mean anything by it. Just habit is all."

I thought she sounded a bit nervous, but we nodded politely and left the room, both of us feeling a little stupid for even mentioning it.

I started having dreams after that and I'd wake up frightened. There'd be a man there in a blue-piped pajama top sitting on my bed and he'd hurt me in some way, but just as I felt the pain, he'd disappear. Mama still hadn't come back home and I kept asking everyone where she was and they all said that it takes time to get settled. I got a few letters from her, one was postmarked from Georgia and the other one from North Carolina, and Mama called at least once a week, but that certainly wasn't enough for me.

She did call me on my birthday, of course. Carolyn had made me a cake with vanilla cream and chocolate frosting. Grandma Edna had bought me a bicycle, a blue Schwinn with lots of extras, like side mirrors and a bell on the handle bar. Seth gave me a charm bracelet with a palate and paint charm and Elvira and Aunt Earline gave me a real good-looking pair of Fry boots.

I was mad at Mama when she called so I wasn't too friendly, especially when I asked when she was coming to get me and all she said was soon.

We weren't allowed into Beaufort anymore 'cause of all the riots and Aunt El said it was a good thing the school bus didn't need to take the city route to get us to school. They took me down and registered me in the ninth grade. Kyle was in the tenth-grade special-education class, which everyone knew was for retarded kids.

My nightmares became worse each night and one time I screamed out loud 'cause I felt a hand on me in the dark. I didn't know if I was going crazy or not, but I could have sworn that I saw Uncle Liam walking around my bedroom stark naked from the waist down, but then I'd get real sleepy and I wouldn't be able to stare at him anymore through the shadows.

I started falling asleep in the afternoons and everyone was kidding me, telling me I was going to sleep right through adolescence. But then I spit up a pill one day and Aunt Earline said we ought to have it analyzed, that it didn't look like any pill she'd ever seen.

"Where you getting these pills?" Grandma Edna asked me 'cause it turned out to be a sleeping pill. I told her I wouldn't ever take any pills, that I didn't even like them when I got a fever and was forced to take them, so why would I want to take them now? But they got it into their heads that I was suicidal 'cause Mama hadn't come back for me and it had been over a month.

My nightmares were consistent and began to get more vivid. I had them almost every night. I could see a man there in the shadows of the room, after I went to sleep at night and he was making me touch things and he was touching me. I could hear his breathing, but I was groggy, too groggy to see who he was. I wanted to tell someone, but I felt ashamed, like they'd think I was making up dirty things.

Then one night, I felt like I was screaming. Through my screams I heard Aunt El's voice. She was screaming, too.

"Get the hell away from her," she said. "Fuck, Liam, get off her."

When Liam stood up, he pushed Aunt El away and she fell back on the floor. I didn't know if I was dreaming or not, but I could see her by the door where he'd shoved her out of the room.

"Stay out of here," Uncle Liam shouted.

I realized my nightgown was way up over my head. I could hear Aunt El's footsteps running down the hall. I went to pull my nightgown back down, but someone's hands were holding me down and causing me pain somewhere.

The footsteps came back, if it was Aunt El, she was running fast. I heard her say, "Get off her or I'll kill you, you son of a bitch."

But Uncle Liam was pushing my head up into the bedpost, over and over again. I almost couldn't stand more pain, but then I heard a loud pop, and the pain stopped.

I felt the pressure leave my body. There was more yelling and another loud noise. I felt the bed springs fall and rise. I felt someone pull my nightgown back down. I felt someone's arms lifting me up and taking me away.

When I awoke the sky was bright, but I didn't open my eyes to see the sun, I just felt it. I could tell I was in Grandma Edna's bed. I could feel the height of it. I listened to them speaking around me like I was dead and I pretended I was dead. Lord knows, I might have been.

"I killed him," Aunt El said. She was crying. I knew Seth was there too, trying his best to tell her he would have done the same.

"What'll we do?" I heard him ask.

There was silence for a long time. Then I heard Grandma Edna's voice.

"He deserved it," she said. "God, forgive me. He was my son, but he deserved it."

"Mama, I'm sorry," Aunt El said.

"Didn't you hear me, child? He deserved it."

"Should we call the police?" Aunt Earline asked.

Grandma Edna stood up and I knew she was walking around the room even though my eyes were still closed.

"I should have listened to the children, they tried to tell me he was naked."

"What are you talking about?" Seth asked.

"At the swimming hole. I should have put two and two together. I should have thought about that rape charge back in 1956, remember?"

"No one is to blame here but Liam, you hear me, Mama?" I heard the anger in Seth's voice.

"What do we do now?" Elvira said.

There was a long silence before Grandma Edna answered.

"Get Dudley." I could hear the strain in her voice. "Tell him to get rid of everything, the car, the body, everything."

"But Papa is coming back, today, tomorrow, soon," Aunt El said.

"This is the story you tell," Grandma Edna said. "Liam came here for two weeks then he left for the mill in Doylestown, you hear that?"

"Shouldn't we go to the police?" Aunt El asked.

"El," Seth said. "He'll maim you if he doesn't kill you first. Daddy will destroy you for shooting his favorite son."

"Then what happened to Liam? He just going to disappear?"

I knew that was Earline's voice and she was sounding real nervous. She was also stroking my forehead and holding me in her arms.

"You sure you saw what you say you saw?" Grandma Edna asked. "He was raping her?"

"He's just like Papa," Aunt El said. "Don't you know that? Look what Papa did to Vi. Christ, he deserved that fucking bullet."

"God forgive us," Grandma Edna said softly.

"No," Earline yelled out. "God forgive him, Goddamn it! God forgive him."

CHAPTER TEN

I started school three days later. When I didn't see Uncle Liam, I assumed he'd gone back to wherever the hell he was from. I didn't want to believe that Elvira had shot and killed him, not 'til I rode my new bicycle over to Dudley's Slave Town. I think I still thought I'd been dreaming that night, dreaming the next morning, too. Thought I just dreamed it all.

"How'd you know where I was, Sassy?" Dudley shouted.

"I told June-bug to lead me to you and she did."

"Smart dog."

"What are you doing?"

"What'd he do is more like it?" Dudley asked. "Must have done something real bad to get himself shot twice in the back."

I almost fell off my bicycle. The barn doors were partially open. I could see bales and bales of hay. They were nearly covering Uncle Liam's brand-new Lincoln, but not entirely.

"Isn't that Uncle Liam's car?" I walked closer. It sure enough was.

Dudley stared at me a moment before he asked me where Kyle was. I told him Kyle had a new girlfriend he'd been hanging with.

"She's fat, too, but real pretty."

"Was it Kyle that shot him?"

"What?"

"Did Kyle shoot your Uncle Liam?"

I started crying and just collapsed right there on the ground. June-bug was licking my face and I pushed her off. I knew I had to let it in, that Uncle Liam had been shot and killed and it was 'cause of me. I kept trying to force the truth of it back, but seeing his car behind bales and bales of hay made it all too real.

"That is his car, isn't it?" I asked through my tears.

Dudley nodded. "They asked me to get rid of it."

"Can you?" I suddenly shuddered, wondering about what I didn't want to think about at all— Uncle Liam's dead body.

"No one will ever find it," Dudley said.

"His body?"

"That neither."

Dudley stared at me a moment then he sat down beside me, looking into my face and taking the hair out from my eyes very gently.

"What happened?" he asked.

I was scared, but I told him everything I could remember. I knew Elvira had gone and gotten her gun and Earline was running right behind her when Elvira came into my bedroom and shot Uncle Liam. I knew it was Earline that came and swept me up in her arms and led me in to Grandma Edna's bedroom.

Dudley's face looked ashen. "Where was Seth?" he asked. He was rubbing his hands up and down his thighs and I knew he was real upset.

"He must have come in late. He was there in the morning when I woke up, but I don't remember him being there that night. He's rarely ever home after dinner."

"And Kyle?" Dudley asked.

"I don't think he knows what happened," I said. "He's seeing this girl, you know. It's got him preoccupied. He wasn't home that night."

Dudley stared out over the fields, looking at the birds that flew low. I suddenly envied them their grace and their ease.

"I could turn your family into the authorities," he finally said.

I must have looked a little horrified 'cause he reached for my hand.

"No one is likely to believe me, though. If I put my two cents into this, I'd be the one likely to pay for it. No, girl, my lips are sealed. Yours, too."

I nodded my head. I wanted to tell Kyle, at least, but Dudley said that Kyle just might go nuts and come on out and demand Dudley tell him where the body is so he could put five more bullets in Liam's dead corpse.

"Where is the body?" I asked.

"Three towns over got his head, outskirts of a big city got his torso, and five towns to the east got his legs."

I almost threw up my lunch, but I got control of it and held it back.

"Why didn't they go to the police?" I asked. "He was doing something wrong to me, wasn't he? He was raping me. I barely remember it, though. It's like a dream."

The grin left Dudley's face for the first time since I'd known him and he nodded his head. "I'd have shot him, too," he said. "Why didn't you scream? Not like you to take something like that."

"He drugged me. I couldn't lift my arms or open my mouth."

"Sick son of a bitch."

"Dudley, Aunt El was protecting me, so why would the police care? They wouldn't arrest her for shooting him, not after they found out he was hurting me."

"Police probably would have let your Aunt El go, but Seamus would sure as hell hunt her down. Seamus would peel the skin from your aunt's body and broil what was left of it on a hot grill. He don't care about you, or his daughter, but his son can run a mill. His son can share a whore and kill his enemies for him."

"But Aunt El is his child."

"Inferno 'bout to come. Watch yourself, Sassy. Seamus is no fool. Truth will come soon enough." Then he added, "Girls are worth 'bout the same as niggers."

I was moved over to Aunt Erin's right before Granddaddy Seamus got to Carter's Crossing. No one knew how long he was staying, but Kyle told me he showed up with a woman and moved up there into the attic rooms and they had a lot of luggage. Granddaddy was telling everyone that the blonde woman he'd brought home with him was his personal secretary, but

Kyle said she didn't appear to know how to spell her own name. He also told me it wasn't unusual for Granddaddy to bring his secretaries home with him whenever he showed up.

"Sleeps right there in his bed," Kyle told me. "Every single one of them shares his bed up there in the attic."

"Why would Grandma Edna put up with it?" I asked.

"If he's got a secretary sleeping with him, then she don't have to sleep with him." He laughed.

Couldn't say I understood the reasoning behind that, but on some level it did appear to make sense.

"Granddaddy is asking all of us what the hell Liam left for. He keeps saying that Liam was supposed to meet him here. Everyone's playing dumb, but Granddaddy is getting real obnoxious about it."

"You know what happened to me, don't you?" I asked and I saw his face redden.

"Yeah, they told me. I would have killed the son of a bitch. El was right to do it."

"I'm glad he's dead. Maybe I shouldn't be saying that, but I'm glad he is."

"You don't ever want to see Granddaddy angry, Sassy."

"Guess not," I said. It was all I could think to say, knowing I was the one with more right to my anger than that nasty old man.

Now that Granddaddy was back at Carter's Crossing, I was barred from the premises and that hurt me a lot 'cause Aunt Erin wouldn't allow me to keep June-bug at her house, so I had to sneak back over to the Crossings to see my dog.

I didn't like living with Aunt Erin and Uncle Austin, but I didn't have a choice. Aunt Erin's cigarettes made me cough and Uncle Austin told one joke after another 'til my eyes crossed. I just couldn't stand one more "Knock, knock, Sassy."

I didn't really understand why I was kept out of Granddaddy's sight, but Dudley said it was to make sure I never said a word about Liam or mentioned Mama and Aaron. I never would have, but I guess they didn't trust me not to.

So I started Wade Hampton High School having to take the school bus ten miles further away from Carter's Crossing. The school was a big, old brown building on a dead-end road somewhere in Hampton County. The only thing I was looking forward to was taking art classes. Art was an elective I was able to choose. Everything else was mandatory.

I once passed the classroom where Kyle sat in his special-education room and he was sitting there staring out the window, drooling from the mouth. I almost started to laugh, especially when his teacher asked him where his homework was and he pulled a crumbled ball of paper out of his back pocket and started eating it.

Kyle's girlfriend, Marjean, didn't go to Wade Hampton High School, which was a good thing 'cause of the way Kyle was teased there. I liked Marjean and told Kyle she was the best girl in the world for him 'cause she wouldn't take any shit from his family. If they'd tried to make fun of her the way they did his last girlfriend, Marjean would have retorted in kind. Why how nice of you to compliment my big behind, Grandma Edna. Your sagging tits are lovely, too.

I knew who Thomas Tierney was the moment I saw him, of course. I was walking up the school drive with Kyle on the very first day I started at Wade Hampton High and Thomas came running over behind us, just the way Kyle said he might.

"Hey, Claw, how was your summer?" he called out.

I looked up at the tallest damn boy I'd ever seen in my life. He was grinning out from a face 'bout as handsome as a magazine model. But his good blond looks wouldn't mean a damn thing to me. I hated him on sight.

"Don't call him that," I said.

"It's all right, Sassy," Kyle said and took my arm.

"Sassy?" Thomas ran in front of us, turned around, and kind of ran backward. He was staring at me and laughing.

"You haven't done bad for a dummy," he said to Kyle. "She's not half-bad at all."

"Shut up, fool," Kyle said. "She's my sister."

"Sister? Don't look much alike."

I really wanted to punch this guy a whole lot. "She don't have a claw hand, either."

That's when I spun my lunch box around and around by the strap that was attached to it. Thomas was still laughing at me. I guess he didn't understand what I was going to do to his pretty face.

"Wow, she's got talent, don't she?" Thomas kept laughing. "Whatcha going to lasso with your lunchbox, Red?"

He was laughing so much he had to stop in his tracks. That's just where I wanted him, with his chin up. I hurled my lunch box into it and he fell back and landed on his ass with his long legs spread.

"Ow," I heard him cry out.

Kyle stopped and stared, like he couldn't believe what he'd just seen.

I curled my lips up over my teeth and snarled at Thomas. Then I walked up to him and put my foot between his legs.

"You take good notice of my new boots, Thomas Tierney. They're my new Fry boots and they're hard as hell. I got 'em for my birthday and if I kick you in your crotch with my right foot, wearing my new Fry birthday boots, you're going to know just how hard they are."

He was gaping at me when I walked off, rubbing his hand on his chin where I'd clipped him and shaking his head. Never said a word more, but he did spread it all over school that I was a crazy girl, so making friends was harder than it might have been.

CHAPTER ELEVEN

After not hearing from Liam for several weeks, Seamus McLaughlin insisted on a full investigation into the disappearance of his son. The family said that Liam had come to town, stayed two weeks, and then told everyone he was off to Pennsylvania to check one of the mills and then, back over to Tennessee where he lived with his wife and two sons. Unfortunately, his wife told Granddaddy she hadn't seen or heard from him in weeks.

I was stuck at Aunt Erin's for the whole six months Seamus was there at Carter's Crossing vigorously working with the police to find Liam. The whole time I was at Aunt Erin's, I didn't see Granddaddy at all, but I met secretly with Grandma Edna once a week, usually on Saturday afternoons. Grandma Edna made Dudley pick me up at Aunt Erin's and drive me to wherever she was on the property. She always brought June-bug with her. I was so happy to see my dog I just about split a gut. Grandma Edna and I went all over Carter's Crossing painting barns and landscapes with June- bug in happy pursuit. Grandma Edna had bought me a very professional set of paints and enough canvas to keep me painting a long while. We'd often go up to the hill where the baby was buried. I never asked her about the baby. There were just some things we didn't talk about, like Uncle Liam's murder and what was buried under the unknown cross at the sycamore tree.

Sometimes we talked about what was going on in the world and how the Civil Rights Movement was a good thing, even though it was causing a lot of bloodshed.

"Don't want you going into Beaufort alone," she said to me. "They're trying to pass desegregation and they'll be a lot of violence before the world makes sense of itself. I just wish this whole Negro mess hadn't of happened."

I knew that Littleton & Son wasn't turning blacks away and the Klu Klux Klan had been there throwing bricks through the front plate glass windows because of it. At that point in my life I preferred the back roads of South Carolina where I could think however the hell I pleased and no one could tell me I couldn't walk down the street with a Negro or drink from the same goddamn water fountain. There were signs all over the place telling Negroes what restrooms they could use and which ones they couldn't.

"Why can't Mama come back here?" I finally asked her. "What's taking her so long?"

"Obsession," she said. "You know what that is?"

"Yeah," I said. "It's like being real focused on one thing."

"Or one person," she said.

"Yeah, sure," I said, but I still didn't know what that had to do with Mama and Grandma Edna sure didn't explain herself very well.

"You mean she's obsessed with Aaron?" I asked.

She looked at me and I could tell she was trying to figure out how to explain herself. True to fashion, she changed the subject.

I heard from Mama pretty regularly, even though I would have preferred her flesh and blood self to her phone calls. She always had an excuse to not be driving back to South Carolina to pick me up and take me to wherever the hell she was. She never mentioned Aaron, but I knew they were together 'cause Franklin Littleton had told us that. I stopped asking her about Aaron 'cause I was tired of not getting answers and then one day, right out of the blue, Mama told me they were coming back married. I was so shocked, I just about fell over backward.

"What?" I said.

"Look, honey, it will all make sense one day, but I can't let myself be controlled by…Daddy any longer."

I noticed that when she said "Daddy" that the word kind of stuck in her throat.

"I don't want you broadcasting this news all around town, but me and Aaron are going to come back to Beaufort and live up over the store. His father has to be moved over to the nursing home. He's pretty sick, honey, and there's no one else to run the store but Aaron."

"But that's dangerous," I said. "People are getting real hurt in those riots, Mama."

Mama just laughed. "We'll be fine," she said. "Next time I call it just may be from around the corner."

I couldn't believe what I'd heard, but I was so happy my feet didn't touch the ground for days. I didn't tell anyone either, just Kyle, who had a right to know. I hardly thought of anything else after that, nothing else but living on top of Littleton & Son with my mama and, now, Aaron, who would be claiming me as daughter.

I was biking back from the Slave Town a few days after Mama told me she was returning to Carter's Crossing. I was taking the back road to Aunt Erin's singing one of Mama's favorite songs out loud, feeling just as high as geese flying south. I'd just gone over to see Dudley to tell him Mama was coming home and right out of nowhere, this big, ole, fat Lincoln comes roaring past the stop sign and cuts me right off at the corner. Someone yelled something out at me, but I was lying on the ground at least three feet from where I'd been, so I couldn't hardly hear him. My bicycle was lying on its side with its wheels spinning. It was Pike that came over and asked me if I was all right.

"Sassy," he whispered. "You know I never stop at that stop sign. You all right, girl?"

After I said I think I only bruised my knee, he went and got my bicycle, which appeared to be fine. When I tried to stand though, I realized I couldn't put any weight on my ankle.

While Pike helped me up on my one leg, he motioned to the car with his eyes. "Say as little as possible, Sassy."

I kind of nodded and looked to the car. I immediately recognized the man who was in the back seat of the Lincoln; I knew who he was the moment he opened the door and stepped out. It was Granddaddy Seamus all right. I could see the goddamn scar Dudley had told me about from where I was hobbling. It was deep, like a scissor mark.

"Your bike seems to be okay," Pike said loudly. "But how are you?"

I watched as Granddaddy walked over to me. He looked pretty much the way he did in the photograph, 'cept he was older. He still had all his hair, but it was white. He was handsome, like Kyle, with those light green eyes.

"Who are you?" he said to me.

"Sassy Sweetwater," I said.

"We'll take you home, live far?" I shook my head.

"Think you need to go to the hospital?"

"No, I can walk just fine," I said and limped around a bit.

"Pike, put her bicycle in the trunk and find out where she lives."

"Oh, that's okay, you don't have to take me home," I said.

"You won't get far on your own, you've twisted your ankle." He looked back at me and pointed at my foot.

"Oh," I said.

He stared at me for a bit and I noticed that his face was tight, like he'd tasted something foul.

"What were you doing over here, by the way? Nothing here but the trees on my land."

"Just biking," I said.

He stared at me awhile longer. "Go on and give Pike your address, we'll drive you home."

Granddaddy Seamus went back to his car and got in. I just looked at Pike; he knew where the hell I was going. He picked me up and put me in the backseat. Granddaddy didn't look at me, he was reading some papers on his lap, but right before we hit the next town, I felt him staring at me like I was a rattlesnake 'bout to strike.

I don't know when it dawned on Granddaddy that we were headed to Erin's house on Blackberry Lane in Dawson, but I still tried to save myself.

"Stop here," I called. "I can get home from here."

"Keep going, Pike," Granddaddy ordered.

Pike stopped the car right in front of Aunt Erin's. Granddaddy sat still as midnight on Main Street, while I prayed for him not to put two and two together, but one thing Granddaddy wasn't was stupid.

"How's your mother?" he asked me.

"Fine," I said.

"And your father?"

"Fine," I repeated.

"Give them my good wishes," he said.

"Yes, sir," I said and got out. Pike had taken the bicycle to the front door. When Aunt Erin opened the door she seemed to turn whiter than a fresh snowfall.

"Why'd you let Pike take you here?" she asked. "Was that my Daddy in the back?"

"Hurt my ankle," I said. "No one I know in the back. I mean. I don't know."

I knew by the look on her face that she didn't believe me one bit. I watched as she went to the kitchen phone and dialed the farmhouse, real quick like. I heard her say, "Shit," before I skipped on one foot up to my room.

Chapter Twelve

Aaron's father died in the nursing home. In the previous year, he'd developed a bad cough and it eventually led to a diagnosis of throat cancer. Everyone thought Littleton & Son would be closing after Franklin Littleton's death and the town could rejoice 'cause they would no longer have to deal with Negroes being served food at the hangout of choice for Beaufort's youth. Unfortunately, for the town, Aaron and his new wife, Violet McLaughlin, had returned to Beaufort to run the café. And it was quoted from the mouths of Mr. and Mrs. Littleton, in the local newspaper, that no one with the money to buy a hamburger would ever be told they couldn't get one at their establishment, the recently renamed Littleton's Café.

Mama said she and Aaron were looking for a house, but in the meantime, there was a two-bedroom apartment above the store and we'd be living there. Mama even told me that June-bug was welcomed as long as I walked her three times a day and I promised that I certainly would.

The apartment wasn't that large, but I would have lived in a tree house with Mama. The small kitchen was right off the living room and shaped like the letter U, but we had a lot of windows looking out on to the street from the front room. The two bedrooms were down the hall. The smaller one was mine and it didn't face any mountains or trees, but when I looked up at night I could see stars that glittered like they were chattering in star talk and when I woke up in the morning I could see all the people opening up their shops on Bay Street. Contentment was a presumption on Bay Street. At least that's how it felt.

Sometimes happiness is a determination. You don't own any rights to it, you have to earn it. It's not necessarily there to be slipped on everyday like your undershirt and no matter how hard you try to hold on to happiness, it surprises you with rude awakenings. Happiness is fickle. I learned that young and that's why every time I know I'm happy, I relish in it, like sunshine and lazy days when you're walking on a country road, not even knowing the challenges you're going to face avoiding the loss of happiness and its illusive staying power.

I chose to forget that Granddaddy Seamus's Lincoln had knocked me off my bicycle and he had probably put two and two together, that I was his daughter's child, Violet's child. I didn't understand why he hated my mama so much and I didn't really want to think about it. I was back where I belonged with Mama and my biological father, even though neither Mama or Aaron wanted to discuss my parentage. They kept saying we'd talk about it when the time was right, but it seemed the time never became right.

No matter. I had the truth now and I had a lot to keep me busy, so I wasn't harping on it. I was loving school and walking June-bug by the river when I got home. Life was actually good. I had a crush on a boy named Jeremy and sometimes I even went to the movies with Kyle and Marjean where I could watch them hold hands and kiss each other. Yep, life couldn't get any better for me than it was. Aaron told me I could work in the store when I turned sixteen and after batting my eyes at Jeremy for a full two weeks, I finally got a date out of it. I had the happiness feeling for sure and I was wearing it well, sort of like the way I wore my best pair of jeans, the ones I showed off 'cause the denim hugged my body so tight it didn't show a crease or a wrinkle, the ones I could wear now that Mama had returned and Grandma Edna wasn't around to give me her death-to-me stare if I didn't take those jeans off immediately.

I was still meeting Grandma Edna on Saturday afternoons up at the sycamore tree. We took long walks, all the way around the Crossing, and every time we saw something unusually quiet and alluring, we'd stop to paint it. I'd almost forgotten about Uncle Liam, until Grandma Edna told me the police wanted to question me about his disappearance.

"Why now? It's been nearly six months," I said.

"New evidence."

"Oh," I said.

"You're not to say anything about the…"

I knew exactly what she was talking about, so I nodded my head. It was understood, it never happened.

"I don't want you to be afraid," she said.

I wasn't exactly afraid, but I was nervous. "What'll I tell 'em?" I asked.

"As little as possible," she said. "Uncle Liam was here for about two weeks, then he left, said he was going to Pennsylvania. We never heard from him again."

"Okay," I said, hunching up my shoulders, like it wasn't any big deal or nothing.

We sat in silence a while. We had settled about ten or fifteen feet from the big Sycamore tree, but we were facing out, toward the farmhouse. I was sketching it, something I hadn't really done yet. It was interesting how differently Grandma Edna and I were seeing things. My farmhouse looked lonely all by itself in a field of tall overgrown grass, but Grandma Edna had given her farmhouse gardens and foot bridges and the grass was clipped. My farmhouse didn't have a thing to offer but itself and the imperfections I seemed to find along with it.

"Our house does not sag, nor is it gray," she said.

"Just the way I see it, Grandma Edna," I told her quietly.

"Kyle wants to marry that girl," Grandma Edna said all of a sudden as she dipped her brush into a yellow slab of paint. I hardly knew what she was talking about; Kyle hadn't said a thing about marriage to me.

"He's too young to get married," I said. Grandma Edna smiled.

"Keep telling him that."

"Whose son is he?" I asked, sudden like, like suddenness would shock her into giving me the answers I sought.

"Was he really left on the porch?"

Grandma Edna sure didn't want to answer that question, so she kind of answered it. "He's a part of our family," she said. "That's all you need to know."

"We got the same bloodline?" I asked.

"Sure enough," she said.

I felt very unsatisfied with that answer, but Grandma Edna was soon to redeem herself.

"Who's buried under the sycamore tree?" I asked, as nonchalantly as I could.

"A child," she said.

"What's his name?"

"Her name," she corrected.

"What's her name then?"

"Charlotte," she said, softly, and something in the way she said it made me keep my mouth shut and refrain from asking any more questions. I'd heard the break in her voice and I wasn't so young I couldn't hear pain. There'd be time enough for answers and another afternoon like this one, another opportunity for Grandma Edna to fill in the blanks 'bout that poor little baby.

Happiness isn't natural, necessarily. There's an ebb and flow to it. I'll never forget that Saturday Kyle came over to Littleton's with his suitcase. Mama had announced just that morning that she was pregnant and happiness was certainly hers, but Kyle had to forfeit his. And mine, well, mine was up for grabs.

Mama was behind the lunch counter and she looked up and turned paler than summer haze when she saw Kyle walking toward her with his suitcase in his hand. Aaron was behind the cash register counting money 'cause the busy breakfast hour was done. I was helping Mama bring some dishes to the kitchen, but came back around when I saw Kyle. He walked right over to Mama.

"Hi," he said.

Mama nodded. "Hi, Kyle."

Kyle seemed nervous. But that was the least of it. He had a black eye and a horrible bruise on his cheek. He looked disheveled, like he'd dressed quickly to get where he needed to go.

"What happened to you?" Mama asked.

"Hello, Sassy," he said, avoiding Mama's question.

"What the hell happened to you?" I asked.

"That son of a bitch tried to get me to tell what I know, but I didn't tell him a thing, no matter how hard the bastard hit me."

Kyle pulled his lips in and looked about to cry.

Mama was clearly confused and she looked at Aaron, who had walked over to join us. I noticed that they both had the same expression.

"Tell who what?" Mama said.

Kyle raised his eyes. "Doesn't she know?" he asked me.

"Know what?" Mama jumped in quickly.

At first, I was taken off guard, then I realized that Kyle must be referring to Uncle Liam's murder.

"Uncle Liam isn't missing, he was murdered," Kyle said in a fierce whisper.

Mama's eyes got round as marbles. I saw her grip the counter. She turned those peering blue eyes of hers at me and penetrated my very soul.

"What?" she said, and leaned in close enough to smell the bacon on my breath.

I knew she wanted me to verify that Kyle had just spoken truth, so I nodded my head.

"Why was Liam murdered? Who did it? What did he do?" Mama asked, looking from me to Kyle.

I hadn't really wanted to deal with the fact that I was raped by Uncle Liam, but having Mama peering at me like that, I lost all my resistance and I broke out into tears.

"'Cause of me," I managed to blurt out. "He…he…"

Next thing I knew, Mama was holding me tight. "That bastard," I heard her say.

"It's okay, honey," Aaron said and stroked my hair.

"Who killed him?" Mama asked, turning to Kyle.

"Aunt El," Kyle said.

We all just stood there staring at each other for a few moments. I could hear Mama taking these long, deep sighs.

"He didn't get it out of me," Kyle said.

Mama started pacing. "But he could get it out of you, Kyle."

"No, he never will," Kyle said. "Can I stay with you?"

"No," Mama said quickly. "We don't have the room, Kyle. I can't take you away from…your family. He'd only come after you. It would make matters worse. You're just going to have to be strong and stand up to him."

"You're my real family, my mother and my father," Kyle said, and turned to Aaron defiantly.

I noticed that Aaron blushed deeply and walked away. Mama stepped back. I was just standing there wondering why Mama wouldn't let Kyle stay with us.

"I'll share my room with Kyle," I said.

"Go sit outside for a bit, Sassy, I need to talk to Kyle." Mama tried to smile, but I could see that her mouth was drawn, like the shape of our kitchen.

I looked back through the window from the pretty white bench Mama had put out there for customers and I could see Mama talking. Kyle's back was to me, so I couldn't see his expression, and Mama's eyes were downcast; she never looked at him once. But I could see she'd begun to cry.

Their conversation was brief. After shaking his head for a bit, Kyle stood up and turned toward me. The expression on his face frightened me to death. He slammed his fist into his hand. Mama must have said something very upsetting 'cause the next thing I knew Kyle was running out the door and he had tears streaming down his face.

"Kyle," I screamed after him and took off running behind him, but he didn't stop. I almost fell to the ground I was chasing him so hard, pushing my legs as fast as they could go. He finally stopped running long enough to drop to his knees. When I went up to him he was screaming and I was breathing so hard I thought I'd faint.

"I'm going to kill that son of a bitch," he yelled with his fists raised up in the air.

"Kyle, what is it?" I said. "Please, Kyle, tell me what's wrong."

"She wanted to take me away with her and he threatened to kill the both of us if she ran off. She's my mama too, Sassy."

"Who threatened to kill my mama? Was it Seamus threatened to kill her? What right did Seamus have to take you from her if you were her child?"

Kyle sat still. I could tell he was struggling with himself, but he finally put his arms around me.

"He raped her all her life, since she was five years old."

"What?"

"I am the product of his frigging perversion. I swear, I'm going to put a bullet through his fucking heart."

"What are you saying, Kyle?"

"That's why she hid her pregnancy and took you the hell away from here. He was fucking jealous of Aaron."

I just stood there staring at the ground, listening to his words, feeling the taste of his tears on my lips.

"I'm a freak, Sassy. I'm an inbreed, a bastard. She said he'd never let me live with her, that he'd kill me first."

"I love you, Kyle," I said. I didn't know any other way to comfort him.

I watched him get into the blue Impala and screech off, revving up to about eighty miles an hour as he picked up speed. My blood was running cold.

When I got back to the store, I told Mama what Kyle had threatened and she sent Aaron out in their car to try and intercept him. I told Mama what he said about being an inbreed bastard and Mama started crying even harder than she had before.

"Granddaddy is his father?" I asked slowly. "Is that what he's saying?" Mama wiped her eyes with the back of her hand.

"And you're his mama?"

"We've got customers over there in the corner, Sassy, will you take their order? I need to go upstairs. We'll talk later," she said.

I don't think anything in my brain was working, but my legs and my hands did their duty.

When Aaron got back that evening, Kyle was with him. It seemed Kyle had driven back to the house and had confronted Granddaddy with one of his own guns. Granddaddy got the gun away from Kyle and beat the hell out of him with it. Aaron kept ringing the bell, but no one would let him in. I can only assume they were all hiding upstairs. Aaron could hear the fight from the outside, things crashing to the floor and the two men screaming at each other. Finally, Aaron watched as Granddaddy opened the front door and kicked Kyle to the curb. When Aaron ran over to help Kyle to his feet, Granddaddy pointed the gun at Aaron and fired. He might have killed him, but Aaron jumped back. Aaron told us that Granddaddy missed him by an inch.

Mama had no choice but to take Kyle in and nurse his wounds. I think she loved him with all her heart, but it shamed her to look at him, to see so much of Granddaddy in his eyes.

I didn't ever expect to see Granddaddy again. I certainly prayed I'd never see him again, but he showed up at Littleton's about three days after Kyle had tried to kill him. Mama lost all color when Granddaddy walked through the door. I saw Aaron's whole body stiffen up and he went right over to Kyle and put a hand on his shoulder. Aaron stood there, looking like he was protecting all of us. He stared at Granddaddy and it wasn't a good stare. I didn't doubt he'd beat hell out of him if Granddaddy moved one muscle in the wrong direction.

School had been out for at least a half an hour and the café was filling up with kids. I felt myself get weak at the knees when Granddaddy looked at me.

"So, the girl on the bicycle," he said. "Seems like you've recovered?" I nodded my head and turned away.

"It's been a while, Violet," he said to Mama, but I didn't hear Mama answer him.

"I've come to apologize to you, Aaron. Almost killed you the other night," Granddaddy said and sat down on one of the stools. "Could use a cold beverage. Any root beer back there?"

"You're not welcomed here, Daddy," Violet said.

"Hum, serve Negroes here, don't you? Should be serving me. Oh, by the way, this isn't their end of the counter, is it? I don't see any signs here."

Granddaddy got up and looked around.

"I don't believe in segregating people," Aaron said.

"Best beware of the Klan then. They don't like to hear things like that, just might burn you to the ground, every last piece of wood. Gone," Granddaddy snapped his fingers, "like that."

I watched as Granddaddy got up and went over to Kyle. I think we all held our breath and didn't move. He put a hand on Kyle's shoulder and turned him away from Aaron. "I ever find out you know who murdered Liam, I'll kill you, Kyle."

"Why don't you just threaten to cut off my other seven fingers?" Kyle spat at him. Seamus looked into his eyes. "You want to redeem yourself, son?"

"Don't call me son," Kyle yelled out at the top of his lungs.

Suddenly, everyone was staring over at us and I felt like crawling under the counter and hiding my face.

Granddaddy looked at Aaron and then he looked at me. "Image of your father," he said to me. "Guess you're no longer a bastard, girl."

We all just stood there staring at him, wishing like hell he'd leave.

"But whose little bastard are you, Kyle?" Granddaddy stared hard at Mama.

"He knows," Mama said. "I told him the truth. Can't threaten me, Daddy. Can't blackmail me." That seemed to shock Granddaddy 'cause he started laughing nervously.

"Always been a liar, my Violet. She's got a vile sense of humor," he said and laughed so loud I swear I saw a cup rattle. "She tell you I raped her?" He looked right at Aaron. "She's a whore. Kyle's daddy could be any man in this state."

No one answered him. We just watched him.

"She's a seductive little bitch, you should know that, boy." Granddaddy sneered at Aaron. "Had to keep her under lock and key as a teenager."

"You need to go Seamus," Aaron said.

I don't think any of us moved or took a breath 'til we heard the door slam behind him.

We heard from Aunt Erin that Granddaddy Seamus was growing dangerously frustrated by the police's lack of information as to the whereabouts of Liam McLaughlin. When the partial remains of a body was discovered over by Goose Creek, Granddaddy became more anxious and started his own investigation beyond what he termed "the inadequacy of the state police." He started brutally questioning everyone in the family for a start. Every waking hour was an interrogation, but at least he never came back to Littleton's.

I kept trying to put everything out of my mind and go on with my life. I didn't want to think about Mama's sadness. I just wanted to be like everyone else and everyone else didn't have disgusting secrets to hide, so neither would I. Unnaturalness is something found in the deep, dark recesses of a bad person's soul. I buried my brief encounter with it and faced myself in the direction of the sun.

Besides, I had other things to think about, lighter things, things that didn't make me sad. Like Jeremy Holden, for one. He was in my social studies class and we all knew he was destined for success like his well-known father. Why Jeremy might even grow up to be President of the United States. He played basketball and hockey, too; neither of which I liked much, but I started going to games and screaming at the top of my lungs every time he scored and I always talked Mama into giving him a third scoop of ice cream at Littleton's. Most of the kids went to Littleton's after school, except for those whose parents didn't like that Mama and Aaron served black people. I was so happy to find out that Jeremy came from a family of real bona fide politicians, all of whom were Democrats. His father was a senator and his mother was on some committee fighting for civil rights.

I guess it was fitting then, how me and Jeremy first got together in that intimate way. It was the day John F. Kennedy was assassinated. I had taken June-bug out to the river after we were all dismissed from school. I was crying, mostly 'cause no one should have been gunned down like that and especially not a Kennedy; someone who was only trying to make this a better world.

I guess Jeremy saw me through the window of the café and he followed me out to the place I always took my June-bug. It was a little private corner, just where the stream turned and a medley of trees hid its journey toward the river. Jeremy sat down beside me and took my hand and that made me cry harder.

"It's a sad day, Sassy," he said. "Do you feel that sadness?"

I looked at his leg, covered in tight brown pants. His socks were white and his shoes looked like caramel-colored taffy. I noticed his hair was straight and dark. My heart started pounding real fast when I felt his thigh against my leg.

"The world is going to change forever. Do you know that?"

I nodded.

"Do you think Castro had him killed? What is your opinion, Sassy? Do you agree?"

"No," I said softly. "I don't think Castro had him killed."

"Who then?" he asked. "Think carefully now, Sassy. You don't want to sound ignorant."

"Don't know," I said and noticed that he had taken his other hand and put it over mine and he was rubbing my hand with both of his.

"Last I heard it was some guy up in a warehouse window. Don't you listen to the radio, Sassy? You surely would have heard it."

Then he took my hand very innocently and brought it to his lips. I thought I was going to pass out.

"I think you're pretty," he said.

I turned all shades of red, I'm sure. I noticed how well-proportioned he was, muscular and broad. His nose turned up and a dimple in his left cheek was long and deep.

Next thing I knew he was kissing me and I was learning how to use my tongue in answer to his requests. His tongue made me tingle all over even though I thought he put too much of it inside my mouth.

"I can tell you haven't been kissed much," he said. "We'll have to change that."

By the time we got back to the café, we'd learned that they'd arrested the man from the warehouse building in Dallas, but somebody named Jack Ruby had gone and shot him. We all sat around a big round table discussing how unfortunate it was to have silenced the assassin and that now we'd never know who might have ordered the hit on President Kennedy 'cause none of us believed it was some lone gunman.

Throughout the whole discussion, Jeremy held my hand where no one could see it and every time I said something, he leaned in close, as if he wanted to kiss me again, but wouldn't dare, not in front of all our friends and certainly not with my mama staring at him from the counter.

Chapter Thirteen

News was all over town that a severed head had been found on the outskirts of Charleston believed to be that of Liam McLaughlin. Granddaddy Seamus knew how to get answers. Without Kyle there to torture, Granddaddy turned his attentions to Seth. When I met Grandma Edna up by the sycamore tree, she was pretty shaken.

"He would have tortured us all 'til he got his answers," she said. "He knows one of us did it. I don't know how the hell he knows that. Liam had enough enemies, could have been anyone. But I guess the devil has special powers." She looked at me long and hard. "He took a pistol to Seth's temple. Seth had no choice, Sassy. He had to do something. Oh, I hate that man with all my heart. Darkest day of my life was when I married him."

"Why didn't you ever divorce him then? He wasn't nice to you, he beat up on your children, he had perverted feelings for my mama."

Grandma Edna looked shocked for a moment, but then she got hold of herself. "Catholics don't divorce, child," she said.

"That's pretty lame," I said.

"What did the police ask you?"

"Same thing they asked me last time."

"You did good."

"What will Granddaddy do to Seth?"

"Won't do anything now."

"Well, that's good," I said.

"You know, Sassy, it should have been a common man shot to death, not John Kennedy. If it could have been a tradeoff, it would have been a good thing 'cause we need Kennedy a lot more than we need some common man that's no good to society. You know what I'm saying?"

I wasn't sure I agreed with her, but I nodded. Though I did tell her that one man shouldn't have to die for another.

"Sometimes the better man needs to be saved," she said. "And the lesser man needs to be sacrificed."

"Sure," I said.

"The police have their suspect in custody," Grandma Edna said carefully. "The murder of my eldest son has been solved. Police couldn't do it, we had to."

"What murder?" I asked.

"The man that shot Liam is in custody."

"Aunt El?" I said. "They arrested Aunt El?"

"Lord no, Sassy, they arrested the criminal, the one who actually committed the crime."

"What are you talking about? Aunt El shot Uncle Liam."

Grandma Edna got up and sat beside me. "Sassy, she didn't shoot anyone. Now I want that ingrained inside your head when the police question you about it."

"So the police aren't going to arrest her?" I asked.

"The perpetrator is in custody," she said very seriously. I stared at her.

"Aunt El?"

"No, Dudley is in custody."

I jumped up. I couldn't believe what I just heard. "Dudley? He didn't do anything."

"Try to remember, Sassy. He killed your Uncle Liam, called him a bigot. You know how Dudley talks, thinks his kind are equal to ours."

"What are you saying?"

She grabbed my arm fiercely and pulled me close. "Listen, Sassy," she said. "Your Uncle Seth came up with this idea and we all need to follow it to the letter now. It's the only way to save your aunt from Seamus."

"No!" I shouted.

"It's going to be okay, Sassy, Seth assured me. Dudley is safer in jail than he is at Carter's Crossing. The Klan will string him up for killing Liam McLaughlin, you can count on that."

I ran to my bicycle and jumped on, without responding to her anymore. I rode as fast as I could over to Slave Town where I was praying I'd still find Dudley. June-bug was in hot pursuit behind me. I guess I was too upset to be thinking straight. I wouldn't find Dudley anywhere but the county jail.

Just as I feared, Dudley wasn't at Slave Town. I didn't know what I was going to do to help him. I needed assistance, Kyle's assistance. But I didn't have any way to get in touch with Kyle without having to go all the way back into Beaufort and that would take too long and I might be seen and locked up in my room, so I settled in to Slave Town, hid there, determined to die there if I had to.

All I could do for days was sit and stare at the sky. My brain was in slow motion and as far as helping Dudley, it provided no answers. I was nearly soaked through to my skin from the torrential rain that decided to fall from the sky when I needed it least. I had protection from the slapping sound of its song as it soaked through the rotted wood of my shelter. Rain came almost nightly and I thought my bones would never warm. I slept on a straw mattress that Dudley must have made. I slept whenever I could 'cause it was better than being awake and I ate berries all day and night. There was a fresh stream about a half mile away and I had to go all the way over to that stream to get water and bathe myself and I couldn't even do that until the damn sun came out and provided me the warmth to leave my little shack.

The days were hot after the rains ended and bugs were having a field day on my flesh. I was turning redder than a lobster fresh out the pot and I'm sure I stunk, even with the springwater baths I took.

I wasn't really thinking straight at all; my mind had shut down all together. After a while, I didn't even know how long I'd been there at

Slave Town. Maybe three or four days. By the fifth day, or maybe the sixth, June-bug got disgusted with me and she ran off. I kept seeing things out toward the field, hallucinating angels playing in the mist. It got so that I couldn't even stand on my feet, I was so weak. I called to the angels to help, but they were elusive and indifferent to my suffering.

I didn't know it then, but my dog had been worried about me, 'cause next thing I knew she'd brought back Grandma Edna. There she was running beside the Rolls Royce, just a few hours after she'd left me, barking up a storm. Pike was behind the wheel and he was driving right up to me. I could hear the ground crunching beneath his tires. June-bug must have led them straight there. I hated to admit it, but I was happy to see the car.

It was Grandma Edna that got out from the backseat and looked around after Pike quit the engine. I was easy to see, lying in the middle of the road the way I was. I watched her whole body go loose when she spotted me. I could tell she was so relieved to see me she looked about to faint.

"Thank God," she said.

"Where's Dudley?" I asked, though I could barely speak at all.

"We thought you were dead, Sassy. We thought something had happened to you."

"Well, I'm not dead, just angry."

She walked over and took her hat off. I watched as she looked around. "I used to play here as a child," she said. "Haven't been here since."

I looked at Pike. I couldn't understand how he could get in a car with any member of our family. Seth lied, put Dudley in jail. I couldn't understand the look Pike gave me; it was almost like he was telling me it was okay.

"Dudley didn't do anything," I said to him, suddenly feeling my strength return.

"He knows that," Grandma Edna said.

"Then what's he smiling for?" I asked.

Pike kind of chuckled and picked me up in his arms and set me down in the back seat. If Pike had anything to say he wasn't saying it.

"I have some bad news," Grandma Edna said as she got in beside me. "I need to tell you something. It isn't good."

I didn't want to hear any more bad news so I closed my eyes.

"You ever hear of the Klu Klux Klan?" she asked as Pike turned the car around and headed back toward the house.

"Of course," I said.

"They burned down Littleton's."

It didn't register at first. She wasn't talking sense, just torturing me for running away. I sat up. "You don't mean…?"

"There's nothing left of it."

I knew it was true by her expression. I started yelling and screaming. She put her arms around me and held me to her.

"Your Mama is fine," she said, over and over again, through my sobbing and choking. "She's fine, Sassy. Aaron, too. They're okay."

"Where's Mama?" I asked and pulled myself together as best as I could. I looked into her eyes. "I want to see Mama."

"We couldn't find you, Sassy. We looked all over the place. They wanted to take you away with them, but we didn't know where you were. Your mama thought you'd been killed. She was beside herself."

"Who would kill me?" I asked.

"No one now," she said.

I just looked at her. "Where's Mama?" I asked again.

"Sassy, in this town there's one man that has more authority than anyone else, more than the damn mayor. He's with the Klan, been with them for years. I'm sure he ordered the fire."

"Who ordered the fire?"

I could tell she thought I was too volatile for the truth 'cause she avoided it.

"There's nothing left of the café," she said. "It was burned to the ground. Your mama and Aaron were lucky to get out of there alive. They had to shimmy down the roof and jump two floors."

"Oh my God," I said.

"Kyle…" she began. She turned her head away from me and stared out the window. When she turned back to me I could see the struggle in her eyes, the pain inside her.

"He must have been out with Marjean," I said, my heart beating on overtime. "His girlfriend? He sees her almost every night."

Grandma Edna shook her head. "No, Sassy, he wasn't out with Marjean. He was asleep in his room."

"Oh my God, he isn't? He isn't…"

"They found a body in his room. He's gone. He never had a chance."

She seemed nervous. Her voice seemed to shake, like she was still hurting from the deep breath she'd taken.

"That's the way that bastard wanted it, wanted all of you dead, I'm sure. It was only a matter of time before he did it."

I collapsed in her arms. Someone must have taken me to bed, 'cause when I awoke the sky could not have offered up anything else but happiness, it was so blue, so clear, but then I noticed Kyle's room had been cleaned out and I felt the emptiness in the contradiction.

Chapter Fourteen

udley was charged with the murder of Liam McLaughlin and was sitting in a goddamn jail cell about to be tried for a crime he didn't commit. Seth had just offered him up to the police, said he just couldn't protect him anymore. Mama and Aaron had fled town. They must have 'cause the apartment we lived in was nothing but black, charred wood. Everything had been destroyed. There was just one body found, burned beyond recognition in the back bedroom where Kyle slept. It was hard for me to accept that Kyle was dead, but they were putting a coffin in the ground with his name on it.

Mama wasn't calling me to tell me how she was, or when she was coming back for me. Grandma Edna said she may never come back, too much sadness to feel in Carter's Crossing. The only good thing was that Granddaddy Seamus got out of town the very next day that Littleton's burned. I was hoping someone would shoot him in the back, especially knowing he was the one had responsibility for that fire, whether or not he held the match to the flame.

"I'm going to the police," I told Grandma Edna. "I'm going to turn that bastard in for what he did to Kyle. It was Granddaddy Seamus set that fire, wasn't it?"

Grandma Edna sat forward and gripped the arms of the chair she was sitting in. "No need," she said. "The fire has been deemed an accident."

"An accident?" I asked. "Who came to that conclusion?"

"Your granddaddy has power in this town, in this state, maybe even in the whole goddamn country. Turning him in for that fire, or not turning him in for it wouldn't have made a damn bit of difference. Don't waste your energy."

"Where the hell is he?" I asked. "Canada, I hear," she said.

Aunt El told me that the family was losing money every day 'cause Granddaddy was lying low in Canada and Liam was dead. She said she had to take over the mills now that there wasn't anyone else to do it.

"Why doesn't he just come back and take responsibility for killing Kyle in that fire?" I was crying when I said it. It seems every time I thought of Kyle I'd start crying.

"I think your Granddaddy is in Canada," Seth said. "We had to have Pike take that ditzy secretary of his back East."

"Why'd he run off to Canada if the fire was deemed an accident," I asked.

"Might get out some day that he set it. Granddaddy's got enemies, could turn on him." Seth looked at his hands for a long time. "He probably feels safer up there."

We were sitting around the dinner table eating blackened salmon and I kept wondering why Carolyn wasn't shedding tears, what with Dudley being in jail and all. She looked nervous, but not at all distraught.

"How are you holding up, Carolyn?" I asked.

She looked right into my eyes. I noticed how gentle the look she gave me was.

"Thank you for asking, Sassy," she said. "I'm praying for my boy."

She looked around the table at the family before she left the room. I saw Seth grab her hand and squeeze it.

"I could do a better job running the mills, anyway," El said, like she'd never taken a breath. "I've always had a head for business. I've been saying this for years: close the unproductive mills and restructure the ones making money. Daddy was going to send us to the poor house."

I was so angry at Aunt El that I could barely look at her. She knew it too, 'cause she kept trying to make amends, kept smiling at me. But goddamit, Dudley was taking her place in jail.

"You'll be making executive decisions now, Elvira," Grandma Edna said. "I have a stake in those mills. They're mine, anyway. I know you don't want the responsibility, do you Seth?"

"I'd rather farm pigs," he said.

"Does that mean we'll be traveling, El?" Aunt Earline asked.

"That it does, honey bun," Aunt El answered and I noted the excitement in her voice.

When I looked over at Grandma Edna she had the strangest expression and she was staring at Aunt Earline and Aunt El as if they'd each picked up a live chicken and broken its neck with their teeth at the dinner table.

"Honey bun?" she questioned. "Strange term of endearment for a grown woman."

I caught the look between Aunt El and Aunt Earline and I couldn't help but giggle.

"Well, Mama," Aunt El began. "I promise never to call you honey bun, not ever."

"Nor I, Mama McLaughlin," Aunt Earline said. "Besides, you're more of a sticky bun."

Grandma Edna laughed despite herself.

The one thing about being young is that things go on behind your back without your knowing or understanding what all the secrecy is about. And all you got when you grow up and look back is a sense of something that happened in a very mysterious way that no one really remembers very well, or so they say. Like that strange night when a bunch of men came to the house and Seth took them into the library and closed the door. I saw Pike go in there with him and even Pike's father, James Leroy. I recognized some of the other men, too.

"What's going on?" I asked Grandma Edna.

She didn't answer me, but she had all the curtains closed.

"Go up to bed," was all she said.

I could hear the murmurings coming from the library and when I looked down out my window I saw five cars leave the property, slowly, like they were all going to a wake.

I was so sad deep inside where they tell you no organ claims your sorrow, 'cept maybe your brain. I couldn't bear to go into Kyle's old room and feel how painful it was to think of him being gone, even sitting in Mama's room hurt me. I didn't know if I'd ever see her again and I had a horrible foreboding feeling about it. If she wasn't calling me, she must be dead, too.

But despite my sadness, I finally fell asleep that night. I was awoken at dawn by loud voices outside the house. I heard someone calling out Seth's name. When I ran to the window and looked out I saw the sheriff's car.

"We're gonna get that nigger," I heard someone say. That's when I realized that a bunch of people were in our living room, not just the sheriff. I tried to listen to what they were saying, but their voices were mostly muffled.

Then I heard Grandma Edna say loud and clear that her son never left the house.

"What's going on?" I said as I came down the stairs. I saw the front door close on some people, all men, maybe about ten of them, just as I hit the bottom step. There wasn't anyone in the living room now, so I headed into the kitchen where I'd heard voices.

Seth was sitting at the kitchen table in his pajamas. He was grinning from ear to ear. I felt I'd come in on the tail end of a good joke. Aunt El was over by the sink, kind of leaning on it and shaking her head.

"Who was just here?" I asked. "Who were you all talking to?"

Grandma Edna put a coffee cup to her lips and took a sip before she answered.

"Someone bombed the jail," she said. "There was a search party here wanting to know if we knew anything about it."

My heart began to go nuts in my chest. "Was Dudley killed?" I cried out.

"No, honey," Aunt El said. "He was freed."

I was shocked silent. I stared at Grandma Edna. She nodded her head.

"Seems a bunch of men bombed the jail right after freeing Dudley. Only one man watching him last night. Guess that was a big mistake." She smiled outright at me. "The commotion caused a bit of chaos."

"So where is he?" I asked. "Is he okay?"

"Must be," Aunt El said. "Had a car there waiting for him and he took off in it. Knowing Dudley, he'll be fine. What luck, huh, the car being there and all?" She smiled at Seth.

"Those fools are searching the woods with dogs." Seth shook his head. "They'll never get him that way."

I quickly looked over at him. "There was a car waiting for him?" I asked.

Seth smiled back at me. "Yep, Sassy," he said. "A car, best way to get anywhere, four wheels and an engine."

I was soon to learn that Seth went out every night 'cause he was meeting with members of some freedom movement and they were doing everything they could to foster civil rights and expose the identity of Klan members.

Seth said he was worried about Dudley's family, that the Klan would torture them into giving out information as to Dudley's whereabouts, but it seemed to all of us that the Klan was losing steam. Several indictments were served against Klan members and there were no more riots in Beaufort anymore, even after black students were bused into white schools. Grandma Edna said the world was righting itself and whether or not we liked it, it was fact.

I was sure that Grandma Edna wanted to spare me the news of Mama's death, hers and Aaron's, but Grandma Edna never mentioned a word about Mama being dead. She didn't say anything at all and that was the worst of it.

"Your mama's safe," she kept repeating, but I had no proof of that.

"Then where are they?" I kept asking and Grandma Edna told me that Mama was too afraid to stay in South Carolina after almost losing her life in that fire and that she and Aaron must have taken whatever insurance money they got from it and left town to start a new life.

"And when they're settled, she'll be back one day for you," Grandma Edna said. "She knew you'd be safe here with us. She had Elvira's word and mine that no harm would ever come to you, Sassy."

"Who would have hurt me to begin with?" I kept asking. "Granddaddy? Would he have raped me like he raped my mama?"

"Sassy, please," Grandma Edna shouted.

"Well, there's no one to hurt me now," I said.

I watched as she got up and left the room, but I heard her say real low, like a whisper, "No, not ever again."

It wasn't long before Aunt El and Aunt Earline started traveling all over the place restructuring the mills and selling most of them off. I kept asking if Granddaddy was ever coming back 'cause he wouldn't have liked that Aunt El was selling off the mills and investing the money in the stock market.

"Hope not," was the only answer I ever got.

"What about Mama?" I kept questioning Grandma Edna. "Where is she?"

"She's having a baby, Sassy. She'll be back in due time."

So there I was at Carter's Crossing, living daily with my broken heart. "She wouldn't ever have left me if she were alive," I insisted.

"Fate," Grandma Edna said. "You should have been here the night they left town instead of making us all worry so much. I guess it wasn't in the stars for you to go off with her, at least not now."

"Well, here I am," I said. "Where is she?"

"Answers come all in good time, girl. There's reasons behind every decision a person makes. And if there's consequences to pay for it, then retribution will come."

So, my life went on, such as it was and happiness reappeared, as it is known to do. And, too, as it is known to do, happiness bit the dirt faster than a Corvette on open road, fickle as a whim.

CHAPTER FIFTEEN

I met my Aunt Peg right before I started my senior year in high school. I'd been living at Carter's Crossing for three years and hadn't heard from my mama since Littleton's burned to the ground. I kept assuming she was dead and wasn't anyone giving me much of an alternative.

Aunt Peg came up for part of the summer that year. She was the one Dudley thought had spirit 'cause she told fortunes in a nightclub in Savannah. Well, as striking as Mama was, was about as ugly as poor Aunt Peg was. And that was my first impression of her, that she was so odd-looking that you had to keep staring at her. Interesting thing, though, is that after I got used to the initial shock of her face, she turned beautiful right before my eyes, sort of like a caterpillar before it morphs into a butterfly. When she spoke, her eyes flashed and in the tilt of her head, she looked regal as a queen.

She was tall and heavyset, though she referred to herself as "big-boned." Her hair was so black it shone in daylight. She wore makeup that accentuated her large blue eyes, eyes that reminded me of celestial crystal balls. Her nose went every which way, kind of long and then veering off to the left when you got to the end of it.

She wore lots of jewelry, bracelets that jangled and necklaces that fell over each other and ended right at the crevice of her large breasts. Her lipstick always seemed a bit too thick. But her teeth were white and straight, like a strand of pearls.

She was staying in Kyle's old room, which had originally been hers. Grandma Edna sent me up there to see if she needed anything 'bout an hour after she'd arrived in an old black MG, the one with the running boards on the side. I thought that car was the coolest thing I'd ever seen in my life.

I took June-bug with me when I went up to see about her, 'cause she scared me a bit. I found her sitting on the bed, looking all around. Her facial expression was strained.

"Oh hello, Sassy," she said.

June-bug went right over to her, so I assumed she was okay. "I came by to see if you needed anything," I told her.

"There's pain here in this room," she said. "I can feel it."

"This was Kyle's room," I said. "After it was yours."

She sighed long and deep. "He was so troubled," she said.

"You weren't at the funeral," I said, not as an accusation, but I had been surprised not to see her there.

"Funerals are not what they seem, Sassy. There are no goodbyes. How easy it would be if there were."

I was curious about the gift she had to tell fortunes and I'd been thinking about getting my fortune read from the minute I heard she was coming. Though fortune telling is not what Aunt Erin called it, nor Grandma Edna. They said it was just a cheap way to manipulate money out of people and any con artist could do it.

Then Aunt Peg said the weirdest thing, as if she'd just read my mind. She said, "I don't have to make a living, Sassy. As you well know, I'm pretty independent, but I have a gift the good Lord gave me, passed down for generations. Maybe you have it, too."

"Wow," I said. "You think?"

Her jewelry jingled and jangled all over the place. I thought she was hardy, the way she slapped her legs and laughed.

"Let's find out," she said.

I think she must have sensed my excitement 'cause she stood up and held out her hand.

"Has June-bug ever gone into your Grandma's bedroom?" she asked.

I thought for a moment. "Well, I'm not sure," I said.

Aunt Peg leaned over close to me. "She won't ever go into that room," she whispered.

"Why not?" I whispered back.

She proceeded down the hall to Aunt El's room, still holding my hand. "Come here, June-bug," she commanded.

June-bug ran right on up to her and kissed her all over.

Aunt Peg did that same thing in every one's room and June-bug ran in and kissed her each time.

But when we got to Grandma Edna's room poor June-bug cowered at the door and wouldn't go in.

"Wow," I said. "What's wrong with her?"

Aunt Peg winked at me. "Brutus," she said and motioned over to a corner of the bedroom where Grandma Edna's favorite reading chair stood innocently before the window.

"Can you see him?"

"Brutus?" I wasn't getting it and stared at the chair. I didn't see anything even though Aunt Peg was pointing like I was missing something.

"Years ago, your grandma had an old tom cat named Brutus. The cat adored your grandma and this bedroom was his domain. He wouldn't let anyone in it, especially not a dog. Poor June-bug won't ever want to come in here. She senses that old cat's presence."

"How come I don't sense his presence?"

"I see him clear as day, Sassy. You could, too, if you weren't so frightened by it."

I didn't like her saying that to me, it made me nervous. But my Aunt Peg sure did fascinate me after that.

"You're going to marry a very fine man," she said to me one day, right out of the blue. We'd been sitting in the living room sipping tea before the fire. Aunt Peg insisted that I should have a cup of green tea every day, that it would keep my body pure and my aura bright.

"You finally going to tell me my fortune now, Aunt Peg?"

She nodded. "He's tall and his hair is light."

"That doesn't sound like Jeremy," I said. "I plan to marry Jeremy, Aunt Peg, and his hair isn't light."

"Jeremy? No, that's not his name."

"Will I have children?"

"Yes, I do see that for you, dear."

I smiled. I doubted if Aunt Peg knew what she was talking about 'cause I knew I wasn't going to marry anyone else but Jeremy Holden, but then, I remembered Brutus and her strange ability to know things, to see spirits.

"Tell me, Aunt Peg, where's my mama?"

Aunt Peg didn't give me the only damn answer I really wanted. She just said, "Not very far."

Unlike my Aunt Erin, Aunt Peg sought me out and wanted to be around me and I liked her more and more for it. She was a real talker and told me stories about people who traveled half the world just to have her tell their fortune. She said she even had children named after her.

"Must be a hundred Margaret's in this world because of me. I do hope they favor the sobriquet."

I looked at her blankly.

"The nickname for Margaret is Peggy, dear…or Peg, like me."

"Can you tell if Dudley is okay?" I asked.

I probably annoyed her to death 'cause I kept asking her questions about Dudley and Mama and she did give me answers, though none that really made sense.

"Dudley is rich," she said. "Sign of the times, the way he makes his money."

"How could Dudley be rich? He didn't come from it."

"You'll see," she said.

"Am I ever going to see my mama again?" I asked her.

"Oh yes," she said. "We are all reunited."

Well, with Aunt Peg, I never knew if she was talking about heaven or earth.

"Where is Mama?" I asked. "Right now? Can I see her right now? When will I see her?"

Aunt Peg didn't like questions like that. She told me that fortune doesn't reveal those kinds of direct answers 'cause the future is always up for grabs; it has no static awareness of what's coming round the bend, just a sense of its impact.

"Then what good is fortune telling?" I asked, and she reached over and squeezed my hand.

"Your mama is happy," she said. "She's happy, Sassy, at least for the time being."

Well, that and a bag full of nickels wasn't going to get me anywhere closer to wherever the hell Mama was. Deep down, I believed Grandma Edna was shielding the truth, that they'd all been burned to death: Kyle, Mama, and Aaron, all three of them gone. I began to believe that Grandma Edna couldn't accept it and thought I couldn't, so she just kept lying to me.

Maybe I didn't get the answers I wanted from Aunt Peg, but I did get some I never dreamed I'd get. Grandma Edna and Aunt Erin didn't like hanging out with poor Aunt Peg so they always had some convenient excuse not to be around. Aunt El was restructuring one of the Pennsylvania mills and Aunt Earline was with her, so it was pretty much up to me to keep Aunt Peg entertained that summer.

She and I went in to Beaufort for lunch one sunny afternoon. I took her to Rocket's, which by this time had replaced Littleton's as the 'super hangout' place to go. Also, by this time, I was driving my own car, a 1964 baby blue Impala. Grandma Edna liked Impalas and thought everyone else did, too, so even though I would have preferred a Mustang, I gracefully accepted the Impala for my sixteenth birthday without complaint.

I was pretty much at ease with Aunt Peg. She was fun to be with and she laughed easily, which was still more than I could say for anyone else in that family, except Seth, after he'd had a beer.

"Who's buried under the sycamore tree?" I asked quickly, just after my burger and fries got to the table.

Aunt Peg didn't take a breath and said outright, "Oh, Charlotte is there, poor little baby."

"Who was Charlotte?" I asked, feeling the excitement of finally getting some answers.

"You don't know?" Aunt Peg leaned in close and looked at me. Then she sat back.

"No, I guess they wouldn't have told you." She sighed and bit into the juiciest burger I'd ever seen. I watched the grease from it fall down Aunt Peg's chin.

"Well, who was she?"

"You know your granddaddy was a bastard, don't you?"

I nodded my head; that sure was fact.

"He used to bring women back to the house, pass them off as secretaries, sleep with them right under your grandma's nose." Aunt Peg wiped the grease away and folded her napkin back up in squares. She looked like she was picking her teeth with her tongue as she raised her eyes to the ceiling and shook her head from side to side.

"So the baby belonged to one of his secretaries?" I asked slowly.

Aunt Peg moved her lips before she spoke, as if she might have been trying to swallow the can of worms she just opened.

"No, honey, it wasn't his baby," she finally said.

"Then whose baby was it?" I held her gaze, I didn't want her flaking out on me now.

"Your grandma was a beautiful young woman. Out of all of us children, Violet most resembled her. She was too noticeable a woman not to be loved or desired, sort of like your mama."

"What do you mean?" I asked, not knowing whether or not she'd tell me the truth, but she started talking quickly and quietly. I detected the anger in her voice.

"A man by the name of Clint Woods fell in love with your Grandma Edna. They had an affair and your Grandma got pregnant. Daddy knew it wasn't his and he was furious, but what could he do? He was never around.

By the time he'd gotten back from one of his business trips, Mama had already given birth to Charlotte and was giddy with happiness."

"But the baby died? How?" I asked.

"Daddy thought little Charlotte was retarded, he kept insisting on it, and he made all of us agree with him. He never talked about not being the baby's father, but he knew, we all knew. He was very controlling, very mean, and he was going to punish Mama whatever way he could. I think he just came back for the sole purpose of getting rid of that baby."

Aunt Peg's eyes seemed to be spitting fire. I could tell she hated her daddy, just like we all did. "She has a flat face," he kept telling us. "Mama loved that little baby so much and she'd tell him he was crazy for thinking that, but he was so persuasive that we kids started believing it, too. We'd look at the baby and think it had a flat face."

"How did it die?" I asked.

"Daddy had Seth suffocate it, I'm sad and shamed to say, Sassy."

I sat back slowly. I lost my appetite in an instant. "What?"

"He used to grab Seth by the neck with those large hands of his and he'd squeeze 'til poor Seth screamed for mercy. Seth grew up scared to death of Daddy. He told Seth to kill that baby, like some animal would kill its young if it wasn't perfect."

"My God," I whispered. "How could Seth have done that?"

"You see the damage it's done him, don't you? No one's more alone on this earth than Seth McLaughlin. He was just a teenage boy at the time. Lost his mama's love for doing it, we all knew that, but it didn't gain him anything from his father. Daddy can't love, he's barely human. And Seth has no head for business, which in Daddy's mind made him about as unnecessary as a blind horse."

"Why didn't Grandma Edna leave Granddaddy and run away with that Clint guy?"

"Clint was married. Your Grandma kept going to church and praying to be forgiven for her sins, but it didn't stop her from seeing Clint. They were so in love. Unfortunately, Clint's home was burned to the ground right after little Charlotte was, well…after she died. Clint's wife and two small children were killed in the fire. Clint died three days later in the hospital, his burns were too severe. His death was a blessing really."

"Burned? You mean like Littleton's?"

"You don't cross Seamus McLaughlin. You do, you die. That's just the way it was."

"Didn't he go to jail for that fire?"

Aunt Peg laughed. "Couldn't pin it on him and live, Sassy."

And then Aunt Peg said the strangest thing. She sat back and took a bite of her burger. With a mouthful of it she said, "Don't worry, honey, Granddaddy can't hurt anyone from the grave."

I never asked her what she meant by that. Maybe I didn't want to know 'cause I didn't respond at all. As far as I was concerned, Granddaddy wasn't in his grave, he was in Canada. I guess that's the way I dealt with things. I ignored them and let 'em settle somewhere deep inside before I had to sort them out, or they just might have taken me by surprise and forced me into a drowning pool. On that day, I brought the subject back to something light, like Jeremy Holden.

"Will you come to my wedding?" I asked her.

"If I'm living," she said.

"You're only thirty-nine years old. I think I'll be getting married before you drop." I laughed.

She raised her eyebrows and they went into peaks. Her brows were thick, like bushy roads.

"I see more than one wedding in your future, Sassy. First one won't be good, won't be good at all, but the last one, the real one, oh Sassy, that will be so fine a wedding day."

I looked at her like she was nuts. "One wedding is all I want, Aunt Peg," I said.

Chapter Sixteen

I was in love with Jeremy Holden and I had been since that afternoon he'd kissed me, the day JFK was assassinated and he'd followed me out to the river. He made me think of nothing else but the next date, the next opportunity to feel his lips on mine, though I did manage to get straight As in school despite the amount of time I spent fantasizing about our life together.

The only really sore spot in my social life was still Thomas Tierney. He'd spread it all over school that I was a tomboy and beat up on the opposite sex just to prove how totally unattractive I was. Well, Thomas Tierney didn't have the power he thought he did 'cause I became popular at school despite him and lots of boys wanted to take me out. All but Thomas Tierney, who still hated me to the core for clipping his chin with my lunch box.

"Why do you say such hateful things, Thomas?" I asked him once.

"Just trying to get you to like me," is what he said. I couldn't believe it.

"Do you have your head on backward or what?" I said. "I could never like you."

"Just being facetious," he said and walked away. "I couldn't like you, either."

He and Jeremy were friends, not best buddies or anything, but they did hang out with the same crowd. I refused to include Thomas in any social activities and I told Jeremy straight out that if Thomas was going to be joining us, I was taking a pass. I couldn't truly stand Thomas, especially after he told me he'd seen Kyle in Crawford eating ice cream in a place called Denton's.

"I swear I saw him, Sassy," he said. "But I couldn't get close enough to see his hand. You know, if it was clawed, it was Kyle."

I was somehow able to stop myself from breaking out into tears, but not from punching him hard as I could across his shoulder, so I let him have it.

"You're hateful," I shouted as my fist shoved him forward.

"Ouch," he said.

"You got me all wrong, Sassy, I was just telling you what I saw."

"No, you were just opening up a wound," I said. "So you can watch me bleed."

He stared at me as I walked away. When I looked back he was still standing there, staring.

Maybe it had just dawned on him he'd said something ridiculous. Dead people don't eat ice cream.

Of course I was under pressure to sleep with Jeremy. We made out every opportunity we got, especially up at Slave Town on Dudley's old straw mattress.

"Wow, what is this place?" Jeremy asked the first time I took him up there.

"Slave Town."

"Really? Almost looks too built up to have been a slave town. You sure you got your facts right?"

"It's old slave quarters," I told him. "Dudley told me that."

Jeremy was fascinated with the size of it; it looked as if it had been a whole two city blocks long. It felt empty and haunted when you stared at it. Sometimes it made me sad. Aunt Peg said I felt that way 'cause Slave Town truly was haunted and I was feeling the suffering of the people who had lived and died there. I'd taken Aunt Peg to Slave Town the day after she'd arrived back home at Carter's Crossing. She walked slowly all around picking up her vibes from dead people. She told me she'd spoken to a young girl who'd lived way past the Civil War, but was slaughtered in a gun battle between the FBI and some bootleggers in nineteen twenty-nine.

"My aunt Peg says she can feel the pain of dead people, what they suffered in their lives, what they went through."

Jeremy gave me his broad smile. "Your Aunt Peg have all her marbles? Don't tell me you believe that crap, I'll have to call you stupid."

I laughed along with him, but truth was, I believed Aunt Peg. I believed almost everything she said, except, of course, my not marrying Jeremy.

"What's that?" he asked me, looking around and pointing out where the old cotton fields were. I followed his eyes, but I didn't see anything.

"Holy shit," I heard him say.

He walked out ahead of me toward the cotton fields. Then he looked over toward the barn. "What's in there?" he asked.

"Oh, Dudley's old hobby. I think he called it cannabis plants. Guess he grew them. I'm surprised they're still alive, but I hear tell my Aunt Erin's oldest boy takes care of the plants for him."

Jeremy's eyes got wide as four-lane highways. I had told him all about Dudley, except that I knew who had gotten him out of jail. I kept that to myself. No sense turning in my own family for a jailbreak.

Jeremy walked over to the weeds and started sniffing them. Next thing I knew he had pulled one of the weeds apart and he crumbled it up into what looked like dried thyme.

"You can smoke this, Sassy," he said. "My older brother, Jake, he took me over to a marijuana plantation once."

"What?"

Jeremy took a cigarette from the pack he had in his shirt pocket. I watched as he carefully dug the tobacco out with a pen. Then he put the dried thyme into the cigarette paper and lit it.

"You didn't tell me enough about your old friend Dudley, Sassy. You thank him for me if he ever shows up here again, you hear."

Jeremy handed me the cigarette and I started puffing 'til Jeremy told me to follow his lead and hold the smoke in my mouth before I let it out.

"Take a little breath with it, Sassy," he said. "This sweet weed is going to make you oh so happy."

It was harder to keep my virginity intact after discovering marijuana in Slave Town and sharing it with Jeremy on the old straw mattress, but I succeeded. Barely, but succeeded, nonetheless.

Chapter Seventeen

I hadn't seen Marjean for over two years. She hadn't come to Kyle's funeral and that surprised me, but I summed it up to her despair and how difficult it would be for her to accept Kyle's death. I barely thought of Marjean 'cause I was in too much pain over losing Kyle myself. It never occurred to me that we might have been comfort for each other.

It took me by surprise seeing her in Beaufort one afternoon. It hit me like a ton of bricks that I should have gone over there and befriended her. After all, we both loved Kyle so much.

"Marjean," I yelled out from my car, but she didn't hear me.

As I pulled over and parked my Impala, I watched her walk down the street with her mama, a woman I had met briefly when I used to hang out with Marjean and Kyle.

I was headed over to Rocket's to meet Jeremy for a malt. I quickly killed the ignition and called out Marjean's name again. When she turned back and noticed it was me, she blushed red as a cherry cough drop and looked away. I felt something in my stomach flip; I wasn't going to let her ignore me like that.

"Marjean," I said as I caught up and stood beside her. "I haven't seen you in such a long time."

She nodded her head in my direction. "How are you, Sassy?"

Her mama smiled at me. "Hello, Sassy," she said.

Not a one of them offered their condolences about Kyle.

"What are you up to these days?" I asked.

She shrugged her shoulders. "Not much," she said.

I noticed the look her mother gave her. I also noticed the wedding ring she was wearing on her finger.

"You married now?" I asked. Well, she was entitled. Kyle had been gone awhile now.

"He's not a local boy," Marjean said.

I looked at her mother, who turned sharply away from me.

"Where's he from then?" I asked.

They started fidgeting and pretended to look for something in their purses, then both of them seemed to say at once that they had to be somewhere.

I'm sure my expression was a dead giveaway; I was baffled as a bat in daylight. "Are you living here in Beaufort? I'd like to come by sometime and talk."

Marjean's mama took her arm and starting leading her off, but not before she said, "Marjean lives in Crawford now, a little too far, I'm afraid."

I froze in place. It was like a dagger went through my heart. I remembered back to what Thomas had said about seeing Kyle in Crawford eating ice cream.

"Sorry," Marjean said, "that we don't have more time to catch up. Good to see you, though."

I watched the two of them walk away. I felt weak in my knees and then I realized my legs were shaking so much I had to lean back against a parked car for support.

I was relieved that Jeremy hadn't gotten to Rocket's yet 'cause my head was spinning. I noticed Thomas right away. He was sitting in a booth with four other boys. When I approached, he put his hands up as if to defend himself against any punches I might throw.

"Can I speak to you outside?" I asked him.

Thomas was still being his asinine self as he slumped behind his friend.

"Only if I can bring along a buddy," he said. "You know, for protection?"

I wasn't in the mood for jokes. I almost started crying. Thomas began to watch me carefully while the other boys horsed around. I turned on my heels and walked out. I guess I couldn't expect much from Thomas; he was just too much of an ass.

That evening I barely spoke at dinner. No one seemed to notice but Grandma Edna, who asked if I had a stomachache. I skipped dessert and went up to my room.

Next thing I knew she was knocking on my door.

"I told you I don't have a stomachache," I said.

"You have a visitor," she said. "His name is Thomas. Seems like a nice young man."

Shows what you know, I thought to myself as I went downstairs.

I found Thomas in the parlor looking around. Carolyn had brought him some lemonade and he was sitting in a big, overstuffed chair sipping it. He got to his feet when I walked into the room.

"What do you want?" I asked.

He just kept staring at me. "What is it?" he asked. "You wanted to speak with me at Rocket's?"

"I changed my mind, not sure you'd give me a coherent answer."

"You had tears in your eyes, in the restaurant, you were crying."

"What's it to you?"

He sat back down.

"You're dismissed," I said. "I'm busy."

I heard him sigh. Then he got up again and stood near me.

"Look, I'm sorry if I acted like a fool."

"You did."

"Said I was sorry."

"Apology accepted. Now go."

"What did you want to talk to me about?"

I got up and closed the parlor door. When I looked back he seemed perplexed, but concerned.

"Did you really see Kyle in Crawford?"

He pulled his lips in and remained silent for a moment before he spoke. It was like he was trying to recall exactly what he'd seen.

"Thought I did. I really thought I did. You going to punch me again?"

"What were you doing in Crawford?"

"My mother took me. She has an old friend that lives in town there, some lady she went to school with. We went for a visit. We visit a few times a year. It's a nice town."

"Thank you," I said. "That's all I wanted to know."

"I was probably mistaken, Sassy, but this guy looked so much like him. He was older, had a beard. I know he's dead and all, but it sure did seem like Kyle."

"Like I said, that's all I wanted to know."

He followed me out of the parlor and watched me walk up the stairs. I felt his gaze on my back. Oddly enough, I felt his concern, as if my confusion was a shared burden he'd opted in on.

From my bedroom window I heard when his car drove off.

Something in my entire being was shaking beyond control and I feared the shaking wouldn't stop, not ever. Sure enough, the shakes spread through my entire body 'til I was trembling all over like a leaf in a hurricane. A cry formed from somewhere inside my soul and it crept up to my mouth, carrying with it the shock of an unexpected betrayal. No one heard the release of my cry, but it started slow, down deep in my gut. It traveled like a cyclone through my blood. When I released it, it might have killed me. But no one would have known. My family was downstairs doing whatever nonsense they do after dinner, never knowing the agony their lies had cost me.

CHAPTER EIGHTEEN

Crawford was at least a three or four hour drive from Carter's Crossing. It was up in North Carolina, near Ashville. The town was not easy to find on a map. I left very early on a Saturday morning and told Grandma Edna I was visiting a friend in Charleston and might stay the night. Several hours later I found myself driving around in circles on a road that should have taken me into Crawford, but took me instead to a little town called Hickory.

I'd taken June-bug with me for the company and I kept having to stop to give her water and let her relieve herself. I wore a green bandanna on my head, large sun glasses and yellow pedal pushers. The convertible top was down and my radio was up high. Oh, I wanted to be noticed all right. I wanted to cause a riot right smack dab in the center of town as I drove in, so that if my mama was there in Crawford, she'd have to know that I was there, as well. I had no definitive plan, just wanted the truth. If Kyle was in Crawford, then chances were my mama and Aaron would be there, too.

From Hickory I found Crawford on a sign with an arrow pointing east. I might have missed it if I'd blinked at the traffic light. After about a ten-minute drive, I finally pulled the car over and parked on Main Street in Crawford. It looked like the town was shaped like a T. Going straight would put me on Interstate 77, taking Main Street West would have brought me back to Beaufort, and taking Main Street South would have gotten me on a highway that might have led me into Atlanta.

The whole town looked like it probably went up in the eighteen hundreds. It was a dusty town, full of smoky windows and stores that looked like they surely smelled of mildew. I noticed a bar, a local bank, and what appeared to be an old, official-looking building that was now a little Catholic school called Saint Mary's.

I walked June-bug all the way down Main Street and saw nothing of interest. I turned back and took Main Street West, feeling all the while that I was in the loneliest little town in the world. But when I got to Main Street East, civilization appeared out of nowhere and I saw cars and people all over the place. There was a big supermarket near the traffic light and several women were wheeling their baskets toward it. As I walked, I saw some nice-looking places selling mighty fine furniture, little card shops that sold records, too. I heard Dusty Springfield's voice carrying out onto the street. Next to the record store there was a pretty market selling plates and water glasses tinted in greens and reds. In front of a place called Denton's was a gum-ball machine, a rack with newspapers, and a life- size dummy with a red and white striped shirt, a white cap, a face full of freckles, and a big smile. He kind of resembled the Alka-Seltzer man on TV. I assumed that was Denton himself pointing his hand toward the door and telling people that Coca-Cola was only a nickel and the best burgers in the South were under a dollar at Denton's.

It was nearly noon and the place was crowded. When I stood near the door I smelled eggs and potatoes frying. The Everly Brothers singing drifted to my ears.

I looked inside and saw a young girl behind the counter wearing the same cap the Denton dummy in front of the restaurant was wearing. There was another girl on the floor taking orders, wearing the same cap and the same red and white stripped dress as the counter girl. I remembered Mama telling me once that she'd like to have young girls working the floor in red and white stripped uniforms. I was about to turn around and leave, but something told me not to and I walked inside, standing close to the cash register, as if it might hide me. I noticed a man at the counter talking to another man seated to his right. From behind, I never would have known it was Kyle, not until he turned in profile to say something. It was then I saw that he had grown a short beard, and he was definitely heavier. His hair was no longer blond. He'd dyed it a dark brown, but I knew who I was looking at and it was most definitely Kyle McLaughlin.

After I recovered from the shock, I grabbed a paper off the rack and walked back outside. I didn't know how long I was going to have to wait before my mama crossed the threshold of that café, but I was certain she would. She might have even been back there in the kitchen. I was prepared to wait it out for as long as it took 'cause I knew she wasn't far from me now.

I walked back and got my car feeling nothing short of fury. Slowly, I pulled my Impala up in front of Denton's. I opened up the local newspaper just to get my mind on something other than my nerves. Tears were streaming down my face while I stared back inside the café wondering if I should go in there and beat the shit out of Kyle, or just sit there and fume while I waited for Mama.

Kyle was very much alive, but I was too angry to feel good about it. I put my head on the steering wheel and felt my body heaving uncontrollably. They had all probably changed their names and I was betting money that they were all Dentons now. That little, bustling café must belong to them. They had disappeared like rainstorms that retreat behind a cloud without a thought to me. It took all I had in me to keep from throwing bricks at the glass windows.

I kept trying to pull myself together 'cause I was sitting in a convertible, exposed to the world and people were starting to look at me. June-bug licked the tears from my cheeks. After a bit of a struggle to stop crying, I was able to lift my head and stare back through the front door of Denton's. I felt like I wanted to scream at the top of my lungs, or at least burn Denton's to the ground the way that Littleton's had been burned to the ground. I wanted vengeance more than I wanted love. I might never want love again.

I couldn't tell you what I thought about that day, sitting in my car waiting for Mama to show up, but I can tell you that when four o'clock came, it only seemed like I'd been sitting there ten minutes. Kyle had walked right by my car without even seeing me. Finally, I noticed that a nice-looking Ford was pulling up in front of where I was parked. June-bug started barking. I guess she must have picked up Mama's scent. I watched as two people and a child got out of the green Ford. I thought June-bug would split a gut and I tried to quiet her.

My mama looked like a movie star, dressed in tight jeans and a red top. Her hair had been cut shoulder-length. I guess Denton's was doing so well they'd hired a cook and a manger, too. Aaron had his hair all combed back off his face and he looked like a happy man. He was holding the child, a little girl with dark hair like Mama. Must be my sister. Jesus Christ. That child was taking the family that I had been denied and I hated her for it. I wondered what her name was, surely not Sweetwater. She didn't come from any goddamn summer storm.

No one paid any attention to June-bug and all the barking she was doing, not until she jumped out of the car and ran straight up to Mama, nearly knocking her off her feet. The dog was going crazy kissing her, while Mama's head went every which way looking for me. I saw Aaron point to my car. It seemed all Mama could do was stand there and stare back at me. I sat as still as I could and returned her stare. I think it was in that moment that I began to understand how damaging it is to assume love.

Mama yelled out my name. They were all looking at me now, even the little girl. Mama and Aaron recognized me in an instant, but they were no longer my kin, so I didn't recognize them back. I watched as Mama started toward my car and my whole body stiffened.

"Sassy?" she said like she was walking hot coals.

"You must be mistaken," I whispered.

I sped off and left my mama running after my dust. She ran until I turned the corner and headed back to the highway. June-bug, who'd been so happy to see mama, didn't even know I was gone. I swear, if that dog had followed after the car, I would have stopped and taken her home. But June-bug sat there in front of Denton's waiting for Mama to turn back, so I just kept driving. Mama had already taken enough, she could take my dog, too.

I think Grandma Edna sensed my mood when I got home that night. When she asked after June-bug I said she'd run away in Charleston and I was headed back in the morning to look for her. I kept getting strange looks after that, but Grandma Edna was smart enough to know I wasn't telling her the whole of it and when I was ready to talk, I might.

The following day Mama appeared at the door with my dog.

"I came to return June-bug to you, Sassy," she said as I stood at the top of the stairs staring coldly back at her.

June-bug tore up the stairs and nearly knocked me over. I was happy to see her, but I barely showed it.

"Is that all?" I said to my mother in between the kisses June-bug was giving me.

"Sassy," she began, "I was afraid. Please understand. I was so afraid. I thought I was protecting you, protecting all of us, that you were better off. I thought I was making the right choice, the only choice for now."

She turned and looked at Grandma Edna as though she wanted her to intervene, but Grandma Edna seemed at a loss for words.

"I never want to see you again," I said simply.

She started up the stairs and stopped a few steps before me. I stood stoically, like a marble statue.

"Perhaps you'll change your mind. I'll pray for that."

"I never want to see you again and I mean it. You're dead to me, too." I turned and went into my room as June-bug followed.

Mama must have remained talking to Grandma Edna for a while, but eventually I heard her start her car. I watched out the window as she drove away, slowly at first and then, speeding out of sight.

I didn't go down to dinner that night. At about nine, Grandma Edna came into my room. "You haven't eaten."

"I'm not hungry," I said.

"You have to forgive her at some point. This is very painful for her. She cried in my arms. She hasn't done that for a very long time."

"I will never forgive her," I said. "I'm not sure I will ever forgive any of you."

Grandma Edna sat on the bed beside me. "I understand," she said.

"Who died in that fire?" I asked. "If it wasn't Kyle, who was it then?"

"Seamus," she whispered, but not like a secret, more like a sigh.

I looked at her as if I hadn't heard her right.

"Try and understand, child. We knew what Seamus was planning to do. Everyone in the Klan hated Aaron Littleton for his liberal views. It was only a matter of time before they took vengeance on him. It got back to us through Seth's group that the Klan was going to burn the café to the ground. We all knew it was going to be more than that. I knew that Seamus was going to burn down Littleton's with all of you in it. He told me that himself, as if I'd allow it. But he felt I had no power to stop him. He always felt that I had no power, but he knew me about as well as he knows another language, which he doesn't."

"He was going to kill us?"

"Yes, he was, Sassy. We had to help Violet and Aaron leave the state before Seamus got a chance to do anything to hurt them, or you and Kyle. But Violet said it didn't matter where they went, she'd never escape him."

"She could have tried," I said.

"Yes," Grandma Edna said. "She could have tried, but it's a difficult thing to do, to outgrow fear. She would never be able to believe she could escape him. This last time she tried by coming back here and facing up to him, but see what happened?"

"So she killed him?" I asked. "She killed Granddaddy so he couldn't hurt her anymore?"

"No, she didn't do anything. I did it. I poisoned Seamus."

She'd said it very matter of fact and I stared at her in disbelief.

"What?"

"Arsenic. Dudley kept it in the barn for keeping insects out of the wood. I found a good deal of it in the barn and I made a family decision. I fed the arsenic to Seamus."

She held her head up proud and I knew she wasn't sorry for it neither.

"We had to protect Violet, we owed her that. I owed her that. Until your granddaddy Seamus was dead she'd never be free of him."

I had to stand up. I walked over to the window and looked out, toward the barn.

"You put his body in Kyle's room?" I stared at her as if I'd never seen her before.

"He wasn't dead yet, I don't think, but he was real sick, near death. Seth and Kyle got him over there in the trunk of the car and set him in Kyle's bed. They set the fire. They started it in your old room where Kyle slept. They put a lamp in there with faulty wiring, hoping that lamp would be blamed for it. Luckily, it was. We had to make sure Seamus was burned beyond recognition. He looked a lot like Kyle and we didn't want any speculation that it wasn't Kyle. We even cut off three of his fingers, just to make sure."

"You cut off his fingers?" I felt so faint I had to hold on to the wall. "Was he dead?"

"I hope not."

When I remained silent for several minutes, she got up and stood behind me.

"Seamus would have killed your mama. He was a very vindictive man. He would have killed all of you sure as I'm standing here. He hated that Aaron loved her, saw Aaron as a rival. He was perverted, like his son, like Liam. Do you understand, Sassy? We killed a bad man, not a good one. He wasn't going to take another one of my children from me."

"Why didn't you tell me the truth? Your lies were cruel. Telling me Kyle was dead?"

"You're young. You might have told someone and that could have led to an investigation. It would have opened up a real can of worms if there was any rumors going around. Your despair over Kyle's death was helpful to us. You couldn't have feigned that kind of grief. No one assumed any foul play, except for Seamus's old Klan friends, one in particular." She looked away. "He threatened us bad, Sassy."

"Why didn't she take me with her?"

"She planned to take you, but you'd run away and we all thought it was best to keep you from knowing the truth after that. Having that kind of responsibility is too precarious for a child. How could she have told you what really happened, that we all murdered your granddaddy?"

"She was never going to come for me then, was she?"

"In time she would have, but she was pregnant then."

"Why didn't she call me? What reason did she have to pretend that I was dead, too?"

"Seamus's old friends had to believe he'd set the fire. But they might have found it strange that Seamus disappeared, nothing frightened Seamus. They were watching you, just in case, just to see if you would lead them to Kyle and your mama at some point. If they'd seen Kyle, they could have had the police reopen the case in a minute. It was the safest thing to do to protect all of us. You had to be kept out of it, Sassy."

"Kyle is a damn actor," I screamed. "You don't think he could be recognized? They only went to Crawford, Grandma Edna, just four hours from here."

"Kyle is not Rock Hudson, Sassy. Recognizing him would have been unlikely. His getting a job as an actor would be unlikely. Who the hell is going to hire an actor with less than half a hand of fingers?"

I felt some barely recognizable sound come out of me and I sat on the bed.

"They all have different names now and Kyle is heavier and bearded. His hair has been dyed dark. They wouldn't recognize him if he was standing there in front of them."

"I recognized him," I said, but held back on telling her that Thomas had recognized him, too.

"The Klan knew Seamus wanted to kill his family in that fire," she continued, "but they assume he only succeeded in killing Kyle. But they could start looking at us more closely, order an investigation if there were any suspicions at all, like Kyle being alive."

"So they could have the body exhumed if they could prove foul play?" I asked.

"If they could prove it, yes, but they're finally under too many of their own indictments, they don't want to bother with us. Those old Klan men will have to put those goddamn sheets in a back closet and start defending themselves against murder and arson. And if Kyle is discovered alive, they'd start pointing a finger at us, seeking revenge. They know what we did, Sassy. Rest assured. If we didn't turn Dudley into the police Seamus would have strung him up. We had to keep protecting ourselves from that man and his vicious friends."

"If the clan is losing steam now, who would give a damn?"

"There's one man I fear. It isn't safe, not from him."

"And you thought I'd go around telling people Kyle was alive? 'Cause I'm too young to keep my mouth shut?"

Grandma Edna sat down next to me and put her face in her hands. "I'm not proud of it, Sassy, but if you want to know whether or not I'm sorry, the answer is no. I'm not sorry for any of it. This family sticks together. You are too young to have had the responsibility of the truth. We all just wanted to protect you."

"And am I not a part of this family?"

"You are the only one to whom forgiveness is not owed. Let's keep it that way."

I lay back in my bed with June-Bug in my arms after Grandma Edna left my room. There was a hole in my heart as deep as a mile long crater. Perhaps if I'd waited to find Mama until I was sure those old men were all dead, or in jail, she would have trusted me with the truth. Perhaps, yes, perhaps. But that was something I was never going to know.

CHAPTER NINETEEN

I stared at Jeremy. We were at Rocket's and he'd bought me a hamburger and a coke. We were in our senior year of high school and I wondered why he hadn't yet invited me to the prom.

Ever since my trip to Crawford, I'd been sleeping with Jeremy out at Slave Town on Dudley's straw mattress. After finding out about Kyle being alive, I didn't much care about doing the right thing anymore, like holding on to my dignity.

Giving myself to Jeremy had altered our relationship entirely. What I came to discover was that after months of trying to get past the foreplay, the quest ended sort of like the act itself, in disappointment.

I reached out my leg and rubbed it up his. He got that funny expression, the one that was all horny-looking. I'd given him a signal, I guess. I was ready to put out again.

"Let's go to Slave Town," he said. I detected a cynicism, not the romanticism I had wanted. Nothing about sleeping with Jeremy was romantic. It was like he hated me for putting out even though he wanted me to. I could tell he thought less of me for it.

I smiled. Sex had been an interesting experiment for me, but it seemed to have shocked Jeremy into several altered states. I wasn't who I was supposed to be, not the way I tore off his clothes and rode him like a buck. I was too aggressive for a seventeen-year-old girl. What was worse, I wasn't a virgin. But Jeremy didn't question that.

We went back out to Slave Town night after night. Maybe I kept waiting for it to get better between us, more connected. I doubt if I consciously made the choice, but I soon realized that having sex with Jeremy was an opportunity to vent my fury against Mama. I'll never understand what came over me. I bit him, I scratched him all over his body, and I orchestrated his movements to my own satisfaction 'cause I couldn't have cared less about his needs. If he moved in a way I didn't like, I slapped him. If he didn't satisfy me, I slapped him harder. His eyes were not soft when they stared into mine anymore, they were filled with disgust.

"Who taught you how to make love, Sassy, Joe Lewis?"

"I'm a passionate person," I said.

"I swear, Sassy, I wish there were some other way to get laid. You're killing me."

I knew it was all changing. Where had the naivety of first love gone? I had shattered Jeremy's illusions of losing his virginity with a demure Southern belle. Instead, he had to experience his first sexual encounter with a crazy, whore-like seventeen year old. I wasn't the proper lady he thought I would be, the one he could take home to his politically correct family. I'm sure he didn't expect to be covering up his bruises with Clearasil, either, or hiding his bite marks with bandages.

"How long you been putting out like this, Sassy?" Jeremy asked.

"I love you," I said. "That's how I express it."

Jeremy got up and walked off. I followed him while he rolled a joint and lit it. This was the night it would all be over between us and I knew it was coming, had known it for weeks. He'd started hinting about other girls, the ones with shy smiles and voices so low I could hardly hear them. He didn't want anything to do with me anymore. A part of me was disappointed. I enjoyed acting out my vengeance on him, but that was all I felt.

It was when I got back from Crawford that I started changing. I started listening to everything that Jeremy said about his illustrious future at Georgetown University, his plans to become a senator, the duties of his wife and the mother of his children. "I am not necessarily a Democrat," he'd said. "I'm at odds with my father's views." He'd turned to stare at me. "I expect you to understand the world as I see it." And as he talked, I realized I hated him. I hated him for being so damn indifferent to who the hell I was, for not even bothering to ask what I wanted out of life, or to give a rat's ass what I thought about anything. Maybe, in my own way, I was growing up.

"No way, Jeremy," I'd said. "I want to travel to Europe, become a painter, and have lots of lovers, all of them handsome and artistically gifted."

He gaped at me as if I was Lizzie Borden in the flesh standing there in front of him with a raised ax. Whatever fantasy Jeremy and I had created for ourselves had been blown into bits by my honesty. It was like I refused to live in a bubble in which all of Jeremy's wishes drowned out my own in relentless waves as high as a building.

"Well, we don't have to marry." he'd said.

I stared back at him as he sat on the ground. He had placed a towel under his backside and he sat there in his gainliness. The perfect part of his hair and the way he wiped his mouth of my scent. The licorice he took from his pocket and sucked on, all of it, disgusted me now.

"What's wrong?" I asked.

"It's too soon to get serious," he said. "I think we need to cool it for a while."

I wished I'd been the one to ask for it, but leaving him seemed like a betrayal to myself. I reached up and tore the chain from my neck, the one where his high school ring had dangled on a gold chain between my breasts like a rock against my heart. I smiled as the little gold links fell to the ground, soon to be buried by the dry dirt.

Jeremy's illusions and his perfections had instilled in me a kind of madness, or maybe, fury and rage had just become my natural state.

I'll never know what Jeremy spread all over school about me, but suddenly I wasn't likeable, I was desirable. Every boy in the senior class was now leering at me as if I walked around in my underwear. They leaned in too close to ask a question, snickered behind my back, pleaded for me to show them that place with the marijuana and the straw mattress.

I was disgusted with the horny, pimply, and smelly group of teenage boys who sniffed out their sexual fantasies like addictions, constantly staring below my chin and tossing paper airplanes between my legs.

I never trusted the laughter of young men after that; it was always too sinister, reeking of self- involvement and entitlement. Their laughter was a secret world I resented them having.

I cared only for Betsy Lou Buttercup, my best friend. She was the one who told me that high school was a necessary process of growth, like a bad chapter in a good book.

"You won't ever look back after this," she said. "Just get through it."

I really loved Betsy Lou. Her boyfriend was already in college and she didn't have time for awkward innuendos. She had a real man.

"Oh, Sassy Sweetwater, you will turn so many heads, you won't even hardly remember Jeremy Holden."

I guess she reminded me of Mama with her dark good looks and light eyes. She was always telling me I was special, especially to her.

"You won't be going to the prom with any stupid boy from Wade Hampton. You're going with William Dixon Craft. Yes, William Craft is perfect for you. I'm going to have Jordan fix you two up."

"He's a friend of Jordan's?" I asked. Jordan was Betsy Lou's boyfriend, who was a sophomore at Charleston Southern University.

"His friends call him Dixie and he's gorgeous, much better-looking than Jeremy Holden. He looks a bit like Dr. Kildare. You know, like Richard Chamberlain?"

Chapter Twenty

Dixie Craft was several inches shorter than me, since I'd grown as tall as Mama was, but he was handsome, like some well-built, light-haired soldier. He spoke loudly, as if it might compensate for his short stature. But Dixie was fearless. The first time I bit his lip and drew blood he threw his head back and howled like a wolf.

"Doggonit, girl, you're full of fire."

Dixie and I had been dating for a month and he'd readily accepted my invitation to the senior prom. I didn't bring him out to Slave Town where that poor, overused straw mattress had whittled down to the size of a pillow, but in the backseat of Dixie's Thunderbird, we created more sweat and steam than a sauna. I wasn't shattering any of Dixie's illusions, I was creating a web of mystery and excitement that got Dixie just about as drunk as a pint of straight gin.

"Think I love you, girl," he said in jest, but in the heat of the moment, he said it like it was a prayer, right into my ear, deep and whispery and continuous.

Try as I might to startle him with hard neck holds and rough tugs at sensitive organs, he only yelped out, "Doggonit, girl, you're more fire than hot lava. You burn me up, baby."

Grandma Edna had taken me into Charleston and bought me the prettiest prom dress we could find. It was open-shouldered and showed off my better late than never, well-developed breasts. The dress was a beautiful shade of green, like deep jade. Grandma Edna had even let me chose the dress myself, having acknowledged that I was soon to turn eighteen and she no longer needed to pick out my pedal pushers, much less something as important as a prom dress.

"You look incredible, Sassy," Grandma Edna said as I stepped from the dressing room feeling like I'd finally come into my good looks, like Mama once said I would.

"I wish your mama were here to see…well, I do wish she were here to see how you've grown, how beautiful you've become."

Grandma Edna had never mentioned my mama again after I'd learned what really happened the night of the fire. I finally got to a point where I didn't even think I had a family in Crawford who had deserted me and whom I hated to the core and would most likely never forgive.

"Maybe Earline will do my hair?" I asked.

"Sure she will. I'm glad Elvira and Earline are back for a while. I'm certain Earline will be happy to do your hair. One thing I have to say about Earline is that she can sure style hair. Maybe she should try and find a job doing it."

I smiled. "I guess that's the nicest thing you'll ever say about Aunt Earline, Grandma Edna."

Grandma Edna grinned. We'd come to a point in our relationship in which we could say things to each other full of truth and avoid getting angry or avoid discussing it, whichever was more prudent.

The night of the prom, Dixie showed up at the door with a pink corsage and pinned it on my dress with all the confidence of a Yankee general at the end of the Civil war. I saw Grandma Edna's face darken when his hand slipped over my bare skin, just above my push up bra.

"I know it's prom night," Seth jumped in quickly, "but you get her home at a decent hour you hear, young man? I'm going to be waiting up for her."

Dixie smiled and nodded his head. "Everyone's staying out 'til two a.m.," he said.

Seth put his hand on Dixie's shoulder. "If she's back one minute past, you're in for it."

Dixie clasped my hand and gazed into my eyes. "Well, sir, breaking the rules would certainly be worth the extra minute."

Betsy Lou and Jordan were out in Dixie's car waiting on us, no doubt, smoking a joint. We'd brought along a change of clothes for after the dance and planned on going over to the Beauford River with a six-pack. Betsy Lou and I were squealing the whole ride over to the Carrington Hotel, where the prom was being held. We'd smoked two joints by the time we walked through the doors like visiting royalty. All eyes were on us and I think that was 'cause me and Betsy Lou were bona fide knockouts and Dixie and Jordan were college boys. We were with real older men and you could see that clearly.

I noticed Jeremy avoided me every time I danced near him or stood too close over at the refreshment table. Only one I spoke to was Thomas. Oddly enough, it didn't seem to me that Thomas had ever listened to any of Jeremy's dirty, little stories. Thomas wasn't leering at me. He appeared to be wiped clean of the burden of gossip. So if he'd heard the rumors, he was man enough not to have given credence to them.

"Hello, Sassy," Thomas said.

I introduced him to Dixie and the two shook hands.

Then Thomas turned to me. "I do believe you are the most beautiful girl at the prom tonight, Sassy," he said.

I stared at him, waiting for the punch line. I half expected him to say he'd been paid a hundred bucks to throw me a line of bull. I expected his obnoxious laugh, nearly expected him to turn to Dixie and tell him I threw a mean right hook, but Thomas just stood there smiling at me.

I blushed and turned away. "Thank you," I said.

Thomas walked off over to some girl he was seeing. She had a pinched expression and her nose made her eyes look small. Aside from the fact I didn't like her, I envied her and that confused me more than calculus.

"Who was that guy?" Dixie asked.

"Nobody," I said.

I let Dixie lead me onto the dance floor. He danced like a bull with a fly up his nose, not caring that he stomped over my feet and when he slow danced, he was stiff as a board. I tried unsuccessfully to take the lead from him.

Somehow, all the music we thought would be barred from the prom that night was being played, like Marvin Gaye and the Supremes. When I looked over at the record spinner I saw Betsy Lou dancing around by herself and giving me a thumbs-up. She later told me she'd bribed the chaperone in charge of the music with three joints and a kiss, but of course, you could never believe anything Betsy Lou Buttercup said. She often said things just for effect.

"You think I'm going to dance to my mother's music tonight, you've got another thing coming," she hollered. "Not that I have anything against Old Blue Eyes, but I really do prefer to shake my behind to rock and roll."

Betsy Lou took my hand and started twirling me around. We did some mean dirty dancing to "Wooly Bully" while Jeremy looked on, smiling snidely, and Dixie stared at me, sort of with the same expression he gets after I rip off his shirt and pop all the buttons and bite his nipples like I'm trying to shell a pistachio.

I hardly noticed when Jeremy left the prom that night, but things broke up about midnight. Dixie and Jordan had a fifth of scotch in the backseat of Jordan's car and they kept sneaking out of the dance to take swigs. By the time midnight arrived Dixie couldn't walk a straight line. I decided to take them out to Slave Town and let Dixie sleep it off on the straw mattress, or what was left of it.

"You see that girl Jeremy was with tonight?" Betsy Lou said. "Her hair was so stiff they should declare it a weapon. I mean, lord knows, if that goddamn bouffant of hers fell off her head it would kill anyone it hit."

I laughed. Jeremy had been with the perfect girl for him, about as sexy as a fistful of bean sprouts between two slices of three-week-old white bread.

Dixie had his head on my shoulder and he was snoring so loudly I didn't hear the music in the distance when we pulled off the road that goes into Slave Town. But when the car approached, I noticed that the trees had been parted. I always put the trees back where they belonged so no one would notice the road and possibly desiccate the property.

"What the hell is this?" I said, sitting forward and trying to see through the incredible darkness of the moonless night. The sky appeared like a deep blue sheet of velvet over us. Both Betsy Lou and I had changed our clothes by then and our prom dresses were safely tucked in the trunk of Jordan's car. I was glad I was in my jeans 'cause I knew instinctively that I just might need to kick some butt that night.

"What's going on?" Betsy Lou asked.

"I'm not sure," I said.

I could see a lot of people. I head laugher and music. I could smell the marijuana as we drove up. I realized then that Slave Town had been invaded by the snot-nosed adolescents of Hamilton High. Some of them had built fires inside the shacks and old buildings. Some were dancing on the dirt road, others hung out drinking. Most of the girls still had their prom dresses on and many of them were engrossed in some heavy necking with boys who had taken off their shirts. Others were sitting in groups sharing their latest gossip and joints were being passed around as easily as popcorn at the movie theater.

I got out of the car and started screaming. "What the hell are you all doing here?"

No one answered me. The music was loud and the kids were too preoccupied to even hear me. I noticed my little cousin, Ricky, off by himself sucking on a joint. He sure was taking good care of Dudley's marijuana.

"Hey, Sassy," someone called out.

I went in to one of the shacks and started kicking out the fire. "What the hell are you doing here?" I screamed. "This is my place, my land. You get the hell out of here."

One of the girls got up and looked right into my eyes. "Shut up, Sassy," she said.

Well, she sure pushed my button and I went after her like a wild woman and started throwing punches. The next thing I knew, we were rolling around on the dirt road and I'd messed her up pretty good. One of the boys grabbed me from behind and another boy grabbed the girl.

"Get off my land," I screamed.

I saw Jeremy come running at me. "We got a right," he said.

"You don't have any right at all." I went for him, but the boy holding me was strong.

"Free marijuana here, Sassy. Don't begrudge us free marijuana." Jeremy started to walk away. I guess he'd dismissed me and my request.

I knew I was spitting fire. "Get out of here, all of you. This land belongs to a friend of mine and I don't want you ruining Slave Town. These old buildings are fragile."

Jeremy got a perplexed expression. "You're not talking 'bout that nigger friend, are you?"

I managed to kick myself free from the moron who had been holding me and went right for Jeremy's jaw. I could feel the crack behind my fist as I hit him. He fell back and my knuckles felt raw.

"You need to be taught a lesson," he said and came at me with his fists in the air. "I should have done this first time you fucking bit me."

I was thrown to the ground by the first swing, but I stood to my feet and ran at him straight on and knocked him over. As we were struggling on the ground, trying to get a good punch, I could hear the kids egging us on in the background, screaming for Jeremy to beat the hell out me. I could also hear Betsy Lou yelling and screaming for help.

"Break her nose," some girl yelled out.

I managed to get my knee up into Jeremy's crotch and I let him have a quick kick with it. That got him off me all right; he yelped loudly and cursed me to hell. Meanwhile, I jumped to my feet. Betsy Lou was still screaming for help and other kids were screaming for my blood.

I'd be lying if I said I wasn't frightened. Jeremy looked angry and drunk. He managed to grab me by the shoulders and when his fist came forward, I went flying on my back, tasting blood. I could barely see that there was someone dragging Jeremy away from me. I tried to open my eyes, but one eye seemed sewn up tight.

Betsy Lou ran over to me. She was crying. "Oh, Sassy," she said. "That son of a bitch hit you in your mouth. You're bleeding pretty bad and your eye is swollen something awful."

Jordan handed me his handkerchief and Betsy Lou held it over my mouth. I heard a familiar voice and tried to open my eye again, but it still hurt like hell.

"Get Jeremy out of here and the rest of you go home, every last one of you."

When I looked up through my good eye, Thomas was bending over me.

"You ought to stop picking fights with boys," he said.

I tried to tell him not to lay a hand on me, but I couldn't. It hurt too much to move, but at least my lip had stopped bleeding.

"Thank you for doing that," Betsy Lou said. "You're a true gentlemen."

That time I managed to laugh. "He's no gentleman," I tried to say, but Lord knows what came out; I could barely speak.

"If you don't mind, I'm going to get her to a doctor," Thomas said. "Will someone take my date home?"

Some boy came forward and volunteered. "Sure, sure I will, Thomas," he said.

Next thing I knew Thomas had picked me up in his arms and had placed me in the backseat of his car.

"Lie down," he ordered.

He drove me over to the hospital despite my protests.

I noticed the looks I got as Thomas carried me in past the nurses. He didn't even let me out of his lap while we were sitting there waiting to see the doctor.

"Will you put me on a chair, Thomas? I can handle a chair," I mumbled.

"Never thought you'd need me for a moment, did you?" He grinned and I made a face, much as it pained me to do it.

The doctor finally put some bandages on my bruises, but luckily, I didn't need any stitches.

"She get into a fight?" the doctor asked Thomas. I could see the skeptical look on his face as he eyed him with a scowl. *Big boy like this might have been responsible for this damage*, he might have been thinking. But the only thing I was thinking was how gently Thomas Tierney was holding me.

"Yes, sir," Thomas said. "You should see the other guy."

Thomas carried me back to his car like I didn't have legs to walk.

"Put me down, Thomas Tierney, I don't need to be carried."

Of course he didn't listen to me and he placed me in the passenger seat like I was a basket of soft-boiled eggs.

"You okay?" he asked.

I had a split lip and a few cuts and a black eye, but I seemed to have survived.

"You're one hell of a rough woman," he said.

I watched his profile as he drove me home. There was something comforting about him, something I never noticed before, I guess, 'cause he'd always been so rude.

When we got into the driveway at the Crossing, he turned off the ignition. I watched as he asked me what got me so riled up about those kids being on the land. He was leaning forward. In the shadowed night his blue eyes looked black.

"It's just land, Sassy. They couldn't really hurt anything."

Through my swollen lip I told him what that land had meant to Dudley and that it was really mine and some day Dudley was going to come back and claim it for real and I was going to sell it to him 'cause he was too proud not to pay for it.

"I just feel like it's really special, mine and Dudley's. He'd never brought anyone out there before, just me and Ricky, taught him how to tend to the marijuana."

"Why'd you bring Jeremy out there to begin with then?"

I turned and stared out the car window, into nothing I could see clear.

"You really believe that Dudley guy would ever come back here? Isn't he the guy that murdered your uncle?"

"You always believe everything you hear?"

"I try to look behind everything I hear. There's always a reason for what people say. Like when they pretend not to like you, like when they lie to themselves about things that hurt."

"What do you know about things that hurt?" I said. "What do you know about living with lies? What do you know about grief, Thomas Tierney? You're just a spoiled, mean boy."

He looked at me so intensely that I felt more exposed than I ever had in my entire life. I felt like any thought I'd ever have from there on in wouldn't ever escape him.

"Well, what do you know about grief, Thomas Tierney?" I repeated.

"Everything," he whispered and leaned close to kiss my cheek. There he found a tear that I'd shed for him, and for me, but I didn't know its reason for being there, not yet anyway.

Chapter Twenty-One

"You're going on a trip," Aunt Peg said into the phone. I laughed. I assumed she'd heard about my trip to Europe, a graduation gift from Grandma Edna.

"Will I enjoy myself?"

I heard Aunt Peg giggle. "How can anyone enjoy themselves with Beatrice McLaughlin?"

"Is she really that bad?"

"Well, put it this way," Aunt Peg sighed, "it will be like traveling with a dead person."

Grandma Edna had decided that my Aunt Beatrice would be the perfect chaperone for my trip through England and France, probably 'cause she had absolutely no personality and didn't seem to like men.

I wasn't so sure I was going to enjoy myself traveling around Europe with a woman who was socially retarded according to Grandma Edna and just about everyone else in the family.

"You have to push her to do things," Aunt El told me.

"She rises at dawn, goes to bed by eight," Seth said. "Never been married or kissed and the only romance in her life is in her books."

"I guess I'll just have to play around her," I said.

The family had not seen Beatrice in seven years, the last time she had been back to Carter's Crossing. I don't think they expected the transformation when she walked through the door. It was a bit of a shock meeting Beatrice McLaughlin, not only for me, but it appeared, for everyone else. Whatever Beatrice had been she had shed like new skin. Maybe it was 'cause she lived up North, where things were different.

Beatrice wore her straw colored hair in a single braid that ran down her back. Her eye color seemed nearly yellow. She wore bright clothes and necklaces of silver crosses and colored beads that she called "love beads." I almost died when she leaned back at the dinner table and lit up a joint.

I noticed how every one squinched up their noses and fanned the air.

"Are those Northern cigarettes, Beatrice? They stink to holy hell," Grandma Edna blurted out, frantically trying to shoo the smell away.

Seth smiled at Aunt El and Earline giggled.

"Good God," Grandma Edna exclaimed. "What's become of you, Beatrice?"

An odd facial expression fell across Beatrice's face, but she said nothing.

"If you must smoke those vile things, please take them to the porch," Grandma Edna finally said.

Beatrice stood up and motioned for me to join her with a tilt of her head. I followed, though I was unsure as to whether or not I should have. She sat in the rocker while I took the white wicker and looked up at the stars. She held the joint out toward me.

"Be here now, Sassy," she said. "Now is all there is, much as that so often disappoints me."

I dared not smoke the damn joint, though I wanted to. It would be just my luck to be caught in the act of getting stoned. However, it didn't seem to matter. The marijuana in the air was so thick I could still get high on it.

"I think we'll go to London first, take in some shows. Would you like that, Sassy? Your grandmother requested I expose you to culture."

I nodded my head while she put her feet up on the railing. There was something sexy in her movements. I could not believe she'd never been kissed.

"I can't wait to see France," I said. "I'll be bringing my sketch book."

"What will you sketch?"

"Churches, old cobblestone streets, Frenchmen in their berets, small village gardens, the Pyrenees Mountains. Shall I go on?"

"Will you sketch me on the lap of my black lover?" she whispered.

I was completely startled. "Are we meeting up with someone?" I asked nervously. Lord knows who Beatrice knew.

I watched her rise and put her hands up toward the moon. "He's there," she said, "where nobody else can have him. That's where I keep him. My Southern kin can't lynch him, enslave him, or belittle him. He's in the moon, Sassy, where it's safe to be."

She bent down to kill the fire on the joint she'd been smoking. I watched as she took a silver case from her pocket. She opened it carefully. I could see that several roaches were in it, to the pile she added the one she'd just smoked.

"Do you have a boyfriend?" she asked.

I immediately thought of Thomas, but shook my head.

"I hear his name is Dixie." She smiled, though I hadn't answered her.

She pulled the rocker close to me and reached for my hand. "I don't like Southern men," she said.

"They can't all be bad," I said.

"Of course they can."

I wondered if I should be taking her seriously.

"You are so much like Violet," she said.

That made me sit up straight. "What do you mean?" I asked. No one had ever said that to me before.

"Did you know that blood is sometimes a deep purple in color and certainly is thicker than water?"

I noticed her upper lip, how it curved up and made her appear slightly grotesque, but only from a certain angle.

"Actually, blood is blue inside the body." she said. "Turns red when it hits the air, then if it is exposed for too long, it turns brown."

"And what does blood have to do with any similarity to my mother?" I asked, feeling put off by her remark.

She leaned back against the porch railing. "If you bleed too much, you'll die."

I wondered how I would get through Europe with her. I felt I'd been insulted, but I wasn't quite sure in just what way. I tilted my head back up toward the stars. How dare she assume to assume anything?

"Do you always answer questions by not answering them?" I asked.

"But I did answer your question," she said.

We sat there in silence for the next thirty minutes staring at the sky and its glittering, quiet chatter.

From the corner of my eye I saw her light another joint. This time, when she held it out to me, I took it.

Beatrice and I planned our trip together at the cove. We'd take a picnic basket of fried chicken, fruit, cheese, and Carolyn's homemade blackberry wine. We'd map out our stops and write down all the must-see attractions. It took nearly two weeks to plan our itinerary and to be satisfied with it.

"Now, nothing is set in stone right, Sassy?" she said with a wink. "I may want to take you out to the countryside before we leave France. There's a beautiful old stone cottage in a little village, right near the border of Spain. If there's room there, we'll go. You're going to love it."

I watched as she dangled her legs in the water from one of the high rocks; they sprouted out from under her ankle-length skirt as she held the skirt up to her thighs. The material was light, like the cheese-cloth Carolyn used in stews that held spices.

Everything was long on Beatrice, her nails, her legs, and her arms. Her fingers were alluringly poetic and appeared as fragile as silk. She spoke with her hands, sometimes holding them in midair while she paused to remember something she'd wanted to say. Sometimes she spread them out and stared at them.

"Next to El, I was closest to Violet," she said, running her hands over the water, as if music might suddenly appear from her touch. "Your Aunt Peg and I fought and clawed our way through adolescence and none of us cared much for Erin. But Violet seemed detached from trivial emotions."

I didn't discuss Mama anymore, but I didn't want to tell her that.

"Did you know that once she wanted to be a veterinarian?"

"Mama?"

"Um-hum."

"She never said that to me," I said.

"Oh yes, she was young then, maybe about twelve or so. Daddy told her it was a man's profession and he wouldn't ever send her to school for it."

That didn't surprise me. "Granddaddy was a bastard," I said.

"Was?" she said. "So you know then?"

I avoided giving her an answer. I certainly didn't want to discuss Granddaddy. Apparently, she didn't, either, for she picked up the conversation where it had left off, as if his demise had never been hinted at.

"He was the worst kind of bastard, your Granddaddy. He was a chauvinistic bastard."

Beatrice had begun to grow on me. I was mesmerized by her enchanting disassociation from everyone else. When the family spoke to her, she never really answered them. It might appear as if a response had occurred, but it really hadn't. She seemed to have mastered the art of detachment. I never really felt that Mama was detached from anything. I felt that everything hurt her.

"I don't agree what you said about my mama, that she was detached from emotions. She wasn't detached at all." I looked at her and caught the sadness that fell on her expression like a shade slowly closing.

"I said trivial emotions, Sassy, not the ones that make you bleed."

"Oh," I said.

She sighed long and hard and looked off.

"Why didn't you ever marry?" I asked her. "Do you not like men?"

"Men are fine, but why marry them?"

I laughed. "You're not romantic at all?" I asked.

"Why, yes, I am very romantic," she said.

I watched as she took off every stitch of her clothes and swam out naked in the cove, way out to the middle, her long braid trailing her like a white cat's tail.

When she swam back, she was smiling. In her smile I detected a hint of recklessness.

"That's romance," she whispered as she flopped beside me stark naked. "I could never get that from a man. Men are burdensome, swimming naked is like letting your spirit loose on nature. Loving a man is too much the weight of him."

I wasn't sure I understood her. Swimming naked just made me think of Uncle Liam. I shut my eyes quickly.

"You'll see what I mean one day," she said.

"Don't you want children?" I couldn't imagine she wouldn't.

"Children? God, what a thought."

"I guess not," I said.

I watched as she stood in the sunlight. She ran her hands over her face, a pale, plain face with freckles the color of wheat.

"That isn't to say I don't respect a good mind, desire a good body, or am never in need of a good friend." She grinned at me. "I don't live in a vacuum, Sassy, despite what my family thinks."

"I think that they think that anyone who would choose to live all the way up there in Vermont isn't normal."

It intrigued me that she lived in Vermont. Vermont seemed to me like a special place with white, picturesque churches at the center of old villages and more hills and mountains that led into still more pretty villages with yet another white, picturesque church. And the people were just like Grandma Edna said they were, stoic and difficult to understand.

"I prefer to keep my anonymous life to myself. My family need not know me for they could never know me well. And I don't have the patience to be assumed by those too shallow to grasp my entirety."

She slipped on her skirt and tied her blouse at the waist. I noticed she didn't wear a bra, but her breasts were small, like Aunt El's.

"And what do you think?" she asked as she put a towel to her hair.

It was then I noticed that her toes were long, as well, like fingers that ended in red tips, fingers instead of toes that ran out beyond the sandals she wore.

"I think you're the sanest person I've met in a long time, maybe ever."

"There's hope for you then," she said quietly.

Chapter Twenty-Two

I hadn't told anyone that Jeremy had beaten me up, but of course, word got around that he had. I used makeup to hide my black eye and hid my face from Grandma Edna as much as I could, but I felt her studying me, wondering if I'd suddenly developed some rare skin disease, I'm sure.

"Got a bee sting, Sassy?" she asked. "Your face seems swollen."

"No, Grandma Edna, allergy to something I think, but it's going away."

"Oh, that's good."

Jordan must have told Dixie what happened prom night and Dixie found out where Jeremy lived and split the left side of his lip, gave him a black eye, and threatened to throw him in the Beaufort River if he dared lay a hand on me again.

"I don't need you sticking up for me like that, Dixie," I told him.

"You think I'm ever going to forgive myself for passing out that night? I was there to protect you and I failed."

"You didn't fail, Dixie, you got drunk."

"If a drop of liquor ever passes my lips again, shoot me where I stand, Sassy."

"I forgive you, Dixie, now shut up about it."

"Liquor has become my enemy, the foul reason I failed you. My lack of self-control might have cost me dearly. I might have lost you to another man."

Dixie was in a stew over the fact that Thomas had taken me to the hospital that night, had been there to protect me instead of him. But sadly, Dixie had not lost me to another man. Thomas had not been by to see how I was after nearly a whole week had passed. I hated myself for the disappointment I felt.

I'd be leaving for Europe in another three weeks and, after days of not hearing from Thomas, I'd given up on his ever caring for me at all. I assumed he'd just been kind that night. I was sure he'd felt sorry for me, like he had in high school, sorry for me not knowing how to act like a girl.

I turned down Dixie's proposal, which followed the night of the prom. I didn't love him at all. I might have if Thomas hadn't kept showing up in my thoughts. I wasn't supposed to be thinking about Thomas. I was supposed to be excited about going to Europe with Aunt Beatrice, who promised to take me to French discos and introduce me to her artist friends who lived in London flats and Paris lofts. We were going to drink French wine on the Champs-Élysées and spend our days at galleries and museums. I should have been beside myself with excitement; I'd finally step foot in the Louvre. I shouldn't be caring if I ever saw Thomas again. I was going to Paris, for God's sake. Who cared about Thomas?

By the time I finally saw Thomas again, my bruises had completely healed, not even a ghost print of the red, open wounds that had been there. I was out on the porch sketching when his old blue Mercury made its way up the drive. June-bug was lying at my feet. Beatrice was taking a yoga class in Beaufort and Grandma Edna was up in her room reading an old copy of Sons and Lovers, though she'd read it twice before.

"Hello," Thomas said, as he walked up the porch steps. I noticed a book in his hand. It was a large leather book, but I couldn't make out the title. He had on faded jeans and a clean white shirt.

He pulled over a chair and sat near me. He was smiling. I, on the other hand, was trying to frown. It was habit; I wasn't supposed to like him. He was supposed to make me frown.

We started talking at the same time and our words fell over each other like spilled beans. "I haven't seen you in a while," I said.

"Your wounds have all healed," he said.

"My wounds have healed, yes," I said.

"Nice dog," he said as June-bug licked his hand.

"June-bug," I said.

"What are you sketching?"

I finally took a breath and handed him the sketch.

"Wow, you're good. It's a footbridge over the stream in the Vista Valley, am I right?"

I looked away. "Yes," I said.

"I've been researching, thinking of you, though."

I could feel what happened to my heartbeats as he said it. *He'd been thinking of me?*

He held the book up. "Slave Town was never a town, but Hammertown was. Hammertown is a real, bona fide ghost town."

I saw the title then of the book he was holding, *Ghost Towns of the South.*

I stepped off the porch. For some reason I wanted to walk, or maybe I just didn't want to be there if Dixie drove up, which he often did unexpectedly.

"C'mon," I said. "Let's go to the cove."

Thomas walked at my side, holding his book, as June-bug aimlessly followed. It was a hot day and we walked slowly.

"Your town was here long before Carter's Crossing was here," Thomas was saying. "Slaves never lived there at all. It was a bustling town in the 1800s, but then people started moving closer to the bigger cities and most of the businesses there started closing. In the late part of the nineteenth century outlaws took refuge there and in the twenties bootleggers came in and opened up distilleries. The town became a haven for outlaws. After Prohibition was repealed, the town fell to wrack and ruin once again. There wasn't any way to make a living in Hammertown. It's out in the middle of nowhere and at that time, there were no roads into

Charleston. People say the old town is haunted now 'cause it has such a rich history."

I thought of Aunt Peg and her vision of the woman who had died in a shootout. Then I looked at Thomas's blond hair, a rich color, like sweet, golden honey, and remembered her prophecy about my future light-haired husband.

"I love to research," he said. "It really excites me to find out about old towns like that."

"Dudley is going to be disappointed when he finds out it was never a slave town, but a haven for old white bandits."

Thomas laughed and then a silence came over us as we walked. I could tell he was struggling for something to say. Finally he told me I could keep the book to show Dudley.

I thanked him quietly. Something was changing and it was in the air. All of a sudden, two people who used to hate each other were shy without insults to toss.

When we got to the cove we sat on the ground and I stared at his hands. His hands were soft and his arms were tan; his tan was rich and deep.

"Isn't it pretty here?" I said.

"Yes," he said.

We sat in silence for a while. Thomas started to hum.

"I know that song." I looked out over the cove. Dark lovely birds flew low in the distance, their wide wings made a wispy sound as they tipped toward the water.

"Yeah, Frankie Valli," he said turning to me. "Can't take my eyes off you." He turned away quickly. "You're just too good to be true," he sang.

We sat more in silence. Potbellied clouds languished over us, drifting carelessly and bumping the sky with soft shoulders.

Suddenly, Thomas sat up. "Been thinking about this all week."

I didn't say anything, but instinctively my heart beat faster.

"We're eighteen now and through school," he said. "We're going to be going our separate ways soon." He stared directly at me. "I have a confession to make."

"What's that?" I asked.

"Time for some truth. You game?"

"Of course," I said. "Let's try and be friends, put the past behind us."

"Okay, how's this? First time I saw you I thought you were the prettiest girl I'd ever seen."

"Ha! If I remember correctly, you were totally obnoxious to me that day we first met."

He held up his chin. "Don't you think it was the other way around?"

"If you thought I was pretty, I never would have known it."

"I liked you so much it made me nervous," he said.

I think my jaw dropped a little. I was smiling inside. I felt I could float up there with the clouds. I wanted to tell him that when he cared for me that night out at Slave Town, I hadn't been able to stop thinking about him. But I chose not to say it. It scared me to say it.

After a long while of silently staring out ahead of us once more, Thomas turned to me again.

"When I was ten years old I used to go over to the cove in Beacon Hill, you know that cove?"

I shook my head. "I didn't grow up here," I said.

"I know."

He lay back. June-bug had just come out of the water and she plopped herself next to Thomas, messing up his white shirt and his light jeans something awful. He didn't seem to mind though.

"Who'd you go there with, anyone I know?" I asked.

"No, no one you know," he said. "We have a dog like yours, his name is Jasper."

"A Border collie?"

"Yeah," he said.

"So you went to the Beacon Hill cove with Jasper?"

"And Tyler."

"A friend?" I asked.

"My brother," he said. "My twin brother."

"You're a twin? How come I never met him? I never knew a Tyler Tierney in school. Kyle never mentioned you having a twin."

"Kyle would have thought he was just seeing double."

"Kyle played at being stupid, but he wasn't stupid," I said, finding myself defending Kyle when I no longer wanted to.

"Why would he do that?" Thomas asked.

"Well, when someone is dumb they don't know what's going on around them, or at least it appears that way to others. It keeps them safe."

"Oh," he said. "Guess he had his reasons then."

"He did," I said.

"Maybe I should have tried to know him better."

"Where's Tyler now?" I looked at his jawline as he spoke. I saw it tighten.

"Tyler died. He drowned out there at the cove, showing off to some girls we'd brought out there one time. It was right before you moved here. I couldn't save him…though God knows I tried. There's a deep end and a current came upon him suddenly. We all watched him go under that day. It was like he was caught up in a water tornado."

"I'm so sorry," I said.

"I know about loss, too, Sassy. I also know what it's like to hate."

I felt how much anguish the loss of his brother had caused him. I suddenly wanted to burst out crying, but I fought it back. I fought it back hard.

"Well, nothing was your fault, Thomas. There is no one to hate for what happened."

"Except everybody on this planet and God, for taking him from me."

I didn't know what I could do to comfort him. The only thing I did know was that I loved Thomas Tierney with all my heart and I was about to burst, keeping myself back from holding him. We both knew that love came with a price.

"I know about grief, Sassy," he said and looked at me.

He saw I was crying and he wiped away a tear from under my eyes with one of his soft, beautiful fingers.

"You ever go over there to Crawford?" he asked me.

"Yes," I said. "I went to Crawford."

"Was I right? Was it Kyle?"

"Kyle's dead," I said. "Kyle's dead to me."

"Someone looking an awful lot like him living in Crawford."

"They say everybody has a double."

"Yeah," he said, "'cept me, now."

I reached out my arm and put it around his shoulder. I moved him toward me and held him tightly. I could hear his breath. I could read his thoughts. I knew the exact moment to turn my head and find his eyes. I knew what he wanted, exactly what he wanted. When he moved his mouth close, I gently stroked his face. I'd never felt like that before in my life. He knew how much I wanted his mouth to find mine. He knew exactly what I was feeling. He kissed me there at the cove and I felt myself falling into an abyss, the kind of abyss loving Thomas would always provide me. His touch was more tender than any I'd ever known. I had no urge to strike him or to hurt him in any way. He was my precious friend and he always would be. And from that moment on I would cherish him, if fate would allow it. If only fate would allow it.

We walked back from the cove hand in hand, laughing and spinning in a circle, June-bug following us and trying to figure out what kind of happy juice we'd helped ourselves to. We were barely back at the house when I heard a car in the distance. I swallowed the happy juice quickly. No way I was going to share it with anyone else but Thomas.

"When am I going to see you again? God, I'm leaving for Europe in two weeks."

"Two weeks," he said. "Wow."

"Um-hum, so when am I going to see you again?"

"Tomorrow," he said.

"And tomorrow?"

"And tomorrow?" He laughed.

We came down off the path just as Dixie drove up. Dixie slammed the car door shut as he got out. I dropped Thomas's hand. I noticed Beatrice on the porch. She looked from Thomas and I to Dixie and raised her eyebrows.

I could see the redness come into Dixie's cheeks as he glared at me.

"This why you did not accept my proposal?" he asked.

I turned to Thomas. "I'll see you soon."

Thomas looked a bit embarrassed, but he turned and started toward his car. I watched him drive off. Dixie was walking in a small circle and I could see the smoke fuming up over his head.

"Come here," he said and led me off, away from Beatrice's prying eyes. I noticed that she seemed somewhat amused by Dixie's suffering.

"So is this why you won't marry me, you're in love with that kid?"

I told Dixie as best I could that I was indeed in love with Thomas Tierney and that I could no longer see him.

Dixie didn't say anything for a full three minutes. I watched him get madder and madder as his cheeks puffed out and his teeth clenched so tight together I thought he'd crunch them right on out of his mouth and they'd fall, like little pebbles to the ground.

"We were never promised in any way, Dixie," I said.

"So you slept with me without shame, knowing there was someone else?"

I shook my head. I was speechless. "No," I said. "I didn't know there was anyone else then."

"Of course you did. And now you spurn me?"

"Spurn you? What the hell you talking about?"

"I clearly have more to offer. His family has little."

"I don't care about that."

"But just maybe he does. Everyone here knows what the Mc-Laughlin's are worth."

"Just what are you saying, Dixie?"

"Betsy Lou Buttercup says Thomas wants to be a lawyer and go to law school and his family doesn't have the money to send him. Betsy Lou and I think the same, that Thomas won't amount to much."

"What?" I clearly wanted to haul off and hit him. I walked up close, my fists were in the punching position.

"You and Betsy Lou can go fuck yourselves," I said.

Before I could defend myself, Dixie grabbed me and kissed me. I pushed him off and kept my lips closed.

"You're breaking my heart," he cried.

"I'm sorry," I said, "but you need to go."

"I will forgive you when you return to me, when you find out that Thomas Tierney is going to wind up washing cars for a living. I will forgive you, Sassy. I will. And I will take you back, despite my better judgment. Do not forget that I am a college man."

I watched Dixie race on out of my driveway on practically two wheels. I felt as if a weight had been lifted off my shoulders. It is never love that burdens the heart, it's the wish for it and the knowledge of its loss. I felt for Dixie, I truly did, but my heart was light with my love for Thomas.

CHAPTER TWENTY-THREE

Everyone knew it, it wasn't hard to see. I ran to the door when I heard Thomas's car coming up the drive. I wore a grin 'bout as long as a lazy stretch of beach. Grandma Edna told me I was as mellow as a July morning, but she could hear my heart fluttering at the mention of his name like storms coming up out of nowhere. Seth teased and went around singing, "Sassy's got a beau, Sassy's got a beau."

"That's what love does, makes you a total contradiction," Grandma Edna said.

"There is no contradiction," I said. "I just love him, plain and simple."

"Keep your dignity, girl. If he loves you, he'll wait for you." Grandma Edna winked at me. But fortunately she hadn't noticed the color that I know came to my face; it must have been pink as a cat's nose, for waiting was no longer an option.

Aunt Earline smiled so wide I could see her silver fillings. She knew it, too. She was sitting there in the corner of the room, pretending to be disinterested in my love life. But she knew damn good and well that Thomas and I had been screwing ourselves silly.

We'd made love every day, more than once a day, too. There were those early afternoons out by the cove, those unplanned moments in the back seat of Thomas's car, all those stolen kisses in his bedroom and mine, keeping an ear out for any unwanted footsteps, and then, not caring at all as we fell back on the floor and fornicated carelessly.

There was no question that I adored Thomas Tierney. I sighed when he touched me and I melted like a stick of butter in the sun when I looked into his eyes.

"I love you, Sassy," he said. "I want to marry you."

"Okay," I said. "I accept your proposal."

He looked startled for a moment, then he smiled. "I've got a scholarship to Washington and Lee University. I have to work my way through school for the most part, but it shouldn't be too bad."

"So you are going to college then?" I asked, thinking of how smug I was going to feel letting Dixie and Betsy Lou know that.

"Sure am," he said proudly.

"Where's Washington and Lee?" I asked.

"Virginia," he said.

I felt myself getting nervous. "When will you be going, Thomas?"

"August."

I looked down at my hands. I wasn't quite sure what this was going to mean to us. I didn't want any separations coming between us, 'cept what I couldn't help, like my trip to Europe.

"I'll be going to the art institute in September," I said.

"The one in Charleston?" he asked.

I nodded my head and took his hand.

"Charleston's not so far," he said. "I want to marry you. I don't want to wait six years for you, but I will if I have to."

I felt sad, as if there were suddenly something that was going to keep us a part, like ambition.

"If it wasn't for the scholarship, Sassy, I swear, I wouldn't go."

Suddenly, it came to me. I could go anywhere on earth. I wasn't confined to South Carolina.

"There must be an art institute in Virginia," I said, feeling my spirits rise. Nothing was going to keep me from Thomas Tierney a day longer than needed.

His face brightened. "I'll be going to law school once my undergraduate studies are done. Think you'll like Virginia? We may be there a while." He laughed and kissed my cheek. I noticed that he smelled like a field of orange trees.

"You going to be a lawyer?"

"Yeah."

"Wow," I said. "I'm impressed, didn't know you were that smart."

He reached out and jumped on me and there we were, rolling around on the grass and laughing and soon after, we were making love. I'd stopped counting how many times we'd made love, but each time, it mattered more.

We lay there afterward looking at the sun set out over the cove, talking softly. We'd decided that we were going to get married and I was going to move to Virginia and find an art school close by.

"We can't have children for a while, Sassy. I won't be able to afford it."

"I don't care, but I'm really looking forward to having a little baby that looks just like you someday."

He took my hand in his. "My family is so proud of me. I can't ever give them Tyler back, but maybe I can ease their pain. I'm going to buy them a house and they'll never lay out a nickel more in their lives. They struggled so hard for us. Mama worked as a teacher at an elementary school and Daddy drives a truck. They mean everything to me, Sassy, the way you do. I'm going to give them everything they never had. I'm going to be a defense attorney. I like the study of law."

He turned and looked at me. He looked so proud of himself. I hated Dixie with all my heart in that moment for insinuating that Thomas was a loser.

"I'll love you 'til the day I die," I whispered.

"I'll love you longer," he answered.

Betsy Lou called me on the phone and said she wanted to spend some time with me before I left for Europe, that she had some good news. So we planned on meeting at Rocket's for lunch. Thomas was going to pick me up there afterward and we'd be spending our last day together before Beatrice and I got on the plane.

I was sitting at Rocket's for about five minutes, but almost died when I looked up to see Betsy Lou walking through the door with Dixie. I was just flabbergasted as the two sat opposite me in the booth. I hadn't seen Dixie since the day he'd sped off my land in a huff.

Betsy Lou looked a little embarrassed as I glared at her.

"I ran into Dixie up the street," she mumbled. "He said he was headed here, anyway."

I took a deep breath and tried to smile at Dixie. "Hello," I said.

"I wanted to see you before you left for Europe." Dixie leaned in toward me and I realized that he was going to pretend I was still in his life.

"I got you a little going away present."

I gave Betsy Lou a sideways glance while Dixie reached into his pocket.

"Oh, how sweet," Betsy Lou said.

Dixie handed me a small, square box.

I thought about telling him I couldn't accept his gift, but his expression made me feel guilty enough to eat a raw smelly piece of squid if he'd asked me.

I took the paper off the box carefully and opened it.

"Go on and put it on," he said. "Better yet, let me."

Dixie slid out of the booth and sat beside me. He clasped a necklace around my neck.

"It's pure quartz crystal," he said. "It will bring you luck."

"Thank you," I said, trying to be gracious, but I knew the moment I got home, it was going in a back drawer.

"Guess what?" Betsy Lou said sheepishly.

"What?" I said, wondering if she and Dixie were in some sort of conspiracy to get us back together.

"Mommy and Daddy have given me a trip to Europe for graduation. I'll be in France same time as you, Sassy. I'm going with my three cousins, Flora, Cindy, and Mary Jane, but I can ditch them easy."

For some reason it didn't excite me to be meeting up with her. "That's great," I said, anyway. "Let's try and coordinate a meeting."

We ordered our food and I listened to Betsy Lou's next bit of news, that she'd broken off with Jordan.

"He's no gentleman," she said.

Apparently Jordan was seen with a blonde woman two towns over and Betsy Lou was so beside herself that she burst into his house, unexpectedly, while he was having dinner with his parents. She threw a few dishes to the floor and made a scene.

"I thought his mother was going to have a heart attack right then and there. I was screaming at Jordan so much and I'm sure she thought I was there to kill him. Turns out the son of a bitch had been engaged to the blonde for months."

"'When the hell were you going to tell me, Jordan?' I screamed."

"I'm sorry, Betsy Lou," I said.

"I never knew Jordan could do something like that." She looked at me and pouted.

"You deserve better." Dixie took her hand and squeezed it. I could tell that they had gotten pretty friendly and I was hoping for the best, that he'd fallen for her and vice versa.

Betsy Lou sat up and cocked her head. "Yes, I do deserve better. I deserve a man like that nice Thomas Tierney that helped you the night of the prom. Jordan was useless that night."

I noticed how Dixie seemed to blush. His skin seemed on fire with his discomfort.

"I thought you didn't like Thomas Tierney," I said.

"Why where did you get that impression? I think that Thomas Tierney is handsome, courteous, and kind." Betsy Lou said with a coy smile.

I smiled, too. I hadn't said a word to Betsy Lou about Thomas and I being in love and apparently Dixie hadn't said anything, either. He'd also lied about Betsy Lou agreeing with him, that Thomas was a loser, that was obvious to me now. Perhaps I would call Betsy Lou later and inform her that Thomas and I were an item.

"I do agree," I said. "He sure is handsome, courteous, and kind."

"Oh? I thought you didn't like him either, Sassy. All through school you called him a stupid oaf and a fool." She sat back with a pout on her face.

"He's neither," I said. "I was mistaken."

She gave me a strange look and stared at Dixie. "It seems to me you have competition." Dixie gave her a stern look and turned his head away.

"Does he have competition, Sassy?" She stared at me, and I suddenly got it: Betsy Lou had set her eyes on Thomas.

When Thomas walked through the door, I thought Betsy Lou would faint.

Thomas stood there and stared at Dixie until Dixie finally got up from beside me and slid back beside Betsy Lou. Thomas finally sat down and took my hand.

"Guess so," Betsy Lou whispered.

I had to sit there and watch Betsy Lou flirt with Thomas, despite the fact he never let go of my hand. She kept saying that Dixie and I made such a nice couple. I wondered why she'd be fool enough to say something like that after it was obvious that Thomas had come to Rocket's to meet up with me. I could feel Thomas's unease beside me.

"Don't Sassy and Dixie make the perfect couple?" she said to Thomas.

Thomas got a coughing fit and Dixie got up and excused himself.

I knew I had to call Betsy Lou sooner rather than later to tell her that Thomas and I were engaged and she needed to stop trying to pair me off with Dixie.

I imagined Betsy Lou would be thrilled to death that it was serious between Thomas and I. But much to my surprise, she was not happy at all.

"How could you do that to Dixie?" she said with a disappointed tone to her voice.

I didn't know if Betsy Lou had taken crazy pills or what.

"Thomas and I are in love," I said. "Didn't you hear me?"

"Oh, he's not in love with you. Dixie is in love with you. I hope you come to your senses over there in Europe, Sassy. Thomas is probably a gold digger. Now, I like him and all, but he's a goddamn gold digger, must be. He never liked you in school and all of a sudden he's in love with you? Oh, Sassy, please. I bet he's trying to get money out of you for his college tuition."

"Please don't talk that way about Thomas," I said, feeling my anger rise. But Betsy Lou continued to run her mouth like an open faucet.

"Now, if it were me, it'd make sense. I'm not rich like you, Sassy, though my family is certainly more well-off than Thomas's family, he still couldn't get a damn thing from me. So if me and Thomas got together, it would be true love. You'll never know if it's true love with him. You following me, Sassy?"

"I am not following you in the least, Betsy Lou," I said.

"Don't be absurd," she said. "You and Dixie are so suited and he loves you so much. His family is about as wealthy as yours Sassy. You'll never need to wonder over his motives. Don't do something you'll be sorry for later. That's my advice."

I figured that Betsy Lou must have thought she was protecting me. She must have believed that Thomas was some sort of a cad, at least when it came to me. But how far will people go to get what they want? A thousand miles, I'd say. And soon I'd discover, a thousand miles and much further.

CHAPTER TWENTY-FOUR

Aunt Beatrice had rented a house in France with seven of her closest friends from Vermont, something she didn't disclose to me until our third day in Paris. We were sitting in the hotel room when she started chatting up her own agenda. Perhaps she thought I would not have wanted to surround myself with university professors for two full months listening to them pontificate on the theory of Russian Formalism and New Criticism, subjects droned into my consciousness by Aunt Beatrice as she insisted on explaining what she taught and how she taught it. I watched as she nonchalantly reached for her suitcase.

"Why didn't you tell me we wouldn't be spending any time in Paris?" I asked. "We are not doing anything we planned. We haven't even been to London yet."

"I'm meeting up with my lover. You remember? I mentioned him to you?"

"Vaguely," I said.

"Well, I have a Black lover and he's in Saint-Lizier so Saint-Lizier is where we're going. You'll like him, he's sweet as can be."

"I don't care if he has honey dripping from his tongue, I prefer to stay in Paris."

It was clear that everything we did would be what Aunt Beatrice wanted to do and my plans might as well be flushed down the goddamn toilette. She was conveniently ignoring me by finding a lose thread on one of her gauzy shirts.

I wondered just how angry Grandma Edna would be if I took off on my own and left Aunt Beatrice to her black lover and her boring professor friends from Vermont. I thought of blackmail. Wouldn't I be justified for betraying the sacred information she'd given me? Why all it would take would be a simple slip of the tongue. Oh, we're heading toward Spain, Grandma Edna, to meet up with Aunt Beatrice's black boyfriend.

Aunt Beatrice gave me a sour look; she must have known I was plotting something.

"You and I sat by the cove and planned out a trip that did not include staying in some old farmhouse for two months," I shouted. "For God's sake, Aunt Beatrice, I could have stayed in South Carolina in some old farmhouse, I didn't have to travel to France for that."

She avoided my glance and put her suitcase on the bed. I could see the colorful tank tops and the long, bright skirts neatly folded and the blue and white scarves she'd bought from a Paris boutique that must have been secretly packed away the night before.

"You could have told me," I said.

"I did. You must learn to read between the lines, Sassy."

"Well, I do not remember being told anything of the sort," I said.

"Look, Mama gave me a list of things I absolutely had to do with you. If she wanted them done, she should have brought you here herself. I am no longer the dutiful daughter. I don't do what Mama tells me to do anymore."

"Why didn't you just happen to mention to her that you had a lover and the real plan was to go see him?"

"Well, I did in a way and Mama thought that was just perfect," she said. "So, you see, I'm not lying, I'm just omitting information. She thinks we'll be going to the countryside for a week, staying with an old French couple. No need to tell her we'll be there a couple of months." She stared at me. "You're not going to betray me, are you?"

"A couple of months?" I shouted.

I watched as she set her jaw and tried to smile at me. She spoke as she packed her underwear, as she walked back and forth from the closet to the open suitcase on the bed, as she went into the bathroom for her tooth-brush. I sat there silently stewing in the regal room with its high-back chairs and silk upholstery, wondering if she'd noticed I wasn't packing anything.

"Mama cares about things that are inherently wrong…like the color of a person's skin. I could never tell her the truth. She's no liberal, Sassy. Besides, the French countryside is the real France. Don't you want to experience the real France, Sassy? Mama thinks there's nothing to do in Europe but visit churches and nothing to do in Paris but visit museums."

"I agree with her," I said, but Beatrice shrugged me off. I was certainly, in her eyes, just as *bourgeois* as Grandma Edna.

She sat on the bed and put the top of her suitcase down. There was a sticker on the top that had nearly peeled off, but I could still read it, *Peace and love*, is what it said.

"You're a goddamn hippie," I said accusingly.

She ignored me. "I promise to take you back to Paris before we leave and even on to London for a few days. Will I be forgiven then?"

She stared at me with her golden eyes and I reluctantly nodded my head. Maybe spending time in the French countryside would give me more time to paint. If I stayed in Paris I wouldn't get any painting done at all. Besides, weren't some of the greatest French artists influenced by countryside flowers?

I bought myself some oils and canvas that afternoon and I packed them away in the trunk of our car for the trip to Saint-Lizier. But even though I tried to talk myself into it, I didn't really want to leave the city of Paris, I wanted to rent an apartment behind a winding row of old buildings where the flower boxes overflowed with tulips and the laughter from the cafés trailed behind my steps.

I watched reluctantly as the bellboy took my suitcase down to the lobby and lifted it into the car we'd rented for the rest of the summer. I could have remained behind, but it frightened me to do so and I imagine it would have opened up a real can of worms for my Aunt. I pouted in the front seat while Aunt Beatrice turned on the radio and started singing along to French music. It didn't take long for my attitude to shift 'bout as easily as gears in city traffic. Much to my surprise, not long after we'd left

Paris behind and drove the Pougeot toward Spain, I began to feel the lightening of my mood and I sang along in my broken French, feeling free as wild horses on open land.

"This is pretty," I said, taking in the views.

"Told you," Aunt Beatrice quipped.

I had to admit, even to Aunt Beatrice, that it was a privilege to simply be there in France at all and I appreciated it. As the country unfolded before me, I felt as if the description I was hungry for had suddenly landed in my lap, enfolding me in its magnificence. For there, behind the enchanting, historic old villages and the story book colors of the sky, I was absorbed and utterly consumed in description. If only I had the words for it, but there would never be words for it. I couldn't wait to get to my canvas and paint everything I couldn't describe with words, mere words. Everything we passed seemed to belong to another space and time. I couldn't help myself, I kept asking Aunt Beatrice to stop the car so that I could get out and explore the countryside and the streets and all the little shops along the way. I was completely enthralled with the French people by this time, how they laughed at my undecipherable French, how life seemed lived more intensely in these villages than anywhere else on earth. The French were in love with life, with their food, the cobblestone streets they walked, the bread they carried from the Village store, and the wine they lazily sipped. I was enjoying myself so much I'd forgotten Aunt Beatrice had lied to me.

"We'll never get to Saint-Lizier at this pace," she complained.

"But I've forgiven you. Please Aunt Beatrice, just one more café up there on the hill. There's an incredible view from up there."

"And another on that hill and another on that, oh, and please Aunt Beatrice, can't we stop for a white wine here and a bit of pastry there 'cause the view is just so incredible?" she mimicked me.

We arrived at Saint-Lizier, three days later than expected and I knew she was eager to see her lover, but I did not feel badly for detaining her. She had, after all, tricked me. As we drove into the village, up a steep hill, I could see a Cathedral in the distance and my heart was pounding to put that on canvas. It was so invigorating for me to be driving the narrow streets, to pass by the ancient houses that had been home to centuries of families, and to see everything that was spread out before me at the top of the hill, like an offering from a God.

St. Lizier is a small village so it didn't take long to drive through it. As we got to the end of a road that seemed to veer off into the sea, Aunt Beatrice made a sharp right turn. I wondered what we'd find at the end of the winding road she had taken. I wanted to come back and walk the village we'd left behind, set my easel up overlooking the *River Salat* on the *rue du Pont*, find the colors, if I could, to reproduce what I saw. I was actually tingling with excitement.

I had asked Aunt Beatrice a dozen times if there were going to be enough bedrooms for all of us when we arrived at her mysterious cottage in the countryside with her seven professor friends. She had shrugged her shoulders, giving me a sinking feeling, a vision of a small cramped cottage with only one bathroom, but as we stopped before the meadow it wasn't exactly a cottage I saw in the distance, it was more like a castle.

"That's it?" I asked.

"It's called a Chateau," she said. "We've rented it."

I couldn't believe it. This could prove to be quite enchanting; I was surrounded by an artistic paradise. I had Aunt Beatrice stop the car for just a moment so I could take a photograph, a long shot of distant mountains.

As we drove closer toward the Chateau, I noticed a bathtub in the middle of the meadow. It could just as easily have been a hallucination from too much heat. The bathtub had little legs, it was absolutely alluring. I wondered if the bathtub had just been dumped there. It seemed unabashedly comfortable in its oddness and it belonged to the landscape as much as the flowers and the bugs that hovered on the petal's edge. It seemed to me that that particular bathtub could never belong anywhere else on earth. Its function had been completely transformed, and it might have been a bird bath, or a lovers moonlit meeting place, or simply just a thing, sitting in a meadow, that added to the landscape much as color to a quiet canvas.

"My God, we're here," Aunt Beatrice said as she approached the Chateau. "Isn't it the most beautiful place you've ever seen?"

We stared out at the large, old stone chateau nearly hidden by pink, purple, and white flowers.

Wild grass leaned in the breeze with thin, narrow leaves.

"How do you know we're here for sure?" I asked.

"It looks like the photograph De sent me."

"It's unbelievable, like a fairytale."

"Look at him, my darling De. Look, look, there he is."

Her lover's name was Demarco, but everyone called him De. Aunt Beatrice had talked of nothing else for the full three day's drive, whenever I gave her the space to talk, that is.

De swept out of the Chateau and held out his arms as he ran to the car. His long bright shirt the color of a tangerine. He was a large man with very black curly hair and nostrils that flared like a furious rain man.

"Come, come," he said and reached for my hand. "We've made bœuf bourguignon and there's wine from a vineyard not far. Oh, and plenty of this."

He handed me a joint, which I politely refused. I realized instantly that Aunt Beatrice's friends would be anything but stiff professors, still boring perhaps, but not stiff.

I followed Aunt Beatrice and De into the old, stone house, which, unfortunately, was filled to capacity with half naked people. I was a bit taken aback and I think I might have gasped. I immediately felt disappointed and tried not to show it. I looked at the faces and the bodies before me, slouched in chairs. Their demeanors seemed to contradict the delicate antiques that filled the gracious room. I at once had an image of a great master's painting, like Rembrandt's *The Storm on the Sea of Galille*, painted in the colors of the American Flag.

"There are naked people here." I tugged at my Aunt's sleeve. "You didn't warn me for that."

Aunt Beatrice, true to nature, gave me her strange smile and didn't answer me.

Though she did intrigue me and I loved her, Aunt Beatrice consistently upset the balance of my life. I should have known not to expect my own assumptions. But couldn't she have told me that her friends were into nudity? The more I got to know my aunt the more I realized that she was really out there, like on another planet. But then again, she herself was unpredictable, I should have known that her friends would be the same.

I would get to know Aunt Beatrice well over the next two months. I would get to sense her moods as they shifted in and out, like a weathervane in a gusty wind. Maybe she thought herself to be, in one moment, who she actually was, but yet, in another, she was someone else entirely, someone too brazen to expose. She seemed conflicted by the lifestyle she'd chosen, coming to me and taking my hand. *Don't hate me*, she'd say. *I need to be truly human.*

Perhaps she really believed the lies she told as she told them, like how many civil war generals there were in her family history. I myself knew of none. *God knows how many well meaning Yankees those confederate bastards slaughtered, she'd say.*

There was a struggle within her to free herself from her Southern roots by claiming every innocent inhabitant of the South to be an enemy of humanity. I sensed her discomfort with her own rhetoric, but she still didn't stop spewing it.

"Don't you see the absurdity in this?" I asked her, referring to her naked friends, but Aunt Beatrice was not about to defend herself and merely shrugged.

"Expand your horizons," she said. "Little Southern belles are passé."

De was getting off on being black. He loved being in a position to hate white people, he loved being on the politically correct side, at least in Vermont. I knew instinctively that he was not there to become a permanent staple in my aunt's life, he couldn't be capable of loving her, he was too bigoted against her. But my Aunt Beatrice refused to acknowledge the truth as it tugged at the hem of her dress and consistently tripped her over.

"You really like him?" I asked. "I'm not sure I do."

She turned to me and gave me her sly smile, the one that was slightly condescending. "You will," she said. "It takes a while."

I was glad not to be asked for my opinion about anything. They assumed I didn't know enough to have any valid thought. Anyway, I was in favor of the Vietnam War. I was quite sure, that if I admitted to that, they would have beheaded me and poor Grandma Edna would never know of my true demise.

De spoke French badly and I was relieved, after hours of listening to him struggle with some bastardization of the language, that he resorted back to English, where his New England dialect was thick. But they all kept going back and forth between English and French, though only one man spoke it well and he looked to be as old as Grandma Edna. I wondered what he was doing there, holding court like some overweight cross legged Buddha whom everyone called "Papa Don."

All of Beatrice's friends were from the same area in Vermont, mostly adjunct professors at various colleges. They seemed to be coupled off, in one fashion or another, except for myself and a quiet young man who sat outside all day and meditated. I could hear him chanting from the window of my room, his soft voice lifted up each morning and landed near my ear like an alarm radio, never jarring, but just as annoying as the real thing.

"You have a stomach ache, Rodney?" I'd call out. "You're moaning something awful."

I wondered if Beatrice hadn't brought me along as an offering, like some southern sacrifice. It was clear that they thought of the American South as the root of all bigotry and there I was, the signification of Southern white royalty, for Aunt Beatrice had long ago lost her southern dialect to broader As and was considered, by her friends, as an Easterner.

I listened to the insults they hurled at me, as if I had nothing better to do than be the recipient for their disgust with the mentality they assumed I represented.

"You all are the bigots," I'd say. "I don't have to go around fornicating with black men to prove my thoughts are on the right side of my brain."

Of course the room would go silent and all eyes would be on Aunt Beatrice, all sympathetic expressions worthy of support for the poor wretched ex-southerner with a bitch of a niece.

I agreed to some level of responsibility, of course, but not without trying to inform them that there were many southerners who were not at all bigoted, southerners like my Uncle Seth and myself. They stared at me, as if I was stupid enough to believe I was ever going to be free of white gloves, Sunday school hats, and drawls as thick as syrup.

"It's in the genes, Sassy," Papa Don said. "The South will never change, not in their hearts. You'll see that damn Confederate flag flying forever."

Papa Don's mistress nodded enthusiastically, as did everyone else.

I didn't have the patience for any of them and took to my room with a good book. It was better there in my small, quaint little space watching the stars flicker and the moon smile, than have to watch a bevy of fools fall in love with their own bullshit.

I didn't like De from the start. He was arrogant. He had two or three facial expressions that clearly expressed his opinion, always negative, always intimidating, or assuming, at least, that he was.

"Why are you afraid of taking off your clothes, Sassy. Are you uptight with your body?" he said to me. I glanced at my Aunt Beatrice who cocked her head at him, as if he'd popped the last secret of Fatima.

"I am more comfortable clothed," I said.

De stood up and stood in the doorway. He spread his naked arms in the air. His body was not perfect, by any means. I hadn't yet worked with nudes, but I knew I would prefer the imperfections, with all the body's birthmarks, sprightly hair, and body fat. Yes, he would be interesting to paint, but I never would have asked.

I thought of Grandma Edna and how appalled she'd be to see this room of naked people. Her daughter and her hippie friends, chanting and smoking dope and most disturbing, her daughter copulating with a black man.

"You should try it." His laughter was like a boom, a sudden drum roll. "It's true freedom, the wind through my thighs, the dampness finding the crack of my ass."

Yuk.

After only my third day at the chateau, De took to following me around. He would appear next to me while I painted and question my reasons for choosing this or that color to depict nature. He'd engage me in philosophical discussions that I had no interest in having.

"Do you believe in God, Sassy?" he'd ask.

"I believe in having the freedom to lock certain people out of my space," I said.

"Ah yes, freedom was always your right, little darling."

At meals he'd sit beside me while I ate and ask for my opinion on his chitterlings and hog maws. Then he'd laugh. "Good nigger food," he'd whisper in my ear.

"Makes my Irish taste buds yearn for a plain steak and something other than what the dog threw up on the rug."

"Charming, Sassy," he'd say. "Southern humor?"

"Do you think your family would find me suitable for your Aunt Beatrice?" he asked.

I looked up. He had followed me out a mile or so behind the house, as he often did, despite telling him I preferred to paint alone. I had been startled by his presence.

"Why not?" I asked as he flopped himself down beside me. "Why wouldn't they?"

I noticed that his skin was black as coal, like his eyes and his hair.

"I smoke grass." He smiled. "And I don't make much."

"Do you love my aunt?" I asked.

"All God's children deserve love," he said. "Don't you think?"

I thought my aunt didn't want to carry any man's weight, but she sure as hell carried De's. She clutched him when they sat together as if he'd just been freed from shackles. She had lied to me. She was not free of his burdens at all, she carried them like bricks. I couldn't wait to get her the hell out of there and back to Paris where perhaps I could restore her to sanity.

"We will never know what it's like to be treated as an inferior," Aunt Beatrice said one night after dinner as they all sat around smoking and I sat by the window thinking about Thomas.

De was the only black person among Aunt Beatrice's friends. He joked often that there were no black intellectuals in Vermont aside from himself.

"I feel your pain, man," someone said and patted De's arm.

I raised my gaze to the ceiling. *You feel my pain? Is it any less than anyone else's, or do I have to be black to gain empathy?*

I stormed up to my room. As far as I was concerned, Aunt Beatrice and her friends were all a bunch of hypocrites. Everyone has got a shitload of pain to bear. It was people like my Uncle Seth who got his hands dirty helping people. All these hippies did was just talk about it.

I could hear their laughter as I slammed my door.

Their nakedness was not uncomfortable for me, but it was distasteful. Maybe they felt less encumbered being naked. De continued to refer to me as a Puritan and if he did show up to dinner in a pair of long pants, he'd grin and announce, "In Sassy's honor."

Even the quiet boy who meditated all day passed in front of me, half-clothed, and shyly raised his eyes, hoping, I'm sure, for an invitation to sit his pretty body close enough to weaken me. As cute as he was, he only made me think of Thomas more. I'd spoken to Thomas only once since we'd been there. It was expensive to call long distance and I knew Thomas would not be able to do it. He sounded happy to hear from me and told me that he was counting the days until my return. He expressed how much he missed and loved me. His voice filled in all the missing pieces I'd felt since being in Saint-Lizier and feeling like an alien. I told him about my aunt's friends and he'd laughed so hard, showing me once again his humor and his trust. He knew I wasn't baring my ass to that crowd and he didn't even have to ask.

I missed Thomas terribly. I decided that If Aunt Beatrice did not keep her word and take me back to Paris soon, then none of this trip would be worth the hours I had lost being without him. The only good thing was the time I spent painting, completely alone, having finally found a way to ditch De before he could figure out in what direction I'd gone.

I wanted to go to the village of Saint-Lizier, but unfortunately, there were only two cars at the house: a large van that the others had driven there in and Beatrice's Peugeot. I wasn't allowed to drive either one and often had to wait for one of the professors to offer to drive me around. Then I had to listen to a lot of gobbledygook about organized religion and its effect on intellect. The professors smoked marijuana constantly and complained about what a terrible world it was and how we shouldn't have wars. I wanted to tell them that without wars we might have all been slaves, but I kept my mouth shut.

I found myself looking forward to the cool breezes that came down off the mountains early mornings. I guess the professors got cold and put on clothes every now and then. I often found them asleep, scattered around the house in their tie-dyed attire and their bell-bottom jeans, their nonsensical conversations gratefully stilled, but their bodies gratefully covered, at least for the time being.

I was quite sure that De had slept with at least three of the four women in the house. They all shared sexual partners the way they passed around their joints. They believed in this free love mentality and resented my judgments.

"You're all no better than animals," I'd told them.

They laughed at me and seemed to agree that I was in for a rude awakening, for no one would want anything other than open marriages in the future.

"In a few years, vows of fidelity will become archaic," they'd said.

"Yawal should have your own planet," I'd told them, in my best Southern drawl.

Early one morning I found Aunt Beatrice sitting in an old antique chair that someone had placed outside. I knew it shouldn't have been there and wanted to bring it back to the dining room where it belonged. It was just the two of us and the sun had risen only moments before. The early morning fog was settling before us and appeared blurry and moist on my skin. I sat opposite her in a white iron chair with a blue-striped plastic seat.

"I believe this is the correct patio chair to be sitting in," I said.

She opened her eyes and smiled, but closed them shut again when she saw that it was me and my judgments come to taunt her. Perhaps she was tired of my opinions, but I didn't care. I felt right. I felt older than she and I thought my aunt was acting like a fool.

"How could you possibly love De?" I asked her. "He's unfaithful. Not only that, he's a bit of a jerk."

"A jerk you say?" She laughed. "I don't think that. Maybe I'm a jerk too, then. Maybe the whole world contains a bunch of jerks and we're two of many."

I gave her a sideways glance. In my opinion she was certainly acting foolish, but I didn't say it. Calling De a jerk was enough, I'd made my point.

"Do you really think it's necessary?" she asked.

"What?"

"Fidelity."

"It is to me," I said.

"Well between you and me, I'm at odds with it," she whispered. "Who I am and who I want to be don't like each other very much. I can't bring them together, try as I might. Don't think I don't know what you think of me. It's not far off from what I think of myself."

"Who is the real you, Aunt Beatrice?" I looked at her. "Don't tell me you think this naked stuff is normal?"

"I bear my family's fucked-up values inside my soul. I was raised to be who I am, not who I claim to be at all. We all pretend. Everyone is a liar," she said. "Let me have my fun and my foolhardy youth. I'm almost forty."

"You think everyone is a liar?"

She didn't answer me, so I could only assume that's exactly what she thought.

"You know that De had a wonderful idea. Would you like to hear it?"

"I can't imagine," I said.

"He wants you to paint us. De and I, out there stark naked in that beautiful field of wildflowers. Will you do that for us?"

I thought for a moment, an opportunity to grant a favor for a favor. "And if I do, will you take me back to Paris?"

"Deal," she said. "When you finish the painting we'll go."

It was my best work ever. Aunt Beatrice and De naked in the white bathtub, sitting in a field of wild and colorful flowers. Her white skin held by his jet-black arms was a startling sight. Their nakedness was blazingly and imperfectly beautiful.

True to her word, Beatrice agreed to drive us back to Paris, sans De. We'd been at the farmhouse only a month and I couldn't wait to get out of there. I don't think I could have stood a month more with Aunt Beatrice's friends.

A few days before we were leaving for Paris, Betsy Lou Buttercup called the house. She must have gotten the number from Grandma Edna. Aunt Beatrice and I had had brief conversations with Grandma Edna and we'd lied about the old French couple's house where we were vacationing for a week. We'd been there thirty days and there was no old French couple, but Grandma Edna didn't question us. I was grateful for that 'cause much of the time I was angry at Aunt Beatrice and might have gone back on my word and told my Grandma Edna everything.

"I'll meet you back in Paris," I said to Betsy Lou. "My aunt and I are returning in two days."

"Oh, I'm already thirty miles outside Paris. I got the address from your Aunt El. I wanted to surprise you, but I got lost. Do you think the old couple would mind if I come for a night? I'll pay for a room."

I literally felt my stomach fall.

"Oh, Sassy, it will be so good to see you."

"What's up?" Aunt Beatrice said as I hung up the phone.

"Oh shit," I said, "that's what."

Chapter Twenty-Five

We had given Betsy Lou meticulous directions to the house and Aunt Beatrice and I were sitting outside waiting for her approach and having lunch. I didn't really want to see her. I had not forgotten how she'd handled my news about Thomas, or her opinion of his deceitful nature. Yet I felt obligated.

"I suppose she'll call if she gets lost again," I said.

"It's really an easy ride up from Paris. I do hope she marked down the right turns, there are several of them."

"I'm sure she did."

I took a sip from the wine I was drinking. Every day at lunch, we had wine and cheese and fresh tomatoes picked from the garden. I gazed out over the French countryside sky and took a piece of cheese. I was mad for France and it had turned into an experience I would never forget, despite my month in the country with Aunt Beatrice and her cohorts. But, out of my frustration, I had done my finest work, my painting of Aunt Beatrice and De.

On that particular afternoon, I was wondering if I shouldn't just go home from Paris. I wanted to see Thomas more than I wanted to walk the Louvre. But there was someone in Paris that I needed to visit, had promised to visit. I had been invited to meet with a Mrs. Dupree for a critique of my work. This had been arranged by my high school art teacher,

Edgar Farmingdale. He had lived in Paris and had received his certificate from Studio Escalier. Mrs. Dupree had been his mentor and had many connections in the art world, according to Mr. Farmingdale. "Just see her, Sassy," he had said. "I'm sure she'll agree, as I do, that you are very gifted. Perhaps she can help you in some way."

I hadn't really given it much thought, but I had promised Mr. Farmingdale. I felt that it would be impolite not to visit his Mrs. Dupree, but I didn't feel I needed help. I was going to study art in Virginia, marry Thomas, and that would be the end of it. Perhaps I'd sell my work some day and perhaps I wouldn't. I didn't really have ambition, only the desire to do what I wanted to do when I wanted to do it.

"Remember that I have an appointment in Paris to meet with Mrs. Dupree Tuesday at four," I said. "We will make it back in time, won't we?"

"Of course," Aunt Beatrice said. "I think you're very talented. I'm sure she'll think the same."

"I think the painting I did of you and De is really good."

"I love it," she said.

"I'm sorry I can't give it to you, but that's what I want to show to Mrs. Dupree. I think it's my best work and, perhaps, I can get it shown."

"Then maybe I'll have to buy it off you." She laughed and took a long pause. "What will your friend think?"

"I don't know. She's never really commented on my artwork. I don't think she realizes how important it is to me."

"I meant about us, this…" She motioned her head back toward the chateau.

"Well, Betsy Lou has always been accepting of…of people who are different."

I thought Aunt Beatrice was going to spill her drink she laughed so hard. When she finally stopped laughing, she wiped her mouth.

"Different? It's you who are different." She poked my shoulder and giggled again.

I stuck my tongue out at her. "Hippie," I said.

"Republican," she uttered.

"Am not," I said.

"They're cooking a roast lamb tonight in your friend's honor, sans any poison. You know how they love Southern girls."

Now it was my turn to laugh. "I guess I'm lucky they're not roasting me."

"I do adore you, Sassy," Aunt Beatrice said. "You and I are the artists of the family and if we never meet again, know that I love and support you always."

"Why wouldn't we meet again?" I asked.

"When I step off the plane in Vermont, I step off the earth of South Carolina. It's like being an alien from a different hemisphere. The only reason I was talked into being your chaperone is because Mama is paying the bill. So I agreed to get to Paris via Carter's Crossing, but I shall never step foot in that dinky little nowhere town again."

"Oh," I said. "If you don't come to my wedding or show up at my first gallery opening, I will never forgive you."

"Don't be hard on me, Sassy," she said. "Love does not turn off or go anywhere when sight doesn't register what it longs to see, like in death, I suppose. I don't even think death spares us from love, though we can't see whom we love, we still love on. It's an energy," she said. "You can't kill it."

She turned to wink at me. "Learned that from your Aunt Peg."

With that, Betsy Lou arrived with a great deal of horn honking. She leaped from the car and began screaming out my name. Aunt Beatrice looked on with a smile as we danced and slapped at each other playfully.

I watched Betsy Lou's facial expressions at dinner. She was unusually quiet. Fortunately, no one came to dinner naked that night. The others kept trying to get her to speak, but soon, they lost interest. That is, after their roundtable discussion over Betsy Lou's name. *"Betsy Lou Buttercup?" they'd exclaimed. "Oh my God, have you ever heard anything so perfect, so disgustingly Southern?"*

Though Betsy Lou enjoyed her first night's dinner, on the second night, they served *cervelle de veau*. After telling her she was eating calf brain, she pushed her plate aside and the others laughed hysterically while poor Betsy Lou nearly threw up. I handed her the bread basket and a joint, which she readily accepted. Earlier that day she'd witnessed naked people talking about Buddhism and the hypocrisy of Christianity. Her mouth had never closed, nor did her expression lose its fixed state of distaste, like she was still eating *cervelle de veau*.

Soon, the usual banter about homosexuality ensued and how two people of the same sex should be allowed to legally marry. I thought Betsy Lou's eyes would drop from their sockets and fall to the ground. She stared at me in disbelief and I shrugged my shoulders.

Since she and I shared a bedroom she was able to express her disgust to me in private.

"Who are these people?" she asked.

"Friends of Aunt Beatrice."

"She the one who writes?" she asked.

"Yes," I said. "She's also a professor at some college up North."

"She's crazy," Betsy Lou whispered. "Like everyone else in this damn house."

The next morning, I watched in amusement as Betsy Lou gaped at the two people in the kitchen having a chat over a café, completely and most assuredly naked.

"Yuk," she said, "how can anyone sit there eating, wiping the crumbs from their private parts, and pretend they're perfectly normal?"

She collapsed in a chair as we stepped out onto the stone patio alone. "I don't think Dixie would ever believe this," she said.

"And why should I care what Dixie believes?"

"Are you sleeping with one of them?" she asked.

"God no," I said.

She raised her eyebrow at me as if, for some reason, I wasn't telling her the truth. I decided to make a mockery of her conclusions.

"Okay, Betsy Lou, I sit around all day naked and when I'm in the mood I grab a body and get laid."

"Even with that old man?" she asked.

"Papa Don? Why not?"

I heard her gasp. It was so loud I was afraid it would make her heartbeat skip. I felt the tears fall from my eyes as I went into a loud and glorious fit of hysterics.

"Oh, don't be an idiot," I said.

She stared at me skeptically. "Thomas wouldn't approve, either," she said.

I took in a breath, even the mention of his name made me weak, made me long for him.

"I think he's fine with it. I have spoken to him and he seems to think it's all very humorous. He said that Aunt Beatrice is probably much more interesting than any of her books."

That seemed to quiet her, and she finished her coffee in silence.

"Do you speak often?" she asked.

"Not really, it's expensive."

"Oh," she said and soon fell off to sleep under the morning sun.

We stayed two more days before heading back to Paris. We all drove back in Betsy Lou's car and De would return Aunt Beatrice's car to the airport. I'd never seen Betsy Lou so somber as she was in Saint-Lizier. I realized that by stepping out of South Carolina, her entire existence was being shattered by things people shouldn't speak of and she'd come too close to its ramifications.

"What if they're right," she said, "and the whole world becomes like them, then how do we preserve ourselves, Sassy? How do we, the righteous, survive?"

I had no answer for Betsy Lou, because I believed that people should be different and, hippies or not, all men and women were entitled to freedom of thought.

"Don't worry about it, Betsy Lou," I said. "There will always be places like Carter's Crossing, places where everyone thinks the same."

Betsy Lou's Southern charm was her cloak of armor, much the same way Aunt Beatrice's new politics were hers. The day we left the chateau I watched in amusement as Betsy Lou kissed every naked hippie in front of her, extended an invitation to South Carolina to one and all, promised several postcards a year to Papa Don, and even accepted an invitation to Vermont from the quiet young man who meditated every day under the full and flowering poppy tree until sunset.

"God, they're so strange," she said as we drove off. I caught a glimpse from Aunt Beatrice in the back seat. She was smiling slyly.

"It is also strange to stroke the cheek of your enemy," she said.

Chapter Twenty-Six

Betsy Lou was staying not far from our hotel and we met up daily to take walking tours. Except, of course, on the Tuesday of that week when I'd had my appointment with Mrs. Dupree. I don't know what I had expected of the day, but Celine Dupree did not meet my expectations, she far exceeded them.

I took a taxi to the left bank. Mrs. Dupree had a beautiful apartment filled with art, most likely from her students. She now taught at the Ecole nationale supérieure des beaux-arts and must have been at least seventy years old. Her hair was white and cut short. She, herself, was petite, but everything in her apartment seemed tall: the windows were huge and looked out upon a backyard garden, the bookcases traveled tall to the ceiling, and I can only assume a ladder was needed to reach the books.

Though at least seventy, Celine was not at all old. She seemed to carry an impenetrable youth, not letting age rob her of glamour. I was completely taken with her and would remain so even if she didn't like my work.

I loved the way she spoke English, with bits of French added, words she could not remember might even be substituted in Italian. Her sex appeal was not lost on me. She wore tight jeans, a man's tailored shirt open low, and high heels. Her belt was wide leather that showed off her waistline. I felt that when she walked, she could just as easily have flown.

After sharing a cup of coffee, I unwrapped my painting and put it on the easel in front of us. Her expression told me everything I wanted to know. She studied my painting carefully. "Exquisite," she finally whispered.

I looked at the painting with her, De's naked, black body, his phallus hidden behind Aunt Beatrice's milk-white flesh. Aunt Beatrice's small breasts, pink at the nipple, and her wheat-colored pubic hair against De's black legs. Her softly protruding stomach and thin arms around him. His striking black hair and chiseled face glaring from the canvas. Behind them wildflowers in vibrant impressionistic color, blustery winds, and white clouds settling in the distance, bright red roses on the ground around them.

"Magnificent," Mrs. Dupree said.

I stayed with Celine many hours, at least four, while we spoke of everything from art to poverty and from cinema to food. By the time I left her apartment, I had promised to consider studying with her at the school. I did not mention that I was in love and that moving my soon-to-be husband to Paris, France, was near impossible. In her exuberance for me, I forgot I came from another world.

I met up with Aunt Beatrice and Betsy Lou at a bar on Rue Bonaparte and chattered endlessly about my meeting with Celine Dupree. I watched as Betsy Lou had glass after glass of scotch and Aunt Beatrice nursed a glass of red wine. I felt myself becoming light-headed, so much so that I began to feel nauseous, but I kept on talking. I didn't have any sense of the ground as it gave way under me when I stood to rise, but I did feel myself falling to the floor.

The next thing I remember was the kind eyes of a man peering into mine, his hand on my shoulder. His blue eyes seemed to dance. He was in white and had a stethoscope around his neck.

"*Vous êtes enceinte,*" he said in French.

"What?" I asked.

"Pregnant," he said. "Did you not know?"

As I walked down the long white hall of the hospital I could see Aunt Beatrice and Betsy Lou seated behind a glass wall, huddled close, talking softly. Of course they knew. I could see it in their expressions as I came closer.

I had been told that I was eight weeks pregnant. It couldn't be Thomas's child. I had been in France for one month, six weeks since I had been in Thomas's arms. Eight weeks before I was foolishly acting out my indifferent sexuality with Dixie Craft, a man I didn't love.

Beatrice took my hand. "Perhaps I can inquire," she told me as we walked outside. Betsy Lou walked behind me. She had been uncharacteristically quiet.

"Inquire about what?" I asked.

She guided me into a waiting taxi. "There are doctors in Germany, I think, perhaps even here."

"Abortion? Is that what you're asking me to do?"

I heard a gasp from Betsy Lou. "Oh, Sassy, you can't," I heard her say.

We quickly dropped her off at her hotel. She was leaving the following day and we'd agreed to meet up for lunch before her evening flight. I was happy to be rid of her by then. I needed my own space. I needed to think and to come to my own decisions.

As Betsy Lou exited the cab she turned back to me, mouthing the words, "Sassy, you can't."

I felt numb with disappointment as I sat on the bed and stared out of the window. I don't think I'd ever been so unhappy. Aunt Beatrice had made several calls from her suite. I had no feelings at all about abortion. I never had to think about abortion. I recalled how Thomas had told me that he couldn't afford children, not until he was through with law school and had a job. I kept seeing his face that day, the earnest commitment in his expression.

I jolted up quickly. God! I was rich! Money would not be an issue. I suddenly felt as light- headed as I had the night before after meeting with

Celine Dupree. But then, I fell back, my eyes filled with tears. I'd forgotten the baby wasn't Thomas's, for a moment I thought it was. Maybe I could tell a white lie. But I knew that I couldn't lie to Thomas. I couldn't tell him the baby was his if it wasn't.

I began to cry as if I'd never stop. I felt Aunt Beatrice sit on the bed beside me and touch my arm.

"I've found someone," she said. "It will be illegal, but we can get it done. It will also be expensive."

I stared at her. My eyes hurt, and I could barely see.

"But he'll only do it if you're less than twelve weeks pregnant. I insisted you were."

"But the doctor said he wasn't sure. I was still hoping for a miracle. If I were four weeks pregnant, it could still be Thomas's child."

"The doctor you saw here in Paris thinks you are seven weeks pregnant. Perhaps he's off by a week, but I think that still keeps you pretty safe."

I thought of Thomas, the burden of a child, a child he wouldn't want, not now, anyway, and certainly not someone else's.

"I want the abortion," I said. "I'll pay the doctor whatever he wants. I must get rid of this baby."

She put her hand to my forehead and bent to kiss the top of my head. "A woman should have a right to her own body. That should never be determined by law."

"Yes, I agree," I said. I felt better already. Soon there would be no child. I couldn't let something that wasn't yet human destroy my chance at happiness.

"I need to sleep," I told Aunt Beatrice. She dimmed the lights and I drifted off immediately, into a deep sleep. I would not have any burdens, any reason not to return to Thomas as I had left him. I would do what I had to do to be with him, as we were before.

When I awoke it was still evening. I carried a deep, dark depression like a damp house with peeling walls and too much mildew. I suddenly knew what Aunt Beatrice felt like when she looked into the mirror wanting to be what she should be and denying who she'd been.

How could I damage the life within me, rob the soul who nestled innocently in my womb? How could I rob its future of possibility? How could I kill it so that it could not run carelessly through the valleys of the earth, feeling as deeply about life as I had felt over the last few weeks? How could I deprive this child of my love?

I sat down at the desk and began to write to Thomas. I told him I was pregnant and I was carrying Dixie's baby. As I wrote, my fingers hurt from the pressure I inflicted on them. I expressed the great sorrow I felt. But if he could see fit to raise the child with me, I would support it and the funds to insure its future would be my responsibility and not his. I told him I loved him with all my heart and sealed the letter, praying this child would not come between us.

I never went back to sleep, I couldn't. I sat in a large chair until dawn, knowing I was about to do the only thing I could do, that I, Sassy Sweetwater, could do. I don't know if it was a moral issue or not, but it came from my heart.

The next morning at breakfast Aunt Beatrice tried to change my mind. "You're too young," she said, "too young to carry this burden."

I disagreed. "This was my mistake," I said. "To selfishly extinguish this baby doesn't seem right."

"Don't be ridiculous, Sassy," she said. "It isn't yet a baby."

"It is, it has a soul. I can feel it."

She sighed. "You're making a mistake."

I ignored her comment. "I've written to Thomas and I've told him the truth," I said. "If I don't hear back I can only assume he doesn't want me enough. Why should he? This will cause him grief when all he needs in his life right now is the freedom to be successful."

"If he doesn't want you 'cause of this, then he isn't a man worthy of your love."

"As if you know what men are worthy of a woman's love," I shouted.

I knew I had hurt her and I turned away quickly. "I'm sorry," I said.

"What will you do?" she asked, ignoring the insult I'd just given her.

"If Thomas no longer wants to marry me, if I know for certain that I'm not going to have a life with him, then I'm going to remain in France. Mrs. Dupree wants me to study here. I'll take her up on it."

"You cannot have this baby alone, Sassy. I have a good-sized house." She was pleading with me. Her yellow eyes grew large and there was a strain in her face not usually apparent. Mostly, Aunt Beatrice always looked slightly drugged, but now she looked fully awake.

"No," I said, "but I do appreciate the offer."

I thought of the last month I'd spent with Beatrice and her friends. What's worse, I thought of De and his insane comments, his dogged arrogance.

"No," I said again.

I heard a sigh come out of her long enough to blow out a candle. "Well, Grandma Edna never needs to know," she said. "Not unless you marry Thomas, of course."

I suddenly felt an ounce of hope. I knew that Thomas would want the baby. I knew he would. Maybe not at first, but he wouldn't want to be without me. It would all work out.

I put the letter to Thomas inside my purse. I would mail it at the front desk later. After watching French television and blocking every thought from my head, I showered and dressed. I'd have to threaten Betsy Lou's life to get her to keep her mouth shut back in Carter's Crossing. No one needed to know my business.

I prayed to hear from Thomas soon. I thought of calling him, hearing his voice, but I wanted him to have the time to think it all through on his own. I didn't want to spring news of the baby on him. I wanted him to have the space to choose me and my unborn child.

"Are you ready?" Aunt Beatrice asked as she came into my room wearing her predictable long skirt and strands of beads, their colors contradictory: green beads bounced against tiny orange stones and red glass wrapped around purple.

We took the elevator down to the lobby of the hotel. Aunt Beatrice held my hand. Betsy Lou was already waiting for us and ran into my arms when she caught sight of me. I didn't want to feel like a victim, but I did.

"What are you going to do?" she asked immediately. "You can't possibly get an abortion. It's a major sin."

I didn't care about sin, I cared only about making the right choice, a choice I could live with. "I'm going to have it," I said.

"It's Dixie's, isn't it?"

I didn't say anything, though she kept her large eyes on me and her open mouth remained static, fixed on my answer. We walked outside where Aunt Beatrice had the taxi door open. I went in first and Aunt Beatrice followed. I realized as I settled myself that I hadn't left Thomas's letter at the desk to be mailed.

"Oh," I said. "I forgot to mail my letter."

"No problem," Betsy Lou said as she reached for it. "I'll bring it."

I instinctively held it back. "It has to be airmail," I said.

"No worry, I'll tell them."

She turned around quickly with the letter in her hand. For one brief moment I feared I had made a mistake and she would lose it, pretend she'd mailed it when she hadn't, that she'd be too afraid to tell me she'd lost it, but the feeling vanished the minute Betsy Lou returned.

"Done," she said.

I breathed a sigh of relief. "Good, let's have lunch then."

Chapter Twenty-Seven

I never knew how long days could be. Hours became eons and minutes became millenniums, as I waited for Thomas's reply. I hadn't expected to wait. I never wanted to wait for anything again.

Aunt Beatrice was getting restless 'cause she was due back in Vermont, but she didn't want to leave me alone. Grandma Edna kept calling and asking me when I was going to be returning to Carter's Crossing. I kept stalling. *Oh, I have to see this, Grandma Edna, and I have to see that, Grandma Edna,* but all I was doing was waiting on Thomas and I wouldn't wish waiting on my worst enemy. Waiting for anything is surely punishment for something.

Aunt Beatrice kept trying to get me to call Thomas, but I felt like that would be putting him on the spot, that he needed to call me, not the other way around. I hadn't made any plans to remain in Paris, remaining in Paris wasn't anything I wanted to do. I wanted Thomas to tell me to come home.

But the days passed without word from Thomas and hearing a phone ring was scarcer than hen's teeth. I didn't know what choices I had if I wasn't going to be returning to Carter's Crossing. I knew I wasn't going back there pregnant. At the back of my mind I was thinking about staying with Celine. She'd hinted at it when I met her for lunch one afternoon, kept telling me I wouldn't have to worry about finding an apartment 'cause she had not only one, but two extra bedrooms. *You must register pronto, pronto,*

Sassy, these spaces fill fast, she kept saying. *To be accepted here is a privilege, please take advantage of it. I can help you get in and get settled.*

I felt the pressure to make up my mind, my time was running out. Finally, at the end of the third week after mailing Thomas's letter, only days away from the end of August, I knew I had to stop acting like a turtle and make a decision. So I sprang into action quick as a bullfrog spying lunch.

I had expected something from Thomas, even bad news would have been something. I expected him to at least write a letter, or better yet, make a phone call. I never would have expected Thomas to ignore my distress. Why, he could have gotten the phone number for the hotel from my family. He surely could have found enough money to make that call.

"Maybe he never got the letter," Aunt Beatrice said, trying to make me feel better. But I had gone to the desk after we'd dropped Betsy Lou at the airport and the desk clerks told me they remembered an airmail letter going out to America at around three o'clock that afternoon. I knew I had no way of knowing if it was my letter they were referring to, but I assumed there weren't many airmail letters going out. People in hotels were tourists, they weren't writing airmail letters, they were sending postcards.

Well, whether the letter went out or not, I knew I had to end the cacophony of emotions I was drowning in. Sometimes, when you feel too much it shuts you down altogether. I was in a dull state of inertia and my life could not move forward without a confrontation, however painful it might be.

Aunt Beatrice promised to sit there while I dialed and to go back to her room when he answered. I was going to tell Thomas that his love didn't go any deeper than an April rain puddle and at the very least, he owed me an honest goodbye, an honest admission that a baby was going to be too much of a burden for him. I would have expected him to have wished me luck, at the very least.

"You know, Sassy, the mail takes a long time. Maybe he hasn't even gotten your letter."

"They told me at the desk it took five days."

"Well, maybe it takes ten."

Aunt Beatrice got up and put her hands on my shoulder. "You need to call him either way," she said. "You need to make plans. You've got to think of yourself and this baby and stop this moping around."

So with shaking hands I had the operator dial Thomas's number. It was his mother who picked up, finally, sounding as cheery as a neighbor come to call wanting a favor.

"He's gone off to Virginia, honey," she said.

I knew then that maybe Aunt Beatrice was right, he might not have even gotten the letter. I asked his mother if she remembered whether or not my airmail letter had reached him before he left for school.

"I don't remember him getting any airmail letter," she said. "You want to leave your number? I'll have him call you."

"No, that's okay," I said. "I'm in Europe, it's long distance. But do you have a number for him?"

She told me he hadn't yet called with a phone number. I said I'd call back, but I knew I was lying. I wouldn't ever call back. He had my letter. The ball was in his court. Why would he have told his mother about my letter, anyway, especially if he had no intention of honoring our love? He wasn't going to accept a woman with a baby. I was water under the dam at this point.

By the time Aunt Beatrice left for Vermont I had accepted Celine's offer to move in with her and I had registered myself at the *Ecole nationale superieure des Beaux-Arts*. I had also given Grandma Edna the news about remaining in Paris to study art. I could hear the disappointment in her voice, but she would not deny me that opportunity.

"I'm proud of you," she said. "I'll miss you like crazy, but you deserve this, Sassy. Every great artist should study in Paris."

In that moment I wanted to tell her the truth about the baby. I wanted her support, I even needed her near. Aunt Beatrice was right, I couldn't do this alone, but I didn't say anything at all. I felt that she would be disappointed with me and demand that I return to Carter's Crossing, the last place I wanted to be with a baby on the way and everyone looking over my shoulder for a husband, when there was none. Maybe I'd return to Carter's Crossing in a few years and I could say I got married in Paris, but my husband left me for another woman. Divorce was somehow easier than saying there was no man there at all.

I was determined to go on with my life, pretending that the brief interlude I'd had with Thomas was going to be enough to sustain me until I grew old and died, because I knew love didn't come often, but if it ever did again, I best hope that the hands of fate weren't still around my neck.

Aunt Peg called me right after I'd moved into Celine's apartment. She sounded happy for me. "Living abroad," she mused. "Oh, my." But she kept saying she'd had a sign, a sense that I was soon to be surprised. "I have ambivalent feelings about you now, Sassy. Are you all right?"

I told her I was, of course, but Aunt Peg wouldn't relent and kept saying that my life was about to change dramatically before the year was out. I couldn't help smiling to myself. I didn't doubt that my life would change. Certainly a baby changes everything, but the only one in the family that knew about the baby was Aunt Beatrice and I was going to keep it that way.

"I promise to let you know," I said. "If things change."

"Remember, the future is not etched in stone. However you see it now, is not how it will be. If you believe that, it will make you feel better."

I didn't admit to Aunt Peg that I saw my future without Thomas and that because of it, I may never feel better.

Chapter Twenty-Eight

Celine had many friends, the majority of them were much younger than she. Their gaiety lifted my spirits, I'm happy to say, but I was still sad, still ambivalent about the choice I'd made. I had told Celine all about Thomas and that I was pregnant. She insisted that I did the right thing not getting an abortion and she kept trying to soothe me. "I am a feminist, Sassy," she said, "but I'm not a murderer."

In theory I understood what she was saying, but I didn't believe that women who chose abortion were murdering their unborn children. I did believe that it was a choice and should never be a law that women weren't masters over their own body. But I fought with this theory constantly, berating myself for not letting Aunt Beatrice take me to her German doctor and then, turning on a dime and feeling my child in my womb. Love would well up out of nowhere and consume me with its ubiquitous warmth and I wondered how this love could come to be for something that was not yet born.

Celine liked having people around her. They talked about everything under the sun. She was exhilarating to be with and she took me everywhere in Paris she thought I needed to go: to every film, to every gallery opening in the city and beyond. "Symbolism is everywhere," she'd say. "Learn to look for it." She introduced me to such fascinating people and took a keen interest in my work. I don't know what I would have done without her. She took my mind off my underlying despondency.

I enjoyed my classes, but I never stopped thinking about Thomas and how much he'd like this and how much he might have liked that about Paris. Some days I'd think about him less, some days I'd think about him more. My heart was broken, yet love kept flooding me with its enveloping presence, as if Thomas was not absent from my life at all.

The doctor Celine took me to said I was about eight weeks pregnant, which contradicted what the first doctor had said, that I was about six weeks pregnant at that time. I should have been ten weeks pregnant then, not eight weeks, which would have made my baby very likely Thomas's. Celine told me it's not an exact science. And what was I supposed to do now, call Thomas and tell him I was having his baby, maybe?

There wasn't a line anymore between sadness and anger, the two emotions had merged and I carried them both whenever I had time to think and to be alone. I both loved and hated Thomas. I longed for him and, yet, felt betrayed and lost. I wondered how long it was going to take to stop wanting what I didn't have.

Celine would take my hand and tell me that love is never without its sorrows, its rough waters, and its unpredictable disasters. And I guess she was the expert on that for she had lost two husbands, one to a war and the other to a plane accident. But I had lost Thomas to fear and that just didn't seem potent enough to justify it.

I'd told Celine everything about my life, all the way back to Mama and how we'd finally come back to Carter's Crossing and how, at first, I was so afraid of Grandma Edna. It was just easy to tell Celine things. She was old and young at once, she was both giddy and wise. She asked me if I ever wanted to see Mama again and I said that I did, but as long as I couldn't forgive her, I wouldn't. And even after all these years, I couldn't forgive her. Maybe if she'd fought more for my forgiveness, I might have, but she hadn't.

"That doesn't seem right," Celine said.

I pushed Mama out of my mind the way I always did. Mama's loss was even greater than Thomas's, just not as new anymore. Even with Celine I changed the subject, took it off Mama and onto gossip or art or the symbolism she was always making me look for. Mama had done wrong and that was the end of it, that would always be the bottom line, that she'd wronged me so.

"Your grandmamma loves you, that's what I think, that's what I think," Celine said, pointing to her head.

I had friends, the ones I met in class, the ones I met through Celine. I ran around Paris with my French girlfriends, their arms through mine, chattering up a storm in their broken English. Even when I didn't know what they were saying they made me laugh. They force fed me joy, force fed it to me until it was really there. Even eight months pregnant I could step as lively as they. Still, Thomas was never far from my thoughts. I felt as much emotion as always, missed him with as much ardent pinning as always. The abyss of Thomas's love, however brief, both filled me up and drained me empty.

I didn't date. Men just didn't seem interested in dating a pregnant woman and I welcomed their disinterest, but I couldn't help but wonder if Thomas was a man about town. He was the perfect catch for someone. Maybe someday I'd hope that he was happy, but for now, all I could wish for him was an unbearable loneliness, much like my own.

My new friends taught me French, a language I had to learn quickly for my teachers did not speak English well. If it were not for Celine, I wouldn't have been speaking French at all. She drilled me constantly and then refused to speak English to me altogether.

I heard from my Aunt Beatrice pretty regularly. She was making plans to return to France for my baby's birth. She kept insisting that I shouldn't be alone even though I told her that I had new friends, not to mention Celine, who was always mothering me. But I knew that my Aunt was my family and, truth was, I wanted her there to meet her godson, so I was glad she was coming. Even though I had all these new people around me, I knew we'd sever ties one day and we'd all look back with fond memories from our present lives. Sometimes, new friends are just like Mama used to say, too new to cash in on.

Every now and then Earline and Aunt El would call and tell me about how much money they were making and Grandma Edna, of course, called me twice weekly. Aunt Peg would call, still insisting on the life change she was sensing for me. I wanted my family to know I was pregnant, but I didn't have the nerve to tell them. "Where was the man responsible for my baby?" they'd ask. "How could I even think I could do it alone?" they'd insist. I heard their questions and I had no answers.

It was only Celine who knew of my restlessness. I missed being home and she was well aware of it, though I never spoke the words. I missed Carter's Crossing. I missed my dog and the creek and the lonely grave under the sycamore tree. Above all, I missed Grandma Edna.

Celine had gotten me a show in Paris at a gallery called *Le Mond du Art*. It wasn't my first show, but it was the first gallery that was going to be featuring my work. I was terribly excited about it and though I was in my eighth month, I was up on ladders making sure my paintings were all lit the way I wanted them to be and hung the way they needed to be.

One night, I came home more tired than I may ever be again. The couch in Celine's living room faced the large window out onto the garden, so that when I walked through the front door I couldn't see who was sitting on the couch. I only heard Celine's voice from the chair behind the wall. I had a fleeting feeling I was looking at a familiar hat, but I dismissed it pretty quickly. I had been at the gallery for hours and all I wanted to do was sleep.

Whoever it was on the couch must have followed Celine's eyes when I walked through the door and started up the stairs. I barely paid attention to Celine's guest because she always had so many and I was so exhausted. Whoever it was, stood to turn and I turned as well, on instinct, but only briefly. My turn had merely been a reaction to hers.

"Sassy," she said and held out her arms.

I stood so still. My God! It was Grandma Edna! How was I going to hide my swollen stomach? I couldn't move. I just gaped at her. I could hear Celine apologizing to me, looking guilty, telling me how much I needed my grandmamma to be there and chattering on about responsibility and trust and my gallery opening and how my grandmamma would have been so hurt to have missed it and before I knew it, I was wailing like a baby in Grandma Edna's arms.

CHAPTER TWENTY-NINE

Patrick Toulouse McLaughlin was born on a bright, blue afternoon, the kind of day that turns a sour mood sugar sweet. It was the kind of day that makes people sigh when they step outside. It was the kind of day that puts a skip to their walk and keeps them seduced by all that fresh, uncompromised air.

"My son is sure to have a sunny disposition," I said. "On a day like this, it's absolutely expected."

I had always loved the artist, Toulouse Lautrec, and I wanted my baby to carry my memories of France for the rest of my life. I called him baby Toulouse, Patrick Toulouse, and silently, to myself, Tommy Toulouse, sweet baby Tommy Toulouse, which is what I would have named him if Thomas had still been in my life.

I could see the sun before I opened my eyes and I could feel it before I awoke fully. It was a warm sun, not the kind that makes you sweat hard; it was the kind of day you embrace.

They had handed my baby to me in a pink blanket. "But he's a boy," I said.

They laughed and told me they'd run out of blue blankets.

I held Patrick Toulouse next to me and nursed him. Grandma Edna was sitting in my hospital room dressed in pressed slacks and a blue cotton shirt. It made me smile, I'd never seen her wear slacks before. She looked good, better than I'd ever expected, and I knew she was up there around

Celine's age. It was all changing. To see my Grandma Edna in slacks, I knew that most certain.

"And who is our beautiful, little boy named after?" Grandma Edna inquired. She hadn't even asked me who the father was, but I knew she assumed it was Thomas. She also knew, or assumed, he no longer wanted me because of the baby.

"I decided to keep the Irish tradition of names," I said.

I knew she was wondering where Thomas was and whether or not we planned to marry at some point, at the very least.

"You'll come back to Carter's Crossing now?" she asked. I saw the intensity in her eyes, the hope.

I saw Aunt Beatrice's head spring up fast. She'd gotten to Paris about three weeks before Patrick's birth, he'd been later than expected, and poor Aunt Beatrice was going to be flying home without getting to spend much time with him.

I nodded in Grandma Edna's direction. I had decided to take Patrick back home to Carter's Crossing. It just seemed so perfect now and I wasn't going to hide myself away in Paris. Grandma Edna would watch the baby while I attended art school in Charleston. I had a year to go before I had my degree in art. I was looking forward to going home. I hadn't seen June-bug in nearly a year and I couldn't wait for a walk by the cove with my beautiful dog. Perhaps it would make me sad to be home, but it's where I wanted to be and it's where I wanted to raise my son.

"I'm sorry he won't marry you, Sassy," Grandma Edna said, taking me by surprise.

I quickly glanced at Aunt Beatrice. Of course, they'd talked. I'd been jilted, not much you could say about that. I knew they were both feeling sorry for me. But I felt joy. I had my son and I was taking him home.

"I don't think about it much anymore," I said.

Grandma Edna and I had had about four weeks together in France before Patrick's birth. I noticed how quiet she'd been, almost pensive. I wondered if she was thinking about her own life and how different things might have been if she hadn't married Seamus, if she'd stood up to him sooner and maybe she could have even become a bohemian in Paris or New York City. Sometimes, I could see that in her, that possibility, and other times, I just couldn't. It made me realize that circumstances and choices begin to define who people really are.

Grandma Edna had come to my gallery opening and had studied each and every painting for several minutes. She finally stood there before the painting I had done of Aunt Beatrice and De. Aunt Beatrice walked away quickly, disappearing behind some people. I watched as Grandma Edna stared from a distance and then moved in close. I tried to interpret her silence. When I approached her, she smiled.

"You always said you wanted to paint naked people."

I looked into her eyes and watched as she put up her hands. "You are a wonderful artist," she said. "Where ever did you find the models for this one?"

I didn't know whether or not to take her seriously. Hadn't she recognized Aunt Beatrice? I had clearly placed her naked daughter in a bathtub with a naked black man. I couldn't interpret Grandma Edna's expression at all, but Aunt Beatrice kept her distance for the rest of the day and went out alone that evening.

I knew how much Grandma Edna had missed me, but I didn't know she'd missed me enough to buy me my own art gallery.

"It's right on Bay Street, honey," she said. "I bought the building. El said real estate is always the best way to make money. You know, she and Earline are doing pretty well. I doubt Liam or Seamus could have figured out what to do with a lot of failing mills, but El sold them off and invested in the stock market and in real estate. I couldn't have had a son smarter than El."

"What about Seth?" I asked. "He's no dummy."

I'd heard about Seth getting an offer to work in Washington, D.C. for one of those nonprofit organizations that protected equal rights. Aunt El had called to tell me he'd moved up there and even had a girlfriend now.

"Oh, I'm proud of him," Grandma Edna said. "No head for money, though. He does well for this world and that's good. And it's about time he left home. All of my children are leaving me. Did I tell you that El and Earline want to buy a house they found in Macon? Well, at least my grandchild and my great-grandchild are coming home." She beamed at the new baby and squeezed my hand.

It was while we were on the airplane flying into Charleston that I told Grandma Edna that I wasn't sure who Patrick's father was, but in either case, Thomas had rejected him and me for having him. If she was disappointed learning of my active, teenage sex life, she didn't show it.

"He didn't strike me like that kind of boy," Grandma Edna said.

I just turned and looked out the window of the plane. I wasn't sure what I was going to tell people about Patrick's father. Maybe they wouldn't ask.

"You keep an air of mystery," Grandma Edna said, as if she'd read my thoughts. She patted my arm. "No one needs to know anything about anybody."

"But what about Patrick?" I asked. "He'll want to know."

Grandma Edna didn't have any answers for that. She fell asleep and left me to the black night beyond the window and the precious breath of my son while he slept.

Pike was there at the airport waving furiously as Grandma Edna and I walked through the airport gate. He beamed wide and his whole face lit up when he took Patrick Toulouse from me and rocked the baby in his arms. I could never look at Pike without thinking about Dudley, without wondering if Pike ever heard from him. I'd never be able to understand how he could forgive us for what was done to Dudley, but one day I'd surely learn that kindness and loyalty beget the same.

"Been missing you, Sassy," he said, hugging me awkwardly and placing the baby back in my arms.

I'll never be able to find words bittersweet enough to explain how I felt as we drove toward Carter's Crossing. It was home. It wasn't Paris, but it was home. No matter how I'd ever felt about it, it was the best place in the world to me now. Carter's Crossing had been where I belonged for a long time. Carter's Crossing felt like some kind of comforting religion, even though there's ambivalence in the embrace of it. The feeling never wears off, that feeling of being contained in a memory, in a genetic pool of emotions. I kept thinking that if I were blind, I could still find it if you placed me miles and miles away. Like radar, I'd be led to it, same way I'm led to God when I'm frightened. Even the black dark things that happened in my childhood were encased within the safety net of my home and made right, the kind of safety net that I would always come to expect, though it contained secrets so heinous. I wondered why I didn't want to flee like my mama had. But the shadows had all lifted away, the evil had vanished, and all that was left for me was the land and the house and the people I loved. I started crying and reached for Grandma Edna's hand as we approached that sign I'd seen so long ago, where all the arrows were pointing to places I'd never heard of. Now I knew them well. I wondered if my Patrick Toulouse would always return here, back to his childhood home, looking for it, always in awe of it. I wondered if some day my own mama would be propelled back, like an old steel magnet pulling her, sweetly owning the largest part of our lives, ambiguous childhood, the times that shape us. There will always be nostalgia for that. So, too, there will always be the weight of it, the familiar but forgotten shadows of it. I could move a million miles away, but I'd always be where I'd started.

I kissed my son on his forehead. His skin was so soft, his little body puffed and pink. He'd been born with platinum hair, which he still had, but it was curly, and I didn't have a clue as to where that came from. His heavily lashed eyes were blue. He looked like a doll any little girl would have wept for, pleaded for. Now he was mine and all the little dolls that had eluded my childhood no longer mattered.

As we approached the house, I sat forward with a start. I wasn't exactly sure what I was looking at. The old red barn had been painted white, had a porch, a garden, and was no longer recognizable. I strained my neck to see it. "What did you do to the barn?" I asked.

I felt Grandma Edna nudge me as June-bug came flying down the drive.

"You better hand me the baby," she said.

That dog went wild, knocked me to the ground, sat on my body, and kissed me 'til I was wet as a creekside swim. She kept barking and kissing me and running wild in circles around me.

I stared at the barn while I kissed her back. June-bug was still jumping up like a jack-in-the-box and I kept trying to take in what was there before me.

"You like it?" I heard Grandma Edna ask as June-bug finally allowed me to walk up to the door.

Grandma Edna followed me inside, still holding Patrick in her arms. I couldn't believe it. The old barn had been completely restored.

"This down here is the main part. You like the kitchen, Sassy?"

I looked over at a brand-new open kitchen with cherry wood cabinets and a stove with six burners. "I'll say," I said.

"There's three bedrooms in the back and a screened patio for outside dining."

"What you going to do with this place?" I asked.

"The studio is upstairs. Want to see it?"

I looked at her with disbelief. *Is she saying this is mine?*

I walked up the long staircase right into a beautiful loftlike studio with open skylights and easels and supplies all just waiting to be used.

"I don't believe it." I shook my head.

"You're too old to live with me. Thought you might like a place of your own."

I threw my arms around her and she held me tightly. The feelings came quick, the ones I got when I kiss my baby son. That's the price you pay for being home, for wanting nothing else 'cause nothing else could soothe my unsettled spirit like this.

Chapter Thirty

I went over to Bay Street the following morning to see the gallery space that I now owned. It was nearly directly across from where Littleton's had been. I had an appointment to meet with a contractor and I was taking notes, getting down everything I'd need. I had decided that I wasn't going to show just my own work at the gallery, but commission the work of other artists, specifically local artists. A good place to start discovering the kind of work I wanted to show would be at the art institute in Charleston where I'd be studying for the next year. I figured by the time I had my degree in art, the gallery would be ready to open and I'd have a big party there and invite everyone in town.

"What you going to call your gallery?" Aunt El had asked me.

"Sweetwater Gallery," I said. "What else?"

"McLaughlin's?" Grandma Edna piped in, sounding a bit too much like a commanding army general. Aunt Earline quickly came to my defense.

"Not the same," she said. "My vote is with Sweetwater."

Grandma Edna scowled and I winked at Earline. There'd been lots of changes in the year I'd been gone. For one, Seth was living in Washington, D.C. and Aunt Earline and Aunt El were buying a house in the countryside, on the outskirts of Macon, Georgia. I think the confidence of finally moving away from Carter's Crossing had provided Aunt Earline with a sharper tongue when it came to Grandma Edna.

"Don't know what the hell you want to live all the way over there for," Grandma Edna had said. "I never heard of a down payment so steep. What the hell you buy yourselves, a goddamn mansion?"

"You're finally getting rid of me, Grandma Edna," Aunt Earline had piped in. "Cause for celebration." She'd reached across the table and poured Grandma Edna more of her favorite wine, a nice, crisp French Chablis.

"We're going to sell off some land for the down payment, Mama," Aunt El said.

I suddenly felt guilty because Grandma Edna would be alone in that big house, not that she was that old, quite yet, or even showed signs of slowing down. Still, I wondered if I shouldn't think about moving back in. She'd given me everything and here I was, leaving her alone.

I had been thinking about that while I was driving back from the gallery, wondering if we just shouldn't sell the house and move Grandma Edna into the new barn with me. I was lost in thought, debating how I was going to approach the subject with Grandma Edna when I noticed a red sports car parked right in front of the barn, real snazzy like. It was clearly a Corvette and sitting there behind the wheel was Dixie Craft, the last man in the state of South Carolina that I wanted to see.

"Hello, Sassy," he said and got out of his car and stood in front of me.

He looked the same, hadn't changed much. He had on khaki pants and loafers without socks. Betsy Lou used to say he dressed so neatly that his clothes looked new off the rack. His white polo shirt was tight around his solid chest and his arms looked big and muscular, like he'd started lifting weights.

I wondered what he was doing in my driveway, but I didn't ask. I think I knew what he wanted. I stood there making small talk with him, expecting him to ask me about Patrick, for surely Betsy Lou had let loose her wagging tongue. Dixie had never done anything to me, but I felt like being nasty and it was a struggle not to be.

"I'd like to see my baby," he finally said.

I think I fell backward, tripped a bit, even though I had expected it. I had some things in my hands and I wanted to put them down. At the same time, I didn't want to invite Dixie inside my new home.

"He's resting," I said and nodded up toward the farmhouse. "My Grandma Edna is caring for him."

He shuffled his feet a bit and then met my gaze head on. I felt his stare might have knocked me to the ground.

"Why didn't you tell me?"

I didn't know if he was hurt or angry, but I didn't want to deal with Dixie's feelings either way. I also didn't want to deal with having to tell him I wasn't sure who Patrick Toulouse's father was.

"I just got back," I said, even knowing that was a dumb excuse.

He looked up toward the farmhouse as if he was hoping to see something he could run up to and embrace. I realized in that moment that it was cruel of me to deny him that, if he was, in fact, Patrick's father.

"Betsy Lou told me you were pregnant."

I wanted to kill Betsy Lou for opening her big, fat mouth, though it had come as no real surprise. Betsy Lou's tongue flapped more than a duck in pond water. The last thing I wanted was for Dixie to be standing at my door claiming parentage for my son.

"Is it a boy?" he asked.

I nodded slowly. "Patrick Toulouse," I said.

He looked shocked and he went back to his car and leaned against it. I knew I'd hurt him again, but I wasn't sure why.

"You married? You married this Toulouse guy? Some French guy?"

I almost laughed, but I didn't. I tried to be kind, to be mindful of the state Dixie was in. His face had turned pink before my eyes and he was breathing heavy, almost like he was gasping for breath.

"No, I didn't marry anyone. That's my baby's name. Patrick Toulouse McLaughlin."

"What the hell kind of name is Patrick Toulouse?"

This time I backed away on purpose. Dixie was furious and his eyes were glaring at me. I noticed his hands had gone into fists.

"Betsy Lou told me how you were living over there in France, having sex orgies with older men, carrying on like a real whore."

I slapped him hard across the face. It was instinct. I couldn't have helped myself if I'd wanted to. He held my hands behind my back and demanded to see his son.

"He's asleep," I said and pushed him off me.

He then insisted that I give him a convenient time and place to come back to see Patrick. I didn't want Dixie in my life or in my son's life. I wanted Thomas to end this misery and drive up the drive and take ownership of his family. But that wasn't going to happen.

I started art school the end of August while Grandma Edna watched the baby. Saturdays I went into town to check on the gallery and the progress that was being made. The builders were putting in storage at the back of the building for paintings being delivered and an office was being built for me on the third floor. The second floor was where I could keep all the paintings that were coming in for the next show. And on Sunday at noon, like clockwork, Dixie came to visit little Patrick Toulouse. It was an ambivalent decision on my part, but I felt obligated to do it. It didn't seem right not to allow that relationship to happen.

From the start I questioned Dixie's motives. He seemed more interested in me than the baby. I watched as he held Patrick in his arms, sort of like he was weighing him or about to offer him up for gold. I knew he was looking for some kind of resemblance to himself, but Patrick still just looked like a little doll. He didn't have anybody's nose or eyes, even though I searched for Thomas's features every day, wanting to see his face stamped on my son's, but my son just looked like a baby.

"Anybody in your family have curly hair?" he asked.

I shrugged my shoulders. I was torn in a million pieces. I wanted to give Patrick a father, but I also wanted the right father for him. I wanted my son to have someone he could look up to, one that would never purposely disappoint him or hurt him in any way. I wasn't sure whether or not I was doing the right thing by letting Dixie see Patrick because I wasn't ever going to marry Dixie. Maybe I'd marry someone, but it wasn't going to be Dixie.

What disturbed me most is that I didn't see any adoration in Dixie's expression when he held the baby. I just saw him searching, looking for the square face and the cleft that materialized in Dixie's chin when he was angry.

But sometimes, it just felt good to be out in town with Dixie and Patrick Toulouse, simply walking around, grabbing ice cream cones at Rocket's or sitting on a park bench looking out over the river. I started to feel that it was normal, being with Dixie like that, like we were a real family just having a usual day. I guess I wanted that so much with Thomas that I fantasized that I was having it with Dixie and I began to get used to his company. Yet it would go no further than that. I would not touch him or allow him to touch me. Much to my surprise, he respected the boundaries that I put up.

"I forgive you for being with other men," he said out of the blue one day, making me laugh and making the sip of the soda I'd just taken dribble down my chin.

"Gee, thanks, Dixie," I said. "But I don't need, nor do I want, your forgiveness."

He looked wounded to the core, but then again, Dixie always looked wounded to the core. It made me feel like I'd done something personally to screw up his life. Even though Dixie had a good job, he was a bank manager over in Seabrook, but he was always frowning. I felt like I was the cause of his bad moods, because I remembered him as being much lighter in spirit and now he brooded more than a once upon a time rich man on a breadline with holes in the heels of his shoes.

It wasn't long before Dixie started showing up unannounced in the evenings. There he'd be at my front door with a bag of groceries. He'd insist on cooking for me and because I was usually so damn tired, I let him. But there were things I was beginning to notice about Dixie that I didn't like. He'd drink a whole bottle of wine and get back in that Corvette and drive the twenty-five miles home. Sometimes he'd fall asleep on the sofa and I wouldn't be able to wake him up, which was fine, because I feared for his safety getting behind the wheel of a car. I hated seeing him there in the mornings, though. He didn't belong in my house. He was an oddity. He was like a hog in a mansion, dropping my crystal and overlooking the Picasso on my wall.

What I liked least about Dixie, though, was that he didn't like dogs. One thing I knew, sure as I knew anything, any man that didn't like dogs wasn't worth loving, wasn't even worth the time of day. June-bug knew it too, and whenever Dixie was around, she went back up to the farmhouse to be with Grandma Edna.

Dixie never mentioned Betsy Lou, but I knew they were still in touch. I told him that if Betsy Lou's name ever crossed his lips, I'd never see him again. Betsy Lou had never made any attempt to get in touch with me and sometimes, when I thought about it, I questioned whether or not Betsy Lou had ever mailed that letter to Thomas. But then I'd tell myself that was just wishful thinking. For if she hadn't, that would mean I could go up there to Virginia and claim him again and there'd be an excuse as to why I'd disappeared, one that we could live with, like Betsy Lou's betrayal. I developed an unnatural hatred for her. I mean, she hadn't really done any-thing to me, but I couldn't stop hating her. It was like I had a premonition that her distance was a time bomb under my foot.

Those kinds of thoughts made me too confused to ponder over and I quickly dismissed them, but I still had a sinking feeling about Betsy Lou. She'd never stopped by to see my son. She'd kissed me goodbye at the hotel that day in Paris and that was it; I just ceased to exist for her. Guilty people are like that, easy to lose.

I tried not to occupy my thoughts with feelings that made me want to stay in bed all day. I tried to go on with my life and enjoy my son and my work. I was excited about the gallery and Patrick Toulouse was the most delightful baby on earth. I had everything I wanted but Thomas. Maybe that's just the way life is, keeping you hungry when you've gotten too full, ample punishment sustains humility, I guess.

I started hiding up in the farmhouse in the evenings so I wouldn't be around when Dixie just showed up out of nowhere. I got real tired of his spontaneous grocery visits. He wouldn't come up to the farmhouse with Grandma Edna there. I think he was a little afraid of her.

Unfortunately, the more I dismissed Dixie, except on the appointed Sundays, the more aggressive he got about marrying me and making Patrick Toulouse his legal son. Lord knew, I didn't want that, but I saw my son getting more and more attached to a man I really didn't like all that much.

Many times I wondered if I should stop the visits before I found myself confronting a lawyer to keep Dixie away from us. His drinking made me so nervous and it terrified me that he'd put my son in harm's way if I ever left Patrick Toulouse in his care. I tried to get Dixie to stop drinking, but he said he didn't drink, he sipped. But that's just the way Dixie was. If I said white, Dixie would say black and if I said he had to leave, he'd say he had to get up every day, but that didn't mean he was going to do it.

Eventually, Dixie tried to get me into bed, but he was always meeting resistance. It got him angry. Sometimes it got him mean and he'd tell me my paintings reminded him of a splattering of vomit or the nightmares of a crazy man. I wondered what can of worms I'd opened letting him into our lives at all. But I wouldn't have to worry about that much longer.

Right before the Sweetwater Gallery opened in July of 1969, Dixie joined the army. I wouldn't see Dixie Craft again for two years. During that time I welcomed the reprieve, but Dixie would return to claim me again and I would wish I'd had Aunt Peg's gift of prophecy when I accepted his proposal. For surely, if I had had Aunt Peg's gift, I would have made a different choice. Yet life does not always reveal that at the bottom of a sewer, lies a jewel. So therefore, what choice is ever subject to recrimination?

Chapter Thirty-One

During the two years Dixie was away he wrote me letters that I put into a drawer and never read. I think I must have been hoping that if I didn't let him into my thoughts then maybe he'd disappear altogether. I'd heard he wasn't serving overseas, he was in Texas where soldiers didn't have it so bad. Yet there was always the possibility that he'd be shipped to Vietnam. I didn't want for that, but I didn't want to see him again, either. I questioned my feelings constantly because he wasn't a bad man, yet I had become increasingly wary of him. Maybe it was his drinking, a sense that he would in some way harm my baby boy. So I hoped that Dixie would forget about me soon enough and settle down with some girl he'd meet at an enlisted men's canteen, have his own son, and make no claim on mine. Maybe he liked the army. Maybe he'd stay in the army forever.

As for me, I could feel myself moving toward maturity like I was letting go of something that belonged to another time and it was a precious something I'd never be able to reclaim. There was an ambivalence to my aging process. I was without the one thing that would have brought completeness to my life. I was without Thomas and the further I felt I was leaving my youth behind, the more in shadow Thomas withdrew. I guess I threw myself into my work so I wouldn't have to confront dating anyone. I still couldn't bear to think of any other man but Thomas Tierney. Every time I looked up, it was Thomas I was hoping to see. I knew he was still in school in Virginia, but I assumed he came home for holidays and just maybe, we'd have a chance encounter. But chance encounters with Thomas Tierney didn't seem to be in the cards for me. At least, not then.

Several of my paintings had been shown throughout the South and I'd sold a number of them. My decision to showcase local artists in Beaufort was a good one. Beaufort was becoming a lively town. The real estate was up and tourists flocked there. People wanted to buy local art, nothing too sophisticated, like the contemporary realism of my work. My paintings were being commissioned by several galleries out of the state and, mostly, that's where I made my money. The art I was selling at Sweetwater's was good, but it was the usual landscapes and humorous depictions of animals, the kind of things people gravitate to for a county house.

Patrick was a beautiful baby boy, but he still didn't resemble anyone in my family. He was a quiet baby, didn't complain much at all. I could take him anywhere and not expect him to make a nuisance of himself. He was a funny little guy, throwing his bottles to the floor just to see me get annoyed. He loved when I got annoyed. Every time I showed my temper, Patrick Toulouse would giggle. It was hard to get mad at him when every time I'd start yelling he'd throw his little pudgy arms in the air and laugh. One day he even rolled over and held his side. I heard the baby giggles that were coming out of him. If I didn't know any better, I'd swear he was in a fit of hysterics because I was yelling into the phone over some delivery that wasn't on time.

Aunt El and Aunt Earline were living in their new house in Macon, so I didn't see much of them anymore, except at holidays. Everyone came home now for the holidays except for Aunt Beatrice, but she always called. Seth had gotten married to a really strong woman. Her name was Agatha Mutton and I swear, she looked like she could take on Sonny Liston in the ring, but she made Seth happy. He'd even put on forty pounds, but hey, I guess he had to.

But mostly, Grandma Edna was up in the big house all by herself. I took Patrick Toulouse up there as much as I could. I spent more time up at the farmhouse than I did in my new home just to keep her company. We'd become good friends, Grandma Edna and I. She was always there at the gallery, watching the baby while I worked. I knew she loved being there, too, especially after I gave a showing of all her barns. Majority of them sold and she couldn't have been prouder.

I got word that one of the best galleries this side of the Mason-Dixon wanted to show my work. It was one we'd all heard of in Ashville, North Carolina. I was thrilled to death and moved into a little bed and breakfast in Ashville for the show. My son was back with Grandma Edna and Carolyn, who'd become my grandma's best companion, aside from me. I'd learned that my family had given Carolyn, James Leroy, and Pike the house they lived in and the thirty acres surrounding it. I guess that was atonement for what was done to Dudley. I realized that Carolyn knew exactly where her son was. Three or four times a year she would disappear on short vacations. She never talked about where she'd been and I never gave it much thought, but after a while I realized she was going to visit Dudley, must have been. I never questioned it or even mentioned my suspicions. I was somehow afraid I'd jinx Dudley's safety if I did.

The night of my opening in Ashville, I was pleased to see so many people. The Ashville Gallery mailing list was sure a lot better than mine and I was standing there thinking how I was going to make a point to build up my list and advertise more when I got back home.

I took a survey of the room, trying to read expressions as people studied my work. Suddenly, I saw something that made me freeze and crane my neck for a better look.

One thing about being a redhead is that you're noticeable in a crowd. People look at redheads. I hear tell that once we were thought to be children of the devil. But the face I was riveted to was too kind to be anyone other than my father, Aaron Littleton.

He met my gaze. I was too startled to move or to even take a step toward him. I instinctively looked at the woman at his side. She was not my mama.

He was standing in front of me in under a second and, I swear, I'd never even seen him walk across the floor. He'd taken the woman's hand and led her over to me. She was way taller than he; a thin, blonde woman with slightly bucked teeth.

"Hello, Sassy," he said.

I had no voice with which to answer. I stared at the woman. She uncomfortably dropped Aaron's hand.

I knew I looked confused. I shook my head, my brows were pinched so tight my forehead hurt. "This is my, ah…wife," he said. "Lillian. You know, my, ah…daughter from my first marriage?" I looked at her without saying anything.

"Your paintings are wonderful," she said to me and then she turned back to Aaron. "I'm going into the other room, dear. I haven't been there yet and I certainly want to see more of your work, Miss Sweetwater."

She looked at Aaron, who nodded, his gaze still on my face.

I kept staring back at him, even after Lillian left.

"I always knew you could paint," he said. "But never like this. I love your paintings, Sassy. And not just 'cause you're my, ah…daughter."

"Where's Mama?" I finally asked.

He looked uncomfortable and rubbed his mouth with his hand. "She left me," he said. "After Lindy died."

"Lindy?"

"Our child," he said. "Linda was her real name, but we called her Lindy."

I thought back to the little baby I'd seen them with that day in Crawford. I felt badly now for the way I'd hated her then.

"She had leukemia," he said.

I looked away. "I'm sorry."

He nodded his head.

"And Kyle?"

"On his third marriage. He works odd jobs, mostly carpentry. He lives about a mile from me."

"Oh," I said.

"He's got a drug problem, Sassy, but he's doing much better."

I looked away again. I remembered how much Kyle had loved the theater, how much he wanted to act. I shook Kyle out of my thoughts. I still hated him.

"Where's Mama?" I asked again.

Aaron took a long breath.

"I just remarried a few months ago. I loved your mother, Sassy, but she just left me, left me emotionally before she ever left me physically. I couldn't reach her anymore. She barely spoke, got down to about ninety pounds."

"Do you know where she is?" I asked.

He shook his head. "She can't deal with pain. She checks out and she won't let anyone comfort her. I'm sorry, but I have no idea where she is."

I felt the floor give way under me. I heard several people sigh as I landed on my side. I'd hit my head against the side of the wall as I fell. I felt Aaron help me to my feet.

"I'm all right," I said, brushing myself off.

"I'm sorry to upset you." He drew my chin up with his hand. "I'm proud of you," he whispered.

For one brief moment, he had acknowledged me as his. I looked over at his new wife, visible in the crowd because of her height. I wanted to hold on to Aaron forever and at the same time, I couldn't bear him. I wanted to scream out Mama's name. Where the hell was she? How dare Aaron accept it, that she'd just gone? Gone where? Why wasn't he looking for her?

"You sure you're okay?" he asked.

I nodded and put my arms around him. One last moment in time to feel my father's arms. I wished him well.

"Will you visit me?" he asked.

"One day," I said.

I walked out of the show that night and packed my bags. I had planned to stay another week, but I couldn't. I wanted to be with Grandma Edna, to tell her that Mama was missing.

It was raining hard by the time I got to my car. I could hear the thunder all around me and I could see the distant lightning flashes. During the long drive home, I wondered if hating Mama all these years had been the right choice. Now I would carry regret for the rest of my life, while my mama was burdened down with sorrow. We had needed each other, but I had chosen to hide behind some insipid code of honor. *You hurt me? Ha! I can hurt you back better.*

"I'm sorry," I cried as the rain fought the wipers of my car and streaked the window and left the night in opaque shadows. "Oh, Mama, I'm so sorry."

I found Grandma Edna in her favorite living room chair watching reruns of that show she loved about some guy chasing a one-armed man all over the place. Baby Patrick was asleep.

I guess I'm one of those people who wore their heart on their sleeve. I must have looked a wreck when I walked in that night soaking wet, with red swollen eyes, because a look of horror came over Grandma Edna's expression. She was clearly surprised to see me. I hadn't called, I'd just taken off from my own show. I sat on the couch after I removed my soaking jacket and put a shawl around me.

Grandma Edna kept staring at me. "Are you going to tell me why you chose to drive all the way back here in a wretched storm when you're supposed to be receiving compliments on your glorious artwork in North Carolina?"

I put my head in my hands and started crying. Poor Grandma Edna didn't know what to do. She came and put her arms around me and held me close. I couldn't speak for at least ten minutes, my tears were coming on so strong. Finally I was able to tell her what happened with Mama, that she'd gone and left Aaron and no one knew where she was.

"Her daughter died," I said. "That poor little girl got leukemia and died."

"Oh my God," Grandma Edna said. She remained quiet for a long time. Then she finally spoke. "Losing two children was too much for her, would be too much for anybody to bear. Vi was always so fragile."

She looked at me. Her face looked strained and sallow. "Look, Sassy, I'll hire someone, we'll find out where your mama is. I'm so sorry."

"She didn't lose me, Grandma Edna, she chose not to come for me. She chose to leave me here with you. I didn't die, I'm the one here."

Grandma Edna got up slowly and walked all the way over to the other side of the room. She looked lost in thought.

"Well, if you hire someone, Grandma Edna, we'll find her. It will be all right. We'll find her," I said, thinking I was comforting her as much as myself.

"Sassy," she said as she came back to sit beside me. She took my hand and didn't speak for at least three minutes while my heart was beating overtime. I sensed she was about to tell me something I wasn't going to like hearing.

"I risk losing you for telling you this."

"You won't lose me," I said.

She wiped the tears away from her eyes. I kept her hand in mine as she spoke.

"Your mama did want you," she said. "She always wanted you. Perhaps if I'd let that happen… oh, God, I don't know. I was the one that didn't let you go. She begged me to send you to her, but I wouldn't. I told her she'd never get you away from me, that I wouldn't put you in harm's way. I wouldn't send you anywhere 'til the heat died down."

She turned away. I was still holding her hand but my mouth was open and my heart was still beating fast.

"What heat? What are you talking about?"

"After the fire, Luke Dawson came over here. Luke was your granddaddy's closest friend. He told me he was going to find Aaron and your mama if it took the rest of his life and he was going to kill Aaron and his whole family, execution-style, for what they did to Seamus. Maybe he was just talking but…I believed him. He tried to get it out of me, where they'd gone, and I said I'd never tell him, that he'd have to kill me first and he said if he had to pay for any murder, it was going to be Aaron's and not mine."

She rubbed my hand at that point. I was trying to take in what she was telling me.

"I wouldn't put you in danger," she said. "Your mama and Aaron refused to get far enough away to be safe. I said I'd give them as much money as they needed to get to the ends of the earth, to Europe, if need be, but they refused to leave the South. I could not put your life in jeopardy just 'cause they were being stubborn, Sassy. I knew Luke was more than capable of doing harm. He'd already murdered enough Negroes and that's about as much as he thought of Aaron, no better than a Negro."

"He thought Aaron and Mama killed Seamus?"

"The only thing he accused me of was covering it up. He never would have suspected me, or any of the rest of us. Aaron was the one being threatened. For a while they were following you; it scared me to death. I'm told that Luke hired detectives to find Aaron. If you had known and you'd run away…I can't even let myself think of it. It was only a matter of time, Sassy. Luke kept calling Aaron unfinished business. Luke was a very brutal man and Aaron was hated in this town for not upholding segregation. The laws changed, but people's thinking didn't. Thank God Luke died last year or we'd never have been rid of him. He was convinced that Aaron killed Seamus to save his own skin and collect the insurance money on his store."

I took my hand away and sat back. I wasn't angry at Grandma Edna. I understood her need to protect me, but Mama fought her on it. They'd argued about it. That's what mattered to me, just hearing Grandma Edna tell me the truth, and that's what hurt most now, that I'd turned my back on Mama when she'd wanted me all along.

"It's okay," I said, even though the regret I felt could have stopped my heart.

"I couldn't risk your running away if you knew the truth and you would have run away. I hated lying to you, Sassy. I know how much it hurt you to feel that kind of rejection."

"It's okay," I said again.

"Life is difficult…sometimes unbearable. All I want to do is keep you safe and untroubled and I come up against fate each time. I can't fight the hands of fate. I can't promise you that it will always turn out your way."

I noticed how defeated she'd become, how she sunk back down in her chair.

"It's okay. I understand why you lied to me, maybe I would have done it, too. I'd do anything to protect Patrick."

"Come here, child," she said and held out her arms to me. I went into them gladly. "Bad news travels like waves, monsoon tidal waves that threaten to take you under, but then they disappear and it's like they were never there. Soon, you're standing in the sun, laughing in the rain. Trust me, Sassy. Maybe not tomorrow, comes the healing, but someday, change just turns out to be what it is."

She reached over and handed me a newspaper.

"I wanted you to see this before you heard it. I want you to be strong."

By that time I truly knew my heart would stop. "What is it?" I asked.

"There's an announcement in the paper, Betsy Lou Buttercup and Thomas Tierney are engaged."

It was like someone had slapped me down hard. I dropped the paper to the floor. I started crying again like I'd never stop.

"These tidal waves just about killed me tonight, Grandma Edna," I managed to get out.

CHAPTER THIRTY-TWO

The private detective we'd hired to find Mama came up 'bout as empty as some old, dried-up well. Her last known address had been in Tennessee. She'd worked as a waitress at a roadside restaurant outside of Memphis. We were surprised to learn that a hospital in Atlanta had admitted her for a nervous breakdown the following year, but she was released after three weeks. She'd been briefly married to some man named Benjamin Morris from Knoxville for six months. But her trail seems to have stopped entirely in 1970. She wasn't collecting any wages from any job nor were there any further marriage licenses nor any other known children. Neither was there a death record for any Violet McLaughlin, Violet McLaughlin Littleton, or Violet McLaughlin Morris.

"Doesn't mean we'll never find her, Sassy," Grandma Edna said. "She'll show up somewhere."

I was determined to look for Mama if it took the rest of my life. I wanted her to know my son. I wanted her to see June-bug again. More than anything in the world I wanted to say I was sorry for being stupid as a choir full of tone-deaf atheists in a Catholic church at Christmas.

Truth was, I found life to bear a weight. I wondered if all lives were as heavy as mine. Oh, I could grab happy moments, cherished for their fleeting tendencies. I think that's why childhood is so blessed; it is natural for childhood to be unburdened by life's unwelcomed torpedoes. One can only pray for that, pray for one's child, that that freedom to indulge in frivolity remain unhindered. Time enough for the world to beat you up, time enough to suffer losses that take you to the bottom of the sea and hold you there like pins to a magnet. Maturity is longer than all the smiles of childhood. All the bombardments that come at you, like stones in your hands and in your pockets, that's the weighted future you face. I was burdened by the lack of buoyancy in my life, but, at least, I was released from the full forces of misfortune by the presence of my son, my sweet Patrick Toulouse.

After I found out that Thomas and Betsy Lou had married, I made great effort to rise above it somehow, to forget the moments Thomas and I had shared. I was determined to put Thomas Tierney out of mind and spirit. I had lost enough, like some threatened wretched organ that had been necessary for the breath I took or the flow of my blood, I had to stand strong and claim it back. Yes, when Thomas married Betsy Lou I was no longer whole, I was wounded. If wounded people don't heal, they bleed for the rest of their lives and between my mama and Thomas, I had no salve for the depths of my scar.

Maybe that's why I married Dixie. I saw no reason not to when he showed up on my doorstep looking like a forlorn wayfarer.

"Hello, Sassy," he said, standing there very much like the last time I'd seen him, except his hair was long, tied back in a ponytail, and he'd grown a mustache. I must have looked as shocked as I felt.

He instinctively put his hand to his hair. "Oh," he said. "I've become a dissenter."

"Oh, really?" I couldn't help but smile. He still wore his khakis and his loafers. It made him an odd dichotomy. He should have been in torn jeans with love beads around his neck.

"War is hell," he said. "May I come in?"

I stepped aside and held the door for him. "I didn't know you went to war."

He stood in the middle of the room and looked around, as though he'd never been there before. Patrick Toulouse came running up to him, giggling with every step and screeching as Dixie picked him up and swung him around in the air.

"Nothing looks the same," he said, "including Patrick. He got big." Dixie looked at me and I smiled and nodded my head in agreement.

"You went to war?" I asked again.

"Hell no," he said. "Doesn't mean I can't be a dissenter, does it?"

We went through the usual small talk about me looking so good and him looking so good and how I wasn't sure I liked his long hair and the whole time we were catching up little Patrick Toulouse sat on his lap and played with his ponytail. In the air between us an electrical charge was snapping. The presence of it surprised me.

"You never answered my letters," he said.

I wasn't sure how to respond to that. If there was any good excuse at all that I could find to get out of my mouth, I would have. Or maybe my best defense was mysterious and ambiguous silence.

"I didn't want you to think…" My voice trailed off.

Dixie stood up and came over to me. I was sitting on the arm of a chair. He grabbed me and kissed me long and hard. I felt my heart pounding in my chest. I didn't push him away. My body responded and why not? I wasn't dead. My true love was a myth. No man is worthy of trust, so why deny myself the simple pleasures of physical fun?

My son was staring at us, giggling as usual. He found my kissing Dixie about as hysterical as he found my temper. He clapped his little hands together. "Mommy kiss, kiss," he said.

Dixie laughed and stood back, still holding my hands. "It hurt me not to hear from you," he said. My body was still trembling, not at all in sync with my head.

"I can bring him up to Grandma Edna. We could be alone." I winked and watched the look that came over his face. He might have been Napoleon at Waterloo, he looked so pleased with himself.

"I brought you something." He reached into his pocket. "Close your eyes."

I felt the ring as he slipped it on my finger. When I opened my eyes I saw that it was a diamond about as big as a dime.

"Absence makes the heart grow fonder, doesn't it?" He grinned. "You can't fool me. You knew the torment of not hearing from you would snare me good."

"Dixie," I said. "I don't…"

He cut me off. "I don't drink anymore," he said. "I know I'm being presumptuous, but I knew you weren't involved with anyone. I have my spies."

I shook my head. All I could think about was Thomas. There I was, too young to have ever shaken the hand of reason. You see mistakes when they pass before your eyes, problem though, is in not seeing them clearly enough. I thought of Mama. *You hurt me? Ha! I can hurt you back better. The hell with you, Thomas Tierney.*

"I'll be right back," I said and picked up baby Patrick, thinking, *Yes, what the hell, what the hell, what the hell.*

I walked up to the farmhouse with nothing in my head but air and some wild, physical desire that needed to be satisfied. Nothing mattered but satisfaction and being able to uninhibitedly respond to the needs of my own body, to react the way I used to with my nails digging deep into Dixie's skin.

He was naked when I got back, standing in my living room with his small and muscular body. He'd let his ponytail loose and his blond hair flowed down his back. It made my heart pound in my chest as I tore off my clothes and jumped into his arms, pulling his hair back, biting on his neck, pulling on his testicles like I was picking apples from the tree. He broke away from me and ran. I chased him, reaching out, slapping his backside. I heard him yelp as I threw him to the floor and mounted him. I pulled his head to the ground and we went at it with a fierce pounding, like a wild bronco ride. He screamed in his satisfaction and I screamed in mine, praying Grandma Edna could not hear my release. It had been so fast, so animalistic, but intensely pleasurable.

"Dawggonit, girl," he yelped, as I lay exhausted in his arms on the living room rug. "That's the Sassy I remember."

CHAPTER THIRTY-THREE

There were concessions, of course, that I insisted on after we married. I would not leave the home that Grandma Edna had built for me and I would not leave Grandma Edna alone. I don't know what Dixie thought of the idea of moving into my barnlike loft, but he agreed to everything I asked, even when I insisted that June-bug remain at the house with us.

"Aw, Sassy," he whined. "I've got allergies."

"Take pills," I said.

We were married by a justice of the peace. I did not want a big wedding, which disappointed Dixie no end, but Dixie did whatever I asked. He even cut his hair and went back to work as a bank manager, which pleased me, because he'd been toying with the idea of doing nothing.

"I don't want some hippie dissenter hanging out in my yard," I insisted.

Dixie treated Grandma Edna with the utmost respect, but he never warmed to her. The only member of my family that Dixie took to was Seth's wife, Agatha, whom we only saw at holidays. Dixie loved to get beaten up by women and Agatha nailed him to the ground on several occasions. I think it was sexually arousing for Dixie to have her refer to him as a misogynistic asshole and a macho ape.

The sexual crescendo I had felt the day Dixie had asked me to marry him had dissipated over the next few years of our marriage and my sexual passion was never to reach such heights again. He was disappointed to have me so unresponsive and he'd often beg me to hurt him, to bite or hit him. I did so, but without any energy behind it. It eventually became mechanical to please Dixie. I wasn't much of a good wife in other ways, either. I didn't cook his dinners, nor did I massage his back, darn his socks. But at the very least, I sure looked good in an evening dress when Dixie dragged me out to his bank's award dinners and company parties. I was the perfect Southern wife for Dixie. By the time we'd begun the fourth year of our marriage, he'd been given a vice president title at the bank and we were living a pretty good life, not without the knowledge that something was missing between us, but it was still pretty good.

We socialized with people I had about as much in common with as I would a Chinese-dumpling chef. Dixie didn't much care for my friends, either, and still referred to my paintings as reflections of a binge walk on the moon or the brush strokes of a hashish addict. I ignored his insults as he ignored mine, insults that increased every year until it depressed me to no end to be sitting there in the evenings, an intolerable, obstinate silence between us like we'd each just received imminent messages of doom. When we did speak, it was angry, reactive, and as scathing as an open wound.

As Dixie watched Patrick Toulouse grow taller every year, I knew he was still searching for gold, for a telltale similarity. I knew what he was thinking, what he still hoped to find. I knew, but I avoided the subject like a discussion of democracy with Fidel Castro.

The insults toward Patrick had begun with sarcasm and snide innuendos after it was clear that whatever Dixie had been searching for he hadn't found.

"You look like a sissy in those shorts. You want to be a sissy, Patty-cakes?"

I stood to my full height and kicked Dixie in the shins, but I knew I couldn't protect my son from this man's stupidity forever. What was he saying when I wasn't around to tell Patrick that Dixie had been a sissy himself and was just projecting?

"Ever hear from that Thomas guy?" Dixie asked, out of the blue, making me blush so fast I didn't have time to bury my face behind a magazine. He rubbed his leg like he was rubbing out a stain. "You kick me again, I'll kick you back," he said with a snarl.

"No," I said. "I never hear from that Thomas guy."

Patrick was growing so quickly that I could no longer call him Baby Patrick or even Patrick Toulouse, without eliciting a scowl, a rare facial expression from my son. He was still such a happy, good-natured boy, still giggling over the most unusual things like monster movies and funerals. He even took Dixie's insults with a grain of salt.

"His wife just got out of some sanatorium in Richmond," Dixie said.

"Sanatorium, Betsy Lou?"

"Yeah, she's a drunk, an alcoholic."

"Seems you two still have a lot in common," I said, staring at the glass in his hand.

"Shut the fuck up," he said.

I stared at my son, who repeated what Dixie had just said. The dysfunction was disturbing me so deeply that I wanted to kill Dixie Craft.

"Take June-bug outside," I said to Patrick.

I found myself sinking into the chair. "How do you know so much about Betsy Lou?" I asked.

"She writes to me."

"She writes to you?" the news brought me to my feet.

"Yeah, over at the bank. She mails the letters there." He noticed my expression. "I guess she didn't want you to know, being that she, ah, snared the man of your dreams." He laughed. "She might just snare another one, you never know."

"What's that supposed to mean, Dixie?"

"Nothing," he said. "Nothing."

We sat in silence for a while. He was reading a book and I was going through some papers, bills that were overdue.

"Can you pay these tomorrow?" I asked. "I'm going to be out of here early, not home 'til late."

He stared at me without answering. "Betsy Lou says she hates him."

My head sprang up. "Who?"

"Your old beau, baby."

I didn't want to talk about Thomas. I couldn't bear the thought that he and Betsy Lou were married, was never able to bear it.

"I asked you never to bring her name up to me, Dixie."

He laughed. "Yeah, I forgot, she stole him from you. Didn't take much, did it?"

Of course I wondered about the state of Thomas's marriage to Betsy Lou, but it was essentially none of my business. Still, how long would he tolerate a wife with a drinking problem? Then again, how long would I tolerate Dixie?

Be that as it may, I had my life now and Thomas had his. Thinking about him was still painful, still felt like an exposed sore dunked in hot oil. Dixie's news was not necessarily surprising. Rumors had gotten back to Beaufort about how Betsy Lou was embarrassing Thomas because she was always drunk, falling-down, nasty drunk, accusing him of carrying a torch for a woman who fornicated her way through France and had a baby out of wedlock with no known father. I couldn't go into Rocket's without overhearing the saga of Thomas Tierney's life with his drunk of a wife.

"God," I mentioned to Grandma Edna, "Betsy Lou is still holding on to the past, isn't she? Still hating me for doing nothing, or so that's what I hear."

Grandma Edna gave me one of those wise looks. "Always a little truth in rumor. He's got you in his heart, Sassy. Seems clear there was never any room for Betsy Lou Buttercup and she knew it. Drinking is no more than a reaction to something."

"Why'd he marry her then?" I said.

"Hurt me? Ha! I'll hurt you back better." She smiled. I had told her what I felt about Mama, that I was so intent on hurting her back I couldn't recognize how much I was needed, how much I loved her.

"Seems you two have that in common, Sassy. It's called pride. When you have too much of it, it bites you in the ass."

My marriage to Dixie was a fog in my brain keeping me stupid. It was like living inside a bunch of boxes that kept getting smaller and smaller. He was cheating on me, of course. After only a few months of marriage, I found it hard to even lay beside him, so I couldn't blame his infidelities. Rumors got back to me that he picked up a woman a week. He would have been the perfect match for Betsy Lou as far as I was concerned; they'd both gotten hooked on the same drug. Dixie had probably never stopped drinking. He always had scotch or Bourbon when he got home from work and it seemed to me that when he picked up the bottle he never put it down. So he'd lied about being on the wagon, same way he lied and said he loved me and Patrick, when it was clear he didn't. He'd won me. That's all I ever was, a prize, a notch in his belt.

By the fifth year of our marriage, he couldn't get to work in the mornings from drinking so much the night before and he lost his job. His father was sending him a check every week to help him feel respectable, but it didn't help. I knew Dixie's downfall was coming, but I couldn't stop it. He was the same man he'd always been, basically a master BS artist. If you told him he drank too much, he'd tell you too much of a good thing is too little of your business. He was losing everything right before my very eyes: respect, prestige, promise, but I couldn't give anything back to help him. I couldn't save Dixie from himself, which isn't to say I wasn't feeling guilty for it, wasn't feeling like I was somehow to blame.

Dixie was withdrawing more and more from Patrick, treating him like he was a nuisance. I could see how much it hurt my son, but I couldn't even talk to Dixie about it. The day I tried, he told me that Patrick wasn't his so why should he give a shit.

"Look at him," he said. "He doesn't look like me."

"He doesn't look like me, either."

He grabbed me by the shoulders and he was holding me so tightly that I thought I'd faint.

"You're hurting me, Dixie," I said. "Let go."

"Hurting is good," he said. "Isn't it? You like to hurt. That's all you do is hurt." He slapped me hard across my face. Next thing I knew Patrick had jumped on his back and was hitting him all over.

"I hate you," he kept screaming, "I hate you."

June-bug took hold of Dixie's leg and started pulling him and growling.

Dixie threw Patrick to the floor and kicked the dog back. I started yelling threats of death as I socked Dixie in his head. Next thing I knew, Dixie had driven off in his newest Corvette and I was on the ground tending to my son's sore knees and making sure he hadn't broken one of June-bug's ribs, knowing it was time to do something before Dixie really did hurt one of us. I knew it certain then. I had to get out of the marriage.

Chapter Thirty-Four

If there was a hole deep enough, I would have jumped into it so my son couldn't see my suffering. By that time, I knew who Patrick's father was and I understood the developing rage Dixie was feeling. I'd found out quite by accident and I still could have been mistaken. There was no proof to it, really, but I knew what I was seeing; it seemed as clear as fresh water.

My pudgy, little baby had grown tall and wiry. He was nearly eight years old at this time. His hair had become more and more curly with the years and he was still very blond; his hair was like the color of champagne, a golden beige. He looked exactly like his personality: cherubic and sweet; there were no surprises. But he still didn't resemble any one in either Dixie's family or mine. Truth was, he didn't look like Thomas Tierney, either, but if I had to say who came closest to claiming his features, I would have said Thomas, hands-down.

One day I was driving over to Charleston. I was taking Patrick with me. It was summer and I had promised him lunch in this restaurant over by the river where he could watch the riverboats pass. I'd decided to gas up at a garage where the truckers go 'cause the gas was cheaper and Patrick wanted a soda from the machine. He loved putting nickels in the coke machine over at the Texaco, especially when he could get change back from it. He said he liked the sound it made.

I pulled up at the pump and Patrick went over to the old red machine. His coins must have gotten stuck because some man came and started helping Patrick try and get the coin out, he started looking up inside the coin drop with some sort of stick.

I couldn't believe my eyes. The man at the coke machine was the spittin' image of my son. I got out of the car.

"What's the problem?" I asked as I stood there staring at the poor guy. He looked to be in his late forties, early fifties. His curly blond hair was streaked gray.

The man laughed. "Case of the missing nickel," he said. "Don't worry, we'll get it."

I studied his face, the laugh line near his blue eyes, the humor in his expression and the handsome, chiseled features, not as perfect as Thomas's had been, but handsome in a non-assuming way. My eyes went to his mouth, the curve of his lip. *My God, this is just too bizarre.*

"Hey, Tierney," someone yelled out, "you coming or what?"

My head snapped back and forth. "Tierney?" I said.

"Yeah, Jake Tierney." He stared at me. "Do I know you?"

"I may have gone to school with your son," I stammered, feeling the heat rise to my face.

"Thomas?"

I felt myself go weak at the knees. I managed to squeak out, "Yes."

"Happy to have him back home now. You can go see him. He lives in Charleston. My son is a lawyer, got a practice there."

He was beaming when he said it. The coin fell to the ground and Patrick scooped it up.

I couldn't believe that I'd just witnessed my son's grandfather standing at a Coke machine. Don't ever think that the absurd and the ridiculous are far from reach. It's everywhere. When your time comes, there you'll be, calling it fate when it's nothing more than the ridiculous coincidences of life.

I found the coincidence to be a sign of something. Out of all the people in Beaufort, I had run into Thomas's father. I had seen firsthand my son's face etched in his. I couldn't explain it, but it made me happy to know this. I'd been holding on to guilt too long. Dixie was not Patrick's father, wasn't even his father in name only. He was treating the boy like crap, taking his frustrations out on my son. First thing I did was call Aunt Peg.

"Look in your crystal ball, Aunt Peg. Find my future."

"Why?" she asked. "You going somewhere?"

"I'm going to divorce Dixie."

"Oh no," she said. "I see you married a long time, Sassy."

"Oh?" Not exactly what I wanted to hear. "Do you see anything else?" I asked. "Any changes?"

"No," she said. "You're not going anywhere."

"Damn."

"Oh, but, there's misfortune. I feel that you will be very sad for a while. I'll read your cards tonight. Maybe there's more."

"I don't want to be sad," I said.

"It will pass. It will work out, whatever it is."

Aunt Peg hadn't helped, she'd just reminded me that life is like a bowling ball on a magic carpet headed into gusty winds with me standing directly under it.

Chapter Thirty-Five

People who never loved a dog will never know how deeply an animal claims your heart. Mine broke and my son's broke the day we lost June-bug. She was fourteen years old and never been sick a day in her life, then, out of nowhere, she was spitting up blood and we were told she had some sort of terminal cancer. The humane thing to do was to put her down. Her spirit was so close to mine that when I saw the life leave her, I thought I'd never smile again. I'd loved that animal so, like a dog soul mate, a companion truly mine. In all the things we make up about heaven, in my heaven my June-bug will always be there, waiting.

I tried to protect Patrick from the loss, but he was so distraught that there was nothing I could do to console him. I took him into Charleston to watch the Riverboats thinking it might cheer him, but he couldn't stop crying and asking after June-bug, making me explain over and over again how she could have ever possibly left us.

"Where did she go, Mama? Please can we bring her back?"

"We all go to God's home," I said. "It's a journey not a one of us escapes. One day though, we may reunite. June-bug had too much spirit, Patrick, too much love, to go very far from us."

He quieted down a bit, thinking about June-bug as an invisible presence, eternally there wherever he turned, seemed to comfort him.

I took his hand. The sky had a smoky, overcast shadow. Suddenly, mysterious life, fatalistic and all knowing, grabbed hold of my soul.

"When pain is there you're much more perceptive," Aunt Peg had said. If there's a bottom inside of us, a place that goes no deeper because you're as deep as deep can get, then I had been tossed into that place. I felt that I might expire. I looked to my son to ground me, but a voice I hadn't heard in years broke through and pulled me back from the depths of my own heartbreak.

"Hello, Sassy."

I didn't have to turn, his voice ran through my veins and flowed within my blood. I began to bawl like a baby, huge horrible sobs. I began to tremble like I had the chills, though the day was hot. Poor Patrick put his thin, little arms around me.

Thomas Tierney had walked in front of us as though I had only seen him yesterday, like he was a natural occurrence in my life. The compassion in his face was sweeter than a lullaby. I cried more deeply as I stared at him; it was as if a dam beneath my skin had broken. My outburst upset Patrick and he cried right along with me.

Our obvious distress disturbed Thomas and he stared at us, not quite knowing what to do.

"We had to put our dog down," I said.

I was overcome with loss, for June-bug, for Thomas, and for Mama. I was crying like I'd never stop from all the hurts and losses I'd endured. These people had caused me too much grief, events had hurt me much too deeply. I knew it was upsetting Patrick to see me so entirely out of control and I tried to pull myself together, but life packs a wallop sometimes and sometimes, you haven't the strength to throw a punch back.

Thomas sat on the bench beside us. "When I lost my dog, it was the worst day of my life," Thomas said. "But it's like with people, you never lose them once they've touched you and you've loved them." He looked at me and I knew I blushed. "Someday," Thomas continued, "it will all come together, all the special things, like your dog and your mama and everyone else that's owned a piece of your heart. It will be there for you to embrace again, all of it."

Patrick stared at Thomas. Somehow he'd been soothed by him.

"Your son?" Thomas asked.

"Yes," I whispered. I didn't know what to say. I knew he'd rise to his feet at some point and walk away, but I didn't know what to say to keep him there.

Thomas stared at Patrick. "You're a handsome young man," he said. "What's your name?"

Patrick suddenly fell into silence, as speechless as I was.

"Patrick Toulouse," I said. "That's his name."

Thomas spread his long legs out in front of him, but he was facing me, staring at me.

"Toulouse Lautrec?" he asked. "Any connection? That's the only Toulouse I can think of."

"Yes," I said. "I always liked him, his paintings."

"Me too," Thomas said.

"Thomas…" I began. "I'm so sorry."

"I always loved his *Rosa de Rouge*. Do you know it? I took an art class in college. That painting stayed with me."

"Yes," I said softly. "I know it." It was a portrait of a woman with red hair. She looked like an artist, I always thought, so independent and mysterious.

"It reminded me of you," he said.

"I've never stopped thinking of us," I whispered. "How we were."

I saw his face change. The compassion was at once replaced with a distracted stare.

"I hope you've been well," he said.

My son sat stoically between us, staring from my face to Thomas's.

"Sometimes," I said.

"I take my lunch here at the river," he told me. "I always sit at this bench." He opened the wax paper and I smelled mustard and baloney. "I don't work far from here."

He turned away from me. "Look," he said, "the riverboat." He looked at Patrick and smiled. "Do you like riverboats?"

Patrick produced a replica of a riverboat from his pocket, a toy I had found him at some tourist trap across the street. "I can build them from scratch," he said.

"I have to go," I said and stood. I wiped my eyes with my hand. I knew I looked a wreck. I knew the worst thing I could have ever said was *I have to go* and I wondered why in hell I'd said it.

He looked up at me and searched my face as I stood there.

"I'm sorry about your dog," he said. Then he put his hand on Patrick's shoulder. "No one will ever take her place, but I'll bet you'll meet another dog someday that you'll love almost as much."

"Yeah, maybe it will be a funny dog, with a flat face," Patrick said.

I looked into Thomas's eyes. In them I saw the same longing I was feeling, but I held to my manners, my pretenses, though I wanted to cling to him forever.

"Or maybe she will be beautiful, with long red hair and eyes like the shadows of dusk." He looked at me and I almost started to weep again.

Patrick laughed. I held on to the bench for support. "Thomas," I began, though I wasn't quite sure of what I wanted to say.

Thomas finished his sandwich and rolled up the paper it had been wrapped with. I remained silent for at least ten minutes, with so much to say and no way to say it. At one point Thomas offered to split his sandwich with me and I shook my head, but he tore off a piece for Patrick.

"I didn't think he liked baloney," I said finally, trying to smile.

Thomas walked a few feet away and threw the garbage into a trash can. I couldn't move. I stood there like a fool. He came back and put his hand over mine.

"Good to see you, Sassy," he said softly and then he turned and continued down the pathway. I watched until he was out of sight. He didn't turn back.

Perhaps I had been touched by madness. Had I actually had a brief encounter with Thomas Tierney or had I imagined it, fallen asleep under the sun and dreamed it?

When I got back home, Dixie was in front of the television with a Bourbon in his hand. I hadn't ever mentioned the word divorce, though I'd thought of little else over the years. I kept grabbling with it and finally, I'd made up my mind to do it, but then June-bug got sick and I knew we were going to have to put her down. It would be difficult for Patrick to lose the only man he'd associated as his father so soon after losing his dog. So I'd put it off, but I wouldn't stall a moment more, not now. It was good for me and for my son, to move on.

Dixie's drinking had escalated and, mostly, I blamed Erin and Uncle Austin for it. That's the thing about drunks, they seek each other out, feed each other's illness. Uncle Austin had been in retirement for years now and it was the worst thing that could have happened to him. He was bored. Aunt Erin, who'd always been a drinker, was now a full-blown alcoholic. They grew more and more fond of Dixie and he eventually warmed to them and confided in them, most likely about me and how miserable I made him. Their remedy was Bourbon and Dixie took to it like a thirsty man in a desert saloon.

"It's only a goddamn dog," he yelled at me as I started weeping again over June-bug. "Shut up." I felt like I was drowning and that seeing Thomas had made me aware that I couldn't swim, couldn't save myself unless I made a plan, a means of escape, found a life vest. Unless I took control of my life and got rid of the one thing that was bringing it down, I would drown.

I took a consensus of Dixie's level of intoxication and came to the conclusion that he was still an hour or so away from total inebriation.

"I loved that dog, Dixie," I said, hating him for his remark. I prayed for just a moment of strength. I listened carefully. I was sure Patrick was sound asleep by now. We'd come back from Charleston tired and drained. I feared that Dixie would start screaming after I asked him for a divorce. I knew I should have taken Patrick up to the farmhouse, but I was distracted and nervous.

I stood to my feet and turned off the television. "Dixie," I said quickly after a deep breath. "I want a divorce."

Maybe seeing Thomas again had given me the guts to carve out a life for myself that didn't include Dixie Craft. Giving Patrick a bad father was worse than not having a father at all. I knew I'd never have Thomas again, but maybe I'd have someone else; maybe just getting rid of Dixie would be all it would take to make me happy.

"What?" Dixie looked at me like I'd said something so low that he couldn't hear. He seemed puzzled.

"I want a divorce," I repeated, louder this time.

I will never be able to describe his expression, it was completely unnatural. He clenched his teeth and stood up. His breathing was erratic. I suddenly became afraid.

"What the hell are you talking about?"

"I want a divorce," I said calmly and for the third time, wondering where I was getting my resolve, my focus.

"You want a what? A divorce, you stupid bitch? You're getting nothing but older and stupider."

He came at me and grabbed my hair. I felt myself being pulled. My scalp felt like it was being ripped from my head. Dixie was dragging me into the kitchen. My first thought was knives. He was going to kill me.

"Please," I begged, "you'll wake Patrick."

He slapped me twice across my face. "Yes, let's wake him. Let's let him know what a whore his mother is."

He turned up the burners on the gas range and held my right hand over the fire.

"You think you can paint? You can't do shit. You can't raise nothing but a sissy, a bastard. Some strange fucking idiot you screwed in France, just like Betsy Lou said, is responsible for that little turd. He doesn't look like anyone. You think I can't see that? He's a product of your sex orgies." His face was red and the sweat was pouring off him.

"Please, please, Patrick may wake up. Please don't subject him to this."

He brought my hand to the fire while I fought him. I screamed. I didn't want to, but I was so afraid of what he was about to do. He was trying to burn my hand off. I kept screaming while we struggled. Suddenly, I heard the door slam. Dixie pushed me to the floor and jumped on me. His fist was in the air when a shot rang out loud and clear.

"Get out of this house and don't ever come back you son of a bitch."

Grandma Edna stood there, her hand was as steady as a clock's tick. The gun was pointed at Dixie's forehead. He was bleeding badly from his arm.

"Get out of here," she repeated. "I'm not above killing you, Dixie Craft, not above burning your rotten carcass in acid. Now get."

"I can't drive," Dixie screamed. "You shot me."

"Count of three or I'll shoot you again."

Dixie tore off his shirt and wrapped it around his shoulder. He stumbled out the door and got in to his car. Grandma Edna grabbed me and called an ambulance. My hand was red and swollen. He'd burned it badly. I passed out. When I woke up I was in the ER all bandaged up.

Chapter Thirty-Six

I filed a police report against Dixie. I also started divorce proceedings. I wasn't going to be able to use my right hand for a while, so I spent a lot of time moping around since I couldn't paint. I couldn't get Thomas off my mind, despite my present circumstances. I'd seen him, had an opportunity to talk to him, and yet nothing but nonsense came out of my mouth that afternoon in Charleston. I'd heard through the grapevine that he'd left Betsy Lou right before leaving Virginia and she'd remained there and remarried. Grapevine also told me that Thomas was seeing someone in Charleston named Rita Marlowe, also an attorney. I had the feeling that Thomas and I had grown apart, that what was, was, and he was on his healing path. Now I needed to get on mine.

It depressed me that Thomas didn't know he had a son and he had no idea I still carried a torch for him. I needed to face facts. I'd lost Thomas eight years ago and I wasn't ever going to get him back.

My son had been awakened from his sleep the night Dixie held my hand over the stove and Grandma Edna shot him. I don't know what he saw, or even what he understood, but he never mentioned Dixie's name again. I think he'd always sensed that Dixie had become contemptuous of him and though he couldn't articulate it, he knew that I had been unhappy and now I wasn't as unhappy. He was resilient, my Patrick Toulouse, and our life went on, almost as if Dixie had never been in it.

I avoided Charleston because I didn't want to run into Thomas again. We were separated by time and I didn't even know what I felt anymore, now that I'd seen him for real. We really hadn't had much to say to each other. Perhaps that was an indication of the miles that had been put between us by life's unexpected misfortunes.

I was still afraid of Dixie; he was too volatile, too capable of showing a very bad temper, fused by alcohol. I heard he was still hanging out with Aunt Erin and Uncle Austin, which infuriated Grandma Edna and I. We banished them from visiting us as long as they were befriending someone as evil and dangerous as Dixie Craft. Thing about alcoholics, though, is that they don't make friendships, they make drinking buddies. All Dixie Craft had to do was show up with a bottle of Bourbon and he was an okay guy who'd just been brought to insanity by the bitch he'd married. Aunt Erin and Uncle Austin had literally chosen Dixie over us and Dixie used that relationship to remain, however loosely, tied to me.

But it wasn't only Aunt Erin and Uncle Austin fueling my fire, it was Aunt El. I'd found out from Grandma Edna that she was about to sell the fifty acres of land that included Hammertown, Dudley's precious slave town, Dudley's special place. I took a trip up to Macon, Georgia to try and talk Aunt El out of selling it. I could never get her on the phone. She said she had an answering machine now and didn't need to pick up the phone anymore. I guess my angry messages about selling Hammertown didn't give her much incentive to call me back.

She and Aunt Earline had a beautiful old Victorian house with a driveway so winding it made my arms hurt just getting up there. I had heard that Earline had bought herself a beauty parlor in town and Aunt El spent her time investing, buying land, and traveling around checking up on the few mills we had left. I didn't even know if I'd find Aunt El home, but if not, maybe I could persuade Aunt Earline to talk sense to her. Aunt Earline didn't travel around with Aunt El as much as she used to. That beauty parlor was her whole life and she got all involved in the lives of her clients, befriending their misfortunes and celebrating their weddings and amateur theater night openings and baptisms and bar mitzvahs.

I was happy to see Aunt El's car in the driveway, sitting there with the top down, surrounded by lilac bushes in bloom and sweeping willows. The second car in the driveway was a white convertible, a pretty sharp little Mustang.

Aunt El was so surprised to see me she blushed red as a beefsteak tomato. I noticed she was wearing shorts down to her knees and a T-shirt. Her hair was all messed up.

"Sassy!" she said and stared at me like I had a shotgun pointed at her.

"Why don't you answer your phone?" I said and walked in.

"What the hell are you doing here?"

She looked confused and her gaze went to the top of the stairs.

My natural instinct was to follow her gaze, right on up to some pert little blonde woman, half-naked, leaning over the banister.

My eyes shot back to El. *What the hell?*

"You cheating on Earline?"

She gulped and I knew I'd caught my aunt in some kind of clandestine lesbian affair.

"Well, are you?" I repeated.

"What happened to your hand?"

"Don't change the subject."

She grabbed my arm and took me into her living room while the pert blonde lady went back into the bedroom and shut the door.

"It's not what you think."

"Yes, it is," I said. I made myself comfortable and gave her a wicked smile. "Now, about Hammertown?"

"He's never coming back, Sassy."

"What?"

"Dudley, he's never going to come back down South."

"Sell the land to me, Aunt El."

"No, we all own it."

"Then I say I won't sell it." I looked up the stairs again. "I thought you people didn't act like the rest of the world."

"You're reading too much into this, Sassy."

"What's her name?"

"None of your business."

"Earline know about this?"

"Nothing to know."

"You sell that land and I'll be putting that to the test."

"Why, you little shit." She stood. "You want to destroy my marriage?"

"Destruction is something we're prone to in this family."

She sat back down. "Okay, you win. I won't sell it. I'm the only one in the family really wanted to dump it anyway. Just keep your mouth shut."

"It's Dudley's town, Dudley's land, Aunt El. He just loved it up there."

"We gave Pike and James Leroy thirty acres plus the house."

"That's Pike and James Leroy. I want Hammertown for Dudley."

"If he ever comes back here, they'll fry him."

"I won't give up the land in his honor." I stared at her. "I believe in honor."

She shook her head. "I'm just having fun," she said, "that's all."

"You stink, but thanks for not selling. I want Hammertown put in my name, along with the surrounding acres."

She made a little sound in the back of her throat. "You speak to your grandma about this?"

"She's left it up to you, you know that. I'll let her know you decided not to get rid of it."

"What? I didn't say I wasn't selling, did I?"

"Yes, as a matter of fact, you did. Hammertown, Aunt El. All fifty acres, or I'll drive right on over to Aunt Earline quick as a tick finds a dog's back."

"You won't."

"Just put it in my name, Aunt El." I held her gaze like a cat about to draw claws.

I couldn't believe that my aunt was no better than a man. I didn't know whether I wanted to laugh or cry. I imagined Aunt El in her travels through Europe, those little suits and ties she liked to wear, now that she felt she had a real set of balls, making eyes at pretty young women, showing off her diamond pinkie ring and flipping her gold-plated cigarette lighter under the batting long eyelashes of willing ladies. I guess making money does that to people.

I had sat there at dinner listening to poor Aunt Earline going on and on about some hairdresser who'd overused the curling iron, wondering what she'd do to my aunt if she knew. I got fifty acres and a town, but Earline would have gotten the whole kit and caboodle, that is, after she'd ridden Aunt El hard and hung her out wet.

I drove back to Carter's Crossing early the next morning, figuring I'd get back by late afternoon. I don't even know why I couldn't part with Hammertown, but it meant something to me. I guess Aunt El was conveniently forgetting that Uncle Liam's old car was hidden behind the hay stacks and that could reopen the murder investigation. Couldn't have anybody finding that old car, traceable for sure. Perhaps Aunt El forgot her own responsibility in that murder. Or maybe Aunt El didn't know there was marijuana all over the place, not that I had any intentions of touching that, but it belonged to Dudley, right or wrong. I had my illusions: Dudley was coming back to claim his town one day, even to claim his vice, fields of marijuana. Someday, I truly believed he would return. Ricky had told me he'd promised Dudley he'd tend to the marijuana plants 'til he got back, damn plants must have been worth a fortune.

As I pulled in toward the barn, I could see Grandma Edna on the porch of the farmhouse where she often sat, but there was someone else up there with her, aside from Patrick. I got out of the car and walked up. The sun was glaring in my eyes, and I couldn't see who it was. My son was playing with a dog on the front lawn.

"Who's that?" I asked Patrick. "Where'd he come from?"

"I hope you don't mind," Thomas said and stood up to greet me. "Frolic had pups. That's my neighbor's dog, Frolic."

I was speechless. Thomas looked so handsome, his eyes against his blue shirt were like magnets seizing me.

"I don't mind," I said. "What kind is she?"

"Retriever," he said.

I got down on my knees and the puppy flopped over in my direction. Thomas sat on the porch rail.

"What you going to call her?" Thomas asked Patrick.

"Foxy," Patrick shouted to us, running around trying to get Foxy to follow. Thomas caught my gaze and smiled. "Yeah," he said. "Foxy seems about right."

Grandma Edna stood to her feet and told Patrick to bring Foxy into the kitchen for some food and water.

"Thank you, Thomas, for your kindness," she said. "You've made Patrick very happy."

I went to the porch railing near where Thomas sat after the screen door slammed behind Grandma Edna, Foxy, and Patrick. I couldn't stop looking at his face.

"I thought it would be too soon to get him another dog." I was being casual, and I laughed a little. "Guess I was wrong."

"I think his broken heart is on the mend," Thomas said.

"Perhaps," I answered bringing my hand so close to his. "But is mine, I wonder." I held his gaze just for a moment. "Is my broken heart anywhere near mending?" For a moment, I felt foolish and vulnerable. "I loved that dog, too," I added.

Thomas looked up toward the sky. "Want to go to the cove?" he asked.

My heart was racing. I didn't know what I expected. I didn't know what I wanted to say, or what I wanted him to say. I jumped off the porch quickly and we started back toward the trail that went down to the cove. We were walking together much like we had that very first time, too shy to speak, too much going on to feel comfortable.

When we got down there some boys were swimming, trespassing on my land, but that wasn't unusual. Where ever there was water, there was going to be people indifferent to signs that warned against stepping one's foot on property that wasn't theirs. I never had the heart to send anyone away, though. The day was hot and I couldn't fault them finding a place to cool off. We walked up several yards from the water and sat down on the ground.

"It's a little damp," Thomas said.

"I don't mind," I said. "It's okay."

I felt awkward. Was this going to be the day I'd tell him that Patrick was his? Would there be any reason not to tell him that?

We made small talk, Thomas and I, like we'd never been so madly in love we couldn't feel the ground under our step. We were blind strangers feeling our way in the dark.

"How's Dixie?" he asked, suddenly.

"We're divorced," I said.

"I'm sorry," he said.

I stood up and walked down toward the cove a bit. The boys were leaving. I turned back to Thomas.

"This is uncomfortable," I said. "You don't give a shit how Dixie is."

"True," he agreed.

"I'm tired of this pussyfooting around, Thomas." He looked at me, a bit shocked, a bit scared even.

"I married Dixie 'cause I was so hurt that you turned away from me, that you married that stupid bitch Betsy Lou. I never loved Dixie."

He was looking at me like I'd lost my mind, that whatever time machine I was held captive by had malfunctioned.

Thomas remained silent, which got me madder. I walked up closer to him. "Goddamnit, Thomas Tierney, why didn't you answer my letter? You owed me that." I slapped him hard across his shoulder. "I never took you for a coward."

"Ouch," he said and stood up to face me. "What letter?"

I had tears streaming down my face, but by this time I didn't care what ran from my nose or my eyes. I was breathing fire.

"I told you everything in that letter, how badly I was hurting, how I didn't want to burden you with my baby, but that I'd take financial responsibility for it."

When I looked at his expression, I could see he was dumbfounded and confused. He walked up to me and put his hands on my arms.

"I never got any letter from you," he said.

I collapsed down to the ground. By this time I was crying and bawling. "I gave it to Betsy Lou to mail for me. We'd just gotten into a cab…and…Oh, god, what does it matter now? She never mailed it? I should have known. I suspected. I just didn't want to believe she'd do that." I looked up at him. "Oh, shit," I said.

"I'm sorry," he said. "She told me a lot of things I never should have paid any attention to, but I was so hurt, so angry at you for not coming back home to me."

"Oh, Thomas," I said. "Can we ever make this right? I never stopped loving you."

Thomas ran his hands through his hair. I wanted to tell him then, about Patrick. In his pause, his unbearable silence, I should have cracked the stability of it, the promise in it. I should have screamed out the truth.

He stood before me and kissed the top of my head. "My marriage to Betsy Lou was the worst thing that ever happened to me. She was so jealous of you. I should have realized that's what her interest in me was all about. She wasn't even someone I liked, but I felt so betrayed by you. I would have done anything to hurt you for not coming back to me. If I'd only gotten that letter, but I didn't. I wouldn't have cared that you had Dixie's baby, it was before my time."

I brought my face to his hands and kissed them, my tears got them wet, but I couldn't stop kissing his hands. I felt him stroke my hair.

"I'm engaged to be married," he said.

I stopped breathing, I know I did. I was so still I could hear my heart pound.

"I'm sorry," he said.

I wanted to throw myself at him and tell him I was raising his son and I didn't want to do it alone, that Patrick needed him, I needed him. But I remained silent. When I picked my head up he had walked away.

"She's a wonderful woman. The wedding is next month."

He hadn't faced me. He was speaking out to the wind, not to me.

I shot up like a thunderbolt and swung him around. When my hand went back there was no stopping the punch I threw. He fell back and rubbed his jaw.

"We're not kids anymore," he said. "You can't do that, damn it."

"You go on and tell me you love this woman, whoever the hell she is. You go on and tell me you love her more than me. Go on and say it."

He looked at the ground. "Can't say it." He looked up at me. "I met her in law school. You were history by then, never wrote, never called. Rita and I dated and got engaged. Plain and simple."

"You're going to marry her?"

"Of course I'm going to marry her. We're engaged."

"That doesn't mean you love her as much as me."

"We had a thing for two weeks, Sassy. I've been dating Rita for two years. We were just a couple of horny kids, you and me."

I took a deep breath. I wanted to kill him, but I restrained myself.

"I want to watch you walk away, Thomas. Don't even look back. You hurt me too much, much more deeply than that punch I threw you. You didn't have to marry Betsy Lou. You don't fight for anything. You don't want anything enough to stay true to it. I can't believe you love anyone more than you love me."

"Sassy, I…"

"I'm going for a swim. When I come out of the water. You best be gone." I turned and started taking off my clothes. I heard the branches snap under his feet as he walked off.

Almost a year later, I took Patrick down to the cove for a swim. I hadn't planned it, but I had been thinking about it. My son deserved the truth and he could do with the truth whatever he chose, but I was no longer going to protect Thomas. Those days were over.

Patrick towel dried his hair while Foxy got us both wet when she shook the water from her fur. I was literally drenched. I took the towel from Patrick and began to dry Foxy off.

"Remember that day we went into Charleston, after we'd put June-bug down?"

"Yeah," Patrick said.

"You remember that man came by with the baloney sandwich?"

Patrick nodded. "Yeah, he came around with Foxy for me a few days later."

"He's your father, Patrick Toulouse," I said. "His name is Thomas Tierney."

Patrick looked at me wide-eyed.

"Only man I ever loved," I said. "Really loved, except for you."

"Then why aren't you with him?" Patrick looked at me like it was just incredulous not to be with the only man you ever loved, the father of your child.

"Blinded by emotion, son," I said. "Blindsided by my own reactionary nature."

Patrick looked off. I felt the relief of finally having told him. I didn't know what he'd do with the truth and I didn't care.

"What are you going to do now, Patrick?" I asked.

"Nothing," he said. "Knowing doesn't change anything, doesn't make him a father, does it?"

CHAPTER THIRTY-SEVEN

Malcolm Marcel Miff said he was a dealer from New Orleans. He walked into my gallery three years after I'd punched Thomas Tierney in the jaw at the creek. I was infatuated from the moment Mr. Miff opened his mouth. But maybe I was just ready to make a fool of myself again.

"Hi," he said. "This place yours?"

"All mine," I said.

"Mr. Miff," he said and held out his hand. I noticed his hands were slender. His grasp felt good, stronger than I had expected. He spent nearly an hour looking at my work and he spent another hour describing my technique and its validity to modern art.

"You're quite a scholar," I said.

He laughed. His gray hair was thick and wavy. His glasses gave him an air of superiority.

"I don't show much of my own work here. It doesn't go over well. But I just happen to have two of my paintings in this week."

"My lucky day," he said. He pulled a rabbit's foot key chain out of his pocket. "Literally."

I looked into his blue eyes, wide and boyish, and I knew he was older, but he didn't really look it. He looked sophisticated, like an old Southern gentleman in white. He wore a straw fedora and in the pocket of his white blazer, I could see a monogrammed handkerchief peeking out.

"You're so pretty, it startles me awake," he said. He took off his jacket and placed it on the back of a chair. He rubbed his eyes.

I knew I was attracted to him the moment he stood near me, put his arm around my shoulder and held me back. "Look," he said. "An interesting choice." He pointed to something on the canvas, but all I could feel was the muscle in his forearm.

I'd been in a dating frenzy for the last three years, almost since the moment I'd walked into the cool waters of the cove and left Thomas to his new fiancé and his new life, his new family that I tried not to think about, especially since our son was growing up without him.

Last I heard Thomas did indeed marry that girl named Rita that he'd met in law school and though I'd hoped he'd come tear assing into my driveway to tell me he'd changed his mind, that didn't happen. There was nothing I could do to alter my unfortunate circumstances but allow myself the luxury of wallowing in my disappointment, which I did, for the next several months. I came out of it because time has a habit, good or bad, of shading the edges of a broken heart with memories that come to mind less and less while we live in the present and forfeit our unfortunate failures in matters of the heart to new dalliances.

I shot through my pining and wallowing for Thomas Tierney like bullets flying and made myself the talk of the town. The farmhouse became known for glamorous parties and for artists who flocked there and flopped there, friends from my days in Paris and my visits to San Francisco and other large cities. My gallery, Sweetwater's, had become a major event in Beaufort and people showed up to socialize and attend my wine tastings as I celebrated art openings and sales of paintings, any excuse to gather a crowd. I was acquiring a reputation of being flamboyant, flirtatious, and fun-loving.

Much to my surprise, Grandma Edna, flowered under the attention of so many people. My son, Patrick Toulouse, showed an interest in art, which thrilled me to death, and he and Grandma Edna went off together to paint barns, just like I had done in my youth. Foxy was always trailing behind, my only memory of Thomas and his kindness that day. I wondered about Thomas, of course, but the ache was gone, or perhaps just covered over with a lot of talk and the whir of my busy life.

Mr. Miff fell in love with my artwork and, not long after, Mr. Miff fell in love with me, or so I thought. I never looked much at older men. Mr. Miff was fifty-five and I had just turned thirty-two. But I never thought of my Mr. Miff as an older man, not really. He was simply my beau, ageless and charming as a Cary Grant film.

He began selling my work at some of the larger galleries in Chicago and New York. He was good to Patrick and they became fast friends. They were alike in so many ways, finding humor, ridiculous humor, in the most mundane circumstances.

"You like him, Patrick Toulouse?" I asked.

"Well, yeah," he said. "I guess."

I don't remember the first moment I realized that I wanted to spend my life as Mrs. Miff. I was comfortable and secure for the first time in my life. I was free from the burdens of misfortune. Wasn't anyone around hurting me that I was aware of. I was about to mount a white charger and steer it into a yellow sun and weep no more.

I seduced Mr. Miff rather quickly, which wasn't hard to do when a man has twenty years on you. "You're easy," I said, and he laughed.

"Were you ever married before?" I asked.

"No," he said, plain and simple. I felt special. There must have been a lot of women in his life, but only I had the ability to seduce him into loving me forever.

We were married in San Francisco, a quiet wedding, with not a one of our family members present. We'd gone out there to visit some museums and quite spontaneously, we'd found a justice of the peace. I knew that my family wasn't taking to Mr. Miff and I thought it was because he was older. I thought they were being biased and silly. Mr. Miff said he didn't have much family, so we were about even. We didn't need them.

"Mr. Miff and I were married," I said as I stood in the doorway of Grandma Edna's bedroom, happy as always to be home. I wasn't sure how she'd take it and I was prepared for an argument. But no matter what, I was still committed to taking care of Grandma Edna, making sure she was not alone in that big house, and since Mr. Miff really didn't care where he lived, we'd remain at Carter's Crossing.

Grandma Edna smiled strangely from her bed. "Why do you call him, Mr. Miff?" she asked.

"It's his name," I said.

"His name is Malcolm," she said. "Is it 'cause he's older?"

"No."

Of course I knew that wasn't true. It was precisely because he was older that I called him Mr. Miff, a joke between us. He'd lecture me, usually about art, but sometimes because I'd say something completely inane, or I'd misjudge someone, so I'd call him Mr. Miff to tease him. *Teacher or husband* I'd say, *which do you prefer?* And he'd grab me and kiss me and I literally would become weak in the knees. He was a bit of a genius, my Mr. Miff. He had made me nearly famous. My art was selling upward of ten thousand a painting. I think I experienced a kind of delirium after meeting Malcolm Miff that I'd never felt before. There certainly was something to older men, hard to explain, but it was very sexy.

"You know I want you to be happy," Grandma Edna said.

"He's done a lot for me." I instinctively felt she didn't think my happiness was going to be found in my marriage to Malcolm and I knew I was pleading his case. "He's really done a lot for me," I repeated.

Grandma Edna nodded her head. "Yes, I suppose he's been around the block enough to know how to help you sell your work. He appears to be a very good salesman."

She gave me a strange smile.

"Does he have any stake in Sweetwater's?" she asked.

"Of course," I said. "He's my husband now."

Grandma Edna sighed. "Yes, yes," she said, "he is." She reached over and squeezed my arm. "What's that?" she asked looking at the little wrapped package I had in my hand.

"It's for you," I said.

I watched her take the paper off the box. She put her head back and laughed. "Oh my God."

"Remember, remember when I was young?" I slid under the blankets with her.

"And you broke my dish?"

"All the way from China," you said. "You have to replace it so you have to go all the way to China for it."

"Oh, I don't believe you remembered that."

"It's from Chinatown, San Francisco, same thing, made in China."

"Looks just like the one you broke." She threw out her arms and drew me into them. "Oh, thank you, Sassy. You are a woman of your word, but the original object of your heart can never be replaced. You know that, don't you?"

I broke out of her arms and stared at her. I knew exactly what she was insinuating, but I pretended not to have heard her.

"Any word about Mama?" I asked, abruptly changing the subject.

"Still coming up empty," she said. "But we won't give up."

"You think something happened to her, she died and we don't know it?"

Grandma Edna shook her head. "I hope to God not, Sassy," she said. "I hope to God not."

I was happy for the first six months of my marriage to Malcolm Miff, and I just assumed my family would come around and accept him. But it was after six months that everything seemed to fall apart.

"Where are you going?" I asked, seeing his suitcase on the bed.

"New Orleans," he said. "I've got family there."

I was confused, he hadn't mentioned it. "I don't know if I can get away right now," I said.

"I haven't asked you along," he said.

It must have been something in my expression because he came quickly to my side and kissed my cheek. "Maybe next time," he added.

The exchange gnawed at me, like a tiresome toothache. He called me from a payphone, conveniently getting cut off before he had time to leave me a number. I realized then that he'd left me no way of getting in touch. Two months later, he returned, as if nothing had happened.

"Malcolm, where the hell were you?"

His facial expression was one I could not interpret. "I told you, New Orleans."

"You stayed there two months."

"I mixed a little pleasure with business," he said and held up a check. "Your *Roses at Dawn*? Sold for twenty thousand."

"What?" I couldn't believe it and grabbed the check out of his hand. I was so excited to have sold a painting for such a good price that I immediately dropped any further discussion, except to make him promise to call me and leave behind his contact phone number in the future.

"Of course," he said, kissing me all over and leading me down on the bed.

It happened again, much like the first time. Malcolm would just take off, sometimes waiting to call me from an airport, and always finding a way not to leave me a phone number. He'd always return with news of a sale. It seems my paintings were selling for ten, fifteen, even twenty thousand dollars.

I didn't tell anyone that I was questioning my marriage. It was too disturbing to admit I'd made another colossal mistake. I went along with it, but not without acting out. I had affairs with other men. Somehow that justified that my husband was never there. Perhaps I should have divorced him, but it felt too much like another failure. Of course everyone around me knew that I was miserable, though I kept trying to pretend that I wasn't.

CHAPTER THIRTY-EIGHT

My problems with men weren't over yet. I was making too many mistakes in my life and I was about to make another one, with consequences far greater than I could have imagined. I had always believed that endings are just what they are supposed to be. Periods at the end of a goodbye. But not all men walk away easy.

The last person that should have been pleading the case for Dixie Craft, a man I hadn't seen since our divorce, was my Aunt Erin, or at least, that's how it appeared at the time. Despite my disinterest in having any kind of a relationship with Aunt Erin, she started showing up at my door. At first, it was just for morning coffee, but then, she'd appear in the afternoons and early evenings. It was obvious that my new husband was never around and maybe she thought she was keeping me company, or maybe she just needed mine. She'd been diagnosed with cancer that year and she was looking pretty sick, though still able to get around. We were awkward with one another and the conversation was strained. I knew she felt uncomfortable with me and I couldn't figure out why she kept seeking me out.

The very last time I saw her, she was wearing a scarf around her head and her eyes were all red and swollen. When she spoke her voice was scratchy, from all those years of smoking.

She sat down on my couch slowly, as if every movement was an effort. She looked around. "You've done a fine job with this space," she said. "It's nice."

I nodded. "What do you want?" I asked. "I don't mean to be rude, but I was in the middle of something."

"I want to redeem myself before I die," she said. "Something is kind of overwhelming me to do it. It's important."

I looked at her, not knowing what she was talking about, wondering whether or not I was going to be the recipient of some good deed, which coming from my Aunt Erin, wasn't going to be such a big deal. Aunt Erin thought a good deed was stopping at a stop sign for a blind man or buying girl scout cookies with an IOU.

"Okay," I said.

"Dixie wasn't happy to hear you married again," she said.

I was so taken aback I almost fell off the chair. For God's sake, Dixie was ancient history.

"Has Dixie been trying to contact you?"

"No, why?" I really didn't believe I was having this conversation.

"Won't be good if he does," she said.

I knew my eyes got small. I hadn't mentioned Dixie's name in years. I felt myself getting short-tempered with my aunt. I had no interest at all in discussing Dixie Craft and resented her for bringing him up. I hadn't seen him and I didn't want to.

"I still see Dixie, you know. He comes around whenever he can. His situation keeps getting worse. It frightens me."

My temper started to sizzle. I still remembered how she'd befriended him even after he'd tried to burn my hand off.

"Listen, Aunt Erin, in all due respect, if you've come here to talk about Dixie I'm going to have to ask you to leave. I have no interest in Dixie Craft. I am a happily married woman."

"Your husband never seems to be around," she said. "That isn't good."

"He travels a lot," I answered quickly.

"Dixie wasn't always such a brute," she said and shook her head.

My mouth fell open. Surely being treated for cancer was making her crazy. She couldn't be in her right mind.

"I can't believe you'd come into my home pleading that bastard's case," I shouted. "I'm going to have to ask you to leave."

She had lost a lot of weight, and I could see the veins in her hands and her face. Her complexion was pale and her teeth were the color of toffee candy. She seemed to be struggling to speak.

"Sassy," she said. "I'm not pleading his case."

"Then what are you doing?"

"You know he's been in and out of the hospital. He's had bad spells."

"I'm sorry to hear he's sick. What's wrong with him?" I wasn't really interested, but I asked anyway.

"It's his mind. He's delusional. They call it mental illness, some kind of disorder. They give him stuff to take for it. I don't think they should be letting him out at all."

I didn't know what to say, but the information began to make me nervous.

"Sassy," she said. "I want you to be careful. He's not talking sane these days."

"Did he ever?" I said sarcastically.

"He's talking about killing you."

I know my head snapped back. She hadn't come to me to plead Dixie's case. She'd come to warn me?

She looked at me sadly and nodded. "Perhaps we never should have befriended him, but he was so forlorn after the divorce. We felt sorry for him. Will you ever forgive Austin and I?"

"Just what are you saying? My divorce from Dixie has been final for four years."

I felt myself getting nauseous. I didn't know if it was her intent, but she was scaring me to death.

"The only thing he ever did when he came over was get drunk and rant and rave about you. We finally began to see how out of his mind he was. He called you every name in the book, said he should do something about that pretty face of yours 'cause you were too stuck up, too much of a bitch to have a good life. We realized, maybe a bit too late, but we realized he shouldn't be there with us."

"He must have moved on at some point, Aunt Erin. I haven't seen Dixie and I haven't been in touch with him for years, like I said."

"He hasn't moved on, Sassy. He's stuck. He's got some deep, twisted hatred for you. Please be careful. Austin says he's just talking, but I think he's crazy as a loon, capable of horrible acts. He says that you ruined his life, caused him to drink. He said you lied to him about Patrick 'cause Patrick was anybody's son and certainly not his. He said horrible things."

"You think he's dangerous?" I asked.

She slowly nodded. "He doesn't want to live, he's so much as said that. He's a horribly depressed man. It doesn't matter who he hurts. That's what I think and that's why I'm afraid for you. I wish your husband was here more often, Sassy."

"You think I need protection?"

She nodded her head slowly. I sat there in a stupor even after Aunt Erin had left. I didn't know if I should take her at all seriously. I didn't know if I should mention what she'd told me to anyone. Why would Dixie give a shit about me? It had been years since we were married and I was now married to someone else.

I kept two guns in the house, one in the upstairs loft, locked away, and the other in a locked drawer in my bedside table. I got the keys to both and started wearing them on a chain around my neck, hidden behind my shirts. I didn't want anyone to know what Aunt Erin had told me. I never confided to a soul what she'd said, but it was on my mind night and day, even after Aunt Erin's death.

Six months after Aunt Erin died, Uncle Austin had a major stroke and passed away. It seemed that with their passing, all that nonsense about Dixie passed with them. After all, I'd never seen Dixie anywhere in town and he'd never tried to contact me. I started to feel it had all been in Aunt Erin's mind, so I finally removed the chain and put the keys back where I'd always kept them. I didn't need any guns to protect myself from Dixie Craft, that was just foolishness.

CHAPTER THIRTY-NINE

I'd be lying if I didn't admit that Malcolm had some kind of control over me. When he was present, he was enjoyable and attentive, fooling me into believing he was traveling for me, to make me famous.

"Malcolm, this is ridiculous, you're never here. This is a marriage in name only."

"Come with me then," he said. "Hop on a plane. You're the one that's tied yourself down."

But I couldn't just hop on a plane and he knew it. I had my own life to consider. He knew I wouldn't just drop everything to follow him around the world. For one, I couldn't take my son out of school like that, and for another, I loved running the gallery and living at Carter's Crossing. It was not my goal in life to roam all over the place just because my husband had a wanderlust, a wanderlust I'd never realized was so intense.

Our marriage, if you could call it that, continued for nearly four years. Malcolm came and Malcolm went and always returned with a major sale of one of my paintings.

"If they're selling so well, why can't I get a show?"

"You don't need a show," he said. "You're selling."

I was totally confused. "But how?" I asked. "How do people know my paintings exist?"

He beamed at me. "What do you have me for?"

"I'm not sure," I said.

Malcolm then accused me of not appreciating everything he did for me. He pouted like a small boy, telling me I couldn't possibly love him, getting me to believe that his focus was always on me and that if he wasn't traveling, he'd be tied to my coattails, not earning a living.

I put up with it all, suffering over my own guilt for sleeping with other men. I was horrified by it and tortured by the fact it would kill Malcolm when all Malcolm cared about was me and my art. During that period of my life my mind was hiding behind a cloud. I was dumbstruck with confusion.

In 1982 Aunt El needed a loan of about twenty thousand dollars to front an investment on some commercial building she planned on converting into several small boutique stores. I said I'd gladly lend her the money. When I went to the bank, I just about died. My account had been cleaned out of over four hundred thousand dollars.

"He's been moving your money around for the last four years," Aunt El said looking between me and Grandma Edna. We were at the gallery where the books were kept and where Malcolm had access to them.

"I don't understand," I said. "He's made me thousands of dollars selling my paintings. Where are those deposits?"

Aunt El shook her head. "I'm not sure he ever sold your paintings. He took twenty thousand out and put it back in as a sale, but that doesn't mean anything. Look here." She showed me the records, records I myself kept.

"How could I have been so careless," I said.

Aunt El continued. "He'd go back in and withdraw the funds. He was just moving your money around, Sassy. He needs to be turned in to the police. He's cleaned you out. He hid his withdrawals. I must say, it was a brilliant scheme, difficult to detect. He's a thief, bottom line. The actual balances are hard to follow, but we can prove it. Why'd you give him access to your funds?"

"He's my husband," I said in disbelief.

I tried to remember the last time I'd gotten something in the mail that showed my balances and I couldn't. Malcolm had taken over the books shortly after our marriage and I'd allowed it.

"Please, just give me some time," I said. "I'm sure there's an explanation."

Grandma Edna stood to her full height. "That son of a bitch has been bleeding you for the full four years of your marriage. Perhaps it funded his jaunts across the country."

"You mean he never sold any of my paintings for any decent amount of money?"

The expression on Grandma Edna's face was all the answer I needed. I felt devastated and furious. "What did he do with my paintings then? Will I ever get them back?"

"He must have just sold them cheaply, or not at all, who knows?" Grandma Edna slammed her hand down on the desk. "Let's get that no-good bastard, you hear? Let's hang him by his goddamn balls."

I took what little possessions Malcolm had left with me and burned them in the backyard. Had I just been reacting again to Thomas's rejection, being dumber than bows on a donkey when I married Malcolm, the way I was when I married Dixie? I'd just been reacting all my life. I realized then and there that I would never be happy, not until I was the one seeing clear enough to find daylight.

Malcolm was brought back to trial in Beaufort county for bigotry and fraud and eventually sentenced to fifteen years in prison. He was the father of two grown girls and a ten-year-old son. He had a wife in New Orleans and he virtually did nothing for a living. He had no background at all in art, just a healthy interest, adept enough to have fooled me. He had lied about everything. He was originally from New Jersey, though he'd spoken to me with a heavy Southern drawl. He was married to a forty-five-year-old woman and his legal name was Tim Hunter.

I would never get my money back. It had been spent on mortgages for two houses in Louisiana, Ivy League college educations for two daughters, and trips to the Bahamas with his wife, the authentic Mrs. Tim Hunter.

What was it about my life that made me so naive? I'd never be able to figure that one out. Only thing I knew for sure is that if your heart isn't holding genuine love in it, you'll never make it up from the dungeons of other people's betrayals. I had my son and the support of my family, despite my stupidity. Uncle Seth called all the way from Washington, D.C. to tell me he could have Malcolm's arms broken for me and I said it was enough to know he'd be sitting his sorry ass in prison for the next fifteen years, but thanked him for the offer.

Chapter Forty

It should have been over then. I should have been able to pick up the pieces and get myself back together, but sometimes it only gets worse. Sometimes, mistakes follow you like demons of the dark night.

I was walking back from the cove one afternoon with Foxy at my side, bounding out ahead whenever she saw a bug. I was distracted by my thoughts, feeling sorry for myself for ever marrying Malcolm, for falling for a total con man. The trial had been over for a month, but I knew it was going to take a long time before I would be feeling like a human being again, before I'd be able to just go on with my life.

The dog suddenly barked and I looked up. I saw a stranger out ahead of me, standing there in my path, blocking my way. I had no idea who it was until I got up close. He was ragged and his clothes were disheveled, but he was no stranger. He wasn't any man I thought I knew, not at first, but under the full, unruly beard I recognized his features.

My heart started pounding in my chest. I remembered what Aunt Erin had said, trying to do her one good deed before she died, trying to warn me against Dixie Craft. I wished I had the gun on me that I'd put back in its hiding place, but I didn't. I braced myself to make a run for it.

I stepped back a few paces. I was afraid for the dog, especially when I saw the gun in Dixie's hand. He lifted it straight out toward Foxy.

"Run, Foxy," I yelled for all I was worth.

I heard a scream in the distance. It was Patrick's voice. He was running fast right for me.

"No," I shouted. "Get back."

"Mom," he yelled. "Mom!"

I saw Dixie turn. I saw Foxy jump on him and the gun went off. I screamed. Dixie smiled at me as he pointed the gun in the air. He'd shot my dog. Foxy lay dead on the ground.

"And now I'm going to shoot your son," Dixie said.

I ran toward Patrick as I heard the shot ring out. I saw Patrick fall and I started screaming for help. Another shot came up loud behind me and I realized Dixie was close and had shot Patrick again. I heard a car drive up and come to a screeching halt behind me. I heard another shot, then another. I cradled my son in my arms. He was bleeding badly.

"Get him in the car! We need to get him to the hospital!" Grandma Edna screamed at Pike. I saw the rifle in her hand.

I was crying hysterically, rocking Patrick's head in my arms. I heard Grandma Edna drop to her knees beside me. "It's okay," she said. "Dixie Craft is dead. I shot him. I killed the son of a bitch."

They'd raced Patrick into the emergency room and Grandma Edna and I paced back and forth in the waiting room. Neither one of us could sit still. It seemed like hours before the doctor entered. It seemed Pike had seen Dixie drive up to the farmhouse and run wildly all over the land looking for me, shouting out my name. Dixie had the gun raised up in the air and they all went into action. Patrick took off to warn me and Grandma Edna went for the rifle. Carolyn called the police and Pike had gotten the car.

"The first bullet only grazed his shoulder," the doctor said. "The second, I'm afraid, did significantly more damage. We don't know for certain, but there may be some paralysis."

Grandma Edna and I stood deathly still, holding each other's hands for support.

"There's a chapel," he said. "On the second floor."

"Yes, of course, it's up to God now." I looked at Grandma Edna, who seemed to be ready to scream, to go back and murder Dixie again and again.

"C'mon," I said and gently took her arm. "We need to plead our case to the only one who can help us now."

We prayed for hours. But God doesn't always listen. I was wrong; he couldn't help us at all. I think sometimes that life isn't about owing God anything, that God doesn't have anything to do with how your life turns out. He isn't a thinking man, he doesn't hear you. He's not bargaining with any one of us and not a one of us can bargain with him. I think the events you create for yourself bring a whole set of consequences that follow. And the gamble is how bad those events will turn out to be, not whether or not life will turn out to your liking, because that's what life is, a series of events. From the moment you're born, you're playing poker with those events, you're gambling with the chips in your hand.

Patrick didn't die, so you might say we had a full house in five-card poker, but he was probably going to be paralyzed from the waist down for the rest of his life, so you might say someone else had a royal flush and wiped us out. It is all a house of cards, this life. The only good news is that you get to play again, that is, if you're still standing.

Grandma Edna and I sat in Patrick's room for weeks, sat there until the doctor sent us both home. The second bullet had entered his neck and had caused spinal-cord trauma. We were told that Patrick was lucky to be alive.

"Will he ever walk?" Grandma Edna asked.

The doctor took a deep breath before he answered. "There are restorative therapies," he said. "It's possible."

"But will he walk?" I reiterated.

"There's hope," he said. "The first six months are critical. We'll know more then. He has some feeling in his legs, that's a good sign."

This doctor didn't know that there was no winning hand called hope. There was just the luck of the draw.

CHAPTER FORTY-ONE

Patrick had lost his humor and remained silent, his face was drawn into a frown. It's a difficult future to face when you're sixteen years old and you don't know whether you'll ever walk again. I didn't know what to say to my son to make him feel any better. If there was anything at all I had to offer, it was patience, the patience to let him get through it in his own way. I did have the support of my family during this critical time. They all fussed over Patrick. Aunt Beatrice flew down from Vermont and was there in his hospital room reading him stories. Aunt Peg brought a Scrabble board and a Ouija board. According to Aunt Peg, Patrick would walk again, but not completely on his own. She said this to comfort us, but we all just got pissed off at her. This was no time for voodoo predictions.

Grandma Edna and I fussed over Patrick. We brought in a radio and magazines and sat there holding his hand, but we couldn't get him to smile. We could barely get him to talk.

We had purchased a special car that would allow for Patrick's wheelchair and Pike drove me over to the hospital the day we were bringing him home. But I was also frightened and harbored ambivalent feelings about how I'd keep myself sane around him.

The barn had double doors in and out of the dining room that would make it easy for Patrick and the loftlike space was pretty well suited for a wheelchair.

As I walked down the hospital hall, I wondered how I would get through it, how the hell I would wake up every day without wanting to hang myself from a tree. I had to live and I didn't want to, not without my whole and vibrant sixteen-year-old son. But then again, he needed me, so I had to shove my guilt aside as best I could.

As I approached Patrick's room, I heard my son's voice and wondered if some of his friends had come to visit him. He sounded so normal. There was a lightness to his tone. There was an energy to the sound of his voice that hadn't been there since he was shot.

I forced myself into a cheery mood and drifted into the room like Loretta Young. I was hoping Patrick would be in a joking mood. God, how that would lift my own spirits to see him smile. I was sorry his friends hadn't come to see him sooner, they'd made a world of difference.

"Patrick, I'm so happy you have company," I said as I walked directly to him and kissed his forehead. I was surprised that only one person stood at the foot of the bed, I had imagined a room full of teenagers.

I started preparing myself to act social when that was the last thing I wanted to be, but I was grateful to whomever it was that had come to visit him.

"Hello, Sassy. I hope you don't mind."

I almost fell over. It was Thomas Tierney standing there. I thought he was a school friend because he had on jeans and a comfortable old jacket. I hardly noticed the beautiful golden hair that fell onto his collar, his familiar stance. But there he was, looking not much different than he had when he'd first kissed me at the cove.

"Thomas?" I stammered.

"I…I hope you don't mind," he said again.

I looked quickly to Patrick. Thomas came around the side of the bed and sat.

"He comes almost as much as you do. Odd how you never visited me at the same time before." Patrick gave me a quizzical look and grinned as if he'd been musing over this for a while. "I guess 'cause you come days and Daddy comes late afternoons."

Daddy? Had I heard that right?

I looked at Thomas. His face was drawn, it was clearly the concern a father would feel for his injured son. I watched as Thomas put his hand over Patrick's.

I remained silent. I was at a loss for words and wondered how long they'd been having a father- son relationship.

"I never understood why you told me about Thomas, that he was my Dad and all…until I went to see him," Patrick said. "I fought it for a while, but then I didn't want to anymore. He looked happy to hear it, told me I looked like his dad and, well, I guess I do. And there was never any question that he wasn't going to acknowledge me. We both decided not to tell you just yet."

Patrick smiled at Thomas and my heart just about broke. There was so much admiration in his expression.

"He's got a mean right-hand pitch, Mom," Patrick said and smiled broadly. "I'm going to miss playing ball with you." He looked down at his legs.

"Why didn't you tell me you got in touch with your father?" I asked my son. "There was no reason not to tell me."

"I wanted some time, that's all. I was going to tell you but the trial and all, I didn't want to upset you, I didn't know if you'd be angry at me."

I looked at Thomas. He avoided meeting my gaze.

"I'll help you get him into the car," Thomas said. "You'll be taking him home?"

I nodded. "Well, I don't know what to say, but this is good, this is good," I stammered like a fool.

After Patrick was released, Thomas helped him to the car, just like he said he would. We didn't speak to each other, although there was cer-tainly enough opportunity. The only thing Thomas said was, "I'm sorry, but he's taking it well…considering."

"Thank you, Thomas," I said, "for caring."

I didn't look back or watch him as he drove off. I imagined now that he and Patrick had established a friendship of sorts, I'd be seeing more of Thomas. I didn't know how it made me feel, but if I had to describe it, if I was forced to describe it, I would have to say that it made me feel like a jumping jack inside a thimble.

It wasn't easy caring for Patrick and it wasn't my son's fault, it was mine. I kept crying and I knew how much it disturbed him to see me weeping like a fool every time I looked at him. I overcompensated, helping him when he didn't need it and avoiding offering help when he did. Our conversations were stilted and I knew I was saying stupid things to make him feel better and everything I said made him feel worse.

"I'm sorry, Patrick, I'll get used to this."

"There's nothing to get used to, I'm just in a wheelchair. I'm still me. I have an incomplete injury, which means I can get some feeling back, even mobility. You're acting like I'm a hopeless case."

Patrick turned around and quickly wheeled himself outside, away from me. I was no help to Patrick at all. It seems every time Thomas showed up to see him, he'd get chatty and friendly and after Thomas left he'd withdraw. When Patrick and I were alone, he barely said a word. When he did speak, there was a distance to our communication that I kept trying to alter, but I was failing miserably. I was carrying the guilt I felt over this like Atlas and his globe.

I was happy to hear the sound of a car pulling up a moment or so after Patrick started up to the farmhouse, where I'm sure he found Grandma Edna's blunt humor much less offensive than my total lack of it. We didn't converse, we didn't even argue. We just sat around asking each other yes/no questions: You need anything? Can you get me the third book from the left in the bookshelf? You hungry?

I knew Thomas was due to stop by, but I was startled to hear a dog bark and assumed Thomas was late and Patrick's friends from school were paying him a visit. Sometimes his friends brought their dogs. But when I walked outside I noticed it was Thomas getting out of his car. Patrick started back down the driveway to see him.

"What you got there?" Patrick called.

Thomas put the little white and brown dog on the ground and it started running around like someone had wound it up.

Thomas looked at me and smiled. "Seems like déjà vu. Didn't I bring you a dog once before?"

I smiled back at him as Patrick wheeled himself over. "I don't want a damn dog," he said. "I can't play with it, I can't chase it."

"What? Are you crazy?" All of a sudden, Thomas ran backward and then he reached in his pocket and took out a ball. He threw the ball right into Patrick's hand. Patrick caught it.

"What the hell are you doing, Daddy?" he said.

"Go on and throw it. Play ball, Patrick." Thomas was dancing up and down and reaching out his hands to catch the ball. At one point he squatted down. "Put her here, Patrick."

Patrick was clearly angry and he threw the ball down on the ground with a slam. "I can't play ball, asshole," he screamed.

From out of nowhere the little dog took off like a bat out of hell and started running with the ball. Thomas started running after the dog. I watched as Patrick stared at the two of them.

"He's fast," Thomas started screaming and laughing as he chased the dog. "He's real fast."

All of a sudden I heard my son laugh, too. And before I knew it, Patrick put that wheelchair into high gear and started wheeling after that dog. The little dog was like a trapeze artist and leaped over the chair and back over again before he let the ball go. Patrick reached for it, and I almost screamed. I thought the chair was going to fall over, but that little dog ran right under Patrick's hand and took off with the ball again. We all collapsed in a fit of hysterics. I didn't know where the dog went, but he returned about ten minutes later without the ball.

"He must have buried it," Thomas said.

That was the first laughter I'd experienced for quite some time. It was the first laughter I'd heard around me in so long, and it felt better than anything good could ever be capable of feeling. When I looked up to the farmhouse I saw Grandma Edna was smiling. She'd apparently been watching us.

"He buried the goddamn ball in my garden," she screamed. "Get him the hell out of here."

We all started laughing again as the little dog sat in Patrick's lap, panting and, seemingly, smiling too.

Chapter Forty-Two

Thomas came to visit Patrick a lot. Sometimes I was home and sometimes I wasn't. We were awkward with one another and avoided spending time alone. Of course, he'd heard about the trial, knew I'd married a con artist, and probably thought I was the dumbest girl this side of the county line. It wasn't easy for me and I wasn't bouncing back from the catastrophes I'd been confronted with. I sold Sweetwater's so I could be there for Patrick even though Patrick said he didn't need me as much as I thought he did.

It hadn't been an easy time for Grandma Edna, either. She'd lost Aunt Erin and Uncle Austin, but then, about a year after Patrick's accident, my Aunt El was killed in a plane crash on her way to one of the Pennsylvania mills. We were shocked by the news. Seth flew home from Washington, D.C. and even Aunt Beatrice flew in from Vermont. Poor Aunt Peg showed up bawling, saying how she never saw it coming and must be losing her gift.

Life changes so quickly. You can't hold it up or take back what it robs from you. Sometimes life seems like a test and, maybe, by the time you're old, you'll get to pass it. I wanted so badly to know where mama was. I wanted to right my wrongs. Sometimes the only thing that kept me sane was my painting and my son and all those walks to the cove where life seemed just a bit less ominous. I felt like I was shadow boxing with fate most of the time. Could I really trust the peace I found by the cove with its unchanging terrain, its steady dose of blue days? Once I left it, my life was anybody's guess, the next loss, the next heartache was always there before me.

I guess I wasn't really holding up for my son. I guess I wasn't who he needed me to be. Whatever the reason, I was never going to forgive myself for it.

"I want to live with my father," he told me.

I'm sure I went into shock because I don't remember moving or speaking. I was finally able to shake my head.

"No," I said. "No, you're not going to do that."

"Yes, I am, Mother," he said. "Yes, I am."

I don't think anyone could have knocked me down harder. We'd gotten news recently that Patrick had regained some more feeling in his legs and that was a good sign, gave us all hope. I was just beginning to feel a little better. I knew he was going to be starting some therapies that could get him back on his feet with the help of braces.

"Please, Patrick," I said. "Please don't do that."

"It's not that I don't love you, Mother, but I don't feel whole around you. You keep seeing my injury instead of me. My father just sees me. I need him now. I need him more than I need you, that's all."

When Thomas drove up to the house to pick Patrick up, I could barely look at him. He didn't know what to say to me, either.

"It's what he wants, Sassy," he said. "Just for now."

"And what about your wife, won't she mind?"

"I've been divorced for a few months now, Sassy. I have no wife."

I felt the earth give way under me. He'd never mentioned a word to me. I hated him more than I ever loved him in that moment.

"You never mentioned it," I said.

"Would it have mattered?" he asked.

I didn't answer. We were no longer in sync. Maybe we'd never been. We stood there looking at the ground until Thomas turned abruptly and went inside for Patrick.

I watched as he wheeled Patrick to the car, the little dog jumped ahead and leaped on Patrick's lap once he was settled. I heard that little dog bark all the way down the road, maybe for a half mile or more. Then it was deathly silent, so silent I could hear the night wind pass through me and I could hear the flowers as they tipped under the moon and their petals fell to the ground, barely touching it.

Chapter Forty-Three

I was there at the hospital whenever Patrick had his therapy sessions. It was really the only time I ever saw him. The doctors felt that Patrick could be helped with braces and we were all ecstatic that Patrick may very well walk again. Thomas was always there at the hospital as well. It was a hopeful time for all of us. Thomas and I conversed like strangers though, like we'd never been lovers. But in all honesty, I think we were both shell-shocked about what had happened to Patrick. I was blaming myself. I was still numb from the experience. Seeing Dixie shoot my son and kill my dog was haunting me every day. I was still nursing my own wounds, feeling sorry for myself, so I wasn't really any comfort for anyone else. I spent a good deal of time alone wallowing over my mistakes, agonizing over what had happened to Patrick. Now, I was the one going over to the sycamore tree talking to Charlotte in the ground, remembering being young, wondering why my life, as good as much of it had been, hadn't ever transformed into the life I had envisioned, one that included the true love of my life, if there is such a thing.

I realized how comforting it was to talk to a grave. I knew that little girl was listening to me and that's why all those still afternoons I watched Grandma Edna up on that hill, she always came back from the sycamore tree feeling better. I always felt better, too. I don't know much about death, but I do know that life has a sense of humor. There you are, sitting at the bottom of a mud puddle not knowing there's a jewel under your ass. That was me, sitting there thinking that life didn't hold any more surprises when it did. If I'd given up, the jewel would have never been mine.

I hadn't been to Hammertown since before I was married to Dixie. Maybe I just never had the time. But something told me to take a drive over there and check on it, make sure none of those old buildings had collapsed. We'd had some pretty bad storms over the years and there was always the possibility of vandalism, too.

I almost had a hard time finding the road again. There were more trees to move than there used to be, but I got out and lugged everything aside and started driving toward the old town. It didn't take long for me to notice a car on the property and some man sitting there drinking a Coca-Cola. I brought my car to an abrupt stop and ran out screaming. I should have known that old abandoned town would attract trespassers.

"I'm sorry, I'm sorry, but what are you doing here?" I screeched. "This here is private property."

The man that had been sitting there stood to his feet. I noticed right away how he was dressed, like someone with a shit load of money. His suit was finely tailored and he had on two-toned shoes and a silk shirt. The car he'd driven there in was a Cadillac convertible and the top was down, the tan leather seats looked rich as fudge sundaes.

"What are you grinning at?" I said. "I told you I own this land and I don't allow any trespassing."

"Sweetwater Sassy," he said. "Still as sassy as a tiger tom cat."

"Dudley?" I stood there with my mouth open. I couldn't believe the vision before me, I guess 'cause I would have never expected it.

"Come here, girl," he said and he held out his arms.

"Oh my God," I wept, holding him tight. He'd gotten much older and it was hard for me to make the connection, but it sure as shit was Dudley.

"Girl, you've grown up. Pretty as a movie star, pretty, little rich girl, I'd say."

We laughed for a full ten minutes and then found an old blanket in Dudley's car that we spread on the ground. We sat there talking and smoking that great weed all around us, 'til we wore each other out and the sun started setting. I told him all about Hammertown, how it had never been a slave town at all, but a place for white bootleggers during Prohibition and how I was prepared to sell him the land.

"How much?" he asked.

"Make me an offer," I said.

"Seven thousand?"

I probably looked shocked. "Can you afford that?"

Dudley laughed. "I may be short, but I'm not dumb, Sassy, nor am I a poor man." He took a fat cigar out of his pocket and lit it.

"What did you do? Where were you all this time?"

"The land of Oz and phallic symbols," he said.

"New York?" I said. I couldn't imagine anywhere else Oz would be holding court or phallic symbols would be more obvious.

Dudley nodded. "Your family set me up with a car, cash, and a whole new identity, which I took to New York City, land of the misbegotten, the holy, and the privileged."

"New York City? I don't believe it."

"Fine place," he said.

It seems Dudley had gotten a job as a chef's assistant in some fancy restaurant and then went on to become a major chef himself. He worked in a very well-known French restaurant and made a lot of money.

"I worked hard," he said.

"Wow, I didn't even know you could cook."

"Came back here to open up the best restaurant in Beaufort. It will serve the best Southern food you'll ever eat."

"Won't they lock you up?"

Dudley stood up and brushed off his clothes. "Clearing my name, Sassy. Your aunt is gone now, no need for me to hide. No one can lock her up when she's dead. Sorry to hear. But it's opened the way for me, I need to stand tall in my home town."

"How do you know you'll get off? It's murder."

"Got a good lawyer, the best." He looked back over at Hammertown. "Where's Kyle?" he asked.

I didn't want to talk about Kyle or Mama, but I told him everything anyway, about Littleton's burning and Mama taking off, pretty much being lost 'cause no one knew where she was.

"Kyle lives in Crawford, about a mile from Aaron. We don't talk, haven't seen him in years."

"You say there's a book on Hammertown, something about ghost stories?"

I nodded and looked at all the gray in his hair. "I'll get it for you. Where you staying?"

"With my folks, right under your nose, Sweetwater."

"You sure you'll get off?" I felt afraid for Dudley and wondered if he just should have stayed in New York City where I assumed hiding was a major sport.

"Your grandmother is going to testify in my defense, admit that El was the one that killed Liam, to protect you, of course." He looked at me solemnly. "I assumed she would have told you."

I started seething. "She never said a word to me, not one goddamn word. Why the hell not? That woman is always keeping things from me."

"Well, I guess 'cause it's going to come out about your being raped. I think she wants to make sure you won't have to take the stand. She doesn't want to see you go through that, Sassy."

As the dusky sky covered the hazy sun we got back into our cars. I promised to be at the trial for support.

"No need," he said. "I'll be fine."

"I want to be there," I said.

I waited impatiently for Dudley to put the trees back when we got to the beginning of the road. When he wasn't moving fast enough I honked. He finally started driving up the road like a damn turtle. I started following him back to Carter's Crossing, but he was going too slowly for me, so I passed him at about sixty on a county road. He honked at me like crazy, but I didn't care. I was feeling the slow boil of my anger. I couldn't figure out why I wasn't brought into this opportunity to free Dudley and I was pissed off. I didn't care if I had to take the stand; all I cared about was seeing Dudley get exonerated for a crime he didn't commit. I wanted to see him open his little restaurant in Beaufort and live happily ever after.

I rushed into the farmhouse and found Grandma Edna in the kitchen with Carolyn.

"Why didn't you two tell me Dudley was back?" I screamed.

Carolyn walked over and looked into my eyes. "It's just enough he's back, honey," she said. "Your old boyfriend is going to give him back his name."

I looked over to Grandma Edna. "What?"

"Thomas is his attorney. I was going to tell you this evening, actually. I didn't want you to be nervous. It's going to come out, about the rape. I'm sure it will."

"Why the hell is everybody keeping this from me?"

"Thomas told me earlier today that he won't need your testimony if everything goes according to plan. He didn't want to put you on the stand and have you relive that."

"When the hell was anybody going to come to me about this?"

Grandma Edna looked sheepish. "I just didn't want you to go through it."

"You're still thinking for me instead of letting me think for myself."

She turned away. "I'm sorry," she mumbled.

"Have you been honest with him?" I asked.

"You aided and abetted a criminal, at least back then, in the eyes of the law that's what you did. And why was everybody so afraid of Seamus? Isn't that why no one went to the police and covered the whole thing up instead? What's a jury going to make of that?"

I gave her a questioning look. I wasn't so sure what Carolyn knew and what she didn't know, but Grandma Edna came right out and said it.

"Thomas is a very good lawyer," Grandma Edna said. "He found a rape victim of Liam's who would testify, if we needed it, but even better than that, he found a man willing to testify to the brutal murder of a Negro at the hands of Seamus McLaughlin. The man was tortured before he was hanged. His crime? Opening a door for a white woman." Grandma Edna stood close to me. "Don't worry, Sassy," she said. "The sun is shining bright."

I went to the trial every day just like I said. Thomas was powerful and charming at one and the same time and I was very impressed with him. He proved for that whole jury, without a doubt, that Dudley could not have shot Liam in the back; he was too short to have been responsible for the entry of the bullet. Liam was shot by someone at least four inches taller than Dudley. Grandma Edna never had to take the stand and it never came out that Aunt El had been protecting me from Liam. So, Liam's murder went back to being a mystery that everyone said was a professional hit, because he had been so like his father, a ruthless businessman, and he'd had enemies and one of his enemies murdered him somewhere and chopped up his body. That suited the family just fine. We were all exonerated.

We had a big party at the farmhouse to celebrate the victory and the champagne bottles were popping. Thomas and I hadn't spoken much during the trial. I'd been nervous about possibly having to testify and greatly relieved when it didn't come to that. I guess Thomas and I were both too preoccupied to even congratulate each other.

The evening was beautiful, alive with stars. I stepped out onto the porch and a minute later my son joined me. He was walking with the help of braces on both legs.

"I'd like to move home, Mom," he said.

I felt the tears come to my eyes quickly. He'd been living with Thomas for over a year. "Oh, Patrick, Patrick Toulouse, how I'd love that."

I put my arms around him. "I've missed you," I said.

"I'm moving home 'cause I think home is where the heart is." He grinned at me.

"I'm glad you've come to that conclusion. A boy needs his mother."

"He's in love with you, Mom." Patrick smiled. "That's the conclusion I've come to."

"What?" I laughed. "Who's in love with me?"

"Daddy told me that when he was a boy, he didn't know how to talk to you so he teased you, pretended not to like you at all. That was his way of getting your attention."

"Yes, that was Thomas's way."

"Don't you see, Mom? He's still doing the same thing. He's pretending not to care when he does."

I was confused. Thomas barely spoke to me at all and when he did, he was very to the point.

"No, I don't see. Your father is not the least bit interested in me."

Patrick shook his head. "Yes, he is. He's wild about you."

"He say that?"

"No."

I studied Patrick's expression. Would Thomas really be too shy to do his own bidding?

"Don't deny yourself the only man you told me you ever loved, really loved. Go for it, call him on it. Men aren't as brave as women. He's hiding 'cause if you hurt him again, he'll crumble."

I kissed my son on the cheek and went to find Thomas. "I'm going to congratulate him," I told Patrick. "That's it. We barely speak to each other, no sparks there anymore, Patrick."

I spotted Thomas in the room and his gaze caught mine. I'm pretty good at reading expressions, but I hadn't been looking for a long time; I'd been too busy counting my losses. I thought of the poker game, the roulette wheel of life, the gamble sitting there waiting for me to spin the goddamn wheel.

"Take a walk with me," I said. If he scorned me, then I would be alone for the rest of my days. There was no more settling for a future without Thomas in it. I was playing for my life that night and all my chips were on the table.

He smiled a bit and nodded his head. I think he knew our lives were going to change too. It must have been in my expression, like a door opening and letting in a warm summer breeze. I took his arm and we walked back behind the house, the same place I had seen Aaron and Mama walk so many years ago. I wanted someone like that then, a person that touched my soul, and I still did. I wanted that magic, that feeling, the one that lasts forever.

I stood there under the moonlight and looked into Thomas's eyes. They shone back into mine.

"I'm through pussyfooting around with you, Thomas Tierney," I said. I was going to say more. I was going to tell him that he was acting like a fool and didn't have the balls he was born with, but I felt his hands on my arms, I felt him draw me into his arms and he kissed me long and deep and hard and the goddamn earth parted, I swear it did. I heard the oceans roar and I felt the volcanoes erupt. We didn't stop kissing 'til the sun came up in the sky and the morning dew on my naked back tickled me and made me laugh like I'd never stop.

Chapter Forty-Four

Thomas and I had a huge wedding right there at the farmhouse. The day he asked me to marry him, he drove up the driveway and took circles around my land, honking his horn. Then he leaped from the car with a small velvet box in his hand.

"I love you, Sassy Sweetwater. Will you marry me?" he shouted.

I ran out of the house screaming yes, yes, yes, at the top of my lungs.

`The whole family, and the whole town, came to see Thomas and I take our vows. It was certainly one of the best days of my life. Patrick was best man and Seth gave me away. Every one cried when Thomas kissed me after the priest said, "And now you may kiss the bride." But no one cried more than me.

We all got happy drunk that beautiful June afternoon. Aunt Peg kept running after Thomas and pulling on his hands and telling him he was the one she'd seen in her vision. "That's him, the one with the light hair," she said to me. "I haven't lost my gift. Beware a daughter as gifted and as beautiful as you. I see it. I do see it, Sassy. It's in the cards."

Aunt Beatrice showed up to the wedding with her husband, Demarco Jones. She'd never told anyone she had gotten married as many as nine years ago and we were all a bit shocked. Not because he was black, but because everyone but me imagined Beatrice as an old spinster, too uptight for anyone, much less a handsome black man who looked like he breathed fire.

"I am not a bigot despite what you think, Beatrice," Grandma Edna kept repeating. "You should have told me."

De had changed quite a bit, which restored my faith in the old saying anyone can change. Gone were the bright lacy shirts he'd worn that summer at the farmhouse, when he wasn't naked, that is. For my wedding he wore a deep blue pin-stripe suit and a tie that looked like it'd been spun with gold. He kissed my hand and told me I was the most beautiful bride he'd ever seen, with the exception of Beatrice, of course. With his hair cut short, he barely looked like the man I had known in France. He looked like a corporate lawyer, which is exactly what he had become, exchanging his life as a professor for something more lucrative.

"He's a black Republican now, Sassy, can you believe it?" Aunt Beatrice told me. "He'll fit right in with this family. Everyone down here is a bigot behind closed doors, even that crazy feminist Seth married."

Thomas and I went to France for our honeymoon. I wanted him to meet Celine and I wanted to show him everything I had loved about Paris. Thomas was beside himself, having never been to Europe. Celine was a charming hostess, but she had slowed down quite a bit. I guess getting near ninety does that to a person.

But, despite the allure of Paris, our best days were spent in the *Provence-Alpes-Cote-d'Azur* region where we'd rented a cottage. It seemed like every year we'd lost together we regained there in the countryside. We were like teenagers all over again, drinking wine, smoking marijuana, and fornicating like bunnies. We did talk, however, for hours and hours and hours as we walked, as we lay side by side, and as we gazed at each other over a candlelight dinner. Those unfettered days will always be imprinted in my mind, like a photograph I can't stop looking at, the one photograph that will never depress me.

My son, Patrick Toulouse, wound up going to his father's alma mater and getting his law degree. He and Thomas became partners in their own law firm and opened an office in Charleston, facing the river, facing the very same bench where Thomas used to take his lunch.

I was thirty-seven years old when I gave birth to Charlotte Violet Tierney. She turned out to be just as gifted and as beautiful as Aunt Peg said she would be. Of course she was beautiful, she grew up looking just like Mama. One of the happiest days of my life was putting my baby daughter into Grandma Edna's arms. She looked up at me and the tears just fell down her face.

"I've got to live long enough to see this little baby grow up," she said. "Oh my, I'd never want to miss that."

She spoiled her great-granddaughter and it was downright sinful what that child got away with, but I let her do it. Charlotte's presence in her life seemed to fill an old wound and she never went back to the sycamore tree, well, not until she passed. I don't think she ever forgot about the little baby she lost, she just got busy with the business of life. She lived almost as long as she'd wanted to, long enough to see Charlotte turn fifteen. She died in her sleep only a year before I lost Thomas.

The poker game I played gave me a royal flush because I had almost twenty years with my beloved husband and our marriage had given us the best years of our lives. Thomas was only fifty-seven when he had a heart attack at the wheel of his car. He might have lived if he'd survived the crash, but he didn't.

My son had married at the age of twenty-nine and I have three grandchildren, all boys. He and his family lived in the barn loft until I gave him the farmhouse years later, after Charlotte was out of school, and I had decided to move to France. Charlotte lives in New York City and she's an artist there. She studies at the art institute. She's a happy young woman. Says she'll never marry, but we'll see. She and I are so close that I know when she's unsettled without her having to tell me, even with so many miles between us.

Dudley not only opened the best restaurant in Beaufort, he had Hammertown restored and put on every tourist's to-do list when they came to South Carolina. That old town became a must-see stop. Everyone had to get tickets to get a tour of the famous ghost town in Carter's Crossing.

Dudley went up to Crawford right after his trial and dragged Kyle back home. I drove up to see Hammertown after the restoration process and there was this man walking around in an old-fashioned suit with a fedora on his head and two-toned shoes on his feet, guiding the tourists through the bootlegging paradise of old Hammertown. He was acting a character named Floyd Mad Dog Demicci and he was happy as a squirrel with a nut to be leading people into the old speakeasies of the 1920s. Sometimes he and Dudley hired actors to play the ghosts of Hammertown and it was Kyle who wrote the scripts and told the actors what to do.

The moment I recognized, Kyle I was flooded with emotion. I held him in my arms and we both started sobbing. He was my brother and I carried only remorse for the years we'd lost touch. From the day we reconnected, he became an important part of the family, my children's uncle, and my husband's brother-in-law. We built him a house on the Hammertown property, where he eventually brought a wife, three sheepdogs, and two babies.

During the first year of my marriage to Thomas I had asked him to help me find Mama, but the search ran as dry as dirt in a drought.

"She was in a hospital for some time, Sassy," Thomas had told me. "That's all we know. She has some sort of disease that causes dementia of sorts."

"What happened to her?" I asked.

"She just walked out of the hospital," he said. "She could be anywhere, even homeless. She losses contact with reality I was told."

I was sorry I had asked at that point. Mama never left my thoughts, but it would be years before I'd see her again and when I did, she wouldn't know who I was. Well, I'd been forewarned, but it didn't make it any easier.

I was still living up at the farmhouse after both Grandma Edna and Thomas were gone. Charlotte had one more year of school to complete. Thomas and I had spent all the years of our marriage living in that house. Now I was without him in it, contemplating what to do with my life after losing Thomas. I'd never expected to traverse to the end of my days without him. I was fifty-seven years old and wondering what to do next. Only thing I did know was that the house I'd loved for so long was haunting me with its memories and in order for me to move on, I had to leave. I had to let go. But it would be a while before I moved on. There was another chapter in my life that Carter's Crossing claimed and I had to wait for it to find me.

Mama was seventy-three years old when she showed up on the road at Carter's Crossing and stood staring back up at the farmhouse like a lost puppy. Charlotte was still living at home then, but she was out back with a friend. I'd been on the porch when I took notice of a single soul on the road. I don't know how I knew who it was that I was looking at. The distance from the porch to the road was quite a ways, but I knew all the same. Knowing is something that many call instinct, but Aunt Peg knew better than that. Knowing is the soul pulling at you and your soul is inside everyone you've ever loved.

I took off running. Mama was so thin, I noticed that right off. Her hair was all gray and it was tied behind her. Oddly enough, she was still beautiful. Her face, or maybe it was her eyes, whatever it was, it was still startling to look at her.

"What a pretty house," she said.

"Mama?" I whispered.

She looked at me strangely. "Do I know you?" she asked.

"Sassy," I said. "It's me, Sassy."

She shook her head. "It's good to be sassy," she said.

I felt the tears fall down my face. "Would you like to see the house?" I asked.

"Oh yes," she said.

I brought her up inside and gave her food and water. She had brought nothing with her except the clothes on her back. I couldn't imagine where she'd come from or how she'd gotten to Carter's Crossing. She was neatly dressed in a skirt and a plain white blouse. She was clean, all except for the white tennis shoes she had on. They were real dirty, like she'd walked miles in mud.

I watched as she looked around. I had no idea what was in her head, but sometimes she appeared to remember something. "That old clock never could tell time," she said at one point.

"Yes, but Grandma Edna always loved the tick of it."

"Do you have a dog?" she suddenly asked me.

I nodded and called for Trixie, a gentle, old black Lab that Thomas and I had had for years.

"I thought you had a dog," she said.

The dog buried her head in my lap and I petted her behind her ears. Mama reached out and petted her too, so close our hands touched. I was hoping she'd recognize me, but she never really did. When I took her up to her old room that first afternoon, she seemed to find new life, she loved it. But whether or not she remembered it, I couldn't say.

"Can I stay here?" she'd asked. "I can clean and cook."

"Yes." I smiled. "But you don't have to do anything."

I had never removed Mama's old clothes from her room and I told her she was welcome to anything she found there. It wasn't long before she started wearing her old cardigan sweaters and her saddle shoes. She looked odd in the old, outdated clothes, odd, but adorable. It touched me to see her like that, happy in some reminiscence or other that had faded like days with too much sun.

Mama never left that old bedroom of hers and I had to bring all her food up to her. I tried to get her to go outside, but she never wanted to. She preferred to sit by an open window instead. I spent hours with Mama, reading to her, talking to her, loving her so deeply it hurt me, and yet the poker hand I held while she was there, was at the very least, a full house. I had her again to care for and to love and sometimes she'd look at me and say, "Sassy?" but before I could say, "Yes, Mama, it's me, Sassy," she'd look away. Once she told Charlotte she looked familiar, but mostly, Mama made little sense.

Mama died in her sleep a year after she'd arrived. I had her buried next to Grandma Edna in the small family plot, under the sycamore tree where Thomas also lay and where there was a place just waiting for me, I guess. I never had Mama back the way I knew her, but I had her in a whole new way. She was mine to love again. And that was enough, would always be enough, would always be a blessing that life granted me.

EPILOGUE

After Mama died, I waited for Trixie, my old black Lab, to pass on. My daughter no longer needed me, she'd moved up north faster than I could say where the hell is Tribeca?

I made my plans after Trixie passed to move to France. I bought a little cottage in the *Provense-Alpes-Cote'd-Azur* region where Thomas and I had spent our honeymoon. My children come to see me during the summer months. Patrick brings his family and Charlotte sometimes brings a friend. So too, I am visited by Aunt Beatrice and De, so often laughing over that first summer when he'd been a naked hippie and I'd been the southern belle whom he couldn't stand.

I lost my Aunt Peg to cancer the first year I'd moved to France, but she told me she would never leave me for very long. She knew she was dying, though none of us wanted to believe her, we just didn't realize she was as sick as she was. One night she called and said her preparation was done and a day later she passed.

"The dead are silent travelers," she'd said to me. "Attached by love. They never go far."

No, I don't believe the dead go far. I speak to Thomas every day of my life. I can feel his response, not so much his words. Words have no place in the next world, where feeling reigns. There is nothing to speak about on the other side, there is only knowing. That's the way to communicate with the dead, or for that matter, with the living.

I am freer here in France, in my new surroundings, in my new challenges, and they are no less anticipated, they are just different and no less exciting. I know Thomas understands how I feel, understands the enchantment I've found here, understands that without enchantment, life closes in and fades.

I'm painting every day and I have neighbors who visit with me, so I'm not really alone or in the least unhappy. I lost touch with Earline years ago when she moved to Missouri with a woman she'd met, but she recently has begun to write to me and that's a comfort. Dudley comes at Thanksgiving to prepare me a feast, as he calls it. He closes the restaurant for a week to visit with me. Sometimes he brings Kyle and sometimes he brings a pretty lady, always a different one. So, no, I am not alone at all.

I am nostalgically happy, if that makes any sense. My love affair now is with news of my family and their visits, with my new dog that I call Abelle. She's a mixed breed and if I had to take a guess, I'd say she was part collie and part spaniel. She makes me laugh. Thomas would have loved her. Thomas was the gentlest man I've ever known. He would have welcomed being here forever with me, with the mountain views, and I am not far from the sea. Oh, he would have loved that. But, I am without him and nothing I can do will bring him back to me. Beauty is my company now. Capturing description, as Mama used to say, is the passion behind it all.

Every day I cherish my mornings. Birds serenade me with such intense chatter, a comforting music, and the sky's blue is so incredibly serene. I tend to my garden, which I love because the colors splash out at me, brightly reminding me that I am a lesser artist. I paint whatever comes into my head these days. Sometimes, it's the flowers I cut from my garden and place in a vase to join me for dinner. Sometimes, it's my fleeting recollection of a girl I noticed in the village, the one with the alluring smile, all young mystery and budding sexuality.

I can often feel the presence of my grandmother and that comforts me. Aunt Peg would have called me a sensitive. I take long walks most days. I take ghosts with me on those walks: my Aunt Peg, my Grandma, my grandma's lost daughter, Charlotte, and, of course, Thomas, who always kept step with me, and still does. Often, just Mama accompanies me, the way she was, and sometimes, the way she became. It is easy to take the dead on a walk, the silent lovers of your heart speak within the stillness. I have the feeling that when I die, there will be no difference, the beauty will remain, the people, too. People are far too stubborn to relinquish anything. Life, like I said, is a series of events, a game of cards. Pain is in everyone's hand. The more deeply it has taken from you, the more robustly you must take it back. I've learned nothing if not that, that life is your one opportunity to soar, even in sadness, it's a beautiful ride. Where ever you choose to go when life gets short, let your spirit take you there. It may be alone in your heartbreak, or it may transcend everything you've ever known.

Yes, I was born near a stream called Sweetwater, but that is not where it all began. It begins now, when the dream fades and the canvas has not yet felt the first brush stroke of color, nor can even imagine the last.

ACKNOWLEDGMENTS

Thank you Ancestry.com for pointing out my Southern roots so seeped in history, and for stirring up my curiosity.

Also, I would be remiss not to thank my main muse, Marianna Young, for listening to chapter after chapter of Sassy Sweetwater and suggesting and adding her poignant insights.

ABOUT THE AUTHOR

Vera Jane's first published novel, Dancing Backwards in Paradise, was the recipient of the Indie Excellence Award for notable new fiction and the Eric Hoffer Award for publishing excellence, both in 2007. *The Story of Sassy Sweetwater* was a finalist in the ForeWord Book of the year awards for 2012.

Ms. Cook, being somewhat torn between fantasy and reality on a daily basis is comfortable writing in the paranormal, speculative, southern and women's fiction genres. Her first paranormal/fantasy novel, *Annabel Horton, Lost Witch of Salem*, was published on December 23, 2011. Her mystery/Science Fiction novel, *Pharaoh's Star*, was published in 2013.

The Story of Sassy Sweetwater is Vera Jane's second southern fiction novel and is followed by *Where the Wildflowers Grow*, and *Pleasant Day*.

Lies a River Deep (women's fiction) is her fourth novel. She is also the author of *Marybeth, Hollister and Jane*, which has been revised and will be republished this year.

The author lives in New York City.

If you would like to communicate with Vera Jane Cook please visit her website at: www.verajanecook.com.